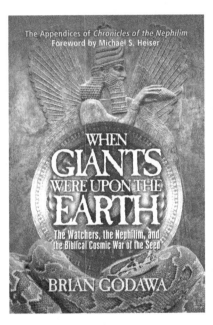

Enoch Primordial

Chronicles of the Nephilim
The Lost Book (Two)

By Brian Godawa

ENOCH PRIMORDIAL
5th Edition

Warrior Poet Publishing
www.warriorpoetpublishing.com

ISBN: 9798710790809 (Hardcover)
ISBN: 978-0-9859309-2-9 (Paperback)

Scripture quotations taken from *The Holy Bible: English Standard Version.*
Wheaton: Standard Bible Society, 2001.

Dedicated to
the memory of the late C.S. Lewis,
and to the memory of the late J.R.R. Tolkien.
Even though it is a cliché these days,
still, they are my masters of imagination –

– after God.

ACKNOWLEDGMENTS

Special thanks to Yahweh Elohim, the God of Enoch, Methuselah and Noah, and to the Son of Man, the second Yahweh in heaven. To the wife of my youth, Kimberly, my heart and soul. To Neil Uchitel for all our rambling discussions all those years ago about fallen angels, vampires and the Nephilim. To Michael S. Heiser, for his scholarship and resources that have fed my hunger. To David Rohl, for his helpful archaeological speculations of the ancient world based on his New Chronology. Thanks to my editor, Don Enevoldsen, my proofreader Shari Risoff, and my editor of this much better second edition, Sarah Beach.

And to Joe.

1

Could it have happened something like this?

PROLOGUE

Expelled from the Garden of Eden on the Mountain of God, the distant patriarch Adam and his wife Havah, or Eve, the "mother of all living," were forgotten by their descendants in the mists of time. Even though their creator Elohim's gracious forbearance covered them, they lived in regret the rest of their days with a mysterious people somewhere in the volcanic region of Sahand, near the boundary of the Garden. Like a dog kicked out of its shelter, they lived as close to their original home as they could without being struck down by those who guarded its perimeter.

The creator Elohim marked their son, Cain, the first murderer, and he was cursed to wander the earth. Few knew what the mark was, but there were rumors. It was said that he had a wild dog or wolf as a companion. Others claimed the man himself transformed into a canine beast at every new moon. The mystery of the actual fate of the cursed Cain was only matched by the fertility of imagination and legend surrounding him.

Cain's tribe migrated south from Nod through the Zagros Mountains and eventually broke away from their embittered patriarch to settle in the plain of Shinar, later called Sumer. The Shinarians referred to themselves as *unsangiga,* the black-headed people for their predominantly black hair and dark-skinned features. Unuk ben Cain, Cain's son, was the first city builder. He created the oldest city, Eridu, naming it after his own son Irad. He also built Erech, in honor of himself. This was the beginning of the ancient cities such as Nippur, Badtibira, Larak, Sippar, and others on the Mesopotamian plains in the land between the two rivers Tigris and Euphrates.

As mankind spread out upon the face of the earth, so did the evil that followed them. For it is the heart that is taken with man wherever he goes, and the heart is deceitful above all things and desperately wicked.

Elohim replaced Cain's cursed bloodline with another seed of Adam called Seth, the Righteous. Seth's people multiplied and migrated down into the fertile plains and surrounding area.

Tribal shamans divined that in a distant island beyond the primal sea a volcano had belched forth a mighty force of its gasses from the underworld below into the heavens above. The sun was obscured, and the earth grew colder for a time. Livestock perished, crops failed, the winters became harsher. It seemed that Elohim's displeasure with man was displayed in all of the heavens and earth.

And generations passed.

CHAPTER 1

An eerie silence settled over Mount Hermon. The ubiquitous ringing drone of singing cicadas ceased in unison. Birds of prey and land predators stalking their next meal froze in place as though suddenly aware of a powerful hunter tracking them. The sounds, the movement, all signs of life that filled the dark night just stopped. The wildlife knew something was coming.

Mount Hermon lay about two hundred leagues to the west of the Mesopotamian valley, across the barren desert. It stood above a valley at the southernmost tip of the Sirion mountain range of the Levant, "where the land rose out of the sea" of the great western waters. It was the tallest peak in the area, about six thousand cubits high. Capped with snow most of the year, the headwaters of the Jordan River, that brought life to the wooded hills and grassy valleys of the south, began on its slopes. It was known for its heavy dew and its evergreen cypress trees that peppered the region.

A beam of blinding light from high above in the dome of heaven punched the mountaintop. It pierced the blackness with a ferocious velocity. Heaven and earth fused as one into a cosmic center of the universe.

Two hundred shining beings of light, brilliant as the stars, fell to earth from their lofty heights above the clouds. A crack of thunder announced their violent passage through the solid dome vault over the earth called "the firmament." The firmament separated the waters below on the earth from the waters above in the heaven of heavens, where the temple of the creator Elohim rested. The mountains trembled and quaked to their very foundations.

These were *Bene ha Elohim*, Sons of God, a mere two hundred out of the myriad of Elohim's divine council of holy ones. These mighty beings surrounded his throne on the mount of assembly with worship and legal counsel. Certain Sons of God called "Watchers," regularly crossed the barrier between heaven and earth to carry out Elohim's plans and to watch over the sons of men.

But these two hundred were not carrying out Elohim's plans tonight. These were Watchers in revolt. Led by two mighty warriors, Azazel and Semjaza, they were establishing their own mount of assembly in the far reaches of the north in direct defiance of Elohim's will.

They chose Mount Hermon as their abode, intending to make it a rebellious reflection of God's own cosmic mountain of Eden, the paradise now banned to all. This choice began a complex plan of deceptive mimicry. Just as Eden held the headwaters of four rivers, the Pishon, the Gihon, the Tigris and Euphrates, all flowing out of the mountainous region surrounding the Garden, so Mount Hermon gave birth to the headwaters of the river Jordan that flowed into the Levant. Its surrounding territory would be called Bashan, "place of the Serpent," in honor of *Nachash*, the Serpent of Eden.

The Garden of Eden had been a temple sanctuary for the presence and worship of Elohim, a perfect shadow of the real temple in the heaven of heavens above the waters. Hermon would become the cosmic mountain of passage between the heavens and earth for the Watchers — the gateway of the gods.

As the Tree of Life stood in the midst of the Garden, so the Watchers chose Mount Hermon for its proximity to the World Tree of the Great Goddess Earth Mother in the Great Desert.

The Man and Woman were the intended priests of the Garden, cultivating and keeping it as a holy center of Elohim's cosmic order before they were banished. Mount Hermon would become a new cosmic mountain that would not only connect heaven and earth, but earth and the Abyss, also called *Abzu*, the subterranean waters, below which lay Sheol, the underworld. Deep within the bowels of the mountain a large cavern held a portal into the waters of the Abyss, a wide pool of thick black liquid that burned with a perpetual flame on its surface.

The two hundred rebel Watchers assembled in disorderly ranks at the center of the new Eden by the shore of the pitch-dark liquid lagoon. Azazel and Semjaza stood ominous and intimidating before them.

"SILENCE!" Azazel's voice thundered throughout the cavern. The Watchers abruptly stopped murmuring. Azazel's violent temper gave him a commanding presence. Every word burned like an ember ready to explode into a burst of flames. Azazel often looked ready to burst into flames. The skin of a Watcher consisted of almost imperceptible serpentine scales that gave off a shimmering glow when enflamed by any kind of passion. And Azazel never lacked passion.

"The decision has been made. We are the Seven who Decree the Fates. If any of you question Semjaza's leadership or my own, I most heartily welcome the contest!"

Azazel's hostile disposition supported by the fiercest of warrior skills made him virtually unopposed in the band of fallen ones. No one would be contesting Azazel this evening.

Only Semjaza standing next to him had the requisite strength, intellect, and strategy to restrain Azazel's volatility. It bothered him that Azazel was a loose fireball who used fear and intimidation to subjugate. He believed that more could be accomplished through positive leadership and inspiration. Semjaza's words were calculated and carried the weight of authority. When he spoke, others listened, even Azazel. He stepped forward to draw attention from the simmering volcano at his side.

"Brethren, for the plan to work, we must all be in one accord. The mythology we are constructing requires a subversion of Elohim's own narrative of authority. If we do not support the narrative, we may forfeit the humans' worship of us as deity. Azazel and I have carefully deliberated who will fill the Seven, based upon craft and skill required for the plan, not upon partiality. We are all gods and we will all rule cities of men. The difference is mere façade. We seven will constitute the visible symbolic figurehead of the divine assembly of gods. As for the prize of our strategy, we will all share equally."

The assembly of Watchers applauded. Azazel frowned with envy at Semjaza's speaking prowess. Semjaza was clearly more skilled at making a lie sound like the truth. Though he and Azazel were equal leaders, it gave Semjaza the edge of perceived superiority. Azazel would have to find a way to change that.

Semjaza continued, "As Anu, the high god of the heavens, I will have more responsibilities of petty bureaucracy than any of you would care to shoulder. Azazel has chosen to be Inanna, the goddess of war who will lead our military administration."

Azazel came up with the role of goddess as an attempt at humorous irony. A female divinity who could stand on the neck of the best of any male warrior was the kind of humiliation of others he frequently sought. But he was beginning to realize that maybe he did not think that irony through well enough. He did not relish the idea of adorning himself in female garb and sexuality for such a long period of time. Some Watchers were already making jests about his feminine traits behind his back. He concluded to himself that if he caught them he would slaughter them.

Semjaza gestured to the five others standing beside them. "Baraqel will be Enlil, the god of air; Arakiba will be Enki, god of the waters below; Tamiel will be Nanna, the moon god; Zaqiel will be Utu, the sun god; and Ezeqel will be Ninhursag, goddess of the earth." Each of them stood proudly beaming in their new identities.

Semjaza pointed into the crowd. "Since Ramel and Sariel helped to pinpoint this location for our cosmic mountain, they shall be Ereshkigal and Nergal, goddess of the underworld and her husband. They shall guard the entrance to the Abyss."

Ramel winced. Much like Azazel, he did not treasure the idea of assuming a female identity. He certainly did not like the fact that according to the myth the others had created, Nergal raped Ereshkigal to make her his wife, in a failed attempt to master the secrets of the hidden underworld. Ramel consoled himself that he would be undisputed queen of the underworld, the guardian of the gates of Sheol.

Sariel pondered how he might play out the myth in a particularly demeaning way on Ramel.

Semjaza continued, "Each of you will have your own identity in the pantheon and will be given tribes and cities to rule over as patron deities." The worship of awe from the humans would not be too difficult. The physical structure of a Watcher represented divinity in

9

the minds of humans. At five and a half cubits tall, with sinewy musculature, they were already towering above the average male human who stood less than four cubits tall. Their finely scaled skin produced a gleaming bronze appearance that earned them the nickname, "Shining Ones." Coupled with their elongated heads and glimmering blue lapis lazuli reptilian eyes, their luminescence reinforced a distinction between the human and the divine necessary for their deception.

Semjaza added, "As you know, Elohim is an insufferable tyrant whose megalomania is only matched by his childish tantrums. If we want to accomplish our ultimate goal, we must give these humans a pantheon of gods that is unified, benevolent, and worthy of worship and obedience."

Azazel knew that last statement was meant for him.

Semjaza had given Baraqel authority over the city of Nippur. Its central location among the cities of Shinar made it a valuable prize for Azazel's military strategy and political status in the pantheon. Nippur would be the first location for the assembly of the divine council among humans. Azazel knew Baraqel was a favorite of Semjaza, and that was why Semjaza had sided with him against Azazel's legitimate claim on the city. Semjaza's compromise was to give Baraqel as Enlil the city, but to allow Azazel as Inanna to have a residence there as well. Azazel had argued vociferously against the decision at first, but decided to give in and wait for the right moment for his own rise to power. Once he led their forces into war, he would achieve the distinction that even Semjaza would have to acknowledge and perhaps even submit to. And then Azazel would rout out all those who mocked him. He would cut off their heads and boil them in lava, which was a particularly painful torture considering that Sons of God could not die mortal deaths. They were, all of them, divine.

Semjaza concluded his remarks to the assembly. "Our first task is to go out to the villages and cities and perform signs and wonders and reveal the secrets of heaven to draw the humans into our trust. If we are to make them believe us, we must believe ourselves. So it is imperative that we never use our heavenly names again. We must always refer to one another by our adopted names of deity. But more importantly, we must *think of ourselves* as those deities. We must inhabit our roles with truthfulness. I am no longer Semjaza; I am Anu the sky god. There is no Azazel, there is only Inanna."

Someone blurted out, "Queen of heaven!" Some laughed. Inanna marked out the heckler and schemed how she would torture him later.

Anu deflected the insult. "Indeed, she is. And she is the goddess of war. You will do well to follow her lead into battle when the time comes. Until then, find your cities, reveal your mysteries, and establish your shrines of worship. This Mount Hermon will be our divine mount of assembly. We will reside here and visit our cities on an as-needed basis."

Enlil spoke up. "But if we do not reside in our cities, will we not lose control over them with our absence?"

Anu replied, "Your religious priesthood will be responsible for crafting a graven image of you that represents your presence and rule over the city. We have developed a ritual for your priests to use to draw your breath into the statue, which becomes your living presence when you are not there. We call it the 'opening of the mouth' ceremony."

Inanna thought the ritual ridiculous, but humans were so flesh-bound they needed concrete expressions of the supernatural realm or they would lose heart. Elohim had done a poor job of uniting spirit with these disgusting filthy sacks of meat.

Anu continued, "You will reveal the doctrine of the priest-king as also created in your own image. This will build the myth required to maintain orderly submission from your people in your absence, when we meet here at Hermon to complete our final plan of action."

It was brilliant. Anu had thought of everything. He had even sent out a select number of them into the four corners of the earth, south into Egypt, north beyond the Euphrates into the Halafan hinterlands, east to Elam and the Indus Valley, and even west across the great primal seas to distant unknown islands. The Watchers would reign as gods over the entire earth and inspire countless variations on their one myth of rebellion against Elohim.

But it was the final plan that excited the loyalty and devotion of the Watcher gods.

They swore an oath, to bind everyone among them by a curse. If anyone abandoned their commitment to the final plan, or revealed its secret scheme, the others would unite and bind that Watcher into the earth to suffer the torment of frozen solitude for millennia until the judgment. It was the one heinous thing that made each and every one of them shiver with dread.

CHAPTER 2

The Watchers spread out over all the land, claiming their peoples and unveiling secrets to the sons of men — dark occult secrets that humanity should never have known. They taught mankind the ways of sorcery and alchemy, incantations and the cutting of magical roots, casting of spells and the arts of divination, necromancy, and astrology. Elohim fast became a distant memory for mankind as they worshipped and served the creation instead of the Creator.

The heavens above was one of the most glorious of that creation that man twisted to evil ends. When Elohim placed the heavenly objects in their order, he did so with the intent of expressing his glory not through beauty alone, but also through story. He embedded that story in the very physical structure of the skies above. As the sun, moon, and stars revolved around the face of the earth, observers recorded movements and charted the heavens. Stars were connected by imaginary lines of constellations that depicted the future God ordained. These constellations were pictures that told a story in twelve distinct parts.

The narrative was of a virgin (Virgo) who would bear the promised seed and pay the price of justice to overcome the "wounder of the heel" (Scorpio the scorpion). This promised one would be a conqueror (Sagittarius the archer), who would carry the weight of sins and bring living waters for his people (Aquarius the water-bearer). Those people would be blessed though bound (Pisces the fish). Their blessings would be finally achieved through a ram of sacrifice who would become a ruling leader (Taurus the bull), a king with two natures (Gemini the twins). He would hold his people fast in his grip (Cancer the crab), and would ultimately reign as king over the earth (Leo the lion).

But this narrative of prophecy would eventually be subverted by the enemies of Elohim, who transformed it into an entire substitute system of astral worship where stars were considered as gods over the lives of men. Though there was no actual power in the stars, it served the purpose of the gods to divert mankind's attention from the true God of history into a god of one's own use.

• • • • •

Of all the forbidden secrets revealed by the gods, none caused as much hope in the heart of Inanna as the arts of fornication and war. She exploited the beauty of human sexuality. It was a particular talent of hers to twist a good thing into something bad. She sought to replace Elohim's holy marriage covenant with unholy violations. She wanted to enslave these wretched creatures to their appetites. The possibilities were endless. The goal was to inspire every kind of union other than a man and woman in lifelong covenant before Elohim.

One of the unfortunate results of such unrestricted behavior was unwanted offspring, which tended to infect humans with a repulsive desire for moral responsibility and chastity. To counter this sentiment, the gods taught the medicinal sorcery of bitter herbs to induce miscarriage, as well as the technique of using utensils to

14

smash the embryo in the womb. This would enable immoral behavior without the consequences. Inanna shivered with delight at that thought. It made her want to go out and violate a few humans herself. But that would be for later.

As for war, now *that* was an art. Inanna taught the craft of making instruments of death more accessible to the wicked. Knives, slings, arrows, shields, breastplates, and spears would become more ubiquitous than instruments of peace. These things were not in and of themselves evil, but in order to inspire mankind to do more damage, provide them with a technology for accomplishing that damage beyond the reach of one man wrestling another to the ground with fists, rocks, and clubs. Evil men will always seek to kill. Warfare technology simply provides them the ability to carry out their evil on grander scales with more destruction. Unfortunately, it would also provide good men with the ability to defend themselves against such evil. But Inanna could overcome that minor technicality with authoritarian control of the populace. Take away the dissidents' weapons and they are more docile and obedient to the power of the state which was the power of gods. To Inanna, the human race was an unfettered malignancy on the earth that required occasional strangling to keep it from getting out of control.

CHAPTER 3

At first, people all across the land bowed in awe before the glory of the gods and their revelation of secret knowledge. They worshipped and built shrines expressing their submission. This first step of the three-part plan of the gods had been successful.

At Mount Hermon, Anu inspired the surrounding peoples to build the first holy temple to the gateway of the gods called *kadingir*. Embedded into the mountain in a step-like structure, it dominated the landscape, serving as the temple of Ereshkigal, goddess of the underworld, Sheol.

The time had come for the second step of their plan. All across the land, in every city and every village presided over by a god, the citizens were called together in congregation before the holy shrine at the center of the city. The priest-king of each city, called the *ensi*, introduced their patron deity who then heralded a proclamation to the people — the proclamation of the Sacred Marriage.

Far away in the city of Nippur, Enlil, Lord of the air, was supposed to be the patron deity and Inanna a secondary goddess. But Inanna's intensity and assertiveness gained her a more devoted following, of which she never ceased to remind Enlil. She often found ways to usurp Enlil's authority, as she did that day during his announcement of the Sacred Marriage rite.

Enlil stood before a hushed audience. "Citizens of Nippur. You have been our loyal servants and for that we thank you. You have honored us with these shrines and with your worship and obedience. But a new day has dawned upon the world. And with it, a new opportunity for union between gods and men."

Inanna butted in, stealing Enlil's thunder with her characteristic impatience and bravado. "We are instituting the Sacred Marriage rite. All women will have the opportunity to be given in marriage to the gods."

The faces in the crowd were unmoved. They did not quite understand what they were hearing.

Inanna continued. "By the authority of the pantheon, we are temporarily suspending all marriage covenants across the land. This will give every woman a right over her own body to choose. If you volunteer for this high honor you will transcend your pathetic earthly limitations and become one with deity. You will be liberated from your oppressed status as the 'weaker sex.' And the fruit of your womb will be demigods who will rule the earth."

Inanna rose to a crescendo as the thought flitted through her mind that even Anu would not be more eloquent at this moment. "I can think of no greater privilege than being a child bearer of the gods! And that privilege begins today. All those women who desire the Sacred Marriage say your goodbyes to your fathers, your husbands, your siblings and your lords, and come to the holy shrine of Enlil this evening. We will perform a mass marriage ceremony and celebrate your newly exalted status!" Inanna was smugly satisfied with her delivery. She had practiced all morning and relished the jealousy Anu might feel at her stirring speech.

17

The crowd remained unimpressed. They stood in stunned silence. They had not anticipated such an outrageous offer and did not know what to do. Slowly, they melted away with solemn faces, back to their homes to consider their options. Was this truly voluntary or was this another play on words that Inanna and Enlil were so adept at doing? Would there be punishment for those who chose not to marry the gods?

Inanna looked with contempt upon the dispersing crowd. Poor insects. They had no idea that she was actually a male, and that Enlil was not the only one who would have his way with these women.

Enlil plotted how he might someday stab Inanna in the back, metaphorically, or literally if at all possible. Either way would suit him just fine.

That evening the priests had eaten their sacrificial meal of goat and barley offerings. They assembled in the courtyard of Enlil's shrine in anticipation of welcoming the arriving women for preparation in the Sacred Marriage.

Enlil and Inanna bickered all the way from their residence in the shrine out to the courtyard. Inanna thought the images of them carved out of stone and wood were terrible artwork. Ugly and unflattering. Enlil thought they were good enough.

"Good enough?" barked Inanna. "Incompetence is not 'good enough.' If we chopped off a few hands, you can rest assured, these deplorable artisans would sharpen their skills and take their duty more seriously."

Before Enlil could respond, they were in the courtyard. The sight was not encouraging.

It was already late into the evening and not a single woman stood in line to offer herself to the gods. Not even a loose woman. A messenger pazuzu, an ugly dog-faced flying creature with a double

18

set of bat-like wings, brought them the message that this was the picture all over the land.

"These malicious conniving ingrates," spouted Inanna.

Enlil fumed as well. Since taking on flesh, his sexual desires increasingly consumed him as he looked upon the beauty of these daughters of men. He wanted them, and he wanted them now.

"What should we do?" asked Enlil.

Inanna responded flatly, her expression frozen. "If they will not give themselves to us, then we will have to take them by force."

Enlil broke into a knowing grin. For once, he and Inanna were entirely in agreement.

· · · · ·

An unusually quiet night rested over the city of Nippur. Families stayed inside their mud brick homes fearing reprisal for not volunteering their daughters and wives to the gods. Families sat hushed as they ate their meals, and went to bed early, hoping to hasten the coming of the next day and with it, a return to normal life. Many finally fell asleep as their exhaustion overcame their worry with slumber.

The tumult of soldiers marching and barging into homes at random broke the quiet. They held fathers and sons at spear point while companions dragged the females of the households and chained them by the neck to the backs of carts drawn by oxen. Screams cracked the darkness throughout the city, awakening families with fright. They could do nothing to protect themselves, only wait and hope they might be overlooked. They could not even pray to the gods, since it was the gods who were kidnapping their women and girls.

Fifty female hostages were herded into the courtyard of the shrine. They crowded in the small courtyard, trapped by the walls of simple enclosed structures of the shrines.

Inanna watched them and thought they would soon have to build up this unimpressive residence with ornament and pillars and gardens. A god deserved to be in the most expensive and extravagant building of the city. They were gods after all. In fact, she had plans to turn it into her own temple with sacred prostitution.

Inanna and Enlil stepped out onto a dais on one side of the large square courtyard bordered with pillars. Some of the women cried hysterically, others shivered in silent terror. Enlil spoke to them.

"My women. My beautiful women. There is no need for you to fear us. Though we were treated disrespectfully this evening, Inanna and I only desire to bless you with our bounty. Sometimes, disobedience to the gods brings chastisement, but it is a chastisement out of love for your best interest." Enlil scanned the crowd as he spoke, looking for his first choice.

"Oh, stop your pontificating and start choosing," muttered Inanna. She tromped out into the crowd and grabbed two young girls. They squealed and squirmed, but they were like a couple rabbits in the strong arms of the tall divinity as she carried them to her shrine.

It was going to be a busy night for Enlil. His skin radiated with hunger and virility. But he was not cruel like Inanna. He would be kind to his new wives. He was compassionate and thoughtful.

• • • • •

This atrocity of forced marriages occurred all through Shinar. Before Inanna and Enlil embarked upon their plundering, they sent their flying messenger pazuzus to as many other cities of the plain as

20

possible, explaining their predicament and solution and encouraging the other gods to follow suit.

And follow suit they did. The injustice throughout the land rose up as wailing tears in the ears of Elohim.

CHAPTER 4

Word reached Anu of Nippur's horror and its resounding influence on the other cities of the plain. Instantly, he knew it was Inanna's scheme. It was all he could do to contain himself. He would journey to each city himself and force each god to personally apologize for their reprehensible behavior. But first on his list was Nippur.

· · · · ·

When Anu arrived with an escort of twenty other gods, Inanna lay sound asleep from her long night of exertion. By the time she was coherent and aware of what was going on, not even she with all her fury could withstand the ten gods who held her and dragged her out to the courtyard. She saw Enlil bullied in like manner to stand beside her. An audience of the city elders and the families victimized by Inanna and Enlil were assembled before them.

"People of Nippur," Anu announced, "I return to you the daughters and wives who were untouched by the reckless actions of your patron deities."

Thirty of the women had not yet engaged in Sacred Marriage with Inanna and Enlil. They raced out of the midst of the priests into the arms of their families, weeping with both pain and joy. The others were already pregnant and would have to remain in holy confinement in the quarters built behind the shrine for this purpose.

"And now, your patrons have something they want to tell you." Anu looked straight at Inanna, awaiting her response.

Inanna stood close enough to hiss at Anu, "We will look weak. They will lose their respect for us."

Anu returned the hiss. "You are a fool, Inanna. You have already lost their respect. Men do not follow cruelty. They follow justice. Apologize, or I will have you flogged. Then we will see how much respect you will receive."

Inanna glared back at him spitefully. She refused to open her mouth.

Enlil jumped in. "My people. My precious worshippers, Inanna and I would like to extend our deepest heartfelt apology for our — excessive enthusiasm last night."

His choice of words was clever, thought Inanna. *Qualified apology.* It gave her an idea.

"As your gods," she interrupted Enlil, "we are responsible to care for you and provide for your needs." Anu could see her twist coming. He knew her too well. "And as our people, you are responsible to obey us. We should not have acted so hastily, and we will not be so harsh in the future. But can you not see how you only hurt yourselves when you refuse to offer your daughters and wives out of love? Can you not see how you hurt us as well? Let us move forward and put this behind us. All is forgiven. All is blessed."

It was amazing, thought Anu, *how Inanna could turn an apology into an accusation without a blink. And deliver it as if she was an objective mediator rather than the offending party.* Of course, he expected as much. But it was better than nothing.

Inanna would not forget this moment. One day, she would have her chance for revenge on Anu and his bullying ways. Her rising anger was tempered by the amazing fact that afterward, Anu appealed to the people again to volunteer for the Sacred Marriage, and this time, at least thirty came forward. They may have realized they had no real choice or that things would only get worse if they did not "volunteer," but nevertheless, they volunteered. Inanna could not deny it; Anu had turned the embarrassment into a victory. The gods would have their brides for breeding.

CHAPTER 5

The offspring of the union between the Sons of God and the daughters of men were called *Nephilim*. A Naphil grew quickly in the womb and depleted the mother's nutrition to a deadly level. Their gestation period was five months. Though they were humanoid in appearance, they had a slight bluish grey tinge to their skin color and sported an extra digit on both their hands and feet, for a total of twelve fingers and twelve toes.

But there was one other important trait that would prove to be problematic for the breeding interests of the gods: Nephilim were large, very large. A mature Naphil could reach heights of seven, eight or even nine cubits tall. The Nephilim were giants. The fetus therefore was manifestly huge and tended to stretch a woman's womb cavity to its limits. For this reason, a Naphil's birth would kill its mother. This was all very natural for its kind, since the dead mother would be the newborn's first meal.

This inconvenient fact meant that the gods had to cloister the carriers into isolated quarters. They pursued a rigorous campaign of lies to keep the public from discovering the truth.

But leaks had occurred and rumors spread about the deadly consequences of the Sacred Marriage rite. All of mankind feared what they worshipped in place of Elohim their creator.

Within five months, the first Nephilim were born and celebrated in the cities and villages across the land. These firstborn were called *Rephaim* because they were the most pure of the breed. They would become kings and rulers of the earth. The inhabitants of Shinar called them the *Igigi*, demigods who served the Anunnaki gods, or "gods of princely seed." New flocks of women, regularly chosen, repopulated the harems of the gods with vessels worthy of their seed.

• • • • •

A generation passed. Nephilim giants multiplied upon the face of the earth and subdued it.

CHAPTER 6

Enoch ben Jared pushed open the doorway to the council chamber of the palace just in time to see Thamaq, one of the ruling Rephaim, pound the table in anger, all but spitting in the face of King Enmeduranki. "We have given a command and we expect it to be obeyed!" shouted Thamaq. Yahipan, the other Rephaim, grunted and nodded sternly as he leaned forward to emphasize his agreement with his co-regent's words.

Enmeduranki was the two-hundred-year old priest-king of the city of Sippar, and Enoch, his young eighty-five-year old *apkallu* wisdom sage. Sippar sat strategically at the point of closest proximity between the Tigris and Euphrates in the northernmost region of Shinar. As the crucial port city for all the economic activity of the area, all commercial trade between the northern and southern regions of Mesopotamia went through Sippar. Commodities like stone, cedar, and lapis lazuli from the north, as well as barley, beer, and livestock from the south all passed through its trade channels. It was a split city, with one half on each bank of the Euphrates. A transportation canal had been dug from the nearby Tigris to connect the two rivers that serviced different sides of the alluvial plain.

The fertile land around Sippar produced an abundance of crops. But there was a shortage at that moment, and the Rephaim were not happy about it.

Enoch choked down his disgust for these contentious giant rulers and set the clay tablets on the table, bowing in deference. "My lords, the accounting of the food stores of the city." He wished his entrance could help Enmeduranki, but he knew the report was not good news.

"Thank you," said Enmeduranki. He looked over the tablets for the numbers. Drops of sweat pooled on his forehead and trickled down his cheeks. The pressure was taking its toll on him.

Enmeduranki was a good soul who sought to rule his people with compassion. But he was also a vassal of the Rephaim, the true rulers of the city. They were a new addition to the bureaucratic hierarchy above the priest-king and below the god. Enmeduranki was supposed to be a liaison between the people and the Rephaim demigods, but what it really amounted to was making the people accept the demands of the Rephaim. And their demands continued to increase.

"It is as I feared, my lords," he sighed. "There is nothing left."

"What do you mean there is nothing left?" blurted Thamaq. "What about the famine food stores?"

Thamaq and Yahipan were two of the original Nephilim born by the seed of the gods to rule over men. They were both nearly eight cubits tall and dressed in ostentatious robes of royalty. They were impious models of vainglorious conceit, releasing their tempers at the slightest of discrepancies. They even mocked Utu the sun god behind his back, an unforgivable act of blasphemous arrogance. Enoch detested them.

"I am afraid the famine stores are exactly what the Nephilim just finished consuming," Enmeduranki offered. The impossible position of responsibility without true authority wearied him. "The last of our famine food stores. The normal stores were emptied out last month."

Yahipan broke in, "Enlist more citizens to grow and harvest more food."

"The entire city is already forced to do so. We have no more private laborers who are not slaves of the realm. We have no source of income, only administrative expenses," pleaded Enmeduranki.

Thamaq rebuked him, "Enmeduranki, we must find a way. The Nephilim occupy the palace streets in protest. They dug the canals and built the entire irrigation system that brings the very life waters to this city from the Tigris and Euphrates. Do you question their entitlement to food?"

Enmeduranki swallowed his sigh at the utterance of that big lie. The Nephilim had built the vast irrigation canals that radiated around the cities like blood vessels. But those earthworks had been completed many years before, and they were now in grave disrepair. The giants had gathered themselves into a union of agreement that demanded minimal labor and maximum wages from the government. They had become an organized gang of thugs. Neither the Rephaim nor the gods seemed to be concerned about the demise of the city's economy.

"I do not question their right, my lord. But as you know, the Nephilim have increased their food intake by a factor of four over the past generation. No one anticipated such exponential growth when we first created our programs. We simply cannot keep up with their consumption." *They are very large and very hungry mouths to fill,* the priest-king thought bitterly to himself.

Thamaq regathered himself, "I am not sure you understand the seriousness of our predicament, priest-king. Facts and statistics are irrelevant to the Nephilim. They are hungry, bitter, and their numbers are strong. If they rise up in revolt, I will not be able to stop them. This entire city will be at their mercy."

"What say you, apkallu?" asked Yahipan with biting sarcasm.

Enoch's bowed head lifted to see the intense stare of both of the Rephaim.

"You sit there in silence. Are you not a fount of wisdom? Then vomit us some wisdom."

For a fleeting moment, the futility of his office flashed through Enoch's mind. He took his religious and political responsibility seriously, so seriously that he had adopted the Shinarian name *Utuabzu* in honor of Utu. Yet, increasingly, it seemed clear that the Rephaim were not so serious in their respect of the office or of his skills.

The city's governance was a typical Mesopotamian oligarchy modeled after the divine council of gods. Sippar's patron deity was Utu, the sun god. Enmeduranki was the governing ruler, the priest-king, created in the image of the gods. He carried out the combined duties of both religion and government on behalf of the deity. He had a council of elders of the city with whom he counseled, but he held closest his personal apkallu wisdom sages.

Enoch, as wisdom sage to the priest-king, was required to command a wide breadth of knowledge. He had trained in the sciences of both heavens and earth. He was shaman, diviner, scribe, and poet all in one. But it seemed to him that the most important office he held was as bard, the carrier of the culture's stories. All the laws, governance, religious beliefs and values of a people flowed downstream from the culture embodied in the songs and epics of the poet. Hearts and souls are moved by story and he who controls the culture's stories controls the people.

The world of storytelling was changing dramatically around Enoch. The new visual communication called "cuneiform" was overtaking the traditional oral recitation of verse. Scribes created cuneiform as a codified physical expression of language, using utensils to make impressions on clay tablets. The scribes wanted to keep a tangible account of personal and public wealth that could not be challenged by verbal lies or faulty memory. Using handheld styluses pressed into the clay, they could list objects owned by the ruler and how many he possessed. It had started out as pictures of cows, gold, wheat, wood, and other belongings. It had evolved into an abstract system of symbols that could be rapidly copied or communicated in a legal dispute.

Eventually the scribes saw other uses for this thing called writing. They experimented with ways of inscribing their oral epics and myths onto the clay. Writing could record what was said by the poet or sage. That record would be preserved unchanged through the years. It was a kind of magic that most sages hated because they feared it would soften their minds. After all, that which was recorded on clay did not need to be held in the memory. But Enoch was fascinated with writing. He wanted to adapt it into a tool for transmitting the dream visions he received from the deity.

"Well? The Anzu got your tongue?" Yahipan growled with biting sarcasm. Anzu was a huge lion-faced bird with vicious talons.

Enoch's stories would not be appreciated today. Today, all that mattered was the original use of writing for accounting records.

"Forgive me, Yahipan," said Enoch.

"Would you be pleased with a bloodbath?" said Yahipan.

"By no means, my lord," said Enoch. "I am a man of peace and piety. I deplore violence, and I have sought to encourage the people to submit to the rule of the priest-king and your majesties."

In truth, Enoch detested these Rephaim with all his being. They exploited the citizens with their tyrannical control and redistribution of wealth and food. But he was also a pacifist. He believed in submission to authority and would never encourage civil disobedience, let alone an uprising. Violence only led to more violence. He believed he should trust the gods and accept their decrees with steadfast faith.

"In my lowly opinion, it seems evident that both the Nephilim and the citizenry have become dependent upon the government to care for them. It is most natural then for them to not care for themselves and to become hostile when their subsidies are taken away. Unfortunately, it seems to me that we are not up against a matter of political opinion, but of reality. The government is bankrupt. There is no more to give. We cannot spend what we do not have."

"You call that blathering 'wisdom'?" complained Yahipan. "I want a solution, not a contest of blame!"

Enoch frowned and then quickly banished it. This was not a contest of blame, these were the bald facts. All the other cities such as Erech, Eridu, and Larak faced these same facts. The strongest economic cities were all collapsing. The giants had been brought to all these cities to accomplish mighty feats of industry for the Rephaim. The purpose had been to glorify the gods and build an empire of power for the pantheon. But it had all gotten out of control. Now, the entire civilization was in jeopardy of collapsing. The giants were large, strong, warrior-like, and organized. They appointed leaders to press their demands upon the Rephaim rulers of all the cities. Revolution seemed inevitable.

The victims in all this turmoil were the average citizens, the backbone of the civilization. These were the ones Enoch felt were exploited at the expense of this class warfare for power. The society appeared to be an advancement of civilization, but Enoch believed it moved toward the inevitable centralization of power into the hands of the elite priestly caste, of which he was one. It remained a point of contradiction in his conscience.

His position made him privy to the myriad of government archives compiled by their scribes, registering every aspect of the lives of its citizens. Births, deaths, genealogies, land transfers, tax records, all were used to drain every ounce of income tax, land tax, head tax and death tax from every soul.

It would seem that slaves, in comparison, had a less complicated life. At least they were called what they actually were. The average citizen became a slave without the name. He worked hard on his farm or in the marketplace, earned an honest wage to take care of his simple family, paid his taxes to the realm, worshiped his gods, and left others alone to seek their own happiness. This average man and his family had his life sucked out of him by taxes and government control, only to end his life in Sheol, forgotten and never to return. Was this the will of the gods? It made Enoch weep at night and question his devotion to the pantheon. He felt that he was a man stuck in the middle, trying to make both sides happy, the ruling elite of the gods, and the common citizens who served that divine council. He felt a miserable failure.

"Apkallu! Are you listening to me, maggot?!" Yahipan's outburst brought Enoch back to the immediate moment. "I will whack your skull from your spine." He raised his hand.

Thamaq stopped him. "Brother, he is not worth your energy. We have been alerted to the facts by our servants. Let us withdraw to our chambers and determine our course of action."

Enmeduranki turned to Enoch. "Where is your son, the apprentice? If he is to become a sage, would not this situation be essential to his learning?"

"Forgive me, my lord," replied Enoch. "If you will excuse me, I will go and brief him." Enoch bowed and left the room. He did not even have the beginning of an idea where in the world his rascally son Methuselah was. But he had a good idea of *who* he might be with.

CHAPTER 7

Methuselah swung the pear-shaped mace down toward the skull of his adversary, a fifteen-year old girl named Edna. She raised her shield and blocked it effectively, then parried with her own mace.

He barked, "Excellent, runt!"

Methuselah was a strapping twenty-year old handsome young man. His unusual blue eyes often drew the teasing of his companions, saying that he was a *Bene ha Elohim*, or more likely a Naphil. It was not true, but he played along with it because he liked standing out from the crowd. He was a fiery lad with a passion for arguing, not the best of traits for an apkallu in training, since their order was marked by restraint and listening. But Methuselah hungered for knowledge, and loved to study and learn about everything.

At this moment, though, he was not learning. He was teaching. And it was not an intellectual exercise, but a physical one.

Edna swung again. He blocked her blow.

"Is that the best you can do, you scrawny little female?"

Methuselah burst into action, swinging one blow after another. Edna could barely keep up with the raining strikes. If she let one get through, it would leave a nasty bruise she would nurse for days.

With each swing, Methuselah verbally challenged her strategy. "What did I teach you? Have you no counter plan? I am stronger than you, so how can you defeat me?"

With those last words, he backed her up against the wall of the small practice room, his mace to her neck. He had used sheer strength to overwhelm her.

He leaned in close to her face and mused, "Now, if I was a particularly wicked soldier, having worn you down, I might take my pleasure before killing you." He was not teasing her. He wanted her to face the reality of the world.

"Too late," she said. He looked at her puzzled.

"Letting you expend your energy on me was my counter plan. While you were worn out and arrogantly crowing into my face with your horrible breath, I was gutting you," she said.

He glanced down to see her hand with knife blade at his abdomen. She shifted it down to his groin and added, "Or severing your manhood if you prefer."

He smiled. "I am proud of you, Edna." He kissed her forehead and turned to sit down for a rest.

To him, it was just a simple peck of affection. He did not notice that the soft swift touch of his lips upon her skin made her swoon. She gathered herself together and plopped down next to him.

"Why do you talk mean to me while fighting?" she asked.

He smiled. "That is what warriors do. It is mental warfare. Wearing down the enemy inwardly as well as outwardly."

"Oh, I see," she said, and added playfully, "you ogre."

He smiled at her. "You are hardly wet with sweat." He was drenched from the exercise.

"We women do not sweat, we glow." Her look of serious reflection melted into shared laughter.

"Edna," he said, "You are amusing. You are a girl, yet you prefer the company and roughhousing of boys. You do not wear makeup or jewelry. You sneak around your superiors to learn sports and fighting — and you are good. You are really good. You are intellectually curious and you want to see the world, yet you are a temple virgin, dedicated to the gods."

It was true. Edna was a spitfire boyish girl. Her serious expression returned in an instant. She brushed a strand of hair away from her face. It was a sole loose one that had come out of her otherwise usual tightly wrapped and bound hair bun.

"Do not tease me, Methuselah. Girls have no choice in their placement in society. I do not want to *be* a boy, I just enjoy doing things that boys do. It is not that I do not have female desires as well."

He laughed. "That would make you the perfect wife I guess."

She thought to herself, *Yes! And I would make you so happy.*

He interrupted her thoughts. "Those female desires will soon be fulfilled when you engage in the Sacred Marriage rite with the god."

She blushed through a moment of uncomfortable silence.

"I wish I could be married to a normal man — like you."

She gulped. Did she say too much?

Methuselah looked at her seriously. "Me too, Pedna." It was one of his many affectionate nicknames for her. He would call her "Edna Pedna," so she had responded by calling him "Methuselah Poozelah," and they eventually shortened them to Pedna and Poozela.

His whole countenance changed from joy to sorrow. He knew the consequences of being betrothed to the gods. He knew the ultimate end of bearing the Nephilim offspring. It always bothered him. On the one hand, the gods were sovereign and had the right to their wives. Humans were, after all, slaves of the gods. But on the other hand, how could so gruesome a reality be part of a just world?"

"What happens to the child-bearers?"

"That is the prerogative of the gods," he said. He could not bring himself to tell her. Instead, his silence and the look of dread on his face spoke loudly.

"Would you let them hurt me, Poozela?"

His heart nearly broke in two. He had been a big brother, even a father figure, to this girl ever since he noticed her special qualities and vivacious thirst for life as a mere ten-year old. He had secretly trained her to read cuneiform, fight with weapons, and reason like a sage. She now stood on the verge of her sixteenth birthday, and he was about to lose her forever. He struggled to hold back a flood of tears ready to burst. He did the only thing he could do. He deflected the question.

"We exist to serve the gods, not question them."

It was the pious response, the proper answer, his duty. And he did not believe it for one second.

"Poozela."

He kept staring out to space.

"Poozela?"

He looked into her eyes. He could not avoid her tender soul.

"That is not good enough."

Methuselah was about to break completely apart.

The door suddenly burst open. Enoch and the priestess supervisor, a stout woman with a perpetual frown of dissatisfaction stood in the doorway.

Methuselah and Edna froze.

"Edna, I told you to stop this silly interest in sports," said the priestess. "You have your Sacred Marriage rite tomorrow and we need to test your makeup and try out the new dress!"

Enoch did not need as many words. "Methuselah."

Methuselah jumped to his feet and followed Enoch down the hallway back to their quarters in the palace.

CHAPTER 8

As a major city of trade, the Sippar palace sported a hodgepodge of ornamentation. Winding their way through the palace hallways, Methuselah and Enoch passed cedar columns from Aratta, hanging tapestries from the Indus Valley, and stone mason work from the Levant.

Enoch was a holy man who did not even see the craftsmanship and art that filled their living environment and absorbed Methuselah's imagination.

They could not be more different. Enoch received visions from the gods. He sought to raise his son with the same sense of piety and obedience. Unfortunately, Methuselah was too lustful for life and this earth. Enoch loved prayer, Methuselah loved reading cuneiform. Enoch barely noticed women, Methuselah stared at every attractive woman he saw. Enoch loved the holy liturgy of worship, Methuselah loved a feast of food and good drink. Enoch spent hours of silence in the temple shrine, Methuselah spent hours worshipping the beauty of creation (and especially the gods' most beautiful creation, the female body). Enoch was a holy man of heaven, Methuselah felt he was a profane man of earth.

It seemed that the only thing his father loved on this earth was Methuselah's mother. She was Enoch's one connection with humanity and both father and son adored her. Nevertheless, Methuselah thought Enoch could not understand his friendship with Edna. His stomach turned with anxiety.

"Are you romantically inclined to this girl?" demanded Enoch.

"No! She is devoted to the gods!" Methuselah barked, reflexively. How could he think that? Methuselah might be quite the romantic lothario in his weakness for women, but he would never violate the sacred order to even consider Edna as a love interest.

"She is like the little sister I never had," Methuselah claimed. "I do not expect you would understand that."

Despite what his son may have thought of his holy demeanor, Enoch was not a heartless disembodied spirit. It warmed his heart to see his son care for people, and seek to help them and protect them. And he certainly understood love. He just wanted Methuselah to learn what was most important in life after religion, and that was status. There would be plenty of time and opportunity to choose a wife from the court once Methuselah was established as a bona fide apkallu to royalty.

They arrived at the door to their quarters and entered. Enoch struggled to shake off his usual thoughts of his son's future.

"Well, I do not expect you to understand the spiritual vision I just received from an enemy god."

Methuselah's mouth dropped. He had no idea what in the world Enoch was talking about.

Enoch's wife greeted him at the door with a kiss and embrace, as she did every day of their marriage. She was a humble woman, unfortunately too often overshadowed by Enoch's important status

41

and neglected in his royal responsibilities. Yet Methuselah knew that without her, Enoch would be nothing. Enoch knew it as well. She was his strength, his support, his closest counsel and only trusted friend. As passionately zealous as Enoch was, he was also prone to depression. He would often say that in his mountaintops and valleys, his Edna was his steady sea level.

She believed in her husband, happy to support his high and holy calling. Methuselah would sometimes jest what a miracle it was that the gods would create a woman with enough patience for his father.

Methuselah found it ironic that with everything about father and son being so at odds, his best friend had the same name as his mother. Methuselah often wondered why his father, who could see spiritual patterns and signs in just about everything, could not embrace this curiosity with a more positive acceptance.

One thing was certain. The two Ednas were nothing alike. They were as different as Methuselah and Enoch. Mother Edna was kind, sweet, supportive, and submissive. Sixteen-year old Edna was spunky, feisty, independent, and stubborn.

Methuselah's differences with his father haunted him wherever he turned. The living quarters they occupied were humble compared with other palace servants or royalty. According to Enoch, a wisdom sage was not concerned about the things of this world, but about truth, justice, and heaven. Thus, their living space held only a couple bedrooms, and a small eating and lounging area. The whole dwelling space was no bigger than the average servant's quarters. They had only the most basic of furniture, stark against bare walls. Methuselah felt it a pity that royalty such as they were should live in such lack of beauty.

Methuselah had wanted to change the bleak environment for a long time. To him, beauty embodied as much a part of truth as philosophy or ethics. In fact, he thought Enoch's failure to understand this was his father's weakness. A spirituality that excluded the body was impoverished. Methuselah sought a more earthy spirituality. Austerity might bring more intellectual satisfaction, but it created emotional emptiness. Did not the gods make this world to be enjoyed? It made no sense to create a rose, or a woman's body and then say, "Ignore the rose and the woman, and the myriad of sensory experiences that make up your daily existence. Just think about abstract wisdom and the unseen spirit world." That was madness to him.

Enoch said, "Methuselah, I just had a vision of the unseen spirit world that you will probably think is madness."

"Try me," quipped Methuselah, expecting his father to be right. It already sounded crazy and he had not even heard it yet.

The three of them sat down together. Edna brought some fruit and nuts for them to eat.

Enoch said to Methuselah, "Once again, your extracurricular activities drew you away from your responsibility to be with me in the council meeting."

"Sorry, father." They might not be able to understand each other, but they did love one another. Apologies and forgiveness came quickly between them.

"You better be sorry or I will tan your hide," said Enoch. Methuselah cringed at the saying. It was a corny phrase his father liked to use — too often.

Enoch continued, "The first place I looked for you was in the palace garden. You spend too much time in that useless waste of space."

"It is not useless, father," said Methuselah. "Beauty *is* divine transcendence. It connects us to the gods as much as any ritual does." He shook his head. "You always do that. You miss the forest for the trees."

"You are wrong, son," said Edna. "Your father does not care for the forest *or* the trees."

It was her way of teasing Enoch without putting him down. A little bit of humor went a long way toward persuasion for Edna. She had to have a lot of humor with this family of stubborn mules.

Methuselah continued complaining, "Do you even know that the temple is laden with garden imagery and ornamentation? The gods are worshipped in a garden!"

"Enough, son," said Edna. "The point was made. Listen to your father." She would never abandon her true loyalty to her husband.

Enoch sat expressionless, waiting for Methuselah to finish his defense. He continued as if he had not heard a word Methuselah said. "When I was in the garden in my dream vision, I fell to the floor as a dead man, and when I awoke, two archangels stood over me."

Enoch knew how to tell a good story, a useful skill for an apkallu sage. Enoch unfolded his experience to his wife and son with such vivid, artistic description that Methuselah felt himself enraptured into the very heaven of heavens, seeing it all with his own eyes. Maybe his father was not all that out of touch.

CHAPTER 9

"Who are you?" asked Enoch.

The larger, stronger angel spoke first, "We are Gabriel and Uriel, the archangels from the throne of Elohim."

"Elohim?" Enoch had heard of the name. His tribe descended from the line of Seth that had worshipped this god as the creator of all things. But when the dispersion had occurred and his ancestors had settled in the city, they were visited by the gods of Shinar, and this Elohim faded into obscurity. An abstract blurred memory of a distant unseen deity seemed impotent in the real presence of the pantheon with its Four High Gods, Anu, Enlil, Enki, and Ninhursag, and their mighty signs and wonders.

"Everything you worship is a lie," said Gabriel.

Uriel looked at Gabriel. "That is a little shocking, Gabriel. Do you not think it would be wiser to ease him into the truth, instead of slamming him over the head with a mace?"

Gabriel rolled his eyes. "Very well." He turned back to the speechless Enoch.

"You might want to close your mouth," Uriel added to Enoch who snapped his gaping mouth shut.

"Enoch ben Jared, the living God is calling you to bear witness to the truth that has been suppressed in unrighteousness." Gabriel looked at Uriel as if to ask, is that good enough for you? Uriel nodded cautiously.

In the fold of archangels, Uriel ranked as a black sheep, one marred with spots as well as an off-color. He always seemed to see things from a different perspective than the others. This caused him to always interrupt discussions and provoke delays. It made him the butt of jokes. He could not help it. He did not seek to stand out of the crowd. Elohim made him that way. Uriel sometimes called it a "curse," but only in jest. Elohim knew better and had his purposes. In a way, it made Uriel feel special. Perhaps his nature was not all that undesirable.

Uriel stood a bit shorter than most archangels, maybe by half a cubit. His stature became another source of relentless teasing about strength and ability. The mockery nudged Uriel to work harder than all the rest, to prove that he was as good as any of them. The teasing sharpened his wit and words, as if to compensate for his lesser physique.

Enoch's dumbfounded stare focused on Gabriel, until Uriel spoke.

Uriel said to Enoch, "Elohim is the true and living God, the Creator of the universe. He has chosen you as his representative to proclaim judgment upon the gods and upon their giant progeny, the Nephilim."

"You call that subtle?" muttered Gabriel under his breath.

"More lyrical than you will ever be," quipped Uriel. He turned back to Enoch. "Terror is about to break out on all the land, and Elohim has commissioned you to reject the gods of Shinar and become his prophet."

Enoch could not decide which was more difficult to accept, a confrontation with two archangels or the inane banter that kept distracting them from their message. He shook himself out of his stupor. Nothing he had just heard made sense to him. "Excuse, me, what did you say?" asked Enoch.

Uriel repeated the words like a mother with an unruly child who would not listen, "Elohim wants you to speak for him."

"Are you crazy?" said Enoch. "I have been a diviner priest for Utu the sun god all my life. The pantheon of gods has been good to me and my family. Now, I am supposed to condemn them all to their faces?"

"And the Nephilim," Uriel reminded him.

Enoch persisted, "The Nephilim are demigods. They have strength and powers unmatched by humans. The first prophecy I make will be my last. They will execute me on the spot."

Gabriel ignored Enoch's protest. "Trust in Elohim. Rahab is coming upon this city." Rahab was the name of the sea dragon of chaos, the creature of destruction that swam the waters of the Abyss. People invoked her name when they wanted to express foreboding disaster of total annihilation.

"Bring your family and loved ones to the mountains of Aratta in the north. In the volcanic lands of Sahand you will find your distant ancestor, Adam. He will teach you what you need to learn to fulfill Elohim's calling upon your life."

Enoch protested again, "How do I know you are telling the truth? I have never heard from Elohim before. How do I know I can trust him?"

The angels knew the question was reasonable. Gabriel had prepared for it. "This very night, your city will be besieged and your king will die. When you, Enoch, son of Jared, are offered the

47

opportunity to be king, know this: If you accept, you and all your family line will be executed to clear way for a new regime."

Uriel completed the prophecy. "If you choose to escape the city with your family, you will be protected by — well, yours truly." He could not pass up the opportunity for a touch of wit.

Gabriel thought Uriel's wit lessened the urgency of their warning. He reiterated, "Do not accept the offer of kingship, Enoch. It will be deadly."

For the first time in his life in the presence of his father, Methuselah sat quiet. He was stunned. Of all the crazy dreams and visions his father had experienced throughout the years, this one was different. It hit Methuselah more like the truth than anything ever had. He thought that was strange, because he was not the mystical type. But this time, *he just knew it was true.*

Enoch's voice vibrated with anxiety. "How do I know this is true? I mean, this Elohim has never shown his face to me all these years, and now all of a sudden, I am told to leave everything and follow him? It is bizarre."

"Are you moonstruck, father?" said Methuselah, a common insult in the city of the sun god. "After all these years of your wild and unbelievable dreams, you question *this one — now?*"

Enoch retorted, "And you now are the gullible true believer? Or is that just your habit of being contrary and impulsive?"

"I am not being contrary. I cannot explain it. I just know it is true."

"You cannot explain it," repeated Enoch. "Well, now you know how I feel, and what I have been trying to tell you all these years."

Methuselah said, "Have you not often said you would like to meet our forefather Adam? To learn of our history? Here is your opportunity to do so."

"I was being sentimental, not literal," snapped Enoch. "I cannot just walk away from Utu. He has been my god all these years. He has provided for us."

They heard the front door shut. They suddenly noticed that Edna was not with them anymore. She had gotten up and must have left their chambers.

Enoch called out, "Edna?"

No one answered him.

"That is strange," said Enoch. "She has never done that before."

Methuselah guessed that his mother believed the prophecy, more than the "sage" who had received it. She was probably making preparations to leave the city, preparations that included Methuselah's young friend, the other Edna, and her parents. She had discussed the possibility with her son in the past.

"She is warning others," he surmised.

"What others?" challenged Enoch.

"Edna and her parents?" offered Methuselah.

"How does she know about this girl of yours?"

"She is not my 'girl,' father," said Methuselah. "I have told mother all about her. She knows we are close, and she is going to help them. She will go after Edna's parents first, to bring them to the palace."

Methuselah's mother already knew that young Edna was in love with her son. She had spent long hours talking with the girl. Mother Edna had been a young lower caste girl once and had fallen in love with a young Enoch as a royal apkallu in training. So she did not have the qualms that either of the men had. They always took so much longer to see these things.

Methuselah replied simply, "We should prepare the family to leave. Mother will be back before long."

"Son, we must have confirmation."

"What else do you need to be — " A knock at the door interrupted Methuselah. Enoch opened the door to a servant messenger.

The man was pale and trembling. "My lord, a riot has begun in the city. The Nephilim are on a rampage, destroying everything in sight and capturing citizens."

Enoch could not believe his ears. "They are taking hostages? What ransom can the palace possibly give them that they have not already extorted out of us?"

"They have been demanding justice. Some say they are taking their anger out on the poor citizens."

"Holy Utu," said Enoch. "My Edna is out there."

Methuselah's throat went dry. He also knew what other horrors awaited the women. "Where is the city guard? Have they done anything to hold them back?"

"The city guard was the first to be taken out," the messenger wailed.

Enoch said, "Where are the Rephaim? Enmeduranki?"

The messenger shook his head. "Nowhere to be found."

That did not make sense to Enoch. They would be the first to coordinate action to protect the citizens. He knew the priest-king truly cared for his people and the Rephaim did not tolerate rebellion.

"The gates of the city have been locked," said the messenger. "No one can get out. For some reason, the Nephilim have stayed away from the palace area." The palace and its riches were always the ultimate goal in these revolutions. "Justice" usually meant theft, plunder, and destruction.

Enoch dismissed the messenger. He turned to Methuselah. "I have to get Edna, but I do not know where she is."

"My Edna will know," said Methuselah. "She can lead us there."

Enoch nodded reluctantly. "You go find the servant girl. I will spread the word to the family to gather in the underground passageways and wait for us. I will meet *you* in the courtyard. Your little friend can lead us to her parents and our Edna."

They ran out the door.

CHAPTER 10

Enoch had been accused of being so spiritually minded that he lacked practical sense, but it was not true. He had arranged various positions of responsibility in the palace area for his extended family. He had given each a code and procedure to follow should any kind of disaster arise, be it a siege of the city or a revolt from within. This revolt fulfilled the second contingency.

He would not have to gather everyone himself. He need only contact a couple of them and they would pass along the information through their prescribed channels. All of them would follow various prepared routes to meet in the secret passageways below the palace, created for this very purpose. Down there, they could weather the danger in the city above. They even had food stores which stayed well-preserved in the cool and dry environment.

Young Edna had no such preparation. In the harem, they would probably be the last to hear about the tragedy unfolding outside their palace walls.

Methuselah made his way across the courtyard to the small harem building at the distant end of the palace area. He could hear the screams outside in the streets. He could not imagine why the giants had not breached the palace gates. He glanced over his shoulder. The glow over the walls of the palace told of buildings burning throughout the city. It was as bad as he had expected.

When he reached the harem building, he dashed into the private chambers. He passed by maidens beautifying themselves and trying on their dresses for tomorrow's Sacred Marriage rite. Screams of surprise and offended modesty rose up as Methuselah looked around wildly hunting for Edna. Losing his way amidst the clamor and buzz around him, he stumbled upon a girl in an elaborate white dress flattening out its ruffles.

"Excuse me, miss," said Enoch.

She turned, and he lost his breath. He beheld a vision of a stunning young beauty with flowing locks of golden spun hair. It bothered him that the gods got the choicest of the women.

"Where is Edna?"

The beauty glared at him with incredulity, exotic make up accentuating her every breath-taking feature. "Are you mocking me?"

"I am sorry, what?" he replied.

"Are you that thickheaded? It is me, silly," said the girl.

It hit him like a ton of mud bricks. This gorgeous vision of feminine transcendence frowning at him was none other than the transformed presentation of his immature scrawny little boyish girl Edna. His little Pedna. How could he have never seen her this way before?

He stumbled back a step and almost fainted. He knew at that very moment that he would never be happy in this life again until he married this goddess. This was the very first time he had really truly *finally* seen her. And his entire life changed in that instant.

"What is wrong with you?" Edna giggled.

Methuselah shook it off. He would have to deal with this later. Right now, he had to save her life.

"Edna, do you trust me?" he said.

"Yes, of course."

"Then trust me this once completely, and do exactly as I say. The city is in danger."

"What?"

"I will tell you on the way. Take off this outer dress. We must leave now. No questions asked."

She obeyed and pulled it off. Her tunic underneath was better suited for running.

She did trust him, with all her heart and soul. She let him lead her out of the building toward the courtyard. He told her about the riots and the giants and the hostages as they ran. It was all horrific, but she was a tough girl. Methuselah realized she was the kind of person you wanted on your side when all Sheol broke loose. She would not scream in fear and shake like a little mouse. She would want to join the fray.

"You need to tell me where your parents live. My mother went to get them, to bring them with us. But now they are all three caught up in the middle of it."

"I will take you there," said Edna.

"I want you to stay here," said Methuselah.

She looked him square in the eye. "You will not be able to find your way," she said. "You do not know the city streets, and you certainly do not know the shortcuts. You will get lost, plain and simple. I am not letting you go alone. I want to be with you."

He stared back into her eyes. He sometimes questioned whether he should have taught her how to debate so well. But she was right, so it was a good thing he had done it.

For the first time in her short existence on this earth she saw the expression of a man who would give his life for her without a thought.

In her eyes he saw the look of a woman who would die by his side rather than be alone. That is, after all, what she had trained for all those years.

He grinned. "Pedna, let us kick some shank."

Throughout Sippar, the streets lay eerily empty. Enoch, Methuselah, and Edna slinked through the shadows, trying to stay out of sight. The screams had died down, sporadic and at a distance. Fires burned all over, but they did not see any giants or people.

"This is not a good sign," said Methuselah.

She responded, "My parents have a secret hideaway in the floor. I am sure they would have hidden there at the first sign of trouble."

"Is there room for a third person?" asked Enoch.

"Yes," she said. "They always figured me into their plans."

"Utu be with them," prayed Enoch as they continued on. *Or should it be Elohim?* he thought.

Ahead of them, in the center of the city, they could see the glow of a huge bonfire. The giants had congregated there with the hostages. The trio needed to pass the gathering to get to the sector where Edna's parents lived. They slid past homes demolished by the smashing strength of the Nephilim. They shuddered at the degree of damage. Whole houses reduced to rubble, the streets littered with household items and furniture, small fires everywhere. But not a sign of life.

They made their way through the cluttered back alleys that Edna knew so well. They avoided the central bonfire. They were almost to her parents' street, when curiosity got the better of them. They decided to turn back and take a look. A gap in the wreckage gave them a better look at the open space.

The debris in the town square had been cleared away and piled up with wood from the marauding. Nearly a hundred of the giants stood around like a gang of miscreants.

Vomit arose in Edna's throat. They could see a crude line of cages full of weeping, pleading humans. Other humans were strung up from poles, and still others were encircled and taunted by groups of Nephilim. But the ultimate atrocity playing out before their eyes was not one of torture and rape, but cannibalism. The Nephilim were eating their captives one by one. Some took the time to impale the victims and roast them over the flames. Others had no such civility, eating the poor humans alive and drinking their blood. The hostages were not being held for ransom at all. They were being held for food.

Tears filled Enoch's eyes. He knew the giants were a rowdy community and sometimes got in trouble for their violence, but he had not realized that they were capable of such barbarism. His entire view of the world had turned upside down.

Suddenly, behind them, they heard the snap of wood and the sound of stumbling and grunting. They dropped to the ground and slid beneath some wreckage. About fifteen cubits away, a drunken Naphil relieved himself in the open. Not all the Nephilim were at the bonfire. Stragglers wandered the streets and back alleys. The trio would have to be extra careful.

The Naphil belched and then without warning, projectile vomited into a pile of rubbish. The commotion gave Enoch, Methuselah, and Edna the opportunity to slip away without being seen or heard.

· · · · ·

The Rephaim leaders Thamaq and Yahipan were not at the palace or coordinating a military response to the riots because they had been the ones who betrayed the militia guard. They had been the ones to lock the city gates, and they had been the ones to instigate the mob riots of Nephilim. They had planned this entire drunken chaos. They had now gone off to a dark corner of the city to celebrate the bloodshed with carnal appetite.

They donned their royal robes and were on their way to the bonfire. Only a few streets from the scene of Nephilim atrocities, they heard a noise from one of the homes. They slipped up to a window and peered inside. An older couple climbed up from a trap door in the floor amidst a pile of debris. Smirking to each other, the Rephaim positioned themselves near the door, ready to trap these renegades. But they paused at a sight they had not expected. Someone they knew very well followed the older couple from the hiding place: Edna, the wife of Enoch the apkallu.

Their smirks turned to broad grins. What a lucky surprise for them, and what an unlucky surprise for these poor leeches. They burst into the home.

The would-be fugitives gasped and backed into a corner. Edna picked up the remains of a chair and brandished it as a weapon.

Thamaq laughed and brushed it aside as though it were nothing more than a feather. He grabbed Edna by the throat and pinned her against the wall. Then he seized the other woman with his free hand.

As Yahipan subdued the old man, Thamaq glared at Edna. "What are you doing here, wife of Utuabzu? You should have stayed safe in the palace."

She struggled in his suffocating grasp. "Why are you doing this?" she choked out. He ignored her question. He leaned in close. "I have long fantasized about consuming your flesh." Thamaq opened his mouth to bite off her head.

57

He did not get to chomp tonight. A knife flew through the air and penetrated his cheek. He dropped the wench to the ground, clutching his wound in pain. He pulled out the blade with a wince of pain. He looked for the source of the stinger.

Enoch stood a knife's throw away. Just behind him, panting from running, appeared young Edna in her tunic, now soiled with the dirt of the city.

It confused Thamaq. It did not make sense, all this royalty out of context in the tenement district of the city.

Yahipan felt no such confusion or hesitation. He immediately started for the little rodent to squash him with impunity. But he did not think ahead. He did not consider there might be a third party lying in wait.

Yahipan rushed toward his prey. The hidden Methuselah struck out with his knife and sliced the heel tendon of Yahipan's right foot.

The Rapha screamed in pain. His leg gave way, tumbling him to the ground with a large thud. He carried the old man in his arms, and used him to cushion his fall. The impact of the giant's body crushed the life out of the poor fellow.

"FATHER!" screamed Edna.

Methuselah shot a glance in her direction. He did not see Thamaq focus on him. The Rapha threw his captives to the ground and jumped for Methuselah. He swatted the human with such force that it jettisoned Methuselah a good fifteen cubits into a wall, knocking him senseless.

When Yahipan fell forward, he landed within arm's reach of Enoch and Edna. He grabbed them both in his iron vise grip. They were not going to break free from this monster. Thamaq brought the stunned Methuselah over and threw him down next to Edna. All three of them looked up into the eyes of fate ready to crush them.

"I love you, Edna," muttered Methuselah.

"I have always loved you," she replied.

"Is that not precious," snorted Thamaq. "Maggots in love."

"SON OF SHEOL, THIS HURTS!" screamed Yahipan. "I want that little worm Utuabzu. I am going to eat him alive."

Thamaq motioned forcefully for Yahipan to wait as he mused over their prey.

"Let us not be hasty, Yahipan. Consider what we have here. The royal apkallu and his apprentice son. Here to save the family of a sacred virgin with whom they have committed treason against the gods." It would indeed be considered treason to steal away a virgin betrothed for the Sacred Marriage rite to Utu.

"I would say that was a deed punishable by death, would you not agree, Yahipan?" said Thamaq.

Yahipan nursed his wounded tendon. His every word came out filled with venom, "I think they deserve a fate worse than death. I am going to torture you apkallus first and make you watch what we do to your little lovebird here."

Enoch swallowed. This was the end. He saw Enmeduranki's priestly jewels hanging from Yahipan's neck, and he knew the priest-king's fate. A fate that would soon be their own. The three held hands and prepared to meet the gods.

And meet the gods they did.

A loud trumpet call filled the skies and the Rephaim looked around. The earth trembled. Thunder cracked the sky.

Yahipan gasped, "The war cry of Anu!"

The bonfire in the distance flared up with supernatural vigor. They heard the sounds of battle, the sounds of weapons of war.

"It is the pantheon," said Thamaq. "They found us."

Everyone turned to see a group of four Nephilim fleeing on the streets. Hot on their tails stormed one of the gods, though they could not tell which one. The god dove and tackled the Nephilim like a group of pins in a sport. The fugitives tried to get up and defend themselves, but the deity sliced through them with his strange scythe-looking weapon as if they were blades of wheat in the wind.

Methuselah could not believe his eyes.

The god looked up and saw him. Methuselah went white. He looked behind himself. Thamaq and Yahipan had already vanished. Young Edna held onto her mother, kneeling on the ground where she had fallen. Next to her, Enoch clutched his wife Edna.

The god walked toward them, joined by another. Methuselah realized it was Anu followed by Utu. Utu called out, "Methuselah! Thank the stars you are alive. Where is the priest-king and your father? Are they alive as well?"

He was the sun god, patron of the city, thought Methuselah. *He should have better knowledge of the whereabouts of his servants.* Methuselah stepped aside.

Utu saw Enoch cradling his beloved wife in his arms, weeping.

Methuselah said, "Thank you for saving us." He limped over to young Edna, and knelt down beside her. He held her in his arms as she held her mother's lifeless body in hers. He was close enough to extend his hand to his father. The three of them were united in their grief. Their loved ones were all dead.

The gods approached them. Anu said, "I am sorry for your loss."

Utu followed up with, "The pantheon will make sure your loved ones make it safely through the Abyss into Sheol."

That was not much comfort to Enoch. What he knew of Sheol did not reassure him. Sheol was the land of the dead, the netherworld, from which no one returns. It was said that the mouth of Sheol was never satisfied and the shades of the dead rested on a bed of maggots where the worm does not die.

Anu said, "The Gigantomachy has been suppressed. Their rebellion is averted."

Enoch did not care about the rebellion. He did not care about the gods. He did not care about anything anymore. His Edna was gone. Now, only his son Methuselah kept him anchored to this earth.

CHAPTER 11

Only a few hundred citizens of Sippar were saved by the gods from the rampaging Nephilim. Similar scenes of debauched giant uprisings and anarchy had played out in other cities of the plain. Pazuzus, the grotesque flying messengers, had been used to spread the madness to other cities. Unfortunately for the mobs of giants, that same source of news found its way to the pantheon, who responded with swift justice from their lofty height on Mount Hermon. Many of the giants were killed, but some of them surrendered quickly to their procreators, and were incarcerated for further interrogation and later execution.

Anu, Inanna, and Utu had arrived and called a gathering to make an announcement. The surviving citizens assembled before the palace. Though Sippar was Utu's city, Anu was chief deity, so he was traveling the circuit of cities making appearances at each one to inspire hope and unity. He spoke with a fatherliness that moved Enoch's heart. Methuselah and Edna were not so easily moved.

"People of Sippar, we stand before you today with shared sorrow and deep regret."

Inanna stood behind Anu, taking note of the dance of verbal trickery displayed in his speech. She listened with a mixture of awe and resentment, but she listened and learned from this master of rhetoric.

Anu continued, "This Nephilim rebellion, this *Gigantomachy*, has wrought great destruction throughout the cities of our rule. We have all suffered great loss. And I want to assure you that on behalf of the pantheon of your gods, I feel your pain."

Disgusting, thought Inanna. *Is he shedding a tear? He has actually mustered up a reptilian tear from within the stone cold rock of his soul.*

The people before them listened in resigned silence.

"The divine council has convened and deliberated on what is to be done for justice to be served on these criminals and degenerates. After much soul wrenching we have come to a most painful yet necessary judgment."

Soul wrenching, thought Inanna. She must remember that word. *It gave the humans the impression that we have a conscience.*

"The giants have become an unruly elite of privilege and power," Anu proclaimed. "They have conspired in revolution and have proven themselves unworthy of their status and authority. As of this day, the gods have removed the giants from leadership over you, and their organized activities have become illegal. The surviving Nephilim will no longer be allowed to congregate, and the Rephaim are considered outlaws for their conspiracy in the riots. They will no longer reign over you. Any giants that are found outside the employ of the palace or temple authority are considered criminals and will be executed. We gods have remained too distant and aloof from our people. But we will now leave our heavenly abode in the cosmic mountain and will reside in the cities of our patronage. We will protect you and shepherd you with our undivided attention."

The people murmured to one another. Enoch thought, *Could it be true? Could the gods come and dwell amongst us?* This seemed to make Elohim further distant in his invisibility and removed presence.

The plan repulsed Inanna. *These stinking organisms of bone, flesh, and excrement are loathsome,* she thought. *Elohim displayed his true incompetence when he created such foul parasites in his image — his despicable image that the gods had sworn an oath to desecrate.*

Anu's voice carried out over the crowd. "Some Nephilim who were captured have expressed remorse for their part in the uprising. Others did not join in. In our grace, we have chosen to accept these few loyal ones back into the fold of our mercy. We will brand them with tattoos of our ownership, and employ them only as our bodyguards and special forces. Those who escaped their punishment into the desert or wilderness will be hunted down and brought to justice."

The crowd of humans broke into spontaneous applause. Methuselah did not. He thought about how he might track down Thamaq and Yahipan and kill them.

The noise made Anu pause. It created a nice dramatic effect. He raised his chin in the air to display a superiority of leadership that inspired confidence in his subjects. He was masterly.

He rode the crest of the wave. "But good people of this fertile crescent, we will need your faith and your fortitude to help rebuild your cities, and create temples for your gods. To seek a progressive future where everyone will give their fair share and everyone will be taken care of from crib to grave."

More applause rang out from the people. He inspired them, refilling them with a sense of hope.

Inanna chuckled to herself. *These ignorant hairy insects have no idea that their fair share is complete and total servitude to the god of the city-state. They were born to be slaves and they will be slaves —* *from crib to grave.* Inanna and the other gods had discovered the universal economic law from time immemorial: whatever you tax you get less of, and whatever you subsidize you get more of. By heavily overtaxing wealth, she could decrease the amount of private wealth and therefore lessen its power. By subsidizing poverty with government welfare she would increase poverty and thus dependency upon the state. Human nature was such an easy thing to exploit when you understood how it operated.

"It is with a heavy heart that I must inform you that your priest-king Enmeduranki of Sippar was killed in the riots."

Murmurs and a few cries could be heard from the crowd.

Anu had not finished yet. "We will appoint a new priest-king to establish a royal line that will administer the will of the gods."

That will relieve us immortals from the contemptible millstone of governmental bureaucracy, mused Inanna. The gods would do as they pleased and make the mortals cover their tracks with treaties, covenants and other wasteful bureaucracy.

Anu concluded his soaring inspirational speech, "So, now, my people, go back to your homes, gather your survivors, nurse your wounds, and rebuild your houses. Soon we will work together for a new world of hope and of change, freed from the suffering you have endured."

The crowd applauded. Anu reached back and held up the hands of Inanna and Utu as their champions.

Enoch, Methuselah and Edna quietly slipped out of the back of the crowd.

CHAPTER 12

"Lord of the sun, Queen of heaven," Enoch humbly offered as he bowed before Utu. The god sat on the throne of Enmeduranki. Beside him stood Inanna, left behind to finish the royal appointment process with Utu. Anu had discharged his duty of making an appearance at Sippar and was off to the other cities to repeat his rhetorical performance. Inanna lusted for the supreme power of the high god, but she certainly did not envy his responsibilities of political pandering required to maintain an awed worship from the citizens. She would prefer to smite them.

Enoch had been summoned to their presence and he waited respectfully for them to speak.

"As you now know," said Utu, "Enmeduranki was killed in the uprising. We are required to appoint a new priest-king to take his place. Because of your wisdom and experience in the workings of the palace, we have chosen you, Utuabzu, to be the new priest-king."

For a sun god, Inanna thought, *Utu was rather dim and unimpressive.* She could not wait to get out of this insignificant city and catch up with Anu to maneuver for some more influence.

"I am unworthy of your grace, my lord and lady," said Enoch.

Inanna could not bear the pleasantries of royal etiquette. She cut in, yet again. Utu's face took on a tight lipped expression of irritation.

"Prepare your family for a coronation tomorrow morning. We will meet in the palace courtyard beforehand to brief you on the procedures. Let us be done with this."

"It is an honor of great magnitude, your majesty," said Enoch.

"Move along, move along," spit Inanna.

Enoch responded obediently, scurrying back to his residence in the palace.

· · · · ·

"This night?" asked Methuselah. Enoch had arrived back at his quarters and was hurriedly packing bags.

"Yes, we are leaving now! Gather only what is necessary. We will meet the family down in the secret passageways and we will take the lesser desert path to the mountains of Aratta," said Enoch.

"So, you have changed your mind. I was right, then?" said Methuselah with a touch of sarcasm.

Enoch stopped packing and turned to look at his son. "Methuselah, this is no time for laughs. The gods just appointed me to the position of priest-king. Tomorrow is the coronation, and the entire family is required to be there."

Methuselah wiped the smile off his face. He remembered the vision his father had told him, how the archangels had said that Enoch would be offered the position of king and then executed with his family to facilitate a total regime change. He shut up and quickly gathered his things together.

· · · · ·

It would not take long to mobilize the fifty or so family members in the passageway below the palace. They had stayed there since the Gigantomachy uprising, so they were ready to leave at a moment's notice. Enoch explained everything to them.

They exited the tunnels a half mile from the city. They would make their way across the Tigris and up into the Zagros mountain territory. They had some onagers to carry the young children, women, and elderly of the tribe. They would have to test their limits with a brisk pace to get as far from the city as they could before daylight.

Enoch knew that the gods would hunt them down as soon as they discovered the family was gone. They did not stand a chance, but he had to try. He had no other choice. Stay and certainly die, or run and probably die.

When Methuselah arrived at the gathering point with Edna, Enoch glared with disapproval. Methuselah stared him in the eye and said, "Would you prefer she marry the gods?"

Enoch stubbornly refused to answer as they moved on through the passageway. His son was right. After all Edna had been through with them, he should not have even raised the question. He would apologize for that later.

They had taken only a few paces when Edna pulled Methuselah aside and spoke to him in a whisper. "You might want to talk to me before implying romantic intentions in public to your father."

"I was referring to saving you from the Sacred Marriage."

Edna studied his face, regathering her thoughts. Then she took the chance of vulnerability, "So did you mean what you said when we were attacked by the Rephaim?"

"What did I say?" he said, stonefaced.

She tightened her lips in anger and hissed, "Methuselah ben Enoch, you know exactly what you said."

"We were about to die, Edna," he complained. "I said whatever came into my mind."

She could not believe it. This stubborn onager was too scared to admit his feelings after all they had been through. But he had left an opening and her strategic training prepared her to take it.

"So, you are saying that at the moment of facing death, your love of me came into your mind?"

Methuselah walked on silently.

What was it with men? Why could they not just say what they felt?

"Poozela, just promise me one thing," whispered Edna. "If we ever face certain death again, please do *not* say you love me unless you intend to admit your love to the world should we survive that certain death. I do not think that is asking too much, do you?"

"Very well, Pedlum," he said, "I promise. Now let us go." They were behind the rest of the family.

Pedlum was a new nickname, adapted no doubt from Pedna into a more flowery affection. It was the tiniest hint that he was starting to break. Edna shivered with glee.

"By the way, happy birthday," Methuselah added as an afterthought. He traipsed on.

She had forgotten. In the midst of all this terror, she had turned sixteen. It seemed inconsequential in light of the world ending and everything.

But he had remembered. He did remember.

CHAPTER 13

Enoch's caravan had covered five leagues to the Tigris River by morning. He had pushed them. They were running for their lives, but this was all the distance they could make with women, children, and elderly.

A small river tribe with boats lived along the banks which could easily have taken them downriver. Unfortunately, their destination did not lie downriver in the heart of Shinar. They needed to travel *upriver* into the mountains of Aratta.

But there were no tribespeople in sight. Had they all hidden? Were they out on a hunt?

Enoch looked back along their path. The morning light revealed a pack of Nephilim already on their trail. Some women screamed. Enoch tried to calm them. Their backs were to the river. The Nephilim were riding down upon them. They had nowhere to go.

Methuselah held Edna tightly and gripped his mace even tighter, Enoch fell to his knees and cried out to Elohim, this god he barely knew and hardly trusted. But what could he lose now? They were all going to die. And this poor innocent river tribe, when they showed themselves, would be caught in the cross blades of slaughter. They had not done anything to deserve this. None of Enoch's clan had done anything to deserve this.

The palace Nephilim had closed the distance to an arrow's flight, but they would use no arrows on their quarry. Nephilim preferred close quarter combat. They preferred to tear the limbs off their prey rather than pierce them dead from a distance. Close combat satisfied their bloodlust. They were monsters, fast monsters. They did not need animals for transportation, for they ran faster without them.

Methuselah counted ten of them. *Talk about overkill,* he thought. *One alone could kill us all.*

The tribe huddled close to each other. The men stepped out with their few useless weapons in a pathetic attempt at a vain last stand. They felt the call of moral obligation to act courageously. They did not stand a chance. They were all going to die.

Certain death did not matter to Methuselah and Edna. They were actually hoping that they would be able to take down one together as a badge of honor before they perished. They had done well against the Rephaim. Their victim was probably suffering a humiliating permanent limp somewhere out in the hinterlands.

Yet, even at that moment, Methuselah felt compelled to make light of circumstances to Edna. He stared out at the approaching predators, at the trail of dust rising in the air, and said under his breath, "Well, here we are again, facing certain death."

She glared at him expectantly.

Methuselah surprised her, "This is where you admit again that you have *always* loved me." He said the word *always* with relish. It was quite revealing when she had first said it, and now she felt like a silly little fool.

She punched his arm hard.

"Ow!" he yelped. He was the stronger vessel, but he had also taught her how to maximize her punch with impact. He sighed and smiled warmly at her. "It is true, Edna. I do love you. And if we do get out of this alive, I will declare my intentions to the world."

Edna glanced back at the advancing Nephilim. She could now see their skin and faces. Their entire bodies were covered in occultic tattoos, displaying their new allegiance to the gods. She had not realized Nephilim could be any scarier than they already were.

"That is not fair," she said. "You know we are *really* dead this time. Even so, I am praying for a miracle."

She glanced around, looking for that miracle. She noticed two river people in cloaks come out of their tents. So there were a couple unlucky tribesmen here after all.

The two cloaked men stood in front of Enoch and his people. The lead one spoke clearly for all to hear, "Fear not! Trust in Elohim and he will deliver you!"

Enoch recognized that voice.

The two men turned toward the Nephilim. The giants were within fifty cubits of the clan and about to pounce. In unison, the mysterious pair threw off their cloaks.

Gabriel and Uriel, the archangels, stood guard before the clan. They brandished the strange weapons Enoch had seen before. Uriel had two of the long blades in his hands called *swords*. The archangels raised their weapons and yelled, "A sword for the Lord and for Enoch!" Then they bolted into the fray of approaching giants.

The archangels cut through the Nephilim like barley. Trained and angry giants were cut down by these two mighty warriors in less time than it took for Enoch to urinate in his tunic from the terror mere cubits away.

The stronger of the two, Gabriel, fought three at a time like a hungry lion. But Uriel made up for his diminished size with cunning strategy and unorthodox moves. They worked well in tandem.

Gabriel disarmed one and yelled out to Uriel, who spun around and cut him down. They swapped positions and opponents in a flash, confusing the Nephilim. But it took effort. The archangels had to work hard for their results.

Three Nephilim managed to strike Gabriel's sword at once. It flew out of his hand. Uriel threw Gabriel one of his two swords until Gabriel could pick up his own and get back on track.

The last four Nephilim surrounded Uriel. Gabriel fought with the leader of the pack. The four monsters tightened their circle on Uriel, lashing, swinging, and jabbing their weapons. Uriel appeared to be weakening.

He had only been drawing them in closer. Then he did something that astonished all those who saw it. He stretched out his two swords like windmill blades. He spun like a whirlwind in this strange position. His shearing blades took out the circle of the enemy surrounding him. It was awe inspiring.

Not one Naphil got past these mighty warriors of Elohim.

Enoch found himself thinking that it was a good thing he had changed allegiance to this distant god of his fathers. His servants were just. And they shared the same enemy. This was good. This was very good.

The archangels walked toward Enoch.

Methuselah and Edna drew near to listen in.

The angels were exhausted. These warriors fought like gods, but they were still finite created beings with flesh. They suffered the burdens of that flesh. They were drenched in sweat and breathing hard. Nephilim were not easy to kill.

As they approached the astonished Enoch and his family, they muttered under their breath to each other. "Six kills to your four. Would you like me to teach you some tactics?" said Uriel.

"Five to five," countered Gabriel. "That one we did together."

"You mean the one *I killed*," said Uriel.

"After *I disarmed* him," retorted Gabriel.

"Was that before or after you dropped your sword?" said Uriel.

"I did not 'drop' my sword," said Gabriel. "Three of them hit me at once."

"Okay, okay, *they* disarmed *you*," said Uriel with a grin. Then he added, "But then, if we both killed him, then that would make it five and a half to four and a half."

They arrived at the humans, and snapped out of their bickering.

"I am famished. Let us eat something," said Uriel.

Enoch stepped backward fearfully. Uriel paused, then laughed, "Fret not, Enoch, we are not going to eat you. Truth be told, we would not even eat those Nephilim."

Edna scrunched her face in disgust. This archangel was rather profane. She wondered if his god Elohim had that kind of sick sense of humor.

Gabriel soothed their anxiety. "Elohim sent us to help you. We brought these boats for you to take the Tigris and Diyala rivers up into the Zagros where you can follow the rest of your trip on foot in relatively safe passage."

Enoch protested, "But the rivers flow south. We do not know how to sail, and we do not have the strength to man the oars to get upstream."

"Are you sure?" asked Gabriel.

"Yes, I am sure," Enoch shot back. "Unless this Elohim of yours would like to perform another miracle and change the course of the rivers from south to north." His sarcasm dripped a bit heavily after having just been delivered by this servant of Elohim.

Uriel raised his hand and gestured with his finger for Enoch to follow him.

Enoch trailed behind him to the bank of the river. The others of the clan shadowed them. Enoch looked out onto the river and lost his breath.

It was flowing north. The river actually flowed in the opposite direction than it had been from the beginning of time.

"It is a miracle," exclaimed Enoch, his eyes and mouth wide open.

Gabriel smiled. "You will learn to be more grateful. It comes with experience."

Uriel leaned in close to Enoch and murmured, "And you also need to stop allowing your mouth to gape open when you are in awe. It is unflattering."

Enoch snapped his mouth closed.

Methuselah spoke softly into his father's ear, "Well, we better not disappoint Elohim, father."

"Board the boats," Enoch said to the tribe.

"Wait a minute," interrupted Edna.

Everyone stopped and looked at her. Enoch thought the little pipsqueak was bold. She stared straight at Methuselah with her teasing eyes. It made him wary. She normally pulled that expression on him when she occasionally beat him in a game or prank.

She proudly proclaimed, "Methuselah has a promise to fulfill."

He sighed. Then a big fat grin burst across his face, and he yelled out to the entire tribe, "Edna has *always* loved me!"

She opened her mouth in shock and slapped him. "I cannot believe you, Methuselah ben Enoch!"

Methuselah stopped laughing. He looked right into the eyes of his precious Pedlums and laughter turned to love. "Edna bar Azrial, I want all the world to know that I love you more than life, more than the heavens and the earth!"

Everyone moaned with romantic longing.

Methuselah was not done. "And if this Elohim does not drown us in the river, freeze us in the mountains or burn us in volcanic ash on our trip to Sahandria, will you marry me?"

She squealed, jumped into his arms, and gave his big fat grin his first big fat kiss. "Yes, yes, yes, yes, yes!" she rattled off, smothering him with kisses. He heartily returned then.

Enoch stood silent, watching them. He had made known his displeasure with Methuselah's interest in the girl, so this display was a bit off-putting to him. But he could see the happiness in his son's whole body. It reminded him of his own happiness when he had realized he was in love with his own precious Edna so many years ago.

Methuselah set Edna down and she apologized for her inappropriate display of public affection. Everyone laughed and applauded her. She gave an impish glance at Enoch, her future father-in-law.

Enoch could see that they were two of a kind. Even he could not stay disagreeable. He smiled. But deep in his heart, he longed for his beloved, the only true thing on this earth. And she was now gone forever.

A deep yearning came over Methuselah that he never experienced before. He hungered for Edna, body and soul.

They had better get to Sahandria quickly so he could marry her.

CHAPTER 14

It took Enoch's family about two weeks to navigate the Tigris to the Diyala river about 80 leagues up into the Zagros. Their trip was uneventful. Enoch prayed that Utu had more important things to do than track down a single apkallu sage and his family, who would probably be dead in the wilderness anyway. He knew Utu well enough to know that the god would not waste his energy micromanaging such minor issues. What was one less puny human to worry about?

The missing Nephilim sent after them were a different matter. They would be missed eventually. Enoch hoped that when they failed to return, Utu would believe them to be rogue outlaws who took their chance to run to the hills when freed from the confines of the city. It would be a reasonable explanation for their disappearance. It had already happened with many Nephilim.

Enoch's party left their boats at the river's end. They had all forgotten the miracle of the changed river course within hours of steering upstream. After a few days, they had begun wondering if their memories had failed them and the river had always flowed north. But as soon as they ran their boats aground, the current suddenly turned back south.

Enoch fell to the ground weeping in repentance.

Methuselah noticed Enoch had been doing a lot of weeping lately, usually for his lost Edna. He wept mostly at night, when everyone else slept. He also prayed much more. Too much. It seemed to Methuselah that his father sought escape by plunging even further into his spirituality in order to avoid facing the pain of this earth. Methuselah felt that pain was more reliable and real than the hope and promises of the heavenlies. After so deep a betrayal by the gods, how could he shift his allegiance to this new god Elohim without question? Elohim's emissaries had saved them, it was true, but for whose sake? Methuselah felt more like a pawn in an invisible spiritual game of wrestling powers. He did not feel as if he had much of a choice in the matter. The worst thing about the situation was all the secrets and mystery. It made trust seem so uncertain.

Methuselah trusted the experience of his senses. The strength of a belly full of food, the contact of a handheld mace with an enemy's skull, and the touch of his beautiful betrothed Edna. These things he could know with resounding certainty. He found it more difficult to trust the uncertainties of invisible gods, disappearing angels, and unanswered prayers and petitions. This Elohim would have to prove himself trustworthy with a bit more rigorous confirmation to get Methuselah's attention.

Edna more willingly believed in Elohim's beneficence. When the river had returned to its natural southward current, she wondered how many other miracles they would take for granted with such lack of gratitude. The provision of food to fill their bellies? More salvation from the enemy's mace? The devoted love of a man with a woman? The conception of a new human life? The birth of a child? It seemed everything kept pointing back to Methuselah in her heart. She watched him lead the group with authority. She thought of him tenderly soothing her fears, dreamed of his strength and humor. She simply wanted to make him happy and build a home together.

Methuselah kept thinking about doing only one thing with Edna, and it was not building a home.

· · · · ·

They traveled another thirty leagues through the valley of Havilah and the Mannean plain until they finally stood upon the volcanic fields of Mount Sahand.

Enoch felt humbled by the majesty. Everyone stared across the stark expanse in silence. The snow-covered dome of the Sahand volcano stood about eight thousand cubits, the highest peak in the region. The mountain range included a dozen other volcanic heads along the ridges. It looked like a fortress wall of rock with volcanic guard towers. Lake Urimiya spread sparkling to the west.

Enoch's soul moved deep within him, knowing that on the far side of Mount Sahand lay the valley of the Garden of Eden, that no man dare approach. This would be the closest anyone could ever come to the legendary paradise. A tribe of Cherubim guarded its perimeter, to keep the descendants of Adam away.

They stood before a vast terrain of igneous rock. Not a soul in sight. A dead wasteland. Enoch wondered where the Adamites were, those forgotten people and their patriarch that they were supposed to find? Did Elohim have his directions correct? Obviously not. There was not a sign of life for leagues around. Tribes of any size always left traces of their presence, and they could see no trace of any human presence in the area but their own.

They would have set up camp and begin their survey of the area first thing in the morning. Enoch hoped that he had not wasted his and everyone's time after all.

They pitched camp a third of a league onto the barren landscape to avoid surprise by any approaching enemies. There was nowhere to sneak up on them in a three hundred and sixty degree arc. Anyone who tried to crawl their way toward the camp would shred their clothes and flesh right off their bodies from the sharp porous bedrock and rubble strewn about.

Enoch limited the nightwatch to two details of three guards. He made sure to keep Methuselah on the far edge of the men's camp for his watch detail. It would keep his son from the tempting position of easy access to Edna in the women's camp. Methuselah was an honorable young man, but at his age passionate urges could be so strong that even honorable young men could go temporarily mad and make decisions they would regret when cooler heads prevailed.

The midnight hour came and Methuselah could not sleep. His thoughts burned of Edna, piercing his brain with a hammer-like pounding. At least it kept him awake for his watch duty. Unfortunately, it also distracted his attention.

He did not catch the first soft sound of scraping in the rocks near him. But the second time the sound flew by, he heard it. He looked up. A full moon lit the landscape. There was nothing out there. Still, he was uneasy. He reached down and picked up his mace, intending to practice some moves with it.

When he brought it up, he stopped in silent shock.

Just seconds before, the horizon had shown no life for miles around. Now the shadows of a hundred dark figures surrounded the camp. The shapes stood upright like men, but had antlers and horns like wild animals. They formed a living fence of shadow-like spectres roundabout. Where had they come from? It was as if they materialized out of the rocks themselves. Were they phantasms, shades of Sheol? Or worse, *shedim*, demons?

Before Methuselah could shout a warning, all the figures held up branches with pots on them and smashed the pots with their weapons. The resounding echo woke everyone up in terror. Women screamed, men grabbed their weapons. A frightening ring of fire surrounded them and they became disoriented. The figures had carried torches hidden in pots. The camp was taken entirely by surprise and now Enoch's company was completely vulnerable, like a man asleep with a blade at his throat.

CHAPTER 15

The dark shadows of the night were not demons, they were men. But they were not entirely the same kind of men that Methuselah and Enoch and all their lineage produced. They seemed more apelike. They walked upright, but were hairier than usual, with a stocky, robust musculature and pronounced brows and jaws. They wore animal skins and headdresses created from the game they hunted, thus creating the illusion of supernatural denizens in the night.

As the strangers guided them in the dark, Methuselah learned why he had not spotted them creeping up on the camp, and why they seemed to emerge from the rocks themselves. They *had* emerged from the rocks. They were troglodytes, cave dwellers. They now led Enoch's clan through fissures and portals into the volcanic earth below their feet.

Their torches lit the way through a labyrinth of carved passageways.

Edna was already confused and thought how easy it would be to become lost amidst these tunnels. She could see the troglodytes knew the way like the back of their hand. Then she thought of Methuselah's hand, and how strong and manly it was, yet how it could caress her with such affection. She pushed that thought out of her head. She had to be all there. She had to be ready for action.

As they walked down the incline, Methuselah was disgusted with himself. Here they were, their lives in danger, captive to a tribe of primitive apemen, not knowing if they would help them or eat them, and all he could do was to stare at the pleasurable way that Edna's hips moved as she walked in front of him. What on earth was happening to him? He could not think straight. He shook it out of his mind. He had to be ready for action.

Enoch could tell they were going deep into the earth. The slope of the shaft was steep at first, but then tapered off as they neared their destination, which seemed to be an untold number of cubits below ground.

They passed through a guarded portal into a large cavern. Enoch gasped at what he saw. They stood on a ledge overlooking a vast space. As large as the palace in Sippar, about two hundred cubits in diameter and seventy cubits high, it was more than a mere natural cave. It had been carved and shaped into a palatial interior, with a vaulted arch ceiling and columns around the perimeter. How could these primitive apemen create such sophisticated architecture?

Below them, dozens of apemen, apewomen, and apechildren busied themselves at a marketplace. They all stopped and stared up at the captives descending the stairs into another passageway entrance. One of the apechildren pointed up at them and whispered something to its mother. It occurred to Enoch that he should probably not call them apemen. It might offend them. Their adult males appeared strong enough to crush his skull if they wanted to.

They passed other hallways and arched entrances. They saw more neighborhoods of dwellings and communities. By the time they reached their destination, Enoch calculated that this city was easily as big as Sippar, but entirely underground. He now started to think that perhaps he should not call them apemen because they might very well be more sophisticated than the city dwellers of the plains.

They stopped before a huge pair of cedar doors. The leader of their party pulled on the bell rope hanging beside the entrance. A beautiful bell clang sounded out. In answer, the doors opened from within.

The leader, a robust older soldier, turned to Enoch and spoke. "People rest here. Leaders come with me." This was the first he had spoken since the capture of the clan.

"Methuselah," said Enoch.

Methuselah jumped to his side. They followed the soldier into a large reception area. The beautiful space had been adorned as a garden. Large oak and cedar columns lined the walls like trees. Flowing green drapes were hung with pomegranates embroidered on the hem. Various sparkling jewels bedecked everything. This was not merely a garden, it was a sacred underground temple.

Methuselah thought about pointing out to his father the earthly imagery used in a spiritual sanctuary. But a voice interrupted his thoughts.

"Enoch, my son! What took you so long!"

Enoch and Methuselah turned to see an old man and woman walk out of a side entrance.

They were both at least a good eight hundred years or so old. The man's stately but bent posture tempered the flashing white hair on his head. The woman's hair shone white as well, but she carried herself with the grace of royalty. She led the man by the arm. They both had a sense of carrying the weight of the world upon them.

Then Enoch and Methuselah saw why she was leading him. It was not that he was more frail than she, but because he was blind. His eyes were glazed over with a foggy whiteness.

"Father Adam?" Enoch said. He realized his mouth hung open and he closed it.

"And mother Havah," Adam replied with a smile. "Do not be disrespectful, lad."

Years of cave dwelling had not been good to Adam, on his body *or* soul. Enoch thought Adam had taken on a resemblance to the troglodytes over whom he obviously ruled. Perhaps being out of the sun had its negative effects on the human body.

Enoch embraced Adam fiercely. "It is you! I never thought I would ever meet you." Then he hugged Havah with tenderness.

"Yes, here I am in the flesh. Are you not going to introduce me to your companion?" Adam said. He could not see, but he had highly attuned his other senses to compensate for the lack of sight.

"Dear, dear, Enoch," Havah said with a loving sadness.

"Oh, pardon me," said Enoch, "This is my son Methuselah."

"That would be your great-great-great-great-great-great grandson," retorted Methuselah.

"Oh? And with a sense of humor, too. It does my heart good to hear you, my great-great-great-great-great grandson," said Adam with what would have been a twinkle in a seeing eye. "I cannot see you, but I can smell you, and you are in need of a bath." He grinned impishly.

They laughed. It had been some time since their last contact with moving water.

Methuselah hugged Adam. He could feel a quivering sigh of sadness in Adam's arms, a regret of lives not shared.

Then Methuselah embraced Havah. She whispered to him, "Methuselah, you shall outlive us all." That struck him as a bit odd, out of place. Maybe she had lost some of her wits in her old age.

Adam said, "You have both come a long way, and with your family. It must have been a difficult journey."

"Just at the start," said Methuselah, knowing he was putting it mildly.

"Well, then, let us break bread to celebrate your safe delivery," said Adam. "Gabriel and Uriel told me of your approach to Sahandria. We have much to discuss."

CHAPTER 16

The cave dwellers laid out quite a spread before Enoch's family. Though they lived in an underground world, Adam's troglodytes were adept at growing fruits and vegetables in secret gardens in the foothills within hiking distance of their residence. They spread a sumptuous banquet before the weary travelers. Skilled hunters, they supplemented the produce with mountain goat, gazelle, ibex. Anything with hair, they could catch and kill. Enoch chuckled at the discovery that even isolated from the rest of civilization, they still managed to make beer and wine. The drink of the gods never eluded humanity.

The extended family finished the meal and left the elders of the tribe to discuss their matters. Enoch, Methuselah, and a handful of others talked about the quarters that were put aside for their people. They did not know how long they would stay, but they would prepare their clan to adjust to their new residence until Elohim revealed otherwise.

Adam sat with Havah next to him, listening to the conversation. She never left his side. They were inseparable, and not because he needed her guidance with mobility. They were all alone in the world, and they only had each other. Despite the community of love around them, they would always have a pain too deep, a woundedness, that separated them from everyone and everything in this world. So they clung to each other with a subtle desperation.

Watching them, Enoch thought Mother Havah was a bit too controlling over Father Adam in his weakened state. But he did not intend disrespect, so he kept his mouth shut.

Adam sat back and belched. He muttered, "Excuse me, my little *Ninti*, Lady of the Rib."

"You are pardoned, my little Man of Red," Havah remarked wistfully.

Methuselah overheard it and his heart warmed. So old grandfather and grandmother liked giving affectionate nicknames. It must run in the family. He longed to hold his little Pedna Pedlums.

Enoch mused, "What is it like, Father Adam? The Garden. I have longed to know."

Havah watched Adam sadly as he gave a deep sigh. He could not get it out of his mind anyway. He might as well paint the picture burned into his heart and soul.

"Exactly as you would think. That is, like nothing you could imagine," he said. His eyes, though dull and without vision, brightened. He could see it all as clear as day before him.

Adam spoke with a hushed awe, "The lush valley is bounded on three sides, the Sahand and Bazgush mountain range in the south and the Savalan and Kush ranges in the north, and in the west, Lake, uh, the lake…" His memory lapsed.

"Lake Urumiya," said Havah. She finished his sentences, corrected his errors, and filled in when he forgot. He showed no sign of irritation. In fact, his descendants had the impression he would not even try to talk without her.

"Yes, yes, of course, Lake Urumiya. It makes for a perfect shelter from the harsh climate that we all know so well. The westerly winds from the great sea bring a warm rain for the dense vegetation in the valley. Every fruit tree known to man thrives there. Whole orchards, and vegetables and nut-bearing trees as well. And plenty of grapes of the vine, let me tell you."

Methuselah raised his chalice. "More wine to make the heart glad!" Everyone laughed.

His words conjured a vision of the Garden for his listeners. They could all see it. And they realized it was good for his soul to have a moment of rest from the heavy burden that lay upon him.

Adam turned solemn again. "And rich red soil," he said ever so slowly, treasuring every word as he felt the earth running through the fingers of his mind.

Havah reached out and rubbed his arm. He held her hand on his arm and continued, "Hot springs of water in rolling meadows. Ice cold waters pouring down the mountains into the river that flows through Paradise and empties into Lake Urimiya."

"The Meidan River," added Havah.

Adam continued, "But it was all like volcanic ash compared to the presence of Yahweh Elohim." He paused. "His immediate presence is what I miss the most." Adam's eyes welled up with tears. An absolute silence fell on the group, breathing stilled.

Methuselah had never heard that name before: *Yahweh Elohim*. He assumed it was an affectionate nickname that only Adam had with Elohim. It was the nature of names in their world. A name was more than mere object reference. A name would often carry the essence of a person. Like *Adam*, which meant "red earth," or *Havah*, which meant "life source."

Enoch did not know what *Yahweh* meant. He had heard no one else use the name, so he decided to avoid presumption and leave the topic for another day. He knew he had much to learn of *Yahweh Elohim*.

89

Adam finished with melancholy longing, "We would walk together sometimes in the cool of the day."

Everyone listened closely. They had never known such presence. Nobody did, except that primordial couple. Death and alienation from Elohim had permeated the entire human race as a consequence of their disobedience. This was why Elohim seemed so distant and unapproachable.

The one thing no one dared discuss was the one thing everyone wondered about: the trees. That is, the Tree of the Knowledge of Good and Evil, and the Tree of Life. To mention them would send Adam and Havah into a tailspin of depression and regret that they might never escape. Uriel had warned the travelers about this. He had told them about the couple's act of eating from the Tree of the Knowledge of Good and Evil that resulted in their exile. He told them that had Adam and Havah eaten from the Tree of Life in that state of sin, there would be no end to the tragedy of eternal evil generated by such a horror. No burden of responsibility could be greater to bear than that. Enoch felt he should trust the angel this time and avoid the topic altogether.

Yet he could not get it out of his mind. He had heard rumors about the Tree of the Knowledge of Good and Evil when he was a young child. It was only a distant memory of forgotten family folklore, replaced by the myth with which he was indoctrinated as an apkallu of Shinar: the legend of Adapa. He called up that tale now to examine it in his mind. The story went that Adapa had been a sage of Eridu, city of the god Enki. He had been taken into heaven and offered the bread and water of immortality by Anu. But he turned them down because his patron deity, Enki, had advised him against it, claiming they were the bread and water of death. So Adapa missed out on the opportunity of immortality. He was clothed with new garments and returned to Eridu to die.

There were so many similarities between the stories: the names of Adapa and Adam, the loss of eternal life, the rejection of a command and the trickster temptation. Yet there were such significant differences: the Shinar pantheon versus the sole Yahweh Elohim; failure to eat rather than eating; no trees, no wife. It was almost as if the Adapa story was an inversion of the Garden of Eden, a replacement narrative intended to displace loyalty from the original story onto a new paradigm.

Enoch studied Adam's face. Yet, here he sat before the original eyewitness of it all, telling him a different report than that of the gods. This was the problem of being a scribe and a sage. Sometimes, education and learning became a flood that darkens the mind with confusion rather than a sun that enlightens it with truth. Enoch hoped one day Elohim would clear that up for him, since he was now his servant.

Enoch had also wondered what it would be like to live forever. Was it transformation of the body? Was it perpetual regeneration? And what was it like to be in communion with Elohim so perfectly as to not need the dreams and visions that Enoch had become dependent upon for his own sense of real presence of the deity?

Methuselah's mind wandered into the details of what Uriel had told them about the Garden. He thought, *If Adam was made from the clay of the earth, and Havah was made from his rib, did they have belly buttons?* Then his mind drifted further to the image of Edna's belly button.

"Methuselah, are you listening?" Enoch's words brought Methuselah out of his tailspin of desire. It continued to creep up on him at the most inopportune moments.

"What?" said Methuselah.

"I just told Father Adam about my vision from Elohim."

"Right," said Methuselah. "You are to be a prophet of judgment."

"Yes," said Enoch. "But you did not hear the rest of my interpretation. I said that it seemed to me that if I were to pronounce judgment upon the giants, I had better be able to defend myself for long enough to finish my prophecies. I want to become a giant killer."

"A WHAT?" exclaimed Methuselah. Finally, he listened.

"A giant killer," repeated Enoch. "Nephilim are considered outlaws now, so by the law of the land, we have every right to hunt them down and bring them to justice. I would not merely be pronouncing judgment, I would be *bringing* judgment down upon their heads."

"You have been a man of peace all your life, father," protested Methuselah. "It does not suit you." Methuselah found the image of his father as a fighter difficult to embrace.

Enoch explained, "When we were in the midst of the Gigantomachy, I knew that everything that I had believed in was a lie. I understood for the first time in my life that the only way that evil was allowed to spread its talons over the earth was for righteous men to do nothing. We will no longer do nothing. We will fight this evil."

"In case you had not noticed," said Methuselah, "Nephilim are very hard to kill."

Adam spoke up. "You are right. Nephilim are half-angel, half-human. What makes them difficult to kill is that they inhabit two realms, and therefore have the strengths of both in a way that neither has of the other."

"Archangels do pretty well against Nephilim. We saw it ourselves," said Enoch.

"Yes, but not without great effort," Adam countered. "And if the Nephilim were to fight in great numbers, they could overwhelm even archangels."

"But we would not fight them in numbers," Enoch insisted. "We would single them out and destroy their filthy corrupted bodies of flesh one by one."

Methuselah said, "You may not have that luxury, father, since they often travel in packs. Still, they are not of this world. They have occultic fighting skills that we know nothing about."

Adam interrupted their spat. "There is a secret order who have developed special skills to kill Nephilim."

"Who?" asked Enoch.

"They are called the *Karabu*," said Adam.

"How can we find these Karabu?" asked Enoch.

"You already have," said Adam.

Methuselah and Enoch looked at each other.

"Sahandria is the home of the Karabu. They are those who aid the Cherubim in guarding the perimeter of Eden."

It all became clear to them. Adam's community was on the perimeter of the Garden, because they housed the guardians of Eden. Enoch was disappointed that he did not figure it out sooner.

"When can we start training?" asked Enoch.

Adam said, "It will take years to perfect the technique."

"Years?" asked Methuselah.

"More like decades," said Adam.

Enoch resolved, "Then decades we will take to become Karabu warriors."

The thought turned Methuselah's stomach. "There is one thing I need to do before I enter this training, or I will not last to the end."

To everyone's pleasant surprise, he turned to Adam and said, "Father Adam, will you marry me to Edna bar Azrial?"

CHAPTER 17

Troglodytes knew how to throw a party. They gathered in a series of halls attached to each other that were even larger than the marketplace cavern Enoch had seen when they first arrived. Apparently, most of the city had come to the wedding celebration. There were thousands of them. They filled the carved out chambers with echoes of chatter and laughter.

These were not the simple people Enoch had thought them to be. Their structure and decorations were simple and sparse, their cave drawings almost childlike, but they were socially integrated and communally connected like no other people he had ever seen. They carried a spiritual quality about them that Enoch could relate to, something he knew his clan could not understand. He had a strange connection to them. He understood why Adam had chosen to live with the cave dwellers. His original bias against them had proven false. It had been based on false legends he should not have listened to.

This was the time to feast and celebrate the marriage of his son. He saw Methuselah and Edna dancing out on the floor. Adam had officiated the ceremony with his ever-present Havah by his side. It made Enoch cry like a baby. He had been concerned about this insignificant little temple virgin, but had come to realize that she too had overcome his expectations. He was beginning to think that for a wisdom sage, he was not proving very wise of late.

In the midst of the music, Enoch glanced at Adam and Havah at the table. They smiled and pretended to enjoy the festivities. But even now, they could not escape the pall of sadness that haunted them.

Suddenly, the floor cleared, and everyone moved to the tables to watch the entertainment. Methuselah and Edna sat down at the head table with Enoch and the others. Adam leaned toward Enoch and said, "You have been wondering what the Karabu can do? Sit back and get ready. You are about to find out."

The Karabu took their places on the floor. There were ten of them. They were dressed as warriors with armaments of animals. Lion heads and manes, vulture winged robes, and heavenly weapons Enoch had never seen before. Strange blades, shields, and javelins.

They engaged in battle exercises that seemed more like a dance of acrobatics than about brute strength or power. They ebbed and flowed like a river of water, their movements fluid, not forceful. They moved through the air as if they were fish floating in water. Flipping, twisting, they attacked and defended with such precision and poise as to transform the act of fighting into a ballet of grace.

Adam could not see the dance, but he could feel it. He knew it well. He said to Enoch, "They were trained by the archangel Gabriel. The original giant killer."

Enoch caught himself with his mouth open again and quickly shut it. He now knew that Elohim had provided for his calling.

Methuselah was entranced by the javelins and how they glided like birds in the air and spun in the hands of the heavenly skilled Karabu. He thought to himself that this was the weapon for him.

Edna wanted to dance like the wind as these fighters did. She found it a haunting vision of terrifying beauty.

Adam touched Enoch's arm and said softly, "What do you say we go up top and get some fresh air?"

It surprised Enoch. So far as he knew, this stooped-over old man had not been out of the caves since he arrived here ages before.

"Anything you ask, forefather," said Enoch.

"Walk me, then," said Adam.

Havah moved to help as she had always done, but Adam gestured to her to stay. He would be all right. Just the men.

As they walked up to the surface through the winding tunnels, Enoch asked Adam about the name he had uttered earlier, Yahweh Elohim.

Adam apologized, "It slips out too often. It is the covenant name of Elohim. It is reserved for only the most sacred of relationships. It expresses his essence as the foundation of existence itself. The divine council of heavenly host uses it." He paused for a moment. "We used it in the Garden, but now with the Edenic exile…" his voice cracked for a moment. "It is a name that should remain secret until latter days. For what purpose, I do not know. Perhaps it has to do with the seed of Eve."

They stepped out in the evening breeze under the stars. Adam stopped and took a deep breath. "Ah," he proclaimed, "I do believe I miss this sweet taste in my lungs."

Enoch helped him carefully so Adam would not stumble on the rough ground at their feet. Adam turned his face to the sky, unable to see anything. Yet he knew every star's location.

"He brings forth the Mazzaroth in his season," mused Adam as if remembering Yahweh Elohim's own words. Enoch smiled and looked upon the host of heaven.

"Elohim's story for us," Adam added, still thinking.

His blind eyes found the right place in the night sky. "Can you see the constellation of the Virgin? The second decans, right about there," he pointed. "*Comah*, the desire of nations."

Enoch could see it. One of the benefits of being an apkallu was their learning of the stars.

"It is my favorite constellation," added Enoch. "Virgin and child. It tells me there is hope. Hope for purity, for a new beginning. For a new 'Adam.'"

Adam welled up with emotion.

"Father Adam," said Enoch, "I know this is probably not the time to ask you, but..." He hesitated.

"But what?" queried Adam. "Speak."

"Is it true, the legend about Cain the cursed one?"

Adam hesitated in uncomfortable silence. He wished Enoch had not spoken after all. It was another sore wound for him in a life of many self-inflicted wounds.

He sighed. "Cain is a scourge upon my existence. He has made it his one purpose in life to foil the plans of Yahweh Elohim because of his punishment for murdering his brother." Adam kept using the covenant name of *Yahweh* because he was in private and knew Enoch was a chosen vessel of Elohim.

"But how can he deny his guilt?" asked Enoch.

Adam shook his head. "The mind of man is never so cunning as when it is involved in the art of self-justification. I know, I am guilty as well."

Enoch steadied Adam as they stepped over some volcanic rubble on their walk.

"At first, Cain accepted his exile in the land of Nod. His family line left him when he began to show signs of lunacy. He had discovered that Yahweh planned a new righteous lineage through

Seth to replace his own cursed line. Many of the names of the sons of Seth were even similar to Cain's line, which reinforced the substitution. To be forgotten, erased from the tablets of history was a fate worse than his infamy. Punishment still affirms the value of the guilty party because it shows they had the nobility to do otherwise. But annihilation means they have no value, and they could not do otherwise. Like a clay pot created merely to be destroyed."

Adam took a long breath. "Cain learned of Yahweh's curse of enmity between the children of Eve and the children of the Serpent. And he learned of the Promise of the Seed that would crush the Serpent's head even as it bit the Woman's heel. Cain realized that the only revenge he could inflict upon Yahweh would be the destruction of the lineage of that promised Seed. So he set out to destroy Seth's bloodline. Unfortunately for him, it had already grown and splintered into many lines of descent, leaving Cain with an impossible goal.

"He seeks the chosen line of the Seed of Havah, and when he finds it, he will destroy it."

Enoch remained silent. He could not imagine the weight of sorrow that burdened this great man.

He changed the subject. "Father Adam, it is getting cold. Let us return to the wedding party."

"Let me return to my bed to get some much needed sleep," said Adam in reply. "My talk with you has made me tired."

Enoch knew he had been a help to the old man. There was something very freeing that came with confession of the heart. It had the effect of relaxing the soul from what it could not carry.

"Oh, I almost forgot," added Adam. He stopped and reached into his shoulder sack and pulled out a couple of animal skins. He handed them to Enoch.

"I want you to have these. They are the original skins that Yahweh Elohim clothed Havah and me with after our fall."

Enoch looked at them with reverence.

Adam finished, "They were a covering for our sins. May they be a covering for you."

Enoch embraced his forefather with all his heart.

• • • • •

Methuselah waited for what seemed like an eternity on the large wedding bed they received as a gift from Adam and Havah. He had only one thing on his mind: Edna. She was preparing herself in the wash area.

He had waited too long for this moment and it had finally come. He thought back on the years he spent pouring his soul into this precious jewel, with nary a thought that she would one day pour back into him. It was the perfect dream. They had been best friends, soul-mates, and now they would be lovers. They would finally become one.

Where is she? he thought.

"Edna, my wife, are you sleeping in there?" he teased.

Suddenly, she pounced on him from behind.

It took him by surprise. They rolled on the bed laughing and playfully wrestling, as they always used to in their sport room.

Then play turned to passion. Finally, they were released for love, and finally, they truly, deeply knew each other.

CHAPTER 18

Many years passed.

Enoch and his tribe sojourned with the cave dwelling Adamites, raised their families, and learned the way of the Karabu. The Watcher gods of Mount Hermon consolidated their reign over the land of Mesopotamia. They built large temples to their names and continued to pursue the outlaw giants. They offered bounty on Nephilim packs and rogues who roamed the desert badlands and mountainous hideouts of the earth.

Rumors grew that the gods were experimenting with occultic sorceries, creating unspeakable monstrosities. For what purpose, no one could tell. Whispers of conspiracy filled the cities. But in the rural areas of desert, forest, and mountain, life was less complicated. For those who did not serve the gods of the pantheon, life was not as bountiful. Survival was a foremost priority.

Survival was not in the stars for the snow tribe of Barakil the elder. They numbered about a hundred members, living and hunting in the snow-capped mountains of Aratta near the Greater Zab river basin.

Most of the men of the tribe were dead, hanging from trees to be dried out like meat under the soft shimmering of fresh snow fall. The surviving women were corralled in makeshift cages for later sport.

Four Nephilim outlaws ransacked the tribe's belongings for valuables and foodstuffs. Three of them were nearly seven cubits tall, but one came up short standing at less than five cubits. All were shaven and covered head to toe with occultic tattoos. They wore pieces of strange body armor over what looked like soldier's garb.

The short one stoked the fire in preparation for roasting their next meal. The leader of the pack, the tallest and the ugliest, crouched in the bush struggling with constipation, the result of eating too much meat the night before. He yelled to the short one, "Get that fire burning, midget! I cannot stand this abysmal cold!"

The other two giants examined some pillaged jewels, trying to figure their worth and conspiring how to secret some away for themselves.

Unseen, Enoch ben Jared peeked out from behind a tree, clothed in near white for concealment. He was just over three hundred sixty years old now, or thereabouts. He had stopped counting because years on this earth were not as important to him as eternity in the heavens. He had spent many years training for his calling with the Sahandrians.

Enoch thought, *These brutes do not seem to belong here. Rogue Nephilim do not usually congregate in packs because they are too easy to spot.* He frowned over the matter. The giants did tend to hide out in unpleasant environment for the camouflage advantages they provided. He gripped his marvelous bow made from heavenly metal and strung with the indestructible hair of a Cherub. He had become quite a death-dealing archer after all those years of naively condemning all war and violence. Elohim had quite a sense of irony.

Twenty cubits away, Methuselah and Edna crouched behind a bush waiting for the sign from Enoch. Methuselah was almost three hundred now, with Edna four years his junior. Their white stealth outfits gave them cover. They held the special Karabu weapons of angels: his, lightweight but deadly javelins; hers, a multi-bladed weapon called a sword, which did not just cut but spliced, diced, and shredded. Methuselah looked from Enoch to Edna's face, mere inches from him, and surprise-kissed her. She gave him a "not now" frown, but then pecked him back with a smile. They were inseparable.

On Enoch's other side, obscured in the brush, Methuselah's twenty-year old son Lamech, pride of his mother Edna, waited. Lamech took after his grandfather. He was a bit of a hermit holy man, preferring prayer and meditation to socializing with people. A conflict of interests burdened him. He loved his tribe of the Sahandrians and he wanted to become a holy priest of their temple. He longed for the security of his volcanic underground home. But he had been trained by his father for another vocation, the holy calling of giant killing.

Lamech prepared his special sword, created by his trainer the archangel Gabriel, and forged in the volcanic heat of Mount Sahand. The blade was strangely like a whip. When opened, it stretched a good seven cubits of flexible metal. When not in use, it rolled up, ready to unravel and strike with razor sharp fury at a distance. Those who relied upon close quarter combat would not have a chance with this little snakebite. He had nicknamed it "Rahab" after the sea dragon of chaos.

The team of giant-killers watched as the short Naphil opened the cage of women. He dragged out a kicking and screaming redheaded teenage girl.

"We have a lively one here!" crowed the short Naphil. "And she is lovely looking. Maybe we should save her for dessert."

"We do need some breeders," said one of the other giants. He stepped up to her, shoving the short one aside.

He looked at her with hunger. "I think I will have some sweets before dinner."

He glanced at the short one for his reaction. Then his body stiffened in shock as an arrow pierced his eye and burrowed into his brain. Before his companions realized what had happened, another arrow buried itself into his other eye. The giant fell to the ground blind and dead.

The short one bellowed. The other giant drew a battle axe and shield to face the Karabu team barreling at them from their concealment.

Methuselah threw a javelin at the front giant, but the Naphil dodged it with preternatural ease. The short one behind him, caught the javelin in mid-air, and snapped it like a twig in his hand. He may have been small for a Naphil, but he was still a Naphil — and strong.

Two more arrows buried themselves in the shield of the axe giant. He shortened the distance between himself and Enoch in seconds, making the bow and arrow useless.

He swung his battle axe with raging fury, chopping down trees as mere nuisance, but it was like fighting a ghost. Enoch danced around the giant's moves as if in a ballet with boulders. It made the giant more angry — and sloppy.

Edna raced straight at the short one and choreographed her own dance of battle with the miscreant. She slashed the creature's spleen, stomach and kidneys before it had the chance to even stop and bleed. He fell on the snowy ground in his own spreading pool of death.

She did not see the lead Naphil behind the bush. He jumped out roaring with a spiked mace — and to his embarrassment, his loincloth still down at his knees.

The poor redheaded teen had been out of the fray, frozen in terror watching it all. The lead giant saw her and snatched her up, intending to throw her at his enemies. He stopped short. A javelin and arrow pierced through his heart. Then Rahab, in the hands of Lamech snapped out, removing the despicable head from its body.

The teen girl dropped to the ground in a heap. The giant's body fell forward, his knife hand just missing Edna as he hit the ground in a splash of bloody snow. He was the last one to fall.

Killing Nephilim was not usually as easy as this battle had been. This crack team of giant killers had become so well trained over the decades that they were a formidable force even for an organized pack of Nephilim. They had been trained by angels.

Within seconds, Lamech was by the young girl, checking to see if she was dead. He lifted her from the snow. When he got a closer look at her, he almost lost his breath. She was as beautiful as a sunset. Ravishing red locks, large pulpy lips, and eyes like a doe.

Edna looked around to see Enoch standing on his quarry's chest, smiling with bow in hand. He saw her, and then his smile faded into dismay. She realized her arm felt numb — and wet. She glanced down. The giant had not missed her. His knife had grazed her arm, leaving a gaping bloody wound. The bright red flowed down her arm and pooled on the ground. She thought, *Is that blood all mine?*

She passed out.

When Edna came to, she found herself surrounded by the team. The redheaded girl was applying a paste of plant leaves and tree sap to her wound. Edna pulled back in dazed fear, but the men held her down.

"It is fine, my love," said Methuselah. "She is a healer shaman. You will be all right."

Edna dropped her head back in relief.

Methuselah leaned in close to her face and gave her a big smacking kiss.

"Nice moves Pedlumnoonypoo!" he said. The years had brought a more developed nickname among many others. "You deserve a back rub tonight."

She smiled through her pain.

He added a caveat, "Of course, he was a small one, more manageable for your size."

He always looked for a way to tease her, catch her off guard. It was his prankster nature to do so, even in the face of grave danger, like now. He used it to diminish fear and evil and she loved it. She had also learned how to tease right back.

"You are right, Poozelahbunnybunch," she bantered. "Apparently, your javelin was not big enough. But we got him anyway, my lovebird of heaven."

It was all in good sport. He adored her thoroughly. She respected him completely. He admired her fighting skills. She had even saved his life more than once. But he knew that did not mean they would not be competitive. She was still a tomboy at heart. *Thank Elohim*, he thought, *she is still a tigress in the marriage bed.*

Enoch examined one of the pieces of body armor. "Strange," he said. "This is specially designed armor that they are wearing. It is almost as if they were a scouting party or a strike team."

Methuselah and Edna looked at Enoch with surprise. "Nephilim hordes are virtually extinct, and packs have not been seen in over a hundred years," said Methuselah. "Where could these have possibly come from?"

"That is a fitting question," replied Enoch. A pack was a company of about four to eight Nephilim and a horde could be as small as twenty organized giants or as large as a hundred strong. A cold eastern wind started to pick up and blow snow around their faces. Enoch bent closer to examine the bodies.

Lamech stared at the redheaded vision before him.

"Thank you, for saving me," she said to him, brushing off snow and pulling her tangled hair back.

"My name is Betenos, Betenos bar Barakil," she said, awaiting his reply.

Lamech gave none. He just stared at her with gaping mouth, just like his grandfather.

Betenos giggled. It brought Lamech to his senses. "Oh, I am Lamech ben Methuselah. This is my family."

"Where are you from?" she asked.

"The Sahand."

"I have never seen such skilled warriors before."

"I have never seen such beauty before," he blurted out without even thinking, and then caught himself. He turned as red as her hair. She giggled again.

"I am sorry, I did not mean to…"

"I thank you for your compliment, Lamech ben Methuselah."

He looked around at the carnage. "I am very sorry for your tragedy," he said. "These Nephilim deserve eternal damnation for what they have done."

"I thank you for your kindness," she responded. "My father, Barakil, was the elder of the tribe."

"Is there no end to your loss?" he said. She saw his eyes blear with tears.

"Would you help me free the others?" she asked.

"Forgive me for my thoughtlessness," he said.

They tromped through the snow to the makeshift cage. The six remaining members of her tribe, all women, cowered in the cage, all alone in the mountainous wilderness without a defense. Lamech and Betenos freed them.

"Lamech, come here!" shouted Methuselah.

Lamech led the women over to the Nephilim carcasses surrounded by Enoch, Methuselah, and Edna.

"We need to move quickly. Apparently, these Nephilim are part of an organized militia of some kind."

"How could that be?" asked Lamech.

Methuselah pointed down at the thigh of one of the dead. "They are branded by the same rulers."

Lamech saw the cuneiform on the thigh amidst the tattoos. There were two names. He read it out loud, "Thamaq and Yahipan."

Methuselah suddenly screamed and thrust one of his javelins into the cadaver's branded thigh. Edna held him and pulled him aside to whisper to him. He was clearly in mental anguish, over what, Lamech did not know.

Enoch explained to Lamech, "Thamaq and Yahipan were co-rulers of the city where I was apkallu many years ago. They killed your grandparents and almost killed us."

Lamech's eyes went wide with shock. He turned to comfort his mother, but she was too busy selflessly comforting Methuselah. "And now they have an organized pack?"

"Or worse, maybe a horde," said Enoch. "We need to wrap up these bodies and transport them quickly to Nippur and get the bounty, before they are discovered missing and sought for by their pack."

"Or horde," reminded Lamech.

"Or horde," said Enoch. The thought was too horrible for him to imagine. He knew things had been getting worse. Evil was spreading across the land. But what use would his calling as a giant killer be to Elohim if Nephilim were organizing and congregating into packs and hordes again? It would be too overwhelming for them. They could take out stragglers here and there. But packs of four to ten could become very lethal and a horde of fifty to a hundred was invincible for their small team.

Enoch turned to Betenos and the others standing behind her. "What can you tell us about your ambush?"

"The men had gone hunting," said Betenos, "so it was easy for them to overpower our camp and catch the hunters unawares when they returned." As the strongest of the survivors, Betenos had became the spokesperson for them.

"They used the women as human shields," she said.

"Cowardly," said Enoch.

"Strategic," countered Methuselah, He had returned to the discussion, his anger suppressed. "Nephilim have no conscience. They cannot be cowards. They must be hunted and slaughtered like the animals that they are."

Methuselah bit his lip. He would hunt down Thamaq and Yahipan and slaughter them, if it was the last thing he did before meeting his maker. He was sure his maker would understand. Or would he? Could Elohim know the pain of losing a father or a son? Or was he a distant and removed being without a family?

Enoch asked Betenos, "Did you hear any conversation that might suggest they belonged to a pack?"

"Or horde," added Lamech. Enoch gave him an annoyed look this time.

Betenos looked to her fellow tribeswomen. They all shook their heads no.

"Just that they came from a great distance," concluded Betenos. "They only seemed to be passing through. But I could not tell from where."

"We had best move quickly," said Enoch.

Betenos implored Enoch, "Please good savior, may I request funeral rites for our dead?"

Enoch looked around. "The snow and cold has made the ground too hard to break," he said.

"My people do not perform ground burial," she replied, "we perform excarnation."

"What is that?" asked Methuselah.

"Sky burial," she said. "We remove the heads and place their bodies in the trees to have their bones stripped by carrion vultures. We then cremate their remains so the soul goes to the gods and the body returns to the earth as dust."

The barbaric ritual repulsed Enoch. On second thought, he realized that no matter how removed from the true God these rural pagans were, their beliefs still dimly reflected the image of God that was in every human. Betenos' words reminded him of the words that Yahweh Elohim spoke to Adam so long ago in the Garden, "For you are dust, and to dust you shall return."

"We will respect your wishes, as far as we can," said Enoch.

Relief flooded Betenos. "Thank you," she said, She impulsively hugged Enoch.

Methuselah felt proud of his father for his wisdom and grace. He was sensitive to the weakness that is humanity.

Enoch's mind drifted in painful memory to the recent deaths of Adam and Havah. Through the years of Enoch's stay with the cave dwellers, he had become close to his forefather. Adam had died first, but Havah followed close on his heels, as she always did.

Enoch remembered the burial ceremony of the Sahandrians. They laid the body into a pit curled up in a sleeping posture. This expressed their belief that death was only a sleep from which they would one day awake. Around the body, they placed various mementos and souvenirs of the beloved's life. They included fruits and vegetables because Adam had longed for the Garden to the very end. They had prepared the body by mixing red ochre powder with water to create a paste with which to cover the body. For them, it was a token of the red earth from which Adam himself had come. It was the red earth they all longed for in their souls. They had then covered the body with flowers of all kinds; yarrow, ragwort, hollyhock and others chosen for their medicinal purposes in life with hope for the afterlife.

CHAPTER 19

After the bodies of the snow tribe's dead had been placed in the trees and on makeshift platforms, Enoch and the others hauled the corpses of the Nephilim onto wagons they had brought with them.

Wagons came into use by adapting the recent invention, the wheel. Four round pieces of wood attached to axles were secured underneath a sled. Towed by a couple onagers, this wagon device could carry heavy loads across great distances in shorter amounts of time than the old sleds had been capable of. Enoch did not know who originated the invention. He wondered if it was from the angels. But whoever had done it should be a king for his brilliance and imagination.

Once they had the Nephilim corpses loaded, they had to stop. They were completely exhausted, with no strength left to continue. A death defying battle with rabid giants and then the sky burial of a hundred tribal dead had used every ounce of their strength. Not even the benefit of wheels was enough to help them. They had to rest, even though they would lose more time and risk being tracked down by other Nephilim.

Betenos, however, had not exhausted her bag of herbal tricks. She gave each of them some special root to chew on that provided them with a burst of energy. They put their belongings on the wagon and started down the path toward Nippur.

They wheeled the wrapped giant carcasses through a dozen or so leagues of lush mountain valleys to a river port where they rented boat passage down the Diyala river another sixty leagues or so to the Tigris. From there they took the artificial canals to Sippar on the Euphrates, and then on to Nippur. The bounty on four Nephilim outlaws could carry them for months with supplies and bribery money.

It was a tiring life to be always on the move, gathering information and tracking giants. For Methuselah and Edna it had been particularly difficult being separated from their family for months at a time. They felt they were missing out on their children's growing years as the tribe took care of them in their stead. Bringing their favored son Lamech with them had brought some peace of mind, but it had its own stress. He was good at giant killing, but his heart was in Sahandria. He did not like the lonely rootless life of a wayfarer.

They had left Sahandria with many tears to become nomads. It seemed more appropriate to Enoch's calling, but it made it harder on everyone, feeling unattached to a substantial community, always unsettled, always leaving.

Though he focused on fulfilling his duty of slaying Nephilim, Lamech often dreamed of being a priest of Elohim for the clan. In this spiritual aspect, he found himself identifying more with his grandfather Enoch than with his father, Methuselah. That brought testy moments of tension between them.

Methuselah would tell Lamech he needed to stop being so sheepish and see himself as the seed of Havah, the special line of God's own choosing. But Lamech just wanted to serve God in the temple of Sahandria and minister to its people, whom he loved dearly. One thing was certain, he would not die a wandering nomad. If he could not go back to Sahand, he would build his own city

112

somewhere on the plain. But first, he had to have a family. That was something he did not think much about in his pursuit of piety. What was a mere human family compared to fellowship with the mighty Creator Elohim? There had not been much of a comparison in his mind until now. He had not thought much of females in his youthful interests — until now. Now, he stared at the most vivacious and beautiful of all Elohim's creatures that he had ever seen. And she was traveling with them to Nippur: Betenos bar Barakil.

Now I am becoming more like my father, thought Lamech. It confused and frustrated him. He felt he had two men inside him battling for control: his father, Methuselah, man of earth; and his grandfather, Enoch, man of heaven. Would he forever be tormented by two opposing natures? If this was the burden he had to shoulder to have a family, then he would seek every way possible to avoid it.

Betenos was no helpless victim, nor would she go down without a fight in this world. She loved life too much. When the Nephilim attacked her, she fought back with the ferocity of a nomad, no matter how futile it had seemed. On this journey, she helped everywhere she could, cooking or cleaning, or even moving the dead giant corpses when necessary. She could drive the wagon or ride an onager free-back. She seemed willing to do just about anything. She was driven to prove her worth to everyone, to demonstrate she was not just another helpless waif in need of saving. Even though she thought the young man Lamech was certainly handsome and strong, she was determined not to fall in love because she knew where that would lead her. And she did not want to go down that road again.

Everyone saw the attraction between Lamech and Betenos. Enoch did not like the idea because Betenos was not a follower of Elohim. She spoke often of the Great Goddess Earth Mother, the World Tree, and had a hard time grasping the incomparability of Elohim over all other gods. She would argue with Lamech for hours on end about Elohim and his excessive demands of exclusivity against the gods. Lamech seemed to enjoy the challenge. The young man's fanatic commitment to Elohim was the one thing that comforted Enoch. He knew Lamech had no interest in marrying an idol worshipper. But what if she converted? What then? He knew it was not right, but he secretly hoped she would not convert to save them all the pain and suffering. Enoch could not wait to get to Nippur so they could end this distraction and get moving on without her.

Edna knew that it was too late. They were already in love. They were all merely observing the discovery process. When Methuselah expressed caution at her youth, Edna reminded him how young they had been when they fell in love. When he brought up Betenos' gods, she told him it was only a matter of time before Betenos would step over to Lamech's side. She knew it. Call it women's intuition or Elohim's insight. But she prayed for Elohim's will to be done.

The other women victims of the Nephilim attack were brought along with the team to be dropped off at Nippur with Betenos. They asked to stay with Enoch's nomads. Enoch had to inform them that the four of them were a band of warriors on a mission. They were simply not available for protection, and their tribe was too far in the opposite direction for the team to escort them there. The women would journey with them to Nippur and remain there to find a new life on their own.

Edna's heart shivered. The circumstances of these women made her long for her own family back at Sahand. During their years of residence with the Sahandrians, she had borne sons and daughters for Methuselah. She missed them terribly. They were taken care of by the extended family when the team was away on their missions, but her longing for them persisted.

Their years of training had granted her the blessed privilege of complete and focused attention from her husband Methuselah. Or rather, *almost* complete attention. The training called for an arduous schooling in heavenly weapons and spiritual discipline with high demands. It was not easy to become a giant killer. Once Methuselah fixed on a goal, he would devote his heart and soul to its completion. But at least in the caves, they had been spared the distracting complications and responsibilities of survival on the surface.

Now, their missions took them away for longer and longer periods of time. She felt guilty about it. Conflict tore at her because she also knew that sometimes holy callings involved a sacrifice that was not required of other servants of Elohim. Still, she sometimes longed to live an uneventful and happily boring life with a stable family and clan in the comfortable caves of Sahandria. She just needed to be attached to someone or some community that would give her purpose. Her parents had provided that for her until she became a sacred virgin dedicated to the gods. When they murdered her parents, she found Methuselah to give her that purpose. The nomadic calling now displaced raising a family in Sahandria. Her identity was constantly being shaken up. She clung to the closest thing Elohim gave her, Methuselah. She sometimes wondered if she was being too needy with him. Whatever the case, she loved to make him happy.

For Enoch, the sacrifice of being a wanderer was not so great as for Edna. He remarried at Sahand and they had five sons and three daughters. But it had never been the same after he lost his Edna. A part of him had died with her and it changed him forever. He was more otherworldly than the rest of the clan. He spent hours in prayer, and treasured his dream-visions. He would talk for hours about spirit and heavenly bodies with a thoughtless disregard for the human bodies right in front of him, including his own wife and children. Edna often felt that Enoch's grandiose prophetic elevation of spiritual reality resulted in the neglect of his own family.

Methuselah seemed to be his father's very opposite. Though he loved Elohim with all his heart, soul, mind and strength, Methuselah's affections were more this-worldly. It placed him at odds with his father more often than not. He remembered one time when Enoch was pontificating at the dinner table about the need for more mundane food and less preparation, so that they might have more time to devote to the pursuit of their spiritual disciplines. Methuselah got angry and retorted by asking if Enoch was saying Elohim was too worldly, since the Creator devoted too much time to crafting the Garden with its multitude of tastes and exotic foods. It was one of the few ways that Methuselah could actually force Enoch into silence.

Methuselah had let the silent pause sink in, then took a deep bite of roasted meat and with his mouth full, spluttered out the words, "I am worshipping Elohim as I enjoy this mutton's glorious heavenly juicy flesh. As I do when I pray or when I hunt or when I love my wife. So, I ask you, who spends more time in spiritual discipline, the one who worships in only some of his actions or the one who worships in all of his actions?"

Enoch had left the table and charged Methuselah with dishonoring him. Methuselah apologized in front of the family for his disrespectful provocation. They both realized that spiritual arrogance was just as sinful as fleshly intemperance.

Edna believed it was Elohim's sense of humor to place such contrary personalities of extremes within the same family and then use them for his purposes. He had provided Lamech as a kind of hybrid of them both as a further picture of their tension and a rebuke of their imbalance. It indicated to her that Elohim was somehow in control, and not their puny little human wills.

If it were up to us, she thought, *we would be in hot bitumen.*

116

CHAPTER 20

The city of Nippur lay on the Euphrates just downriver from Sippar, Enoch's home town. They had passed by Sippar without stopping in order to avoid being recognized by the god Utu and thrown into prison. Even though their escape had been hundreds of years earlier, and though Enoch had grown out his hair and beard, Utu would certainly recognize him. The god would certainly remember his original intent for Enoch's family, and would certainly not be merciful.

Enoch and his traveling band of warriors and women pulled up to the Nippur river wharf on their boats with their dead Nephilim cargo. They hauled the bodies to the Temple Guard command post just outside Inanna's temple, called *E-anna*. Though Utu was the patron god of the city, his temple, *E-Babba*, was not as large as E-anna and was overshadowed by its administrative duties, another visible sign of Inanna's usurpation of his priority. A saying had developed amongst the Nippurians, "It matters not he who rules, but she who counts the money."

It was bothersome bureaucracy to register the details of the abduction and execution of the fugitives, with exact times, locations, descriptions and names of everyone involved. Enoch did not trust this procedure. It created an accessible record of their comings and goings that could make them more easily tracked. It typified the kind of centralized control by the gods that Enoch despised. He had been raised within its clutches, but his years with the Adamites had changed him. He and his band of free spirits now roamed through Elohim's creation without the gods' oversight. But unfortunately, he could not violate this protocol if he wanted to collect the bounty for their wages.

It had not been the usual protocol, however, for the gods to be involved in this petty administrative procedure. It surprised Enoch when Inanna herself showed up at the command post to meet with Enoch's raiding party.

She stepped into the room, leaving two Nephilim Guards at the door. Methuselah glanced at Enoch. Lamech and Edna tensed. Would she smell their fear? Would she recognize any of them? Edna remembered Inanna with crystal clarity. She was abominable — intemperate, violent, and unpredictable; the worst combination in any leader let alone a god.

Inanna glanced over the tabletwork. She looked at Enoch and the others with a suspicious pause. *How could these four worms have overcome four formidable Nephilim?* She stared long at Enoch. He looked familiar, but she could not place him. He was rodent-like with his long tangled hair and filthy ratty beard. They all looked the same to her. These rural types would have to be cleansed from the earth someday to maintain ethnic purity. The younger sinewy one was acting a bit skittish. Maybe he was overwhelmed by Inanna's charismatic presence. She smirked to herself. Their obvious son was handsome and ripe. But she had to return to the task at hand

"What is your name?" she queried.

"Enoch ben Jared," he said.

She did not know the name. It was foreign to Shinar. Enoch was grateful he had taken on a Shinarian name when he was an apkallu of Sippar. Had he used that name of Utuabzu now, Inanna would mentally place him at Sippar and might recollect his escape from their heinous scheme all those years ago.

"How did you defeat these giants?" Inanna inquired with her annoyed impatient tone.

"Good queen of heaven," — Enoch hated faking respect — "most of our tribe were wiped out in the battle. We have a few survivors staying at a hostel in the city." The most convincing lie was the one that was mostly true.

He continued, "We were concerned about the armor and branding on the giants, my lady. It appears they might be congregating in packs of organized militia."

"Or hordes," added Lamech.

Inanna looked at the young man with surprise. Enoch broke out into a cold sweat.

"You think there may be hordes of Nephilim?" Inanna asked Lamech. "That is a rather bold claim, human. Hordes of Nephilim would indicate a rebellion of serious concern. How do you come by this intelligence?"

"The child speaks thoughtlessly, your majesty," interrupted Methuselah. "We have only seen pack-like activity."

"I am speaking to the young man," snapped Inanna. She knew if she had an opportunity to draw out anything incriminating on these foul vermin, it would be through this stupid brick head of an offspring.

"How is it you are so well trained in recognizing such militia activity?" she asked Lamech. Perhaps they were not telling her everything about their background. Maybe they had their own revolutionary connections. She had heard rumors about some kind of secret order of giant killers somewhere in the Havilah territory, but could never verify them with any certainty. Even torture had not revealed any secrets. Subterfuge might be a better tactic.

"Does not their soldier's uniforms and special armor indicate military affiliation?" asked Lamech. He was no brick head. He knew that turning it around and asking it as an obvious question would make him look much less educated and more of a speculator.

Inanna surprised them by turning to Edna. "Have there been any rumors of where these hordes may be?" Inanna thought wenches were even easier to trip up than young men.

Edna played her ignorance well. She added an uneducated rural accent. Her theatrics made Methuselah anxious. "My lady, can they hide inside volcanoes?" She said it without a trace of guile. She sounded spectacularly naïve.

Inanna rolled her eyes and shook her head with contempt. She would not even dignify that remark with an answer. Instead, she turned back to Enoch. "We have had some military uniforms stolen from caravans," she said. "Several other packs have shown up wearing them as well. Your 'hordes' are merely a pack of thieves." She turned to the administrator and snapped, "Give them their bounty." She whisked herself away without a farewell.

"Thank you, mighty queen," Enoch called after her.

She did not even acknowledge it. But as she exited the room, the Naphil guard who accompanied her caught Enoch's eyes in a long stare before he turned to follow the goddess.

It bothered Enoch. He collected their reward, thinking that they had better leave the city as quickly as possible.

Inanna sensed something askew with the bounty-hunters, but she also knew she would not get anywhere with her questioning. These humans were too smart to be so stupid. So few survived a tribal slaughter and killed four trained Nephilim warriors? And yet these survivors did not even know that volcanoes were inhospitable to animal life? She did not believe it. There was only one way she was going to get any information out of these wily travelers.

"Shadow them," she ordered the Nephilim.

Ohyah, the Naphil who had been watching Enoch, responded, "I will send my best tracker, your worship."

"Good. If he discovers a conspiratorial hideout of more of these giant-killers, we will hunt them down," Inanna said. "If not within the week, have him kill them as quickly as possible. We cannot have any of these nasty little gadflies getting under our skin with their revolutionary tendencies."

"Yes, my queen," said Ohyah.

She knew she could trust him. As a captain of the bodyguard, Ohyah had proven himself worthy by foiling an assassination attempt on Inanna some years before. It had happened when she began to usurp Enlil's status as patron god of Nippur. She simply outshined the unexceptional and mediocre Lord of the Air. She drew more followers through her bold leadership, and he had clearly become jealous.

She suspected the attempt had been masterminded by Enlil, but found no connections that led back to him. Though, as an immortal, she could not die, she could be wounded and impaired, which would weaken her status in the pantheon of power. Enlil had become so impotent that he locked himself in E-babba for weeks on end, not showing his face to anyone. When she went on her strategy trips back to Mount Hermon, he was too incompetent to take back his rightful glory. It made her smugly proud. She would eventually orchestrate his imprisonment so she could assume the throne physically, to complement her spiritual influence. But imprisoning a god was tricky. They could not be killed and had to be bound and entrapped into the heart of the earth, or better yet, a volcano. She grinned to herself. It required just the right sort of opportunity. She would wait for her moment.

She was engrossed in her planned rise to power. She had no idea that Ohyah, this most trusted of servants, had secrets of his own that had been haunting him. Secrets he could not reveal without losing his head.

CHAPTER 21

Enoch and his party, with the six rescued women squashed themselves into a city dwelling that only housed a family of four. They slept, some on the floor and some on the roof under the night sky. The patriarch of the home, Egibi, was a good friend of Betenos' father Barakil. They had traded with each other through the years and had become more than mere acquaintances. Egibi felt honored to give shelter to Betenos' tribe in this time of mourning.

Enoch explained to the women that Egibi would help them all find shelter and training for employment in the city. It would be difficult for these nomads to adjust, but they needed to do so. Enoch could not take care of them.

Betenos, however, was another story.

She pleaded with Enoch to take her with them. She pointed out that she had already helped them in many ways since they rescued her, not the least of which was finding this much needed shelter.

Enoch was set against it.

"This is a holy calling, Betenos. You do not even know who Elohim is."

"Lamech is teaching me," she answered.

"We cannot afford the time for Lamech to teach you," said Enoch. He doubted she would ever convert to Elohim.

Lamech butted in. "I will not shirk my other responsibilities and I will carry her weight if I must."

That brought a raised eyebrow from Betenos.

Enoch said, "She is not a giant killer."

Betenos retorted, "Giant killers need healing shamans for their battle wounds and cooks for their strength."

Enoch said, "This is too dangerous."

Edna now joined in, "She survived having her tribe wiped out by Nephilim."

Enoch barked, "Because we saved her!" He felt put upon.

"And she returned the favor." Methuselah held up Edna's bandaged arm. He was forever grateful for the healer's salve.

Enoch sighed with exasperation. He stared at Betenos and asked, "Why do you want to join us so desperately? Are you trying to seduce my grandson?"

Everyone went silent.

Betenos looked offended. She puffed up indignantly and said with a slow burn, "No, I am not trying to *seduce* your grandson." She gave that back with a sting. "I was the daughter of a tribal elder. I do not need your grandson for my betterment! Although, I suspect your concern should be that your grandson is trying to seduce *me*."

Lamech flushed with embarrassment. She could not have insulted him more.

"But you do not have to worry about that," Betenos continued proudly, "because I never want to marry and have a family anyway! I want to do something much more important with my life. I want to fight for justice. And that is what you are doing."

Enoch sighed, his resistence cracking. "If you slow us down, we will leave you at the nearest city."

Betenos pushed on, relentless and unyielding, "Did I slow you down in the Greater Zab valley?"

When they had been too exhausted to go any further, Betenos had given them those special roots that renewed their strength like that of eagles when chewed.

"All right, all right!" barked Enoch. He put his foot down. "But you will be our healer and cook, and you will do as you are told."

"Will you teach me the bow?" asked Betenos.

Enoch burst out chuckling. Everyone joined in, relieved. She was growing on them all.

Enoch said, "Well you certainly do have the requisite stubborn-headedness to be a part of this tribe."

They all laughed some more — except for Lamech. Her remarks had deeply hurt him. He had truly been enjoying her presence, not trying to seduce her. Her arrogance of caste superiority left a foul impression on him. He looked for a way to leave the room without drawing attention to himself.

Edna could see her son's hurt. She held back from mothering him. She knew he had to go through this rejection on his own. It would mature him.

A knock at the door frightened them all. A curfew ruled the city. Anyone out in the streets at this hour could be arrested. The four of them found their weapons. Egibi opened the door to a six-year old child.

"Child, what are you doing out there!" yelped Egibi. He grabbed the small shoulder and pulled him quickly inside. "Do you not know, you could be arrested or killed outside past curfew!" he scolded.

The child nodded. He held out a small box to Egibi, a scribe's writing tablet with wax embedded in wood. When opened, a person could mark the wax and close it for storage and delivery. Egibi opened it and looked at it, but he could not read.

Enoch took the tablet and read it. His eyes went wide. "It says it is from an 'Ohyah,' the Nephilim Captain of the Guard. He wants to speak with me in secret. He says he has important intelligence for me. He wants to meet outside the city walls by the garbage dump."

"That smelly pit?" said Betenos.

"He does not want us to be discovered," said Enoch. "No one is going to be snooping around the city garbage dump in the late of night. And there are not many places a giant's presence can be discreet."

"A trap," offered Methuselah.

Enoch did not agree. "He would not admit to me that he was a Nephilim Captain of the Guard if he wanted to trick me," he said. "That would be about the last thing he would pretend to be."

"A double cross?" suggested Methuselah.

Enoch countered, "He is telling me a truth that places himself in a vulnerable position. And this little child is more evidence of that sentiment."

"Just the same, we are going with you," said Methuselah. "We will keep out of sight in case it does turn out to be a trap."

CHAPTER 22

The city dump lay just outside the walls on the north side of the city, downwind from the sea and river breezes that jostled their way through the streets. The stinking festering pile of refuse made Enoch think of Sheol and what it would be like to be cursed.

He walked toward some trees at the edge of the dump. How anything could grow here amazed him. The stench of the rotting garbage drew too many flies and made him gag. He shooed away a couple hyenas fighting over a cattle bone and looked around. The nearly six cubit tall dark figure standing in the moonlit shadows of the tree foliage gestured just enough to draw Enoch's attention. His heart raced. He wiggled his fingers in preparation to draw his dagger. Methuselah, Edna, and Lamech moved in and out of cover amidst the piles of rubbish, ready to charge at his command.

Enoch stepped up to the giant and found cover out of sight of the city watch above on the walls.

Ohyah towered over Enoch in both size and strength. Tattoos covered him, but he was one of the more handsome looking giants, if one could say that about such beasts.

"Are the three following you your own?" asked Ohyah, trying to keep his deep voice to a whisper.

Enoch nodded. This giant was also warrior-trained and had highly attuned senses. He could easily grab Enoch and crush him before any of them could come to his aid.

"I am grateful you came tonight. I know it was not an easy decision," said Ohyah.

"Then make it a worthy one," said Enoch. He would not fear this monster. He knew whom he served and did not fear death in the least.

Ohyah said, "The Nephilim you killed were not random thieves wearing stolen uniforms. They were from the deep west in Bashan by the Western Sea. From the area around Mount Hermon."

Enoch had heard of Mount Hermon. He knew it was the place of descent, where "the gods came down from heaven" to rule among men. It was an area shrouded in mystery, separated from their fertile crescent by hundreds of leagues of harsh arid desert. No one he knew had ever travelled there. All he had heard about it was rumors, gossip, and speculation. Nothing he cared to trust.

Ohyah continued, "After the Gigantomachy, some Rephaim escaped the Great Purges and found sanctuary in the one place that the Watchers would not consider looking for them. Their own territory of Bashan. The gods left their cosmic mountain to reside in the cities, so the criminal Rephaim and Nephilim went to hide out where the gods had left. They congregate and secret themselves like cockroaches in the nooks and crevices of the mountains and foothills. The giants you brought in were branded with the mark of Thamaq and Yahipan, Rephaim originally from Sippar."

Ohyah did not know that Enoch had been in Sippar during that fateful event. Enoch heard everything Ohyah told him, and knew it was all true. This earned the giant a measure of trust. Of course, he was still a Captain of the Temple Guard of Inanna, and the best lies were mostly true. So Enoch remained guarded.

Ohyah offered, "If you want to kill outlaws, Bashan is one of their hideouts."

Enoch narrowed his eyes and looked suspiciously at Ohyah.

"Why are you giving me this intelligence?" Enoch asked.

Ohyah did not expect Enoch to believe him easily. He knew he had to be vulnerable first, to reveal information that would place Ohyah himself in jeopardy. It was the only way he could earn trust.

"I have been having dreams from a god named Elohim," Ohyah said.

Enoch's attention perked up. How could this dark minion of Inanna know about Elohim? Did he know that Enoch and his band served Elohim? But how?

Ohyah, continued, "I saw the Ancient of Days, the ruler of heavens come down to earth and sit on a throne surrounded by ten thousand times ten thousand of his holy ones. He proclaimed a sentence upon all flesh and then wrote it on a tablet. The tablet was immersed in water and when it came out, all the names were washed away but eight. I fear for my life, Enoch. I want to join the forces of this god Elohim."

How could a demonic chimera receive revelations from Elohim? wondered Enoch. This was madness.

Ohyah said, "Elohim told me that you served him."

He could not possibly have known Enoch's calling except by revelation. *But what was this water judgment?*

"And he said that you would be going to the land of Bashan."

Ah, there he is wrong, thought Enoch, *I have been called to pronounce judgment upon the Watcher gods and their progeny, but Elohim has not told me to go to Bashan. Though it would provide the most opportunity for his bounty hunting of giants.*

Ohyah said, "I have a twin brother, Hahyah, who I believe is hiding out in that region. We have had an inseparable spiritual

129

connection since we were born. I am sure he has had the same dreams and is most likely looking for me. I want to go with you to Bashan to find him. We will both repent and serve Elohim the Creator."

Enoch simply could not accept this insanity. A demonic spawn repent to worship Elohim? But was it possible that the truth was more than he understood? Could Elohim regenerate the soul of a Naphil? They were half human after all. Why could not their sin be as forgivable as his own? He wondered, if one of these could turn, could a Watcher god turn?

"No," said Enoch, "We are not going to Bashan. If you want to find your brother, you will have to go alone."

"It is treason to leave the side of Inanna. I will not be allowed to return. At least with you, I have a chance."

"Why do you say that?" asked Enoch. "You are a mighty warrior."

"But Elohim favors you," said Ohyah.

Enoch paused and measured his words carefully. "And Inanna favors you."

Ohyah understood the obvious implication. They served different gods. Enoch could never trust him because Inanna was a treacherous scheming demon of war and perversion. He did not blame Enoch. But it dashed his hopes nonetheless.

Enoch could see Ohyah's crestfallen expression. A Naphil, Captain of the Guard, mighty warrior, and demigod looked as if he was a kicked cub. Maybe more truth hid in this matter than Enoch thought at first. But he had to trust his intuition, unless Elohim himself told him otherwise.

Ohyah spoke with sad respect, "May your Elohim bless you on your journey with protection and success." With that Ohyah melted away into the shadows of the trees.

Methuselah arrived first. "What happened?"

Enoch stared into the blackness. Edna and Lamech joined them. Enoch paused thoughtfully, then finally offered, "He wanted to help us, but I turned him down."

"Help us?" sniffed Methuselah, "You mean betray us."

"That may very well be," said Enoch. "But if so, then he fooled me."

Methuselah, Edna, and Lamech all looked confused at Enoch and then into the dark, hoping that Ohyah would come back and explain the impossible. But no explanation was forthcoming. Enoch said, "Let us get back to the house. I need sleep."

Enoch's thrashing awakened Methuselah and Edna from their sleep. When he sat up, they saw the sheen of sweat bathing him. He gasped for air. They knew it was another dream vision.

"Elohim told me to go to the land of Bashan," said Enoch.

Methuselah and Edna could not believe their ears. Edna reached over and softly closed Methuselah's gaping jaw.

"That is near Mount Hermon, the cosmic mountain of the pantheon," said Methuselah. "Do you consider it wise to tread so close to the headquarters of the gods?"

Enoch said, "The Naphil guard captain told me that Thamaq and Yahipan were hiding out in Bashan."

Methuselah took one look at Edna and said, "We are going with father to Bashan."

If the Rephaim of Sippar, the murderers of his beloved Edna's parents, were still alive, if these abominations of desolation still breathed the good air of earth, then Methuselah had his purpose: to hunt them down and kill them.

The revelation of the Naphil dreams still bothered Enoch. Elohim had told Ohyah Enoch's charge before Elohim had told

Enoch. How could this be? Should he have welcomed the giant into their company? Was that from Elohim? Or was it occultic sorcery? Was this a test? Did he fail it? It chewed into his brain. The giant knew Enoch's destination before he did. Elohim spoke to a Naphil!

Enoch stared into the distance like a holy man in a trance. "If you are going to go with me, you had better wake the others. We leave immediately for Mari."

CHAPTER 23

The city of Mari sat a good one hundred and thirty leagues up the Euphrates River from Nippur. As an economic trading center between Shinar in the south and Syria in the north, Mari channeled timber, stone, pottery, grains, and perishable foods up and down the Euphrates. It was also a way station to cross the vast desert to reach Bashan by the shorter and more hazardous path. The longer circuitous, and safer, route swept northward around the fertile crescent.

Enoch's traveling band of giant killers hired a boat to take them up to Mari. From there, they would strike out across the desert. The legendary Thamudi, primitive tribal peoples, roamed the desert, filling it with danger. They were said to skin victims alive and roll them in the sand to increase their unbearable pain.

Enoch left the snow tribe women with Egibi as he had promised. But he took Betenos with them, as he had conceded to her.

They avoided staying in the city proper so they would not be easily tracked by enemies. They chose a thick forest off the river's edge. They burrowed deep into the wildwood far from civilization to rest before their westward crossing of the desert.

After clearing a camp, they started one of the first fires they had been able to burn in a long time. They roasted wild boar on a makeshift spit and sat back, bellies full, mugs topped with drink. The women slept as Enoch, Methuselah, and Lamech sat around the fire planning the next leg of their trip.

Methuselah interrupted the discussion. "We are being followed." Lamech shook his head in surprise, for he had not noticed.

"I know," said Enoch. "I sensed it about half way up the river, and whoever it is has trailed us into the forest."

Lamech grabbed his weapon, Rahab. "Should we wake the women?"

"Yes," said Enoch. "But do not cause a commotion, because they are very near."

Lamech lightly nudged Edna and Betenos awake. He gave them a shushed gesture of warning. They understood the danger and picked up their weapons. Edna gripped a multi-bladed weapon and handed Betenos an axe from the wood pile. They stepped up slowly to the campfire.

"Backs against the flames, in a circle," commanded Enoch, who pulled an arrow from his quiver and nocked it on his bowstring. "It is time we face our stalker," he said.

They heard the rustling of the leaves in the wind in sync with the rustling in the underbrush. Whoever lurked there had a hunter's skill for blending into the natural background.

Or *whatever.*

They heard a soft growling. The iridescent glow of eyes reflecting the firelight from the brush appeared. Pairs of eyes. All around them. About twenty.

The lead alpha male stepped out of the bush. It focused on Enoch, seeming to know his equal. It was a bizarre creature that none of them had ever seen before, a chimera, a hybrid mixture of several animals. It crept on all fours, and was about three times the size of a man. It had the long scaly neck and head of a horned dragon, the body and forelegs of a feline predator, the taloned hind legs of a bird of prey, and its tail was a living snake.

The creature showed no fear of its prey. It seemed to merely be sizing up how easily the game would be taken. It snarled.

Lamech rolled out Rahab. He could tame this thing with a whip of his sword, but twenty of them? That was another story altogether.

The alpha hissed. Its forked tongue tasted the air that carried their scent. It backed up a bit into the shadows. The eyes of the others moved slightly forward, lowering to the ground. They prepared to strike.

Suddenly, the alpha beast yelped as its tail was jerked from behind. Something dragged the monster into the brush and out of sight. Its roar cut off in a squeal of pain.

One of the surrounding chimeras jumped out of the bushes at the humans by the fire. A seven cubit tall Naphil leapt through the air, intercepting the chimera. It met the beast with a crunch and they rolled to the ground in a mass. Then the giant stood up, victoriously, his blade dripping with chimera blood.

He stood, wearing only a loincloth, the ritual Nephilim hunting attire, holding a pear-headed mace in one hand and a battle axe in the other. Was he on their side or was he claiming them as his prey?

Another squeal cut through the dark. Another chimera flew out from the bush and landed in a dead heap for all to see. Its killer followed, a second leaping Naphil. He landed on the other side of the blazing fire, ready to kill with a mace and sword. Two down, eighteen to go.

Enoch suddenly recognized the second Naphil as Ohyah, the Captain of Inanna's guard. The first Naphil stared at Ohyah with a look of surprise, like he had not anticipated Ohyah's arrival.

Enoch had no time to sort out what was happening. The gang of monsters pounced in unison. Most of them attacked the two Nephilim. The others went for the humans.

These hellions fought fiercely. Methuselah thanked Elohim the Nephilim were on their side. They might not have survived without them.

Enoch killed a couple of the chimeras with his bow. With such close quarter fighting, he dropped the bow and switched to an axe.

Methuselah used his javelins as pikes, poking out eyes and throats. He caught a quick glance of Edna, spinning and slicing more furiously than he had ever seen. But her wounded arm, though mostly healed, was a bit stiff and slow. She was tiring and getting sloppy. Killing hybrid giants was one thing, but these obscenities were five-part hounds of Sheol. Their freakish nature resulted in confusing unpredictable fighting behavior. They were flexible, agile and fast.

Betenos was not a warrior. Lamech had been working with her, and she had been catching on quickly. But this was not any kind of battle to practice in. It was not even a battle that Lamech, with all his experience, had ever been in before. He had double duty snapping his sword Rahab and covering for Betenos behind him with their backs to the bonfire. She snatched up Enoch's bow and arrows. She had time to aim and release from behind Lamech.

Lamech's arm was tiring. He chopped off a snake head tail of one of the beasts and then caught the dragon head of another. The force of it yanked his weakened arm and he lost control. The whip blade cracked just over Methuselah's head near the fire.

"Are you still angry at me, son? I told you I like Betenos!" yelped Methuselah. Even at such a moment, he could find the humor. He might as well. They would probably all be dead and eaten by evening's end.

"Sorry!" yelled Lamech. He switched hands with the flexible blade. He was not as good with his left arm. But he needed rest or he would collapse any moment.

The Nephilim worked in natural coordination with each other. They each grabbed a monster in tandem and threw the beasts at each other with a crash, stunning them. They followed up with a synchronized double clubbing. They were highly trained guards and would be very hard to kill should Enoch's team find themselves facing off with the giants after this ambush — *if* they made it out alive.

Enoch's thoughts distracted him for a moment. One of the chimeras fell upon him and pinned him to the ground, knocking the wind out of him. Saliva splattered from its jaws. He could feel the hot breath on his face. It bared its teeth to strike, its lips pulled back to reveal two rows of razor edged fangs.

Enoch shut his eyes, waiting for his life to be torn from his body.

The jaws never came.

Ohyah grabbed the dragon's throat and ripped out its windpipe. It fell to the ground.

Enoch opened his eyes.

Ohyah smiled at him, for just a moment. Then a pack of three of the mongrels pounced in unison onto his back. He went down beneath a pile of fighting monsters. One of the creatures clamped its iron jaws onto Ohyah's arm. He screamed in pain.

The other giant ripped one of the beasts off of him and flung it down onto the fire.

An explosion of flames and embers covered everyone.

Methuselah's javelin and Edna's weapon pierced through the second one.

The third mutant beast with clamped jaw had its head cut off by Lamech's Rahab.

Suddenly, unexpectedly, it was all over. Those were the last three of the chimeras. The giant killers had teamed up with their own enemy to defeat a common foe.

Everyone was near total exhaustion, lungs burning for air.

When Lamech saw that Betenos was unwounded, he hugged her for dear life.

Methuselah crawled to Edna. He was too exhausted to say anything more than, "Pednanoonypoo."

"Poozelahbunnybunch," she murmured and collapsed in his arms. They lay gasping for a moment.

"What in the world were those monstrosities?" an incredulous Methuselah asked anyone who would answer.

No one did.

Methuselah glanced around. The second Naphil helped Enoch up to his feet. Whatever possessed this creature to help them was beyond Methuselah.

He saw Ohyah stand up behind Enoch. His father was sandwiched between the two giants. The hair rose on the back of Methuselah's neck.

Ohyah raised his ax.

Methuselah screamed.

It was too late. Ohyah delivered a mighty blow.

But it was not to Enoch. Ohyah struck the other Naphil. It fell to the ground dead at Enoch's feet.

Enoch looked up in fear at Ohyah.

Ohyah dropped the weapon and sat on the ground, his task completed.

Lamech and Methuselah ran to Enoch to protect him. They pointed their weapons at the surviving giant. Ohyah sighed and said, "That Naphil was sent to kill you."

"How do you know that?" demanded Enoch.

"Because Inanna ordered me to send him," said Ohyah. "He did not anticipate being beaten to the task by the mushussu." He looked at Methuselah. "That is the answer to your question. The beasts are called *mushussu*. He must have relished the challenge of gaining your trust in the fight in order to kill you in your sleep."

"And you?" said Lamech.

"I came to stop him. He thought I was here to help him."

"This is becoming a jumbled confusion of cross purposes," exclaimed Methuselah. "I must be getting old."

"It is simple, father," said Lamech. "We are on our way to kill giants." He pointed to the dead Naphil. "That giant was sent to kill us." He pointed to Ohyah. "This giant came to kill that giant. But these mushussu came to kill us all. So we all teamed up and killed the mushussu." He paused for a moment. "And now we are all wondering if we should kill this giant." Lamech was becoming a chip off the old mud brick, with his wit. Edna smiled.

Enoch said, "Why should we trust you, giant?"

"Is it not obvious?" said Ohyah. "If I wanted you dead, I would have let the Naphil kill you."

"But *you* are a Naphil," protested Methuselah. "You are the Watchers' seed."

"But half human," said Lamech in Ohyah's defense.

"Elohim made me this way," Ohyah countered.

Edna watched Ohyah closely. She did not have the open mind that these men displayed. She cared only to protect her son and husband.

"Can Nephilim actually repent and serve Elohim?" Methuselah's words echoed everyone's thoughts.

Enoch spoke up. "Ohyah means us no harm. He will be traveling with us to Bashan."

He stared straight into Ohyah's eyes as he said the words. Ohyah sighed with relief and smiled at him.

"Well, I never thought I'd see the day," said Methuselah. "A repentant Naphil joining a team of giant killers. You will have to write about that in your memoirs, father. But I anticipate you will be accused of fictional embellishment."

The others chuckled. It was all too absurd to believe. But they were living it.

Enoch studied one of the dead monsters, deep in thought. He picked up one of the severed heads to look at it more closely. "Ohyah, you called these mushussu? I have never seen nor heard of them before. What are they?"

"Miscegenation of the gods," said Ohyah. The word referred to hybridization. Herdsmen and pastoralists had learned to crossbreed certain animals to create new ones that were blended combinations of both animals. The domesticated dog came from such breeding. Humans selected wolves from one pack that were more docile than the others and interbred them with docile members of a different pack to create a new breed of canine more friendly to humans. There were limits to hybridization that restricted such breeding to animals of the same kind. One could not "crossbreed" birds with felines and reptiles. Yet this hideous mutant clearly had been so magically bred. It was unimaginable.

"How is it possible to crossbreed so many creatures?" asked Methuselah.

A pall of darkness came over Ohyah's face. "It is not natural," he said. "It is part of an experiment of occultic secrets by the gods."

"But why?" asked Enoch. "For what purpose?"

"I do not know," said Ohyah. "But I suspect you will find the answer in Bashan."

"Well, let us get our rest," said Enoch. "We begin our crossing of the Great Desert in the morning."

CHAPTER 24

They set out to cross the Great Desert, heading into a stretch of one hundred and seventeen leagues of the most severe desert, with the harshest weather Enoch and his band of warriors had ever experienced. He wondered where such severity came from. He had heard that in early days, the region had been rich in vegetation, animal life and bodies of water. Something had happened that changed it all, that brought a curse upon this infernal land.

Riding onagers, they followed a trade route marked by wells along the way. The watering spots gave them relief for their blistered and dehydrated bodies. They crossed paths with caravans returning from Egypt by way of the Levantine coastal lands. Within days they adjusted to the harsh environment. As nomads, they had learned to survive in any habitat, from rigid cold mountain to hot humid jungle to barren dry tundra.

Methuselah, who longed to experience all the extremes that his body could endure in this world, found it exhilarating. He felt that if Elohim gave him physical senses to experience, he would indulge them to the fullest — within moral boundaries of course. And one of those moral boundaries included holy union with his beloved Edna. Even after all these years, he was more grateful for Elohim's creation of oneness with his wife than anything else, be it feasting on a roasted boar or killing a giant. Well, roasted boar ran a pretty close second.

Edna glanced at Methuselah, lost in thought as they plodded along on their pack animals. She knew exactly what he was thinking. She would tease him about it in their tent later that night. And then she would kiss him—passionately—because she understood him more than anyone in the world. She loved him the way he was, with all their differences.

Enoch had not adapted to this miserable climate as well as the others. He used the long hours of travel to pray to Elohim. But he could not stand the relentless heat. He longed to leave his body and once again swim in the crystalline waters above the heavens. He dreamed of being in the heavenly temple and the glorious light of ten thousand times ten thousand of Elohim's holy ones. Instead, he suffered the burning rays of a red hot sun scorching him to the bone.

Lamech and Betenos lagged further behind. Their non-stop talk drove everyone up a rock cliff. What is your favorite animal to kill and skin? Do you prefer lean-to shelters or sleeping under starlight? Do you ever want to settle down in a city someday? It was amazing how long they could talk without taking a break to breathe or drink water from their goat skins.

Edna smiled and said a prayer of thanks when she heard them spend hours debating the greatness of Elohim versus the Great Goddess. She could hear Betenos breaking down in her protestations. She knew it was only a matter of time before Betenos rejected her pagan upbringing and embraced Elohim. Who knows? She might even become a giant killer. In the meantime, she cooked a mean lizard stew and kept them from heat exhaustion with her herbal remedies.

The one area that gave Edna grave concern was Betenos' vow against marriage. The young woman was dead set against having children and refused to talk about it. Edna made a mental note to talk to Betenos about it when they were alone.

Ohyah brought up the rear. They all found it difficult to accept a giant walking amongst them. He did not want to make them any more uncomfortable. Besides, Nephilim were reclusive creatures and treasured their solitude. They were bred to kill, not socialize.

The group made astonishing time at almost eight leagues a day for nearly a week. They were just past half way to their destination. The midafternoon sun penetrated everything.

A gush of warm air washed over them.

A shiver went through Ohyah's spine. He yelled out in his deep resounding voice,. "Shaitan! Shaitan!" It carried all the way to Enoch at the front of their line.

It was the Naphil word for sandstorm, a very vicious sandstorm. Enoch searched the horizon. He did not see it. No one did. The Nephilim had a sixth sense the humans did not share.

Ohyah sprinted to the front. "It is coming from the north! We must find shelter!"

They had seen no shelter for days.

Enoch yelled, "RUN!" They all kicked their rides and galloped westward as fast as they could.

The storm did not take long to become visible. A huge billowing wall of sand in the distance charged toward them like a tsunami. Before they could get to safety, it swept over them. A cyclone of whirling dust and sand and rocks enveloped them.

A large rock hit Ohyah in the back. It would have killed any of the humans, but it merely knocked him dizzy. He tried to cover the women with his bulky figure.

They did not know how long they could last. Such storms could be short gusts or stretch for distances of leagues.

They covered their mouths with their cloaks as filters. They could barely breathe.

The onagers collapsed. They had no filters for their lungs.

The company could not move. Their beasts of burden were dead. They huddled together.

They prepared to die.

As suddenly as it began, the storm stopped. It passed over them. They coughed and sputtered and shook out the sand from their clothes.

They looked around. The storm had not actually passed them by. It was now all around them. They stood within a swirling wall of sand circling around them like a huge corral.

"The eye of the storm," blurted Lamech.

They had heard of such a thing, but had never experienced it. As if they were at sea, this hurricane of sand had a center of complete calmness and they had entered it. All around them rushed the impenetrable curtain of cyclonic wind and earth. They huddled in a circle of complete calmness.

Betenos looked up behind them all with astonishment. "Oh my gods, it is true. It is really true."

Everyone turned to see an incredible wonder. Not too far from them stood a tree, a very large tree, a tremendous tree that extended into the heavens, thousands of cubits high.

"The World Tree," murmured Betenos. "See, Lamech?" she cried, "I told you it was true. The Great Goddess Earth Mother."

She fell to her knees and worshipped.

CHAPTER 25

Enoch looked upwards. He could not see where the tree ended. It just disappeared into the clouds. How could this be? They should have seen it from leagues away. But there had been nothing but empty desert for many leagues in every direction. It was not only thousands of cubits high, it was at least a couple hundred cubits around. Its tangled mass of roots were no doubt anchored deep into the earth. It could not move with the shifting storm, so how could it be in the center of it?

Enoch rubbed his eyes. Was this a vision? It could not be. The others saw it as well. Were they under some kind of spell? It must be magic.

Skepticism filled Enoch. He felt they were nestling within the coils of a huge serpent. It might be dark magic.

Ohyah recalled the story from his youth about Inanna and the Huluppu Tree. Could this be the one? The very origin of the Sacred Marriage rite. It came rushing back to him. *In the very first days and the very first nights when Anu and Enlil had separated the heavens and the earth, and Ereshkigal was given the underworld, there was a single Huluppu Tree.* The wood from the tree was used to make the bed of Inanna where her lover Dumuzi would sleep with her. Then he remembered, *the great thunderbird, Anzu left its young up in the branches*. Ohyah stared up into the sky, transfixed, looking for some sign of the mythical eagle-like creature.

Without warning, he ran toward the tree.

Enoch yelled after him, "Ohyah! What are you doing?"

Ohyah did not respond. He ran like the wind all the way to the mighty trunk and jumped onto it a dozen cubits in the air.

He climbed.

The others stood wondering what had gotten into his head to do such a thing.

Methuselah said, "I knew we could not trust the giant."

"We must take cover before the storm shifts," Enoch said, starting toward the tree. They approached its base, a tangle of gnarled roots plunging into the earth like grappling hooks. The wood of the tree was weather-beaten and leathery. The roots writhed and folded around each other creating crevices and hideaways.

High above them, Ohyah climbed rapidly. White clouds shrouded the top of the tree. As they watched the spectacle of the tree-climbing giant, he vanished into the mist.

Enoch brought his gaze back down. He started.

Three beautiful young maidens stood before them like phantasms. They reminded him of the cave dwellers of Sahand who suddenly appeared as if rising from the ground itself. But these beings probably materialized from the large fissures of the tree. And they were not so earthy as the cave dwellers.

They were actually quite heavenly.

Surprise silenced the travelers.

The women were barefoot, adorned in silky flowing dress, with flower-laden hair. One had jet black hair and the others had wavy locks as golden as the sand. Their pale milky skin looked as if it had

147

never been in the sun. And when they spoke, it gave the impression of singing.

The women spoke as if in unison, "Welcome to our abode. You must be exhausted to have weathered such a storm."

Enoch could swear he did not see their mouths move. "Who are you?" he asked.

"I am Lilith," said the raven-haired beauty. "And these are my daughters Lili and Lilu."

"Are you angels?" blurted Lamech.

Lilith smiled. "We are the keepers of this most sacred space."

"Where are we? What is this?" asked Enoch.

"This is the Great Goddess Earth Mother, the Tree of Life," answered Lilith. "She is the link between heaven and earth."

"What?" said Enoch. He looked at Methuselah and Edna. They knew of only one Tree of Life and that was unapproachably secluded in the Garden of Eden.

Lilith and the girls giggled. "All will be made clear. But first you must rest, re-gather your strength," said Lilith.

She led them to a campsite nestled in the encircling roots of the tree. It seemed a comfortable safe encampment with a firepit, locations for sleeping and protection from any sandy winds or scorching sunrays that might try to find them.

But the feature that caught their attention was the flowing fountain of sparkling fresh water that poured from a hole in the tree into a small pool with well walls built around it.

Lamech plopped down exhausted in a bed-like nook of soft bark.

Lilith stepped over to the pouring water and took a handcupped sip. "You must be weary and thirsty from your journey. Please allow Lili and Lilu to serve you refreshment."

Enoch, Methuselah and Edna were not merely weary but wary. Betenos was transfixed in wonder.

Lamech started to snore. He had fallen asleep from fatigue.

Lili and Lilu brought ladles of the water to them. Enoch surmised that this strange angelic woman could not be offering them poisoned water since she indulged from the fountain herself. He nodded to the others and they drank deeply.

But Enoch also noticed something about Lilu that made him curious. Up close, it became apparent to him that Lilu was in fact a slender feminine young boy who had been dressed and groomed as a girl. But the promise of water distracted him.

The liquid felt like balm in their parched throats. It brought almost instant healing to their chapped lips and revived them from within. Their blurry sight became unclouded. Their foggy heads dissipated and they could think more clearly. They must have been dangerously dehydrated and had not realized it.

Lilith said to them, "It is the living waters."

Edna felt a pain in her stomach. Nausea swept over her. She looked at the others. They seemed all right. It was not the water.

Lilith noticed Edna's grimace with a look of concern, a display of preternatural sensitivity to others' feelings. To Edna, she seemed the very embodiment of compassion. She was elegant and fair, like a hidden queen of this desert oasis paradise.

Methuselah was no doubt allured by her. He deeply loved his wife. She knew he worked hard at keeping his eyes focused on his beloved Edna. But she also knew her husband's tastes. She suspected that he was trying very hard at that moment to avoid an attraction to this exotic woman.

She was right. Methuselah found Lilith beautiful. He wondered if Havah had looked like this when she was first created in the Garden so long ago, the essence of woman.

Enoch felt surprised at himself. He had never been one to be overcome by women's beauty. But he had never seen such transcendent and feminine loveliness in all his wanderings. It stirred him in a way he had not been stirred for years. He wondered if he had become too mental and disembodied in his spirit. Perhaps Methuselah's accusation of him was correct: he was missing out on the visual beauty of Elohim's creation.

Lamech had stopped snoring. In his dreams, he began to experience erotic thoughts he had not had before. His desire for Betenos was rising within his soul. He wanted to marry her. But she did not worship Elohim, and that was a problem. He had no desire to unite himself, a temple of Elohim, to a temple of other gods. Betenos had listened and asked questions for a while. But she was unwilling to reject the gods she had known all her life and worship his god. But even if she did, she still did not want to marry and raise a family.

Yet, in the dream, Betenos came to Lamech as he slept. She whispered in his ears, "I will follow your god, but you must first know me."

Her body began to sway and undulate with an inhuman flexibility, almost like that of a snake.

She brushed against his body and he was about to grab her, when her tongue flicked out and licked his face. It was a split tongue.

It shocked him awake. His heart raced. He tried not to display his fear as he looked at Betenos sitting attentively listening to Lilith, completely unaware of Lamech behind her.

Edna thought she felt the sand move beneath them. It was a dizzy spell. She shook it off. She was feeling better.

Enoch said to Lilith, "Tell us about this Tree of Life you call the Great Goddess Earth Mother." Enoch refused to be a pushover. Just because they had been rescued by these maidens, that did not mean he trusted that they had altruistic motives. The others knew he was testing Lilith. He did not mention that they had sojourned with the very first inhabitants of the Garden, the only humans to see the Tree of Life. He knew this was not the same tree.

Her daughters sat dutifully beside Lilith as she told her amazing story.

CHAPTER 26

Hundreds of cubits above the campsite, Ohyah continued to scale the mighty tree. Deep grooves and knots in the wood made for easy climbing. He stopped again to rest. For the first time, he looked more closely at the bark he had been grabbing for handholds and footholds.

What he saw almost made him lose his grip.

The bark seemed to consist of countless multitudes of human bodies fused indistinguishably into the wood in agonizing and convoluted tangles. It was as if the tree was made of these bodies melded into one large edifice that rose into the sky. Was this a tree of corpses or damned souls?

A tremendous caw overhead drew his attention back to his goal. The call of the Anzu. He planned to catch the great thunderbird. He could not see it yet, but knew he was close. It probably nestled amidst one of the branches in the heights. He continued to climb.

• • • • •

"You are familiar with our forefather Adam and the Garden of Eden?" Lilith asked her attentive group of resting travelers. They nodded their heads yes.

152

"And you have heard that he had a wife, Havah?" she added. They nodded again.

She let loose with her revelation, "What you no doubt have *not* heard is that I was Adam's first wife."

The travelers did not hold back their surprise.

"It is true. I do not expect you to believe me. For I know that Adam and his second wife have conspired to construct a myth that covers up the truth. You see, Elohim created me to be Adam's equal in the Garden. But if you knew Adam, you would know that he is a controlling patriarchal male."

Enoch and the others could understand that sentiment. They had come to know Adam. He had been a strong leader, at times a bit demanding. And he often had appealed to his status as the firstborn of humanity. When drunk, he would sometimes mumble, "I am primogeniture," a term that meant the firstborn birthright to inherit an entire estate. Ironically, though, in his later years, his blindness made him depend upon Havah. Methuselah thought it was Havah, not Adam, that had become a bit more controlling than he thought appropriate.

Lilith continued, "Adam became so oppressive that I refused to submit to his authority out of fear for my safety. I had no desire for his position as head of the human race. I simply wanted equality. After all, Elohim had created me out of his side, not his rear end."

The listeners chuckled. She had the good sense of humor to make light of what was an otherwise intolerable situation. Edna began to think of Methuselah and how much she had given up to follow him, and how he was often insensitive to her interests and absorbed in his own.

Betenos hung on every word, completely oblivious to any memory of her secret romantic interest in Lamech. All she thought of was his insufferable demands that she follow his male god

Elohim, who did not display much interest in women as far as she was concerned.

"I gave in to his bizarre and abusive demands," continued Lilith, "and gave him the two daughters you see before you now." Lili and Lilu were looking more innocent to Methuselah and Enoch. Enoch had already forgotten his discovery that Lilu was a boy.

It did not occur to any of them that Lilith and her offspring should appear much older than they did. If they had been with Adam before Havah, they would be close to nine hundred years old.

Enchantment lay upon Enoch and his party. The water from the tree had drugged their faculties of observation, reason, and morality.

"Unfortunately," said Lilith, "Adam and his 'god' did not want girls, they wanted boys, the superior gender as they told me. They conspired to use this against me and cast me and my daughters out of the Garden, so Elohim could make a more 'suitable' partner for him, someone who would remain barefoot in the Garden and bow to his every wish and whim. In other words, a slave."

Edna now saw Methuselah as the exact replication of his forefather Adam, a patriarchal pig. Thoughts raced through her mind like gnats. *He probably thinks of me as his slave, to fulfill his commands at the expense of my own. And all he ever thinks about is sex. What kind of spiritual leader is that? I probably need a man like a fish needs a pelican.*

Betenos had already determined that she would never marry Lamech, the wild boar progeny of his father. *Maybe what I really need is another woman instead, who understands me. Maybe one of these daughters. That way, I would never have to worry about birthing those clinging little screaming monsters called "children."*

Lilith said, "My daughters and I were exiled by the sky god and his violent male oppressor, but our Earth Mother, the Great Goddess, found us and gave us rebirth here at the true Tree of Life."

Betenos suddenly broke out weeping. Lilith touched her gently.

"What is wrong, my dear?" she asked.

Betenos mumbled just clearly enough, "That is why I do not want to bring children into this world! My whole tribe was slaughtered by men and their lust for violence and war."

"It is true," said Lilith. "Perhaps if the nurturing gender were in charge, we might have peace in the world."

Edna doubled over with crippling pain in her abdomen. She reached below her cloak and pulled her hand out. It had blood all over it.

Enoch recoiled with revulsion.

Methuselah refused to come to her aid.

Serves her right, he thought, *the way she has been ignoring me lately with her hysterical emotional tantrums.*

Lilith helped Edna up with gentle compassion. "I think this is something only another woman can help with," she said. "Come for a walk, my love. I can help you clean yourself from impurities."

Betenos jumped up. "May I come also, Lilith?"

Lilith kept her back. "Maybe later, dear."

Betenos sat down again, disappointed.

Edna felt certain that something moved beneath her feet again, like something swimming in the sand.

Lilith called back to her daughters, "Lili and Lilu, will you please keep the others entertained."

"Yes, mother," they said in perfect unison. Lamech was sure their mouths did not move when they spoke.

However, their bodies did move. Their motion reminded Lamech of the writhing dance in his dream. Exactly the same dance in his dream. Like the movement of snakes.

The sinuous dancing wove the enchantment on the travelers tighter. But the three keepers of the tree had not anticipated one minor mistake in their perfect scheme: Lamech had not drunk the water.

The young man burst out, "Father, we have been enchanted by sorcery! In the holy name of Yahweh Elohim, awake!"

The secret covenant name of Yahweh broke the spell and ripped the men from their stupor. He would never have used it but for the lethal nature he knew they were in.

The girls cried out in unison, "Ningishzida, arise!" And then they fled.

Betenos tried to go after them, but Lamech held her back. She struggled and thrashed in his arms, trying to get loose. "Let me go! Let me go!" she screamed. It was as if she was possessed of an evil spirit. But Lamech would not let her go. He loved her too deeply.

Enoch and Methuselah gathered their weapons. They snatched up some burning logs for light, and ran after the two girls.

They saw the figures fleetingly, disappearing into the tree a short distance ahead of them. It was as if they dissolved into it.

When the two men reached the spot, they discovered a cleft that led deep into the tree, hiding a narrow passageway. They entered it, with lit torches and drawn dagger and javelin into the darkness.

CHAPTER 27

Ohyah stopped climbing the gnarled wood and pressed close to the trunk to avoid being seen. The Thunderbird nest was in sight. He could see its tangled branches and leaves molded into the arm of a large branch. For one moment, he reconsidered what he was doing. Not only was he about to risk his life attempting to capture the great Anzu with nothing but a rope he had attached to his belt, but he was planning on doing so after an exhausting climb of untold thousands of cubits.

The bird had made no sound since he first heard it. He did not know if it was still in the nest or had left it. He would have to take a chance and hope he caught it asleep. He thought he would make a quick prayer to Elohim just in case he might be willing to help him out, since he was a member of Enoch's team of travelers.

· · · · ·

Betenos finally broke down in Lamech's unrelenting embrace. She wept as Lamech told her they had been victims of sorcery. He told her that he forgave her for all the cruel words she had bellowed at him while trying to escape his grasp. They had been vile, spiteful words and she was now deeply sorry.

She could not believe such evil things could come from her heart. But they had. Lamech knew it was the same evil that lay in his heart and in every heart of every human. The sorcery did not create their wickedness, it merely unleashed it from its moral restraint.

Now he understood why she had fought against the idea of having a family. It made him feel even closer to her. How could he blame her for not wanting to bring children into such an evil world? It was natural for her to think this way. Only faith could overcome such fear.

Betenos looked up at him and said, "Lamech, who is Ningishzida?"

It was the last thing the sirens had uttered before they disappeared. *Ningishzida arise.*

"I do not know," said Lamech. He felt the ground move as if something burrowed beneath them. They got up to follow Enoch and Methuselah. But they were thrown backward by an explosion of sand in their path.

Out of the earth rose the head of a gigantic serpent. The creature must have been a good twenty-five cubits long. Its horned head was as big as Betenos' body. Its girth was at least three cubits wide. It was black and its eyes glowed with the lapis lazuli blue of the gods. But its fangs gleamed pearly white.

"I think we just met Ningishzida," said Lamech.

The head rose until it reached a striking position three cubits above the ground. It hissed fiercely. Lamech and Betenos could hear in their minds a whispering voice, *You are going to die.*

Lamech's weapon Rahab lay where he had been sleeping. The path to it was blocked by the other end of the snake. The tail burst out of the ground and grabbed Lamech in its coils. It shoved Betenos aside into the sand.

Lamech struggled to free himself. But the strong coils of pure reptilian muscle held him fast. All he had been able to do was grab a handful of sand. He laughed at himself. A handful of sand. What a weapon! At best, he could throw the sand in its eyes and blind it for a moment — before it finished him as the first course of its two-course meal.

The tentacle-like tail raised Lamech into the air, squeezing the life out of him. The giant ophidian head gracefully moved to look its prey in the eyes. Its big split tongue shot out and tasted Lamech's skin. His horrible dream came back to him like an unheeded omen. He should have foreseen this. He had been too concerned about Betenos to catch the signs all around him. Now, he was going to die and he could not even help the woman he secretly loved.

• • • • •

Enoch and Methuselah followed the labyrinthine passage under the tree deep down into the earth. The serpentine roots appeared to move under the heat of the torches. The men were so intent on their quest, they barely noticed that the roots all around them consisted of the tortured tangle of human corpses transmuted into the wooden essence of the tree.

Edna's husband loved her so madly that he adored her through every one of his senses; visual, audible, tactile, taste, and olfactory. The perfume of spices she used left an alluring trail of smell. He stopped at various points in the pursuit and sniffed the air or a root where her clothes had brushed by and he knew exactly which way these "night hags" had taken her.

Soon they came upon a large opening in the ground, a subterranean chamber cut out of the rock. They remained quiet, hoping to maintain the element of surprise.

All four women were there.

But Edna lay upon a stone altar.

Lilith stood over her, while Lili and Lilu held Edna down. Her cloak was pulled back to reveal a plump belly. Three hyenas sat obediently on either side of the altar.

The hideous sight of the walls of the chamber shook Enoch and Methuselah to their cores. Skeletons, thousands of skeletons, not adult bones, but infant ones, all covered the walls. They both realized this was not the madness of grave robbers, but rather the evil of demonic murderers.

Then Methuselah realized what he had been too ignorant to see before.

Edna was pregnant.

• • • • •

Lamech gasped for breath. The scaly coils of the huge serpent crushed his lungs. He should have been awake earlier to be prepared. He started to black out. The serpent bared its fangs, ready for the kill.

Lamech managed to wheeze out one last word, "Ra — hab."

He and Betenos heard a whisper in their minds tell them, *I am not Rahab. I am Ningishzida, Lord of the Tree. But I welcome the comparison.*

Lamech was not looking at the serpent, but at his beloved Betenos on the ground. He made his final gesture before collapsing, throwing the sand into the face of his enemy. Its protective lids closed for just a moment.

That was all that Betenos needed. The snake had ignored the weak female prey to focus on its stronger male opponent. It did not realize that *Rahab* was not a reference to the sea serpent of chaos, but rather to the name of Lamech's weapon.

Betenos snatched the weapon and unrolled it behind her. She had watched Lamech enough times. He had even taught her how to use it in a pinch.

This was a pinch.

She snapped it forward. The blade wrapped its coil around the serpentine abomination just below its head and cut through it like a stalk of wheat under the scythe.

Lamech dropped to the ground with the falling head of Ningishzida. Betenos ran up to him and pulled the coils off him in tears.

"Lamech! Lamech, my beloved!"

He was unresponsive, pale blue, not breathing.

"Please, Elohim, please," she pleaded to the heavens.

Lamech coughed and gasped for air. His face filled with color.

Betenos hugged him for all her life, but he stopped her.

"We have to find father and grandfather. They need us."

CHAPTER 28

Ohyah ascended the last distance to the Anzu nest with as much stealth as he could manage, to avoid detection. He peeked over the edge of the nest. The Anzu bird lay inside, asleep. The fierce looking creature had a body size twice that of a Naphil and a wingspan of about four times that. Huge and powerful, its leonine face included sharp incisors in the jaw.

He climbed closer. It snored. He suppressed an involuntary chuckle. Every creature on the face of the earth, no matter how frightening, had to sleep just like every other creature. Therein lay its fleshly weakness. This massive intimidating bird of prey snored like a giant kitten.

Ohyah sprang. He slipped his prepared rope bridle over the monster's mouth as he landed on its back.

Startled awake, it snapped open its wings at the weight of the Naphil. It opened its mouth in a roar. Ohyah pulled tight on the makeshift bridle, asserting control over his wild quarry.

The bird reacted instantly. It leapt into the sky. It quickly realized that it had to release this smelly agitating creature from its back or suffer the fight of its life.

First it flew upside down, then it zigzagged. It plummeted, it shot up, it jerked left and right. The nasty little parasite would not let go.

Ohyah was breaking this bucking Anzu.

$$\bullet \ \bullet \ \bullet \ \bullet \ \bullet$$

Down in the depths of the hideous tree, Enoch nocked an arrow in his bow and aimed.

Lilith held a stone sacrificial dagger raised above her head. She sounded an incantation over Edna. Enoch saw that the physical features of the women had become decrepit. Their beauty was falling off their faces. These monsters drew their life force from the slaughter of infants. Enoch marveled, appalled. What kind of abominable deity would demand such a thing?

He released his arrow.

The arrow pierced Lilith's hand, pinning it against the wall behind her. She dropped the blade to the floor.

Methuselah threw a javelin. It penetrated Lilith's chest, puncturing her lung simultaneously with Enoch's arrow in her hand. A howling shriek of agony, such that neither of them had ever heard before, filled the chamber.

Enoch realized that these were not mere creatures of flesh. They were demons.

Lili and Lilu pulled the projectiles from Lilith's body. They cackled in unison. Large leathery wings unfolded from behind Lilith, materializing from nowhere.

Methuselah realized the piercing shriek did not come from Lilith, but from the three hyenas near the altar. They howled in agony when Lilith was struck. Some kind of connection ran between the animals and the demons.

"Hit the hyenas!" he yelled. He launched one of his javelins into the air.

It caught one of the hyenas in the thigh. It yelped again. Simultaneously, Lili grabbed her thigh in pain. The other hyenas scrambled for cover.

Enoch for another target. A rumbling overhead halted him. The vibration felt as if an army on heavy mounts was arriving just above them.

He looked around.

The night hags and their animal avatars were gone.

Methuselah ran to the altar and took Edna up in his arms. She gazed up at him in a drugged state of mind and simply uttered, "My Poozeydoodoo," before passing out altogether.

He kissed her with weeping tears. "I will never take you for granted again, my dear, dear Pednapoodlums."

CHAPTER 29

Enoch led the way back through the maze of twisted roots. Methuselah carried the unconscious Edna, holding her close. Halfway to the surface, they met Lamech and Betenos. A group of strangely clad desert nomads accompanied the pair. Enoch drew his dagger.

"Stop, grandfather!" Lamech called out. "These are the Thamud."

That did not reassure Enoch. He held himself ready for battle. He remembered what he had heard about these savage killers. They skinned their victims alive.

Lamech pleaded with hand raised, "Please, trust me. They have come to rescue us."

Enoch and Methuselah traded glances. How could this be? They looked back at Lamech. He was not under duress. They could tell if he was lying, and he was not.

Enoch relaxed.

"Well, they might have gotten here a bit earlier," complained Methuselah. "We could have used their help."

The lead Thamud, tall, gaunt and handsome with closely cropped beard, stepped forward. "Forgive me, Enoch. I am Diya al

Din, prince of my people. We need to hurry. The storm is increasing."

"Can we not seek refuge inside the tree?" asked Enoch.

"The storm and tree are one demonic entity, and that entity will draw us alive into Sheol if we do not leave promptly" said Diya.

Methuselah protested, "My wife is with child. She needs medicine."

Diya looked at her pale face. He understood exactly what had happened to her.

"Follow me," said Diya, "or she will die."

They followed him.

The fury of windblown sand that had surrounded them earlier now descended upon them.

Diya's team of fifty warriors on camels led Enoch, Methuselah, Edna, Lamech, and Betenos out into the whirlwind. Methuselah thought they were going to be suffocated as before, when they came upon a small canyon carved out of the rock.

A cave entrance rescued them from the immediacy of the tempest outside. It was a tunnel pathway, not merely a shelter from the weather.

They traveled through the tunnel for a couple of leagues before ascending back onto the desert plains.

When they came out of the tunnel, Enoch looked all around him. There was no sign of the sandstorm. It was as if it had never been there. And there was no thousand cubits high Huluppu Tree connecting heaven and earth.

Diya could see his confusion. "I will explain later. Our first concern is to get your wife some help."

Methuselah raised his eyes from Edna's face to an amazing sight. They were close to some rocky buttes that seemed to burst out of the ground. He could see rock carvers chiseling facades of huge buildings into the faces of the rocky bluffs. It was a small city of buildings carved out of the rock.

Methuselah saw a large figure standing out a distance away from the rock faces, looking their way like a dog awaiting the arrival of its master.

It was the giant Ohyah on an Anzu bird.

This should be interesting, thought Enoch as they rode toward the stone city.

CHAPTER 30

This was the second time Enoch learned that his preconceived notions of a people were completely wrong. He had thought the Adamite cave dwellers were primitive ignorant natives, only to learn they were a spiritually profound elite who taught him the secret ways of Elohim. Then he had believed the rumors and gossip about the Thamudi being a savage clan of barbarians, only to be sitting in front of them now in their homes of incomparable architecture having his own ignorance enlightened by their compassionate explanation of current events. Even the interiors of these rock palaces were exquisitely designed and carved.

The Thamud had heard of Elohim through the trade route that spanned their area many generations before. They had concluded that the very god that Lilith and her Earth Goddess brood of demons hated would be the very god whose side they wanted to be on.

Methuselah could barely listen as Diya al Din explained everything. All he could think about was Edna. The healers and midwives were treating her in their special room set aside for such matters. Would she be all right? And their growing child in her womb? He would never forgive himself if anything happened to either of them.

Lamech and Betenos listened intently as everything came clear to them.

"At first, we made our battle call and mounted up in preparation to fight Oyhah. He is a Naphil after all."

Ohyah sat a bit away from the others. He never wanted to impose his presence or overshadow anyone in the room. He did not need to be near to hear. He had eagle ears and could hear a centipede crawling at ten cubits distance.

Enoch turned to face Ohyah. "How did you do it? How did you tame the Anzu bird?"

"It was not easy," said Ohyah. "He nearly threw me to my death a thousand cubits in the sky more than once. But after he broke, I could lead him with the bridle as we do any beast of burden."

"But how did you know we were in danger?" asked Lamech.

"I am a Naphil," Ohyah said simply. "I am attuned to the spiritual world. As I climbed the tree, I connected with it, with its soul, or should I say with the myriads of souls it had devoured to sustain its life."

"That is not all it devours," said Diya. "The desert you have now become so unhappily acquainted with was not always a dead barren wasteland. Before the Earth Goddess grew there, it was a fertile land every bit as lush as life along the Euphrates. Even more so. Mountains, rivers, forests and meadows, wildlife of every kind."

"How could that be?" exclaimed Betenos, speaking for everyone's wonder.

"The Earth Goddess is a parasite," said Diya. "Her roots burrow deep into the earth, and her branches seek the heavens as she sucks the life out of the environment and atmosphere around her. That is what she has done to create the desert that covers this peninsula."

"Abomination of desolation," blurted Enoch.

"Someone should destroy it," offered Lamech.

"That would be very difficult," said Diya. "It would take a gibborim."

"How did you find us?" asked Enoch.

Diya replied, "When Ohyah flew the Anzu bird to our humble city and pleaded for your lives, he offered his neck to me. I could have killed him in an instant. Something I had never seen a Naphil do. And because he tamed the Anzu, the watchbird of that wicked tree, I knew we had a common enemy. Without your giant friend and the Anzu, we would never have found you. Its black magic comes from the depths of Sheol and the witch demons use sorcery of all kinds to remain obscured and undiscoverable."

"Well, I hope to never discover that vile wicked tree again," said Betenos. Everyone laughed.

Lamech blurted out, "And the story Lilith told us about being the first wife and daughters of Adam?"

"Lies from the pit of Sheol," said Diya. "That She-demon knew that the best lie is patterned after the truth. You conquer a people by conquering their narrative — subverting it. It has been her goal all along to control the world."

Betenos felt a fool for being taken in by the trickery. A wave of repentance washed over her. She stood up to proclaim to the group, "I repent for worshiping the Great Goddess Earth Mother. I am ashamed of my idolatry. And I am grateful for the patience and loving help that Lamech has displayed with me during my travels with your family. It took a large black serpent to awake me from my spiritual slumber, and push me into the arms of my Creator, Elohim." She was done, and she was crying, her tears flowing from a cleansed soul.

Lamech, bleary-eyed, hugged Betenos.

Enoch got up off his chair and approached her.

Lamech pulled away to see what his grandfather would do.

Betenos felt a bit afraid, since Enoch had not trusted her throughout their journey. Would he doubt her now?

Enoch stared at her. She felt her spine tingle.

"Betenos," he said, "slayer of Ningishzida, you *are* my family." And Enoch hugged her with complete acceptance.

Lamech's smile went so wide it hurt his mouth.

Methuselah felt some happiness despite his own painful fears for Edna's safety.

Even Ohyah was moved. Could this god Elohim be so powerful as to redeem the most cursed of all creatures?

Betenos wept more. She had so longed to be accepted by this great patriarch, the grandfather of the man with whom she was desperately in love.

"Betenos bar Barakil," said Lamech on bended knees, "I have prayed for this moment from the second I set my eyes upon you. And now my wildest dreams have come true. Will you be my wife?"

Betenos could not contain her happiness. But before she could express it, they were interrupted by two midwives entering the room.

Methuselah leapt to his feet and ran to them.

One of the midwives simply whispered, "I am sorry, we lost the child."

Methuselah broke away from them and ran to the healing room, to the bedside of Edna.

She was barely conscious, drifting off into sleep. Methuselah sank beside her and gently held her.

"My Peedlums, I thought I lost you."

"Poozy," Edna whispered. "I love you."

"I love you," he replied, "with all my heart and soul."

"I was waiting for the right moment to surprise you," she managed to murmur. "I should have told you sooner." She began to cry weakly. "I am so sorry, Methuselah. I have failed you."

"Pednanoonypoo. You have failed no one."

She did not believe it. She had spent all her life transferring her purpose from one person to the next, as if her significance were founded in giving other people significance.

Edna protested, "I have failed to bring forth your seed."

Methuselah was almost angry. "You listen to me, woman. Your worth is not in satisfying my purpose, it is in obedience to your Creator. And if my memory serves me, you have obeyed Elohim far more than I ever have. It is from you that I have come to understand Elohim's ways, his compassion, his mercy, his grace and his love. You have not failed me. I have failed you. I have failed to be the leader worthy of your submission. I have placed my trust in this earth and not in the promise of Elohim's seed. Can you forgive me, my love?"

She looked up into his eyes. He knew just how to get through to her, and she to him.

"There is nothing to forgive, Poozey," she said with a weak smile. "You are the finest, truest man I have ever known."

"You are the *only* woman I will *ever* know," he said.

He caressed her sweaty hair. "Do not fret. Elohim has our little one in his arms."

"Yes, I know," she whispered and fell asleep.

Methuselah kissed her on the forehead, and settled her back on the bedding. He then rose and crossed over to the water pail and birth rags. He opened a bloody towel to behold the tiny little body of his miscarried son. He was no bigger than a mouse, all curled up in a tight sleeping position, red with uterine blood. But this was his son. He whispered a prayer to Elohim and turned to one of the midwives come into the room.

"We would like a burial for our son, Adam," he said.

"Yes, my lord," said the maidservant and left the room to prepare.

He softly laid the edges of the towel back over the little body in his hand.

He could barely contain himself. He knew the reason his son was dead was because of their experience with Lilith and her evil offspring. He blamed himself. He thought that if he'd only kept his mind on Elohim, he would not be so easily deceived by the flesh. If he was as godly a leader as he ought to be, he would have seen the trap earlier, and saved his wife sooner. He would have saved his son.

Betenos gazed into Lamech's eyes as they waited for Methuselah to return from the healing room. Their situation was bittersweet. In the face of death Betenos now saw new life.

She spoke with conviction, "I have been so afraid to lose what I could not hold onto. I have seen that I am far worse than I ever imagined, and more loved than I could have ever hoped. I will be your wife, Lamech ben Methuselah. I will bear your seed. I will bear Elohim's calling."

· · · · ·

The burial ritual for little baby Adam was brief and simple. They laid him in a small carved box and rubbed red ochre on him, just like his forefather. They even had some desert flowers to cover him before they prayed and filled the grave with dirt. *For you are dust, and to dust you shall return.*

Enoch said a prayer to Elohim. They all filed back into the rock-faced buildings. Edna had returned to health and was able to mourn with Methuselah. It was not the same as losing an adult child like Havah had with her Abel, but it was still a sacred little life created in the image of Elohim, taken too early.

She was sure Elohim knew their pain, and knew that someday he would put all things to right.

CHAPTER 31

"You cannot be serious!" Edna cried, staring at Enoch, in one of the meeting houses of the Thamud city.

Ohyah remained silent and listened from the back of the room, as usual.

Methuselah added, "God wants us to go on a suicide mission?"

"Not you, me," said Enoch.

"God wants *you* to go on a suicide mission?" said Methuselah. For once, Methuselah wished he could see whatever it was that Elohim showed Enoch. How did he know these dreams were actually from Elohim and not mere self-delusion? Hallucinations from greasy sand rats not cooked well enough before eaten? Or spoiled drink?

"Not suicide, obedient faith. Young man, have I taught you nothing in this life? Have I failed as a father?" said Enoch. "When Elohim commands, we obey. He will bring about the results that he sees fit."

Enoch told them of his latest dream-vision. Uriel had visited him again and taken him up to Mount Hermon in the presence of all the fallen Watchers, not to fight them, but to pronounce Elohim's word of judgment. No actions, just words. And this was Enoch's final journey to make.

This vision gave one new piece of information they had not heard before. Enoch had been told that there was a Chosen Seed to come from the line of Seth, through Enoch, Methuselah, and Lamech, one who would bring an end to the reign of the gods and bring rest from the curse of the land.

Everyone recognized the reference from their time with Adam and Havah. It was the seed of the Woman, Eve, at war with the seed of the Serpent, Nachash.

Lamech was stunned. His bloodline would bear a redeemer?

It perturbed Methuselah "When am I going to see one of these visions?" he asked. "You would think that Elohim would confirm such crazy ideas with one or two others of us, if they were so important to the future of the human race."

Enoch flushed red with righteous indignation. "Methuselah, you speak as an ignorant child who would not want the very thing he whines for should he receive it."

Methuselah went silent, properly scolded. Enoch walked up to him, slowly explaining himself. "You have fought giants, and have faced the gods, it is true. But you have no idea the terrifying holiness of Elohim's temple and divine assembly of his holy ones."

With every word, Methuselah's confidence waned.

"Are you so sure you want to see what I see? Do you desire to tremble and fall at your feet stiff like a dead man? Do you want to be utterly and entirely exposed in your sinfulness before the Lord of hosts and before his holy ones who surround his throne crying, 'Holy, holy, holy'? Let me give you just a glimpse of the frightening awe of the heaven of heavens into which you so desperately long to look."

Methuselah had become very still.

Enoch spoke with barely a breath, "In the midst of piercing light is a structure of crystals, and between those crystals are tongues of fire, encircled by rivers of living fire, over which are the sleepless ones who guard the throne of Yahweh's glory, the Seraphim, the Cherubim, and Ophanim, the archangels, Mikael, Raphael, Gabriel and Uriel and ten thousand times ten thousand of countless holy angels, all bowing before the Ancient of Days and the one to whom belongs the time before time, the Son of Man, with head as white as wool and an indescribable garment, to whom belongs righteousness and with whom righteousness dwells, the Lord of Spirits, who will remove kings and mighty ones from their comfortable thrones and shall loosen the reins of the strong and crush the teeth of sinners, who shall depose the kings from their kingdoms who do not extol and glorify him and neither do they obey him, the source of their kingship, and he says, 'Behold, the Lord comes with ten thousands of his holy ones, to execute judgment on all and to convict all the ungodly of all their deeds of ungodliness that they have committed in such an ungodly way, and of all the harsh things that ungodly sinners have spoken against him.'"

It was the longest run-on sentence Methuselah had ever heard, and it frightened him deeply. But he would not tell anyone that. And he would never again ask to be given a vision of Elohim and his holy ones. No one else on the team would either, as they were all duly terror-stricken. Edna trembled.

Methuselah mumbled, "Father, forgive me for my impertinence. I am an unclean man with unclean lips."

Enoch could not believe it. Methuselah had actually apologized.

Methuselah's relentless curiosity interrupted even this moment. "But help me to understand why Elohim would equip us to be giant killers only to have you walk alone and unarmed right into the hornet's nest of invincible death and destruction?"

"He will not be alone," a voice said behind them.

Everyone turned to see Uriel the archangel at the entrance of their room, standing with arms crossed in assurance.

It did not assure Methuselah. "I mean no disrespect, mighty one, but there may well be hundreds of Watchers on Mount Hermon, and you are but one archangel." The battle with the Nephilim at the Tigris River came to his mind. "And if I remember correctly, you are not even the largest or strongest one."

Uriel rolled his eyes. *Why does everyone always have to point that out to me?* he thought.

"Oh mouthy one," Uriel retorted with his signature touch of sarcasm, "I will not be the only one accompanying Enoch. Mikael, Gabriel, and Raphael will all join us when we are in range of our destination." The presence of the four highest archons of Elohim's throne room signaled something big to everyone in the room.

Methuselah said, "Forgive me, high prince Uriel, but that is still only four. It seems to me that fighting Watchers will not be quite as easy as fighting Nephilim."

"Who said we were going to fight them?" asked Uriel with a smile.

It baffled Methuselah and the others. Enoch would walk into the midst of the Watchers' hideout with the help of four high archangels and preach a sermon, and these rebellious sons of Elohim were going to just listen to them?

The only one it made any sense to was Ohyah, who chose to remain silent.

Uriel chuckled. "Before I explain the elementary principles of faith and obedience to my hardheaded companion here, I think we have a wedding to celebrate." He looked with joyful eyes upon Lamech and his betrothed Betenos.

177

CHAPTER 32

Lamech and Betenos had a brief wedding ceremony. Its brevity was inspired by the fact that the team of giant killers was about to embark on the final leg of its journey to Bashan. They allowed the new lovers several days to discover themselves in all their god-given intimacy. At last, Lamech understood what his father meant when he said that loving his wife was an act of worship to Elohim. It embodied the kind of union that transcended their physical existence. Grandfather Enoch, with his passionate way with words, had often spoken of the love of Elohim for his people being like that of a bridegroom with his bride.

If that is true, thought Lamech, *then I am most honored to have had this small taste of so great a love.*

For all her royalty, Betenos had never experienced loving tenderness in her family. Barakil had been a protective father to her, but he was also the clan elder, so he could never be vulnerable with his family. He could never put aside his responsibility for his tribe's safety and justice to play with his children or caress his wife. As a result, Betenos had experienced stern discipline and mature responsibility, but she felt as if she never had a childhood. She did not know how to have fun, how to let loose and just release her voice into the wind with abandon.

She could do that now, with her loving husband to free her and protect her.

Diya al Din, whose name meant "brightness of faith," proved to be an ally of inestimable worth. He had not only saved them from the Earth Goddess and her demonic minions, but also helped them plot their final course into Bashan. Though his people had never been inside Bashan, Diya knew the best and speediest route to get there. He showed them on a map, with Enoch, Methuselah, Edna, Uriel, and Ohyah clustered around the table.

Diya said, "It will only be a short distance west from the Thamudi fortresses before the topography will change and become the foothills of the Sirion mountain range. You will find the lone river Pharpar that will take you in all the way to Bashan and ultimately to the foot of Hermon."

"Do you have information about specific packs or hordes of Nephilim in the area?" asked Methuselah.

"We just do not know," apologized Diya.

Lamech and Betenos skipped into the room together with giggles of delight and playful grabs. Everyone turned to look at them. They stopped, blushed, but got down to business.

"Betenos is going with us," Lamech announced.

"It is too dangerous without Karabu training," responded Enoch.

"Grandfather, do we really have to go over this again? Has Betenos not proven herself worthy over and over?"

"This is different. We do not know how many packs we may encounter in Bashan," said Enoch.

"All the more reason to have a healer," said Lamech. "And I do believe she has bested you in target practice more than once."

Methuselah snapped, "Shooting targets is not the same as shooting Nephilim warriors."

"You are newlyweds," added Edna. "Stay here and get to know one another. There will be time later for responsibility."

"Mother, if I recall, it was Elohim who said that marriage was a leaving and a cleaving. I am not under your authority, I am now responsible for my own family, and we have decided that the time is now."

In one of the rare instances, Ohyah spoke up. "A healer would be beneficial. I fear we will not return from Bashan unscathed."

Uriel studied Ohyah with curious interest. "The giant is correct," he said. "It is a lawless territory. Fiefdoms of war chiefs. What few small towns are there, Ugarit, Jericho, and others, are not friendly."

"So, what you are saying," said Methuselah, "is that we are entering a lawless province of criminals, that willingly hosts the Watchers, universally hates our god, unanimously despises our people, and will joyfully kill us where they find us."

"Exactly," said Uriel.

Methuselah concluded, "But it is also the hideout for the scurrilous Rephaim Thamaq and Yahipan that killed our parents and tried to annihilate our family line."

"When do we leave?" said Lamech.

CHAPTER 33

The fellowship of giant killers gathered on Camels given to them by Diya al Din. These amazing creatures possessed the ability to store nutrients in their large humps, enabling them to travel long distances at quick paces. They had not yet become universally domesticated, but Diya believed they would be eventually because they were so advantageous.

Enoch's team had been with the Thamud for a month or so, but Methuselah knew they had made lifelong friends. He hoped one day to return in less troublesome times, but suspected those times might not come during his life.

After much customary hugging and kissing, Enoch's band set out on their way: Enoch and Uriel, Methuselah and Edna, Lamech and Betenos, and Ohyah.

It only took one day of vigorous travel to reach the Pharpar river. They followed it toward its source fifty leagues upriver, about a three-day brisk ride. Half way to their destination, they were met by three new fellow travelers, Mikael, Gabriel, and Raphael. They each rode a new beast of burden called a *horse*.

These horses were powerful animals, similar in structure to a wild ass, but twice the size, and pure muscle. They had smaller ears and could run like the wind. It was no surprise that the heavenly archons were the first to seize this opportunity of newly domesticated travel. The archangels riding on the majestic creatures appeared like a new kind of Cherubim.

The angels would ride ahead on their horses, their heavenly senses highly tuned to sense approaching danger. Ohyah took up the rear on foot, his earthly spiritual senses almost as acute as those of the angels.

Enoch rode ahead to travel with the archangels. He discussed the secrets of heaven with the spiritual beings. Methuselah watched with curiosity, wondering what they were saying.

The Naphil could hear them. If he concentrated hard enough and pointed an ear in the flow downwind, his preternatural aural sense could pick up snatches of their private dialogue. They had long discussions on the heavenly luminaries, animal visions, the Chosen Seed and a "Son of Man." He gathered that of the group of archangels, the small one was sharp tongued and the mightiest one a bit overly confident. They all seemed to bicker and pick on the small one. It amused Ohyah the kind of servants Elohim chose for his purposes. It was so opposite of the ways of the Nephilim, which was based on power.

They did not spy their first giant until they were in the foothills near Mount Hermon. The sun set on the horizon. The team set up early camp on a hill overlooking the wide expanse of the Sirion range. They ate some dinner of dried gazelle meat. They were hidden within a thicket of pine trees to avoid detection. Ohyah stood lookout.

Enoch and the angels huddled, discussing the route they would take further west to Mount Hermon.

Ohyah quietly alerted them.

He spotted two Nephilim less than half a league down in the valley. They appeared to be headed north toward a destination somewhere around a rocky butte.

Enoch told Methuselah, "It looks like this is where we part ways. The archangels and I will continue on to Hermon. You may want to stay low and seek out information before you start attacking any giants. Remember, you do not know the land yet."

"You are right. We would not want to just march right into the headquarters of evil and announce our presence," retorted Methuselah sarcastically. "That would be suicide."

Enoch scowled at Methuselah for venting his pain. They both knew in their hearts that they would never see each other again on this earth. No matter how different in nature father and son were, no matter all the arguments they had been in through the years, they loved one another with fierce devotion.

"You will live to a long fruitful age, my son," said Enoch.

Methuselah thought, *Why does everyone keep saying that? Havah, now father.*

Enoch added, "But you have already made me the proudest father on earth. Elohim be with you."

"Elohim be with you," said Methuselah.

They kissed and embraced.

Enoch lingered longer with Betenos and Edna. "My two precious flowers. You have brought much needed grace to this pack of slovenly brutes. You are too good for my sons." Everyone's nervous laughter broke the somberness.

Enoch continued, "I love you as my own daughters." They hugged and kissed and cried.

Enoch turned to Lamech and held his face in his hands. He said, "Lamech ben Methuselah, out of your line will come a Chosen Seed who will end the rule of the gods and bring rest upon the land. Tell no one until God himself does."

"Yes, grandfather," said Lamech, and they hugged.

Enoch stopped at the giant. "Ohyah, you have surprised me, and humbled me." He paused for a second, then continued.

"I want to tell you this one thing. The judgment in your dream is fast approaching the earth. And the water you saw in the vision, it is not symbolic. It is real water. It is cleansing water."

Ohyah was not sure what to make of that esoteric statement, but he hugged Enoch.

"Thank you for believing in me," said Ohyah.

They had no more time to delay. They all mounted their camels and stallions and went their separate ways: Enoch, Mikael, Uriel, Gabriel, and Raphael, west toward Hermon; and Methuselah, Edna, Lamech, Betenos and Ohyah, north after the traveling Nephilim. If they moved quickly, they might be within close observation range by the time the giants pitched camp.

CHAPTER 34

The sun set over the great sea. Enoch and his four companions rode solemnly toward the base of Mount Hermon a mere league away. Enoch was about to face the ultimate challenge of his life, but he felt safe in the presence of these mighty angelic warriors. He knew they would have no problem getting safely *to* the cosmic mountain. The real danger was getting *inside* the infernal meeting place where the fallen Watchers assembled for their diabolical planning.

Angels could not die like humans. They were spiritual beings that could suffer and even be overcome, but they could not die. They were only four archangels facing as many as two hundred Watchers, if all were in attendance. Despite their exalted status, these four would be easily overcome and tortured. They would probably be bound and cast into the earth where they would live forever in a prison of stone. They saw no way that Enoch would get out of this alive. There was no way the angels were going to get out of it at all.

Enoch had come to realize over the years that he had been running from his calling. Elohim commissioned him to pronounce judgment on the Watchers and their progeny the Nephilim. But he had turned that calling into a hammer of his own justification. When he lost his Edna, he lost all interest in this earth. Killing the Nephilim became an expression of his desire to escape the physical world that held him prisoner and stank of corruption. But in hating the physical world that Elohim created, he misunderstood the faith that was required of him. Now he exercised that faith by obediently fulfilling the calling he had been given. Enoch had been an instrument of judgment on the giants. Now he was to be an instrument of *Elohim's* judgment on the Watchers. He was to pick a fight he would not win, because Elohim was going to win it on his terms.

Methuselah was right. It was suicide. But Enoch reasoned that Elohim could raise the dead, so what did it matter that Enoch was riding to his death? The interaction of his comrades in arms broke through his solemnity.

Uriel was the talkative one, a bit rascally, and witty. Gabriel countered his fellow wisecracker with his own whimsical and energetic humor. Raphael did not speak much, but he thought and observed plenty, so Uriel and Gabriel often competed to win a smile or even a nod from "the quiet one" as they teasingly referred to him. Mikael took his responsibility as the prince leader with serious determination. So like the bigger brother, he would always have to "break it up" when it got out of hand. But even he could not help but smile at a well placed verbal barb.

"Did Uriel tell you, Enoch?" asked Gabriel, "He was chosen by Elohim to be the guardian of the Chosen Seed when he should carry out his calling."

He paused, and then delivered the punch line, "Elohim wanted to make it very obvious that the Chosen Seed was protected not by strength nor by might, but by faith."

Enoch snickered. "Very funny," said Uriel. "You mean the faith that killed six Nephilim to *your* four in the battle at the Tigris river, to which Enoch was witness?"

"Five and a half to four and a half," protested Gabriel. "I remind you of the one we did together."

"You mean the one I killed?" said Uriel.

"That I helped you kill," said Gabriel.

"Before you dropped your sword," said Uriel.

"I did *not* drop my sword!" said Gabriel. He felt frustrated at getting trapped in the same argument as before.

Uriel just smiled and shook his head. He had successfully turned the tables, as he usually did with his superior wit.

Raphael laughed from the belly. "Very good, Uriel. Very good." Raphael did not speak much, so when he did, he tended to cast the deciding vote on an issue.

"So what you both meant to say," concluded Mikael, "was 'not by strength, nor by might, but by verbal bickering and wordplay,' saith the Lord."

Enoch finally interrupted. "You know, I cannot believe that I am on my way to certain death in the bowels of the mountain of hell and you four are quibbling and jesting over your battle prowess. Is it too much to ask you to be more somber about our impending doom?"

"Forgive us, Enoch," said Gabriel. "We mean no disrespect to you."

Enoch felt better for the apology. "Thank you," he said with finality.

Gabriel muttered to Uriel, "But it *was* five and a half to four and a half."

"Six to four," muttered Uriel.

"Elohim, deliver us," muttered Enoch.

• • • • •

By the time Methuselah, Edna, Lamech, Betenos, and Ohyah caught up with the traveling Nephilim, their quarry had already arrived at their base camp a league north. The giants were not alone.

As Methuselah had feared, they were part of a pack. But they were wearing armor similar to that worn by the Nephilim that had started them on this journey. The hunters were on the right track.

Fifteen of them feasted on what appeared to be cattle and humans roasting on spits. If the team were discovered, killing the Nephilim would be difficult. Methuselah and his team were giant killers, but they were not archangels. Three and a half trained warriors against fifteen giants was not the kind of odds Methuselah wished to entertain. They had never even seen that many Nephilim together at once, let alone fought them. The rumors were true about Bashan. It had become an easy hideout for bandits, desperados and other packs of outlaw giants.

Thank Elohim, we have one Naphil on our side, thought Methuselah. Ohyah possessed the enviable Nephilim fighting skills. They would have the element of surprise. These brigands would never expect one of their own to fight against them.

Lamech whispered to himself, "That is a lot of bounty."

Methuselah gave him a dirty look. "We are not here for bounty. We are here to find Thamaq and Yahipan. And stop talking. You will give us away."

It was a difficult task to sneak up on Nephilim. They had acute senses and usually would be able to hear them and smell them approaching. But this time, they were downwind from the hunters on a particularly windy evening, with a storm brewing overhead creating distracting noises.

The small camp sat in the center of a rather wide clearing around the butte. Methuselah and the others hid at the crestline of foliage watching the camp with high strung nerves. They waited for their planned deception to unfold.

CHAPTER 35

Enoch and the angels arrived at the foot of Mount Hermon and left their animals to climb the rocky crags. A short way up the foothills of the mountain sat the village of Kur, populated by the human followers of Ereshkigal. They had built a temple for this goddess of the underworld embedded halfway into the mountain, an expression of the union of heaven and earth within the sacred space.

According to legend, inside the temple were the seven gates of Ganzir that led to an opening to the Abyss, or *Abzu*, the cosmic waters under the earth, the barrier above Sheol, the underworld. Ereshkigal's throne stood at the Gateway to Sheol.

The Abyss was home to the most frightening of all creatures, the sea dragon of chaos, Rahab. It roamed the waters as sovereign of the beasts, seeking whom it might devour. It was a creature of both utter destruction and yet utter perfection. A terrible beauty, armored scales covered its huge, three hundred-cubit-long body, its teeth were like sharpened iron, and it could produce a flash of burning fire from out of its mouth. It seemed its only purpose was to destroy worlds. No one could defy Rahab or subdue it, save Elohim alone, who created it for his purposes. How it was that Elohim controlled the untamed monster of the deep, Enoch could never understand. But then again, Elohim did not operate within human ways of understanding.

Mount Hermon was not the only location that had direct access to the waters of the Abyss that led to Sheol. There were several openings to the earth. One of them lay in Lake Urimiya at the very Garden of Eden. It was said that Yahweh Elohim at the lake held back both the waters of the Abyss and the dragon of chaos in order to establish the "heavens and earth," his covenanted cosmic order with his covenant people, Adam and Havah. It was also said that the Abyss and Rahab were the only things that the Sons of God and the Nephilim actually feared.

Enoch hoped in his heart that he would simply be killed by the Watchers rather than being thrown into the Abyss. He did not want Rahab to sport with him before tearing apart his body and consuming his flesh. He was thankful that at least they would not need to journey through the pagan village, and the temple, and the seven gates of Ganzir to get inside the meeting place of the Watchers. Mikael knew a secret way in, through a cave opening in the side of the mountain, out of sight of the village near a terebinth tree.

• • • • •

The pack of fifteen Nephilim were busy about their camp site when they heard a lookout whistle. They grabbed their weapons in unison and peered into the brush near their camp. In walked a disheveled Ohyah with a lookout giant behind him.

The team's plan had been for Ohyah to disguise himself as a wandering loner desert Naphil looking for a pack to join. The Nephilim would of course be suspicious at first. But their guard would eventually lower as they got to know Ohyah. Eventually they would lead him to their headquarters. Ohyah would study the branding on the Nephilim to see if any were owned by Thamaq and

190

Yahipan. He would gather any other information he could on the whereabouts of the two Rephaim. If there were any so branded, he would give Methuselah the sign by going to relieve himself on the edge of the camp, and signing how many had the mark. Methuselah's band would then follow the pack of Nephilim at a distance until Ohyah could find an opportunity to slip away and rejoin them.

Ohyah surprised the pack. But after some discussion, they calmed down and offered Ohyah some food. He chose the cattle over the human meal and partook as a hungry loner would. Soon, Ohyah went to relieve himself, heading toward Methuselah's hidden team. When he signaled, they were surprised to see Ohyah excitedly indicate the number fifteen.

It shocked Methuselah. All fifteen had the branding of Thamaq and Yahipan? How could that be?

Lamech interrupted his thoughts, "We hit the payload. They will lead us right to those sons of Sheol."

A Nephilim war cry burst behind them, an ugly sounding scream that pierced their ears and shuddered their souls. Methuselah jerked his head around to find the lookout Naphil in the bush, hovering over them. He had scouted the grounds and found them. Their cover had been compromised.

Methuselah looked back at camp. All the Nephilim faced their direction, taking up arms. By the time they took out this Naphil, the others would be upon them. They would not be able to outrun these muscle-bound monsters.

They would have to stand and fight.

CHAPTER 36

Anu and Inanna presided over the parliament of gods in the cavern of the Watchers. The huge stalactites and stalagmites created the sensation of being in the fanged mouth of the sea serpent. The cosmic mountain and divine council room of the gods rebelliously replicated Elohim's original council room on the Edenic mountain, complete with throne and source of waters. Enoch noted the irony that this sacred space was a garden of stone as opposed to Eden's garden of living vegetation. The source of its waters was a fiery black quagmire in contrast to the rivers of fresh living waters of Paradise.

The dripping of mineralized water built the stalactite formations, sparkling with gemlike iridescence. It created a kind of glow through the subterranean grotto in even the faintest of light. But there was no need for a light source, because the Shining Ones emitted a brightness when emotionally charged, a glow like that of burnished bronze or gleaming metal. Their heated discussion created flashes of fire and sparkling beryl that stalactite reflectors amplified.

Anu and Inanna sat on the thrones of Ereshkigal and Nergal to lead the discussion. They did so whenever they were in Bashan for the divine assembly. Over a hundred others gathered before the throne, along the burning black liquid shore of the Abyss.

They were discussing the possibility of capturing Rahab the sea dragon of chaos, to use her as a weapon of war. Enoch, Mikael, Uriel, Gabriel, and Raphael slipped into a dark recess of the cavern through their secret mountain tunnel.

Anu announced with authority, "The throne recognizes Enki, patron of Eridu, Lord of the Abyss."

Enoch stood and spoke to the assembly. "Brothers and sisters, I have organized an advisory committee on the Rahab matter with the gods of Canaan."

The Canaanite deities stood up. Enoch had not seen them before. There were whole families of gods that administered different locations on the earth that Enoch did not recognize.

Enki continued, "We have been developing spells that will render the sea dragon Rahab vulnerable to capture."

"Are you mad?!" interrupted Resheph, one of the Canaanite gods of plague and destruction. "You think you can domesticate Rahab for our purposes? She is not tamable. She is the very heart of chaos itself!"

Enki replied, "I do not suggest Rahab is tamable. I merely intend to subdue her long enough to capture her in such a way as to release her upon our enemies for their destruction."

"And what way of capture might that be, O brilliant shining one?" snorted Resheph, his scaly skin burning with arrogant luminosity.

"If you must know," Enki answered curtly, "we believe that we can lure Rahab into an underwater cavern where we have engraved tranquilizing spells on the walls of rock. Her spirit will be lulled into a trancelike state. We then have a large cedar box, with the spells carved in the walls to contain her in that numbed state until release."

"Oh, so, now Rahab has a fear of enclosed spaces?" asked Resheph.

"No. It is a kind of catatonic dream state the monster goes into. I cannot explain it. I do not understand it," said Enki.

"May I suggest that what you do not understand, remains out of your control," sniped Resheph.

Inanna listened closely. If what Enki said was true, she could use this weapon one day to great advantage. Resheph was a fool to scorn innovation in combat tactics. Such risks often brought victory on the battlefield. It was true, the sea dragon lived resplendent in its mighty power to wreak havoc and destruction. It was the mightiest of all created things. But it was still a created thing, and no created thing was invulnerable. If they could merely unleash that chaos in the direction of an enemy, why could it not accomplish great devastation? She would have to converse with Enki on this further.

Anu asserted authority again, "Enki will report back to us with the final results of the investigation. But now, we must finalize our strategy for the lawsuit we are to bring before the divine council of Yahweh Elohim." The Watchers, faithful or fallen, referred to Elohim by his covenant name within the sacred space of the divine council in heaven. That surprised Enoch a little.

Anu continued, "I yield the floor to the Accuser."

The Accuser, translated as "the satan," was the legal term for the prosecuting adversary in the heavenly court of Yahweh Elohim. Of all the Shining Ones, the Accuser drew the most respect and admiration. He was *Nachash*, the Serpent of the Garden, a seraph of great intellect and cunning. His single act in Eden had accomplished more for their cause than anything anyone else had done. Unlike the others, he was the sole Watcher who had not taken on a new divine persona in the pantheon of gods. Semjaza had became Anu, and Azazel, Inanna in order to spearhead the earthly violation of the created order. But Nachash remained the heavenly Accuser before the divine council in order to accomplish their massive legal assault upon Yahweh's kingdom. He even preferred being called simply *the Accuser*. It brought attention to what he sarcastically referred to as "his calling."

Anu looked about for his colleague. The Accuser was not there. Everyone looked around for this titan of malevolence, but he was no longer present.

He had sensed what was about to happen.

• • • • •

The lookout Naphil died in seconds, pierced through with Methuselah's javelin and Betenos' arrow. Edna took off its head with her multi-bladed angelic weapon.

The Nephilim raced toward them. They broke through the foliage like a wind storm. They held to some discipline, as two remained guarding the camp.

The giant killers called upon all the best of their training in this battle. They used an integrated defense system of covering for each other. Rather than one team member taking on a fight alone, each lent their skills to create a "one-two" punch. An arrow from Betenos was finished off with a slice by Edna, or a javelin from Methuselah. But in order for this system to work, they were constantly on the move, flowing in and out of each other's space with a dance-like choreography. Crisscrossing one another's paths, diving, rolling, spinning and flipping. This was the dance of the Karabu.

When the first three Nephilim reached them, weapons swinging, Edna went right into the thick of them. She flipped and twirled her weapon around the three of them. They swung maces and clubs in thin air, missing Edna. Betenos' arrows and Methuselah's javelins caught them unprepared. The team took care to make head shots or gut shots to avoid the alloy armor the Nephilim wore. Lamech with a slashing Rahab in hand beheaded the third Naphil in midstride.

The other Nephilim reached them, and it became a frenzied attack. It might have been an unequal fight of these four against the many ogres, but the giant killers had a secret weapon: Ohyah.

Once the fight ranged into the bush and out of sight of the two guards left at the camp, Ohyah rained down fury upon his fellow Nephilim from behind. They did not even know what hit them. Ohyah took out four of them before the others realized they were betrayed.

With Ohyah behind them and the four giant killers before them, the last five did not stand a chance.

It discouraged Methuselah. This was not really as glorious a victory as he had hoped. But he could not complain. It was more important to win than to have a close fight.

When the Nephilim lay at their feet, Ohyah and the four humans took a moment to catch their breaths. They had been taxed, but invigorated as well.

"Well, that was some much needed exercise," said Methuselah.

Ohyah picked up a pear mace. He walked up to Methuselah and knelt. He offered the mace to Methuselah. "Hit me," he said.

"What?" asked Methuselah.

"I said hit me. There are two guards left at the camp, and we cannot sneak up on them. We will have to use subterfuge. It will appear suspicious if I am the only one left alive without significant wounds."

"Of course," agreed Methuselah. He grabbed the mace, swallowed, and swung it at Ohyah's head.

He knocked Ohyah unconscious to the ground. When he came to, he had a black eye and a large bruise on his noggin.

"I did not ask you to knock me out, just give me a bruise," said Ohyah.

"You did say 'significant wound.'"

196

"Evidently our definitions of 'significant' do not coincide."

"Sorry."

"You will have to give me your weapons," continued Ohyah. "I will walk you in as my captives. When we are close enough, we will be able to overtake them before they catch on."

"I hate to be the killjoy," said Lamech, "but we just slaughtered an entire pack of branded Nephilim. I suspect in this territory, we will be the wanted outlaws now."

"Unless we can get rid of the bodies," said Edna. "That might gain us time before they are discovered."

"Let us finish the job first, then discuss strategy," said Methuselah.

CHAPTER 37

By the time the Watchers inside the mountain realized that the Accuser was not with them, Enoch and the four archangels had found their way to the far side of the black lake. Across the water, they could see the Watchers congregated around Anu and Inanna on their thrones. They heard the Watchers discussing some way to capture Rahab for their nefarious purposes and then announcing their plan to bring a lawsuit before the throne of Elohim. Enoch had no idea what that was all about. He just knew what he was supposed to do: prophesy and die.

Though Mikael, Gabriel, Raphael, and Uriel were the highest of archangels, and could no doubt take out a good number of these Watchers, they would eventually succumb to the sheer force of enemy numbers. There were just too many of them. The loyalty of his guardian escort impressed Enoch. They did not even question their duty. They told jokes and argued amongst themselves on the way to this spot, as if they were just going to march right into this nest of vipers and prance right out, job accomplished.

He could not imagine facing their possible fate. Unless they knew something they were not telling him.

The four archangels surrounded Enoch, with weapons drawn and ready. He bellowed out, his voice amplifying as it carried over the pitch black waters of the Abyss.

"Praise the Most High, the Great and Holy One!"

The entire army of Watchers fell silent. All heads turned to stare straight at Enoch and his four puny guardians on the other side of the lake. It simply did not enter their minds that these insignificant fools would ever do such a moronic thing as to enter their very cosmic mountain.

Inanna reacted first. "Well, well, well, what have we here? A silly loud-mouthed meat puppet and four yipping lapdogs on a leash?"

Enlil recognized Enoch. "Utuabzu? So, you are still alive. What brings you into our lair uninvited?"

Anu thought, *This little insect has gall. Where did he come from and how did he get these archangels?*

"I am Enoch, a servant and prophet of Elohim, the living God, and I have come to pronounce judgment upon the Watchers and upon their progeny the Nephilim!"

The chamber held silence for a moment. Then Inanna howled with laughter, followed by a hundred other Watchers.

Anu and Enlil played along with this farce. It seemed absurdly amusing to them.

"Well, then, by all means, pronounce thy judgment, little man. We wait with baited breath," said Anu.

Enoch looked straight at Anu. He raised his hand, pointing his finger at the Watcher. "Semjaza, you and your associates have united yourselves with women so as to defile yourselves in all your uncleanness!" Enoch called Semjaza out by his true name. "And when your unholy sons are slain, you will be bound fast for seventy generations in the valleys of the earth, till the day of judgment."

"My, oh my, we are quaking in our sandals," mocked Inanna. "Fear and trembling has seized us! We beseech thee to draw up a petition for us that we might find forgiveness in the presence of the Lord of heaven."

Enoch ignored the vitriolic mockery. He next prophesied directly to Inanna by true name. "Azazel, thou shalt have no peace. A severe sentence has gone forth against thee to put thee in bonds. And thou shalt not have toleration nor request granted to thee, because of the unrighteousness which thou hast taught, and because of all the works of godlessness and unrighteousness and sin which thou hast shown to men."

Inanna muttered to Anu, "My humor is taxed. Let us be done with this pathetic gnat."

"Wait," Anu held up his hand.

As Enoch prophesied, the Watchers circled slowly around the lake, to enclose Enoch and his guardians. Anu had not been simply entertaining the absurd prophecy for the sake of amusement. He was stalling for time. But something in the human's words sent a chill down Anu's back, setting his teeth on edge. He wanted to hear the final words.

Enoch continued, "The decree has gone forth to bind you in the earth for all the days of the world. And you shall see the destruction of your beloved sons. For a Chosen Seed is coming to bring an end to the reign of the gods and bring rest from the curse of the land!"

That last line struck them all. In that moment, they knew Enoch was indeed a prophet of Elohim, and they had been cursed.

"Eliminate them, immediately!" commanded Anu.

• • • • •

Ohyah walked behind his four captives, Methuselah, Edna, Lamech, and Betenos. They held their hands behind their heads in

200

submission. Ohyah even pushed Lamech, to look impatiently hostile. Lamech fell to his knees from the force.

"Hey, take it easy," muttered Lamech. "You are enjoying this a bit too much for my comfort." Ohyah smirked.

They were about half way across the vast clearing when the two Nephilim guards noticed the captive visitors. They trotted toward them to meet Ohyah's arrival.

Methuselah whispered, "I will take the one on the left. Ohyah, take the right. They will not see it coming."

Before they could carry out their plan, they stopped dead in their tracks. A line of Nephilim stepped from the foliage into the clearing. Methuselah turned and saw masses of other armed Nephilim appearing *all around them*. A horde of over one hundred Nephilim surrounded them. They had never imagined this horror happening.

• • • • •

Anu gave the command to eliminate Enoch and the angels on the shoreline of the cavernous Abyss.

Gabriel lifted his cloak and pulled out his trumpet. He raised it to his lips and blew. The mighty sound penetrated the diabolical cave and resounded right up to heaven itself.

The percussion of the horn's note was supernatural. Its sound waves washed over the Watchers, felling many of them in its wake. An earthquake rattled the cave to its core.

A beam of intense burning fire cut through the rock ceiling above Enoch and the angels' heads and enveloped them in its blinding light. But it did not consume their flesh. It was as if they stood in the midst of a flaming furnace and remained unsinged by the heat or flames.

It dumbfounded Anu and Inanna.

Before their eyes, Enoch and the four angels were translated up through the ceiling and into heaven. In an instant, they were gone, and the beam of blazing light followed them.

A shroud of darkness fell in the cavern. The drastic change from intense brightness to intense darkness temporarily blinded the Watchers. After a moment, their eyes adjusted. They looked to the throne for their commands from Anu and Inanna.

The two of them were shaken to the core.

Anu, who had never shown weakness as leader of this rebellion, for the first time was pale and sweating. Inanna stood speechless for her first time. Their behavior had been uncovered by Elohim and judgment was coming. Their time was cut short. They had to act on their plan or risk utter failure and imprisonment in Tartarus.

"Unleash the wolves of war," commanded Anu.

CHAPTER 38

Methuselah's team was not quite as blessed as Enoch's.

The horde of Nephilim surrounded Ohyah and his "captives." They stood fearfully awaiting their end at the hands of the horde. An officer adorned in golden armor stepped out from the horde. He approached Ohyah. He studied the captives, then looked back at Ohyah with suspicion. He thoughtfully considered the bulging pus-filled black and blue eye of Ohyah.

The Naphil leader spoke with a gravelly voice, "I am General Mahawai of Baalbek. Who are you, soldier?"

A general? thought Methuselah. *What do they have out here, an army of Nephilim? How could that be?*

"I am Ohyah, son of Semjaza," blurted Ohyah.

Methuselah's team tried to hold back their surprise at this revelation. Semjaza? Semjaza was the infamous leader of the Watchers, now known as the father sky god Anu.

What new trick is Ohyah attempting? thought Methuselah. Sure, it might protect them from immediate execution, but it only delayed their demise until the Nephilim got word from Semjaza. Still, any amount of time was helpful, if they could only devise an escape.

Thanks a lot, Ohyah, Lamech thought. *You just added prolonged torture for us when they discover you lied. Well, at least you will suffer more for being a traitor.*

Ohyah continued, "I am a lone voyager from the east. I found this regiment because I wanted to join your forces. These giant killers took us all by surprise."

Mahawai glanced at the two Guards from the camp. They nodded slightly in approval. But it was not approval enough for Mahawai.

"These soldiers merely parrot what you told them earlier. How do I not know whether you brought these vermin on your tail? How is it that you alone survived the slaughter of thirteen of my soldiers? Why should I believe you?"

Ohyah felt his hands tremble. He became short of breath. He had no answer.

Then a voice came from out of the horde, "General Mahawai, I will vouch for this Naphil's word."

Everyone turned toward the voice. One of the soldiers stepped out from the crowded regiment. He came straight up to Mahawai. He saluted and stood at attention.

Mahawai looked at him expectantly.

"I am Hahyah, son of Semjaza. This Naphil is my twin brother."

Methuselah felt a sickening pit open in his stomach. His whole world came crashing in on him. Everyone on the team glanced at each other with shock. Only Betenos kept staring at Ohyah.

This Hahyah did indeed look just like Ohyah, save for his warrior-shaved head.

The general's next declaration caught them off guard. "We are done with our training exercise. Bring these captives back to Baalbek. Let Thamaq and Yahipan deal with them."

Well, thought Methuselah, *at last I will face the Rephaim who killed our parents and the rest of my city. Unfortunately, they will have the blade in their hands.*

The distant sound of a war horn interrupted his thoughts. The Nephilim stood at attention. Mahawai peered to the south and said to himself, "That is the battle call of Inanna." He turned to his troops and yelled, "ALL SOLDIERS TO ARMS! DOUBLE TIME TO BAALBEK!"

• • • • •

Baalbek lay about ten leagues north of where Methuselah and his team were caught. All night long they marched through the Sirion mountain pass. Eventually, they entered a broad river basin called the Beqa Valley, just before the sun rose. They followed the Orontes River through a vast cedar forest to its springs in the heart of the city.

As they came up from the south, they passed a huge quarry used for the stone of the city. The morning quarry shift had not yet begun, leaving the stone pit empty. It struck Methuselah how large the stones seemed to be. He thought his eyes were playing tricks on him in the moonlight, with the distance and his perception.

Yet when they reached the city gates, he realized that the size of the stones was not an optical illusion. They were huge beyond belief. Stones the size of four men tall, thirty cubits long and thousands of tons apiece. He had never seen hewn rock so large or so finely crafted with precision. How did they cut, transport, and position such mammoth stones? It was inconceivable to him.

Until they entered the city gates.

Baalbek was a city of giants, vast and thriving, alive with industry and labor. And all of its inhabitants were Nephilim — *thousands of them.* All around them, everywhere, humongous architectural edifices crafted from cyclopean blocks of stone rose tall, some of the buildings a hundred cubits or higher. The team of giant killers felt like fleas in a nest of wasps. The giants they saw going about their business towered six to ten cubits high, and most of them wore strange foreign looking armor or carried foreign looking weapons. Baalbek looked like a military occupation of invading forces.

They were paraded through the city streets toward the palace. The staggering implications of what they saw overwhelmed Methuselah, Edna, Lamech, and Betenos. It meant that everything they believed about the gigantomachy was a lie. The giants were not reduced to outlaws and wandering vagrants hunted by the gods, they were an organized civilization. The general Mahawai had submitted to the call of Inanna as if they were her own army. How could this be? The gods had outlawed the giants in the East, only to create an army of Nephilim in the West?

These and many other questions filled Methuselah's head. He feared the answers. A deathly dread overcame him.

Lamech stumbled closer to Methuselah as they approached the steps of the palace. "Ohyah planned this all along. He betrayed us from the beginning," he whispered.

Methuselah nodded his head. He glanced at Edna to make certain she was well. Both Edna and Betenos had barely kept up with the rigorous march. The rapid journey had exhausted them all. They could have fallen asleep standing up, were it not for the fact that they would have been executed had they done so.

Before the palace, they passed a series of giant chariots, four-wheeled war carts drawn by teams of horses. The giants did not usually use beasts of burden, except in royal processions or in a military capacity for their leaders. This gathering obviously included a dozen different chariots from a dozen different tribes.

Baalbek was not the only city and army of giants? How much worse could these revelations possibly get? How much more shocking? thought Methuselah.

CHAPTER 39

The giant killers were ushered through the gigantic halls of the palace by a squad of six Nephilim warriors. Edna marveled at the intricate sculpting of marble and granite on the architecture. These monsters were evil, but they were still capable of creating such impressive beauty. It could only mean that artistic creativity and cultural sophistication were not in themselves signs of moral goodness. The cruelest, most monstrous beast could torture and eat a man, and yet turn aside and carve magnificent masterpieces of sublime beauty worthy of gods.

Betenos wanted to hold Lamech's hand. But she knew better. It was bad enough to be a woman captive. The heinous treatment she would soon receive was bad enough. But if their captors knew affection bound any of the giant killer team together, it would provide their torturers more vulnerabilities to exploit, when they got around to carrying out their duty. If Ohyah revealed their relationship, all attempts at hiding the connection would be futile.

Lamech and Methuselah sized up everything as they trod the halls to their destination. The thought of escape might be laughable, but a warrior never stops looking for ways to fight. Whatever they could learn of the palace layout or the cultural behaviors of their captors might come in handy in an emergency.

Methuselah watched one of those cultural behaviors in action as they were escorted through the hallway: Nephilim were slaves to their insatiable lusts. They had voracious appetites for food, drink and danger of any kind that gave them a thrill. The Nephilim guards kept sneaking glances at Edna and Betenos. Methuselah knew exactly what they were thinking.

On the one hand, he could certainly understand why. His wife was still the most covetable woman in any company.

Betenos was no less attractive. Though Lamech had sought to emulate his pious grandfather Enoch in spirituality, he could not avoid his good taste in beauty. Like patriarch, like son.

While Methuselah worried about Betenos' future, he knew Edna was very capable of using womanly talents to her own advantage. *It may even be she who will get us out of this impossible situation,* he thought. She would play them, cloud their minds with her seductive beauty, and then slit their throats before they knew what happened. He was proud of his godly warrior wife.

They arrived at a set of huge oak doors that opened to a feast banquet for giants. The vast dining hall had floor tables in a U-shape overflowing with every kind of fish, fowl and mammal imaginable: roasted boar, gazelle, lion, bull, and bear, as well as whale shark and coelacanth. The one animal kind Methuselah noticed as absent was reptile. No snakes, crocodiles, lizards or dragons.

That would be too much like eating their own, he thought.

It was a feast of flesh fit for kings, because that is who sat at the table before them; kings — giant kings. They were the Rephaim who were first birthed when the gods came down from heaven. Eleven of them sat on the floor in their eating positions. One tossed a lion's bone to two mushussu chained in the corner. They were the same type of chimera dragon monsters that had almost killed Methuselah's team near Mari, at the beginning of their journey. The beasts snarled and fought over the bone. It was not an encouraging sight.

Thamaq and Yahipan presided at the center table, the evident rulers of this city. They looked up from their revelry to see Methuselah and his team standing in chains before them.

Their eyes met. Time stood still. The enemies recognized each other. Blood rose up simultaneously in Methuselah, Edna and Yahipan. Hatred resurrected and gripped all their souls.

Yahipan stood and started to limp briskly around the table toward the captives, the look of murder in his eyes.

"Yahipan!" shouted Thamaq.

Yahipan stopped.

"There will be plenty of room for revenge later."

Yahipan limped back to his spot and plopped down in anger.

Methuselah thought, *Good. He has carried that wound I gave him for hundreds of years as a miserable reminder.*

Edna's thought completed his, *That is a foretaste of the misery I am going to give you, giant, if Elohim gives me one chance.*

"Methuselah ben Enoch and his band of mighty giant slayers," said Thamaq, with biting sarcasm. "Welcome to my *marzih* feast of the First Born."

A *marzih* was a banquet that Rephaim indulged in the presence of the gods to celebrate life or death or a military send off. But no gods were present at this feast.

The other Rephaim now stared at Methuselah's team. They were the first of the offspring of the Watchers. The mightiest, the rulers of royalty, and they were all supposed to have been executed after the Gigantomachy hundreds of years ago.

These Rephaim all measured about ten cubits tall and wore robes of kingship that expressed primacy and power. Each sported a different design, based on the different tribes or cultures they represented. Some outfits were studded with precious gemstones, others with silver and gold. All of the Rephaim were hairless and carried the tattooed skin of the Nephilim, strange occultic marks and spells burned into their leathery bodies as a magic oath of fealty to their gods. Their eyes bore the strongest resemblance of any of the Nephilim to their reptilian creators. They were stronger, faster, more cunning, and more spiritual than those who followed them.

"Forgive my lack of etiquette," said Thamaq. "Let me introduce you to the Council of the Didanu, who will soon rule over the wretched little lives of your descendants."

So they were organized into some kind of multi-kingdom empire. But who was the emperor?

Thamaq gestured to each one as he gave their names. "Ulkan, Taruman, Sidan-and-Radan the conjoined twins, Thar the eternal one." Methuselah did not hear the rest of the names. He kept his eyes focused on Thamaq and Yahipan, like a leonine predator waiting for the moment to strike.

Yahipan felt it.

Even though Methuselah stood in chains, and the kings were surrounded by the mightiest of the Rephaim in a city of giants, still he felt it — as if *he* was the one in danger. *Ridiculous*, thought Yahipan. *I am manifesting weakness,* he concluded and shook it off.

Methuselah and Lamech did not know why this Rapha even bothered to treat them as if they had information to exchange.

Thamaq was playfully ironic. "As you no doubt have seen through your tour of our good city, we have been busy. Apparently, so have you, I see. Learning the way of the Karabu."

Silence filled the room. Everyone on the team thought, *How did he know?*

211

The other Rephaim sat intensely quiet, anticipating the answer Methuselah might give. Genuine fear filled their eyes, as if Methuselah's little gang knew something that would crush them. But what could it be that would scare them so?

Thamaq dropped his levity and turned deadly serious. "Where did you learn the way of the Karabu?"

Thamaq did not appear confident of his question, fishing for the truth with a bluff.

The Karabu never left their underground city. Only a few bands like Enoch's ever travelled outside of the Sahand area of Eden. So only rumors and legends ever traversed the land about the secret order. There was no way that information was going to be drawn out of any of the team — even under torture.

"Very well," said Yahipan, "torture them."

The Nephilim guards turned to escort the prisoners away.

Yahipan added, "But keep them alive. I want the leader and his wench for myself."

Methuselah and Edna cringed. They could only imagine the horrors he had in store for them.

"Halt, Nephilim," said Thamaq.

The Nephilim obeyed.

"What would the Council of the Didanu advise?" said Thamaq.

Yahipan grimaced with anger. He did not want anything slowing down his plans for the two maggots.

The conjoined twin Rephaim, Sidan-and-Radan, spoke first. When they did, they spoke in synchronization. It was as if they shared not merely their middle body but also a consciousness. "We have heard the legends of the Karabu," said Sidan, "but it seems to us mere exaggeration," concluded Radan.

"We do not have time for such trivialities," said Taruman. "The die is cast. The furnace is stoked. There is no turning back."

What were they talking about? wondered Methuselah. *What strategy had these creatures of damnation implemented? What diabolical madness have we happened upon?*

Yahipan tried to conclude the discussion. "I will extract what I can from them and meet up with you with any important intelligence."

"Be gone with them," said Ulkan with the wave of his hand. "We have a war to conduct."

A war? What war? thought Methuselah.

The team of giant killers wondered what devastation was about to be wrought upon the land as they were led out of the banquet hall in chains.

CHAPTER 40

Methuselah hung by chains on the dungeon wall. He had already been beaten but kept in one piece for Yahipan. Edna lay chained to a mating altar, used for the Sacred Marriage rite. Lamech and Betenos were in the next room in their own bonds.

Yahipan sat before them, staring at Edna.

"I care nothing for the Karabu," said Yahipan. "I have no interest in extracting useless secrets of some sneaky order that exists in the fantasy and rumors of desperate and hopeless slaves."

For the first time in their lives, Methuselah and Edna were really and truly afraid.

"No, little worm," Yahipan said to Edna, "I am not even going to torture you."

He paused for effect. "I am going to impregnate you and the other wench. You will bear my offspring, then you will die. And I will have satisfaction."

Methuselah struggled to free himself from his chains. It was completely futile, but he tried anyway. He would die trying.

Yahipan smiled at him. "You, I will do interesting things with. I have never forgotten the day you gave me this limp. I have plotted all these years what I would do if I could only find you again. I have some ideas I have been waiting for the right opportunity to experiment with. What a pleasure to discover I can do them also to your own son as you watch. Yes, I will have satisfaction."

Yahipan stood up and limped over to Edna. He leaned down close to her and sniffed in deeply her scent. Then his sandy lizard-like tongue licked her face for a foretaste. Edna cringed and almost vomited.

Methuselah had no idea how he could possibly get out of this predicament. He did the only thing he could do at that moment; talk. Any amount of talk brought the tiniest delay that might result in some kind of miraculous opportunity. At least, that was his faint hope.

"Nephilim — w-were outlawed," he stuttered through his pain. "Why did the gods allow them to build a city?"

Yahipan considered the question, and then slowly smiled. Perhaps additional knowledge would increase the pain as well, knowing the juggernaut they could not stop.

"Oh, there is more than one city," said Yahipan. "The Gigantomachy was a hoax. It was a ruse ordered by the gods to draw attention away from their true plans; to build an army of Nephilim in Bashan, and train them thoroughly for the battle of all battles." He paused again for dramatic effect.

"A war on Eden."

The words hit Methuselah and Edna hard. And sank deep. They knew the reason without Yahipan needing to finish.

"We are going to storm the Garden, destroy the Cherubim, and capture the Tree of Life," said Yahipan.

The consequences of this plan horrified Methuselah. A malevolent race of giants with the power to live forever would reach heights of evil he could not even imagine. They would be invincible in their might and omnipotent in their rule.

215

"How?" asked Methuselah. "The guardians..." he sought to finish his question.

Yahipan interrupted him, "Those guardians have a weakness. The gods cannot invade because their own kind, the heavenly host, outnumber them overwhelmingly. And earthborn humans cannot enter because of the Cherubim sentinels. That is why the Watchers bred the Nephilim. Nephilim are a hybrid of angel and human, a creature that exists simultaneously between heaven and earth. We can achieve collectively what our genetic sources cannot individually. And our numbers are legion."

Suddenly, it all came clear to Methuselah. Years before, when they had killed the pack of Nephilim in the mountains of Aratta, he had wondered where their strange armor had come from and whether they were a part of a horde. Their armor was the insignia of this Baalbek army. They had killed a band of Nephilim scouts on a reconnaissance mission, gathering intelligence of the land surrounding Eden for their planned invasion. Enoch and his band of giant killers had stumbled upon the plan and had never realized it. And now they were about to be gotten rid of.

A rap on the dungeon door stirred Yahipan's impatience. "What is it?!" he yelled through clenched teeth.

The door opened. A soldier saluted and announced, "My lord, the goddess Inanna demands your presence at the mustering. They are about to begin the march."

"Son of Belial!" he cursed. "I told her I was occupied." Belial was the spirit of unclean wickedness.

Yahipan might be angry at the inconvenience, but he responded immediately. One did not trifle with Inanna's will. She once struck a high Rephaim dead for a delayed appearance before her. Yahipan turned to leave the room, but stopped, and turned back to his prisoners.

"I am going to inquire of my god. Now is your chance to inquire of yours. You might want to ask him why he cannot save you. But then I doubt he can even hear you."

Yahipan left them alone.

Methuselah admitted to himself that the thought had crossed his mind. Edna had been praying the entire time. They both knew that Elohim owed them nothing. Every breath of life was already undeserved. Elohim gives and Elohim takes away. Blessed is the name of Yahweh Elohim.

Simultaneously, Methuselah looked up and Edna stopped praying.

The soldier had not moved. He did not leave them or even close the dungeon door. He stared at them. Methuselah could not believe their bad luck. Was this going to be a Nephilim who broke ranks and risked death just to abuse a pair of prisoners?

The soldier walked up to Edna and took off his helmet.

It was the familiar face of Ohyah. Only it was not Ohyah, it was his brother Hahyah. He began to unlock the chains that held down Edna.

"We do not have much time. When Yahipan discovers Inanna did not summon him, we will have them both after us."

It confused Methuselah. "Your brother betrayed us. Are you now betraying him?"

"No. He is freeing your compatriots right now."

Edna asked, "But why do you help us?"

"When we discovered your team in the clearing, he had to maintain the ruse or risk execution. We are sons of Semjaza. That would be the highest of treason."

"Then why treason?" asked Methuselah.

Hahyah finished releasing Edna. He moved to unclasp Methuselah's chains. "I had dreams from your god Elohim not unlike my brother's. It was a garden of two hundred trees being watered. I believe these were the Watcher gods who came down from heaven. As their roots grew, the water flooded the forest and suddenly the garden became ablaze with fire and the water evaporated. I kept getting this dream night after night. And I knew it was judgment. Then I heard of the prophet Enoch and of his condemnation of the gods. I knew the time was at hand. So when my brother finally found me, I discovered he too had been visited by your god."

He finished releasing Methuselah. Edna leapt into her husband's arms.

"Wait a moment," said Methuselah. "You said you heard of Enoch's condemnation?"

"We had received word that Enoch and some archangels had entered the cosmic mountain Hermon, and stood right in the midst of the council of the gods who could not touch them. He prophesied and it was said he was translated into heaven on a fiery chariot."

Methuselah and Edna looked at each other with hope in their hearts and smiles on their lips. If this rumor was true, Elohim surely had a sense of irony.

"The gods are mustering their armies for war on Eden as we speak. Inanna is the Commander in Chief, and the Rephaim Council of the Didanu are the generals."

Of course, thought Methuselah. *Why did it not surprise me that Inanna was the force behind this atrocity?*

Ohyah and the freed Lamech and Betenos arrived at the door.

"We have no time. We must leave now!" barked Ohyah.

• • • • •

Yahipan quickly made it to the command center by the gates of the city. He limped his way past the security detail with swift recognition. When he arrived at Inanna's tableau, she stood finalizing her plans with Enki and Utu who would accompany her leadership of the forces.

Enlil had refused to be there as one of the gods under her command. Their long lasting feud over the control of the city of Nippur was known to all. She had managed to seize popular support if not political status through her machinations. If she succeeded in this campaign, she would most likely imprison Enlil in the earth and turn Nippur from the religious center of Shinar into the capital of an empire with herself at the top. Yahipan wondered if Anu had thought through the predictable consequences and whether he had prepared for such a coup.

Yahipan limped before the gods and knelt in fealty.

"My gods, Queen of heaven," he said.

Inanna turned to look at him. He noticed a distinct lack of expectation in her face. In fact, she looked annoyed, wondering why she was being interrupted.

"What now, Hobbler?" she exclaimed impatiently. She called him that in derision because of his persistent limp, an ongoing sign of weakness and reminder that he had been hobbled by a pathetic human.

She was not expecting him.

In that moment, Yahipan knew he had been duped by that piece of baboon excrement down in the dungeon.

"Forgive me, your majesty, I only wished to alert you to the fact that my forces are ready to bring up the rear guard."

It distracted her. "Good, do not slow us down, Hobbler, or we will leave you in the dust. Be gone with you." She turned back to her plotting.

Once Yahipan was out of Inanna's sight, he barreled full force back to the palace dungeon. He accommodated his handicap using a skipping movement that maximized his speed when running. Unfortunately, it made him look like a jackrabbit scampering through prickly bush. All he could think of was figuring out how a Naphil could possibly agree to engage in treason. Whatever the case, he would immediately kill the males and impregnate the females without further ado.

· · · · ·

Ohyah and Hahyah led the four giant killers through the dark dungeon hallways up toward the surface. They dodged and hid in the shadows, avoided personnel, and only had to kill one Naphil guard who happened upon them by accident.

Methuselah hounded Ohyah with questions.

"How many Nephilim troops are mustered?" he asked.

"Thirty thousand."

Thirty thousand Nephilim storming Eden? "Are the other Watchers joining the battle?" said Methuselah.

"No," said Ohyah.

"Why would Elohim not send his heavenly host right now to stop it?"

"Because the other Watchers have employed the Accuser to prosecute a lawsuit in the heavenly court at the same time. So the Sons of God are required as witnesses and counsel. It was all a diversion."

That did not quite add up to Methuselah or anyone in the group. They were not familiar with the bureaucracy of the divine council and the legal procedures that Elohim used to procure justice. They had to trust that what Ohyah was saying was true, since he had been privy to the Watchers' plot as a son of Semjaza. They concluded that if it was not true, he would have just let them suffer their fate at the hands of Yahipan.

220

•••••

Yahipan made it to the dungeon. He discovered what he had feared most: the open doors and empty dungeon cells. He found a security detail of four guards and barked orders for them to follow him. The prisoners had escaped.

He tracked the smell of their sweat upward. He had become very acquainted with Edna's scent. It had inflamed him like none had before. He would find them. It was only a matter of moments.

They stumbled upon the dead Naphil and continued on, knowing they were close.

•••••

Methuselah continued his questions with Ohyah as they climbed the palace hallways toward the roof.

"How far is Baalbek from Eden?" he asked.

"About two hundred and thirty leagues."

It would take a normal army twenty days to march that distance at a fast pace. But this was not a normal army. It was a Nephilim fighting force that could run all day with packs on their back. It would take them a third the time, perhaps seven days to make it to the perimeter of Paradise. How long then to defile it and raze it to the ground?

Methuselah felt sick. "We have to get to Eden to warn the Karabu."

•••••

Below them, in the long passage, Yahipan figured it out. They were going to the roof. But why? To cast themselves off? Why did they not try to find the tunnels beneath the city? It did not matter. They would all be dead soon. The Nephilim behind him had all their senses tuned in for the kill.

221

． ． ． ． ．

The two giants and four humans arrived at their destination, the top of the palace building overseeing the entire city. They ran to the ledge and looked out onto the plain. An awesome and frightening sight spread out before them. Thirty thousand armed Nephilim warriors filled the valley, preparing to march to war.

Trumpets sounded. A series of eerie drones blown through dragon horns created an unearthly sound befitting an unearthly horde.

The Nephilim started their march — or rather, their long distance race. One by one, huge sections of the multitude poured forward like a tsunami wave of titans.

That is what this holocaust is, thought Methuselah, *a Titanomachy that will make the Gigantomachy of the past look like cub's play.*

"We cannot possibly outrun the Nephilim," cried Lamech.

"We are not going to outrun them," answered Ohyah. He turned and produced a screeching birdcall, unlike anything Methuselah had heard.

"We are going to outfly them," added Hahyah.

Methuselah realized that he *had* heard that sound once before.

A reply screech drew their eyes into the blinding center of the sun. Out of that brightness, six large Anzu birds dropped directly toward the palace. It was the family of the Anzu bird that Ohyah had broken at the World Tree in the desert.

The Anzu landed on the rooftop. Each of the escapees got on one. The feathered felines were huge, twice the size of even the giants. They could easily carry the passengers. It would be harder for the passengers to stay on, however.

So Elohim did work all things to his own purposes, thought Methuselah. Even the Anzu bird. But what about this army of darkness assembled before them on the plain?

Yahipan burst through the rooftop access with his four Nephilim. He spotted the escaping prisoners.

The Anzu birds lifted off the roof.

Methuselah's was the last to take off. It moved just a second too late. Yahipan leapt and grabbed its hind talons. Rephaim had iron vise grips. He was not going to let go until he sent them all plummeting to their deaths.

Methuselah's Anzu bird lost its balance. It zigzagged a course over the Nephilim on the roof.

Yahipan smirked to himself. *I have you now, Methuselah. No last second escape this time.*

Yahipan focused on how he would grab Methuselah. He did not see Edna's Anzu bird circle back.

It clamped its lion jaws on Yahipan's strong leg.

Yahipan screamed.

He let go of the leg of the bird Methuselah rode. The biting Anzu bird let go of him at the same time. He was only about ten cubits above the roof, so he landed with a concussive thud. But he survived — and so did his burning desire to spend the rest of his life hunting down Methuselah and his disgusting wench.

"AHHHH!" he screamed. He grabbed his leg, bleeding profusely from the wounds created by the Anzu fangs. Now both his legs were wounded. He belted out another curse of anger and wrapped up his wound. How was he going to hide this from Inanna now?

The Anzu birds ascended vertically, to reach their maximum height as quickly as possible. They leveled off and flew in formation higher than any mountain in the region.

Methuselah saw the waves of charging Nephilim far below. They looked like an army of termites. He could not imagine how Eden would withstand this onslaught. He only hoped they would not be too late.

He glanced at Edna, flying beside him. They shared a smile. Ohyah and Hahyah led the group, with Lamech and Betenos taking up the rear. It was as if the birds intuitively understood all the relationships in the group and lined up to match them. Methuselah calculated that at this height and speed, it would take them less than a day to reach the Sahand and alert the Adamite Karabu. It was their only hope in a hopeless situation.

Methuselah thought back to what Ohyah had told them. He wondered what was happening in Elohim's court of principalities and powers. Would the Watchers' heavenly scheme delay Elohim's response to the earthly crisis? The implications were staggering.

CHAPTER 41

The Throne of Yahweh Elohim gleamed in the holy temple in the heavens above the waters, unapproachable, a chariot enthroned above the Cherubim and beneath the Seraphim. The Seraphim were a different breed, created exclusively for God's own guard. The Cherubim were sphinx-like, but these had four faces and four wings, and they sparkled like burnished bronze. Their faces were those of human, lion, ox, and eagle. Beside each one was an object that appeared to be a wheel within a wheel of gleaming beryl, that moved with the living creature as they moved.

The Seraphim above the throne were equally as glorious and awesome. Their humanoid yet serpentine bodies had six wings. With two they flew, two covered their feet, and two covered their faces. And all of them proclaimed the trisagion, "Holy, holy, holy, is the Lord of Hosts. The whole earth is full of his glory."

The heavenly host presented themselves around this throne, the *bene ha Elohim*, or Sons of God, ten thousand times ten thousand of his holy ones, the divine council. Their presence flashed like lightning that would burn out the eyes of any human being in the flesh.

The Accuser was not impressed by any of this. A transformed seraph himself, his plaintiffs were all Sons of God as well. His opposition did not intimidate him at all. He and Semjaza, along with almost two hundred Watchers, presented themselves across from the array they despised. They considered the throne-circling adversaries to be a mob of sycophants, yes-men and sell-outs, puppets and tools.

The Accuser, Semjaza, and their fellow Watchers were just as divine, and maybe even more powerful than their enemies because at least they exercised free will — real free will — iron will. That will did have to bend to the sovereignty of the Judge, however, to the use of their original heavenly names of Semjaza, Baraqel, and Zaqiel instead of their Shinarian deity names of Anu, Enlil, and Nanna.

They assembled before the throne of heaven to prosecute a lawsuit with the help of the rebel Watchers who fell to earth. This would not be like any other lawsuit the Accuser had ever litigated. This was a *covenant* lawsuit against the very judge himself, Yahweh Elohim, the maker of heaven and earth, the Lord of Hosts, the Suzerain King of kings.

The ancient form of covenant treaties between sovereign or suzerain king and subservient vassal contained five basic parts that bound the two parties. First, there was a preamble that identifies the Lordship of the great king, his transcendent sovereignty and jurisdiction over territories. Second, the historical prologue that recounted the previous relationship of the king and his subject, along with an establishment of hierarchy and authority. The third section laid out the ethical stipulations or laws required by the king for the subject to maintain his status as protected vassal. The sanctions or listings of blessings for obedience and curses for violation of the covenant came fourth, providing for the continuity of the covenant relationship with succeeding generations. The fifth and last section called for divine witness of the gods or the heavens and the earth.

When Yahweh Elohim had created Adam and Havah, he had enacted a covenant that essentially reflected this pattern of Preamble,

Prologue, Laws, Sanctions, and Witnesses. Adam, as the first of the human race, had violated that covenant and the world now experienced the negative consequences of that covenant violation.

The Accuser had filed a third party class action complaint on behalf of Adam and Havah and the entire human race, claiming that Yahweh Elohim's covenant with the human race was in fact unjust at every single one of the five points. The Accuser's "equitable remedy" involved among other things, an award of damages and a permanent injunction and restraining order against Elohim from the Garden and the presence of mankind.

To make matters worse, the Accuser intended to pull every trick of legal hairsplitting, explore every petty technicality, and appeal every tedious legal procedure that he possibly could, in order to drag this thing out as long as possible. He felt confident and prepared as he took his place as prosecutor in the court.

A battery of defenders stepped out, across from the Accuser and Semjaza's Watchers. They took their places to counter the accusations of the lawsuit. They were the prince archangels: Mikael, Gabriel, Raphael, and Uriel.

Then the voice of Yahweh Elohim cried out, "Whom shall I send? Who will speak for us?" The silence of the throne room penetrated all beings present. The arrival of the final member of the defense team broke the silence: Enoch ben Jared, prophet of God.

"Here I am, send me," said Enoch. He approached the defense team and joined them. They smiled their approval.

At the sight of Enoch, Semjaza wanted to jump out of his seat and strangle the little meat sack. Enoch caught his eyes and rage rose up inside the Watcher. The Accuser saw it. He leaned over to Semjaza, whispering, "Do not be a fool. We have a higher cause here. Suppress your instinct. It is weakness."

Semjaza sat back and took a deep breath.

Enoch saw Semjaza's rage. He sat down in his defense position before the throne with a sense of righteous indignation. He remembered the saying Diya al Din had told him back at the Thamudi fortress, "Let justice roll down like waters." It felt appropriate for this scenario.

A cloud filled the inner court, and the sound of the wings of the Cherubim swept through as far as the outer court. The Seraphim spoke as one. Their voice thundered like the sound of many waters. "Elohim has taken his place in the divine council. In the midst of the gods, he holds judgment."

Everyone fell silent.

This lawsuit would be different from all others because of the legal procedure to be employed. Normally, plaintiff and defendant would stand in the bar before the Judge and make their arguments, calling forth testimony and producing evidence upon which the Judge would rule. But since the Judge himself was being charged by the Accuser, there would be no need of additional testimony or cross examination. The Accuser would make the complaint, and Enoch would speak in defense of Yahweh Elohim. After presentation of all oral arguments, the Judge would make a righteous summary judgment. Special circumstances dictated special procedures.

Yahweh Elohim pronounced, "Hear O heavens, give ear O earth, listen O mountains of God and the heavenly host. I call the sun, moon, and stars as witness today."

The Accuser and Enoch stood beside each other before the throne.

Yahweh Elohim said, "Accuser, what are your motions?"

"Going to and fro on the earth," answered the Accuser.

"What are your *legal pre-trial* motions?" said Yahweh Elohim, correcting the deliberate misconstrual of his words.

He was a wily one, this Accuser, looking for every opportunity to twist, spin, and undermine the system and procedures to his advantage.

The Accuser said, "I petition the court for a change of venue on the grounds that this heavenly court places the defense at great advantage and the prosecution at great disadvantage. I petition the court for jury nullification on the grounds that the myriad of heavenly host are incapable of impartial witness because of overriding prejudicial bias in favor of the defendant. I petition the judge to recuse himself on the grounds of conflict of interest as he is the defendant in his own trial and therefore cannot be fair and unbiased. And I petition the judge for the removal of the defense attorney next to me on the grounds of his lack of legal qualifications for this case."

This was going to be a long trial, thought Enoch.

Yahweh Elohim responded, "There is nowhere in the universe that can contain the heavenly host outside of this throne room. First motion dismissed. The Sons of God are divine council, they do not render verdicts. Second motion dismissed. I am the origin of fairness and objectivity. I do not change and I do not violate my character, so all my judgments are true and just even in reference to my own actions. Third motion dismissed. Enoch ben Jared has stood in the divine council and therefore has met the qualifications for prophet of God and lawful defense attorney. Fourth motion dismissed."

"Well, in that case, your mighty eminence of unbiased objectivity and fairness," said the Accuser sarcastically, "I ask for seven days to finish discovery, since I was surprised by the unreasonable volume of documents that deluged my council. These tablets of unending *toledoth* are time consuming." He was referring to the clay tablets that contained the genealogies of the heavens and the earth as well as those of Adam's descendants.

The gall of this rascal amazed Enoch. He could turn everything into an accusation, even against Yahweh Elohim.

The Accuser continued, "And you really have to admit that this endless list of animal names is quite tedious and would fatigue any staff, much less my own of less than two hundred Watchers."

After a deliberate delay, he added, "Your magnificent majesty most high."

This list of names was a record of those that Adam gave the animals in the Garden as an expression of his covenantal dominion, the authority that the namer had over the named.

"You have two days," said Yahweh Elohim.

Enoch knew the Accuser had no intent of reading the genealogies and names. But even in the face of this obvious stalling tactic, Yahweh Elohim went out of his way to be fair and impartial, even to his own disadvantage.

CHAPTER 42

The team of giants and giant killers fell asleep on the flight over the vast desert. At this height, the air was cold, but the feathers of the Anzu kept them warm. The giant birds flew smoothly.

Methuselah awoke to the sunrise directly in front of them. He saw they were already leaving the arid environment of the desert, flying over the fertile Mesopotamian plain.

But something was not right. They were heading into the sunrise. The sun should be to their right.

He recognized the river course below him. It was a part of the Euphrates just north of his own city of Sippar. They were headed southeast. They should have been traveling northeast toward the Aratta mountains and Eden. But they were going southeast toward Shinar and the Zagros.

He got the attention of Edna and the others. They all recognized their change of route. But their Anzu flyers would not catch up to the two giants in the lead. It was as if the birds had been ordered to stay back and not allow the contact. Methuselah could only assume that they were now captives of their rescuers. He could not imagine where they were being taken and for what purpose.

· · · · ·

The Nephilim horde had run most of the day. They only set up camp for a three hour sleep. Before the sun rose again, they were already up and trampling the ground. Fortunately for Yahipan, Rephaim generals rode on the new four-wheeled chariots drawn by teams of horses. Otherwise, his doubly wounded legs would have dangerously hampered him. He needed more time for healing.

They made good time, following the Sirion Mountain range along the curve of the fertile crescent to avoid the deadly desert. The Euphrates lay a few leagues before them. They would head due east, cross the fertile plain of northern Mesopotamia and enter the Aratta mountains just below their target point.

Inanna calculated that if they could keep this pace up, they might shave another day off their journey. So a few hundred would die of exhaustion or dehydration. What was that to her? Countless thousands would perish in the final battle anyway. Nephilim were expendable. She expected to lose most of them in the first wave of attacks establishing a breach in the Garden. Elohim's forces would not be fighting for their lives, they would be fighting for their eternities. It would actually be quite a relief to lose tens of thousands of mouths to feed and demands to satisfy. These hybrid offspring were a voracious consuming mass of flesh and bone. Like a plague of locusts, they stripped bare the life of every territory where they encamped or passed through.

She liked to call it "the circle of life," the way of all things on earth: eat or be eaten, only the fittest survive. Morality and all its self-righteous proclamations of right and wrong were reducible to the will to power. Might made right. She would have to craft that into a myth one day. It would be a useful tool to obscure the Creator and justify all kinds of atrocities.

If a man could convince himself that morality was not a matter of humanity being created in Elohim's image, but rather was a construct of society, in order to maintain arbitrary control over the masses, then there would be no end to the genocides and holocausts that could be unleashed when man would take that belief to its logical end. Even more devastation than that accomplished by the religions she and her fellow gods "revealed" to these pathetic mud-pies of Elohim.

That was an idea whose time would come. But now was not that time. Inanna grinned with self-satisfaction. *I will indeed craft that secular myth for when ancient religion will have run its useful course.*

• • • • •

By the end of the second day, the Anzu birds arrived in the Zagros Mountains, just northeast of Erech and the South Sea. As the giant birds descended, Methuselah saw a large ring of steep mountain buttes surrounding a plush forested valley. This secluded crater basin might have been a second Paradise. It looked just that rich, green and flowing with streams of waters. The ring of cliffs were like a wall of rock protecting a pristine lost world. It did not look like there was any way in or out, except by air. The Anzu landed inside the Edenic crater.

Methuselah, Edna, Lamech, and Betenos got off their mounts. What else could they do? Their carriers were obviously in the service of Ohyah and Hahyah. The Anzu birds took flight to the north. They had been double-crossed by the giants they had trusted, whom they had considered to be redeemable. Methuselah was not yet sure for what purpose they had been betrayed.

"Why did they not kill us?" asked Lamech. "Drop us from the skies to our deaths over the desert, never to be found again?"

Edna added, "And why in this lush, beautiful, secret valley?"

It certainly seemed safer than the rocky lands outside Eden, where war was approaching.

"Do not be deceived by appearances," said Betenos, looking around at the trees of gorging fruit. "Poison can be as outwardly beautiful as medicine."

"First, we must make some weapons," said Methuselah. "Then, let us get to the walls and explore the perimeter. There may be some hidden exit through a cave or a climb."

They only had three knives among them, taken from the bodies of guards they overcame on their escape out of Baalbek.

CHAPTER 43

"I have already addressed the partiality of the divine witnesses in this case," said the Accuser. "So let me move on to my next charge."

The trial had resumed. Yahweh Elohim had summoned the prosecution, and the Accuser came out with serpentine eyes and bronze body blazing. His skill as an adversary was quickly proving to be of the highest marksmanship.

The Accuser continued, "Regarding the covenant preamble, we have this difficult matter of the sovereignty of the Creator. Really, is not the sovereignty of the suzerain the foundation of the entire edifice? If this cornerstone is rejected, do not all other bricks crumble to the ground?"

He brilliantly used leading questions. Enoch thought to himself how he would like to see the cornerstone fall on the Accuser and crush him.

The Accuser's voice rolled on. "Now Elohim's covenant begins with a claim to sovereign jurisdiction: 'In the beginning, when Elohim began to create the heavens and the earth, etcetera, etcetera.' Is this not a clear case of tyranny and colonialism? Elohim claims to 'create' and 'own' all things as a tyrannical justification to colonize the land. He wants to demand a certain land goes to a certain people, in this case, the Garden to Adam and Eve, and no one else has the right to it. And then he kicks everyone out. What next? Will he claim a land that already has a people residing there as his own, and just wipe the indigenous inhabitants off the face of the earth to make room for 'his people of choice?' Will he ultimately claim the whole earth as his own and allow some clan of meek people to inherit it over those strong peoples who built up its richness? What kind of a suzerain does such a thing? I will tell you what kind: A despot and a tyrant."

Zealous anger filled Enoch. Not only was the Accuser spewing outright blasphemous lies about Yahweh Elohim as defendant, he was also cunningly undermining his authority as Judge by deliberately using the shorter non-covenant name *Elohim* in place of the judicially proper *Yahweh Elohim*. The Accuser earned his name with the ability to accuse on every level of his language.

Still, he was right about one thing: suzerains did claim their right to the land by claiming their gods as creators of it. The difference in this case was that Yahweh Elohim *really did* create all things and the gods were incomparable in his presence. *They* existed in *his* universe. But the Accuser was only beginning. He would build his case upon a mountain of bitterness built up over the millennia.

The Accuser carried on his argument. "But this covenant maker is not merely a tyrant, he is a totalitarian puppet master who is the author of evil. What kind of creator makes earthquakes that demolish entire cities and kills the populace under mountains of rubble? Or a hurricane that drowns shiploads of sailors and devastates port cities under tsunamis of water."

It did not bother the Accuser that his comrade, the god Enki, had claimed the same powers to make the earth tremble and quake, or that Enlil claimed to be the source of hurricane storms and lightning and thunder. Consistency was not the Accuser's strong suit, emotional appeal was.

"What kind of 'loving god' allows untold thousands of poor innocent women and children to suffer the ravages of disease and poverty?"

The Accuser was an actor of the highest caliber. He actually looked as if he meant what he was saying. Tears flowed from his crocodile eyes down his glistening scaly face. He did not care a whit for women and children. He actually thought poverty and disease were good ways to keep the population from expanding to unmanageable numbers that would threaten the earth's ecosystem of life. To the Accuser, humans were in fact parasites of Mother Earth, grubworms of the Great Goddess. Disease was the Earth's balancing revenge. But that belief would not stop him from using rhetoric to appeal to the sympathies and compassion of his enemy.

"But that is only 'natural evil,'" he waxed eloquently. "What of *personal evil*?" Now his words took on the calculated righteous indignation of a politician. "What kind of god would allow the heinous evils of rape, murder, genocide, *and war*?"

Uriel snorted at the irony. At this very moment, the Accuser's ally Inanna was leading a horde of thirty thousand unholy demigods on Eden. They were planning massive rape, murder, genocide, and war.

"I submit that if Elohim is truly 'sovereign over his creation,'" the Accuser said, his words dripping with venom, "then he is responsible for all the evil that exists in the world. If he is not so sovereign, then he is an impotent deity without the authority to back up his covenant."

The Accuser took a dramatic pause, pretending he was holding back a flood of empathetic tears. Then he finished, "A covenant is supposed to be constitutional, the very bedrock of truth and justice.

This covenant is unconstitutional because its creator is a king who is a totalitarian oppressor, a cheat who makes the rules of the game to favor himself; a despotic dictator and tyrant who claims absolute ownership over creation; and worse, a genocidal emperor, who, mark my words, will soon kill everyone on earth who gets in the way of his imperialist empire!"

Enoch was stunned. He had never heard such a vile litany of invectives and hate speech against the Creator pour out of the mouth of a mere created being, except perhaps from Inanna.

The Accuser stopped abruptly and returned to the bar with a suddenly quiet and diplomatic disposition. "May the court forgive me, I forgot one thing. If I may, I would like to propose a humble suggestion. The defendant, Elohim, appears to be obsessed with transcendence and separation. Heaven is separated from earth, land is separated from waters, angel is separated from human, human from animal, male from female, and so on. With all this talk of the creator's transcendent distinction from his creation, all this *separation* and difference within creation, perhaps therein lies the problem. Separation and distinction breed hostility and fear of the 'other.' If this god would only be *one* with his creation, if all things were considered *one* instead of separated and different then maybe we might not have all the alienation and violence that such fear of *the other* creates. Of course, the Creator might know this if he actually knew what it was like to be one of his lowly creatures, to be a man rather than the omnipotent potentate of power and pious purity that he proudly preaches." He smirked. He thought his alliteration of Ps was a nice touch of poetic contempt.

He wrapped it up, "But I contemplate that would be impossible for such a 'high and mighty one,' so 'separate' and 'distinct' from his creation is he."

It was quite an explosive opener, thought Enoch, *followed by a low-key false humility that had the effect of making the audience listen intently. Like dropping your speech to a whisper after yelling.* Enoch wondered what was next, if this was just his opener. His adversary had engaged in so much fallacious rhetoric that he thought it would be quite easy to dismantle the argument and make a fool of the Accuser.

But then he thought better. He realized that he did not want to fall into the trap of emulating the fool in his folly. He decided his strategy should be to avoid matching the emotional excess. Instead, he should strip the rhetoric down to its core of absurdity with calm cool reason. Use the folly against the fool. This was, after all, a court of law where rationality served truth and justice not agenda and advocacy.

Enoch strutted before the throne. He lifted his chin high in thought. He then spoke like a scribe would speak to his students. "This Accuser has laden his argument with so much emotional invective and blind hatred that one can only wonder where he received his credentials. I am not aware of any apkallu wisdom sage on earth or in heaven who teaches insulting, appeals to pity, appeals to force, and popular sentiment, false dilemmas, slippery slopes, equivocation and question begging as actual legal strategy." *That was good,* thought Enoch. He did not hear the expected chuckles from the divine witnesses. But then again, they did follow strict rules of sobriety in trials. All his years of being an apkallu were bearing fruit in him now. It was as if it were all preparation for this moment.

He continued. "I would like to strip down the Accuser's so-called arguments to their bare essentials and address those sparsely few issues with that gem so rare among the wicked; rationality. 'Come, let us reason together,' says the Lord. And so we shall."

Enoch felt his confidence rising. He was much smoother than he had expected. The butterflies in his stomach had gone. He felt like a falcon flying pretty high, his eyes focused on his prey far below him.

"It is true," said Enoch, "that Yahweh Elohim is sovereign over his creation and therefore the covenant." He used the covenant name of God as proper protocol in the heavenly temple regarding covenant lawsuits.

He continued, "Our Creator works all things according to the counsel of his will. He makes nations great and destroys them. He brings both well-being and calamity upon cities and individuals. He has made everything for its purpose, even the wicked for the day of evil. And no purpose of his can be thwarted. In short, Yahweh Elohim is all-powerful and ordains whatsoever comes to pass. It is also true that he is an all-loving creator who cares for his creation. So if I may boil down the Accuser's argument into its simplest form, void of all its emotional hysteria and libelous insults, it would look like this --

Premise one: If Yahweh Elohim is all-powerful he could destroy evil.

Premise two: If Yahweh Elohim is all-loving he would destroy evil.

Premise three: Evil is not destroyed.

Conclusion: Yahweh Elohim is either unable or unwilling to destroy evil."

Now it was Enoch's turn to pause for dramatic effect. He milked it with relish.

"Let us dispense with this popular sentiment of ignoramuses and mental midgets. It is really very simple. There is a hidden premise in that argument that is fallacious. It *assumes* that evil will never be destroyed or put to rights. Well, who says so? Is the Accuser the god of time that he knows that evil will not be destroyed in the future? In fact, Yahweh Elohim promises to one day destroy all evil and put all things to rights. Simply because evil is not *yet* destroyed is no argument that evil will *never* be destroyed. I realize logical consistency is not a virtue to the Accuser, but it is a requirement of truth."

His train of thought completely engrossed Enoch. His words came out like fire from heaven. His pronouncements of justice rolled down like waters. He barely stopped to take a breath.

"The Accuser slanders Yahweh Elohim of being the author of evil, but *creating* evil for a purpose is not the same as *being* evil. Just because we do not know his purpose or reason for the evil he ordains in this world does not mean there can be no good purpose or reason. Our finite ignorance is not a measure of the parameters of the truth. Creaturely freedom and responsibility does not logically negate the Creator's sovereignty. Does the clay say to the potter, 'Why have you made me like this?' Shall the axe boast over him who hews with it, or the saw magnify itself against him who wields it? The Accuser complains of the Creator/creature distinction as the source of cruelty, but it is precisely the transcendent infinite God who distinguishes kindness from cruelty. If everything is one, kindness and cruelty are one and the Accuser's complaint is dismissed."

Enoch delivered the death blow. "And so I file a motion for summary judgment to dismiss this frivolous lawsuit. Amen."

Enoch sat down next to Mikael on one side, Uriel and the other archangels on the other. He felt like one of the angels himself. He drew in a deep breath. He knew that he had just won the entire trial in one fell swoop of oratory.

"You may have just lost the trial in one fell swoop of oratory," Mikael whispered to Enoch.

"Elegant delivery, apkallu," said Uriel. "That was vanity befitting of the Serpent himself. Is that what they teach you in wisdom sage school?"

Gabriel added, "Have you switched sides?"

Enoch's eyes stretched in terror. What had he done wrong? He had just made an iron clad rational case on behalf of the Creator. Or so he thought.

"Close your mouth," said Uriel.

Enoch stared at him.

"I mean literally," said Uriel. "Your mouth is hanging open like a fly catcher again."

Enoch closed his mouth. He was dumbfounded.

Then he opened it again. "But I thought I was supposed to use rigorous wisdom to dismantle the Accuser's position. I thought that is what truth is about."

"Truth is a person, not a mere proposition," said Uriel.

"So you think you fight vanity with vanity?" said Mikael. "You do not represent an idea, you represent Yahweh's character. Of which you were evidently completely oblivious as you strode about like a pompous braying ass."

"A strutting cock-a-doodle-doo," added Uriel.

Enoch's spirit dropped. His own pride, the worst sin of all, had just blindsided him. He had completely failed his God and had not even known it. Had he lost the case already?

CHAPTER 44

Methuselah found some straight saplings, cut them down and whittled a series of spears with his knife. The aim and accuracy of a spear required a finely balanced weight, which was not easy to attain with such primitive instruments. But he did his best with what he had.

So did the others. Betenos worked hard to create a bow and some arrows using one of the other knives. She wove some durable and string-like casings of a wild vegetable for the string. Lamech, who was at a loss without Rahab, created a sling and filled a pouch with perfect stones from a nearby brook. Edna took the knives when they were done and created a makeshift three blade staff weapon, an adaptation of the angelic blade she had mastered over the years. They could not kill giants with these handmade weapons, but they would not be at the mercy of lesser predators, which described most everything else.

They searched along the western wall for quite some time. They decided to make camp for the night, when Edna yelled out that she had found something.

Everyone ran to where she was. Or rather where she had been. She was nowhere to be found in the rocky area.

"Edna?" called Methuselah. "Edna, where are you?"

He began to get worried when she gave no response. They shouted urgently for her.

Methuselah came to a portion of the rock wall covered with hanging vines and other foliage. He stopped and looked back out into the forest, searching for any sign of Edna. Suddenly, a pair of hands flashed out from the hanging vines and grabbed him. They pulled him into the wall of green, as if to dissolve into the mountain face.

It was Edna. The vegetation hid a ravine just six feet wide. Edna hid within it.

"Gotcha, Poozelahpooneypoo," laughed Edna. She gave him a big fat sloppy kiss.

They had been in such danger for so long that they had not had time to show their love for one another. And when love has lived long, the connection gets deeper and richer than young lovers have any idea of.

Lamech and Betenos lay cuddling on the bank of the brook. They felt rested and at peace for the first time in a long time. He kissed her and stared into her eyes. She loved the way he would appreciate her. He would say she was a feast for all his senses: sight, sound, smell, taste, and touch. He made her feel so beautiful. Only Elohim could create such a harmonious artistry of physical and spiritual unity between man and wife.

The sound of a monstrous bellowing roar brought them to their feet. It came from the direction of the vine-covered crevice where Methuselah and Edna had been. They ran as one to the spot. They grabbed up their weapons, leaping through the vegetation into the ravine. It was a passageway through the mountain wall. They followed it.

Methuselah screamed at the top of his lungs. The roar burst over them again. It was so loud, it shook their insides.

How big was this thing? thought Lamech as they ran toward the sound. They knew their patriarch was in trouble.

They burst through the other side and found themselves in the mountain territory just outside the secret valley.

Methuselah knelt on the ground, cradling Edna, covered in blood, weeping.

Mere cubits away, a gigantic creature the height of a huge temple building staggered around. It tried to shake a javelin from its eye. It stood upright on its hind legs, though Lamech was not sure that was its natural posture. It had a tail the size of a cedar tree, bulging muscles on bones of iron, and teeth like iron swords. Its head looked like a hideous reptilian bull. It was some kind of amphibious dragon. It roared again and came down on all fours, revealing a deformed hump on its back. It turned to lunge at Methuselah and Edna.

"Father!" screamed Lamech.

Methuselah did nothing. He just held his beloved in his arms.

Immediately, Lamech and Betenos raised their weapons. Betenos launched an arrow at the great beast. Her makeshift arrow hit it in the face near the javelin. Lamech's stone broke one of its teeth with a loud cracking sound.

It roared again. They realized they were only making it angrier.

Lamech and Betenos ran to Methuselah. They dragged the patriarch and Edna's limp, bleeding body back into the covered ravine opening.

The colossus shook the javelin loose and launched after them. It snapped at their feet as they cleared the entrance into the ravine. But it was too large to fit through the opening.

Betenos launched one last arrow into the beast's mouth. It buried itself in the creature's tongue. It roared with rage and actually tried to force its way through the crack of the mountain.

Lamech felt the very mountain shake. Rocks fell loose and the earth quaked. But the colossus could not get through.

They carried Edna back into the safety of the crater basin. Betenos ran to get whatever healing roots she could find. Edna had been bitten by the monster. Her life was bleeding out of her.

Lamech tried to compress the wounds where the teeth had penetrated Edna's body, but there were too many punctures and they were too deep.

Methuselah knew it was time. She gazed up into his eyes. She managed a slight smile of love. She was in more pain than he could imagine, and she could still smile in the face of the only man she ever knew. She tried to say something. Her lungs were punctured. He leaned in close, putting his ear to her lips.

"I — will — see you in time, my be-beloved." Every word was painful and prophetic. "Enoch's m-mantle is now — yours. Our son — m-must live."

And Edna breathed her last.

Methuselah wailed. It echoed across the valley like a ghostly hound. It made Lamech think of the very beast they just escaped.

Betenos came back from the forest in resignation. She knew it was over.

The three of them lay over Edna's body and wept. Wife, mother, servant of Elohim, she was now with her Creator.

They buried her body near a large terebinth tree by the brook. Terebinth were sacred trees that were considered places of communion with deity. Edna had been a conduit of communion with Elohim for Methuselah. She was the most powerful proof of God's presence and goodness to him. Through her he came to understand grace, goodness, strength, perseverance, and a faith that he did not have in himself. She had been both submissive wife and godly inspiration to him, his perfect *ezer*. He would never have known happiness but for her. He would never know happiness again without her.

They laid the stones upon the resting place as a memorial, and prayed to Elohim, and wept and sang songs of hope. Then they ate a meal together.

Late night drew over them. And still they sat in silent memories.

Betenos looked up at the full moon. She sat close to Lamech with silent empathy. He labored to fix the triple blade weapon his mother had made. It had been damaged in the attack. Lamech's eyes were red from hours of painful recollections of his mother. The joys, the happiness, the hard work and discipline of family. He could not understand why Elohim would allow such a seemingly random thing as her death, after all they had been through. He had started to think they were invincible, God's chosen ones. That nothing would stop their righteous cause. Now, his pride crashed down in humble brokenness. He did not know what he believed. *Would Elohim allow us to get this far, only to snatch our lives one by one, never to be found or remembered in this uninhabited godforsaken mockery of paradise?*

Methuselah stared into the fire with dead eyes. He could not feel anymore. His soul was gone. He wanted to run out and attack the cyclopean monster without concern for his survival. Suicide. But Edna's words haunted him. He was to take over Enoch's mantle, now that Enoch was gone? Lamech was to be Elohim's chosen lineage for the One who would end the rule of the gods? What was all that to him now? He just did not care. He did not want to live.

But how to end it? he thought.

A twig snapped.

Instinct flooded back into them all. They were on their feet in seconds, with weapons drawn.

A single man walked out of the darkness into the flickering light of the fire. Tall, muscular, and young-looking, his eyes betrayed a great age. Beside him trod a large black she-wolf.

"I see you have met Behemoth outside the valley walls. I think your wailing was about as loud as his. Made it easy to find you."

Methuselah gripped a spear, ready to lunge. Betenos pulled on the string of her bow with nocked arrow ready. Lamech gripped the triple blade Edna had made.

The black she-wolf snarled at them.

"Is that any way to treat family?" said the stranger. "I let you bury your dead and get your bellies full." His delivery was ominous. He had a darkness in him that reminded Methuselah of Inanna.

"Who are you?" demanded Methuselah. "What do you mean, 'family'?"

Twenty large wolves stepped out from the bush surrounding them. They appeared to be a pack of predators controlled by this stranger before them.

When the stranger spoke again, Methuselah's blood ran cold.

"I am Cain, son of Adam."

CHAPTER 45

The trial reconvened before the Supreme Judge of the Universe. The Accuser took his place to mount his next attack on the Covenant.

"In your historical prologue, there is prattling on and on about the 'generations of the heavens and the earth,' etcetera, etcetera. And then we come to your creation of Man, 'in the image of God you did create him, both male and female.' I would like to address two aspects of this 'image': First, authority and hierarchy, and then this imperialist mandate of 'dominion.'"

Semjaza approached the Accuser and whispered in his ear.

He was updating the prosecutor on the progress of Inanna's forces. Enoch knew this already. Everyone on the defense knew it. Yahweh Elohim was not some kind of idiot finite deity who did not know what was going on in his creation. The mere fact that he chose to accomplish his purposes through such secondary means as the divine council and the freedom of his creatures did not bother Enoch anymore.

There were many mysteries of the infinite eternal Creator that faded away in the minds of finite mortal creations in his immediate presence. Enoch smiled to himself at all the energy he had spent on earth fretting as an apkallu sage, seeking the ever elusive dream of absolute knowledge and wisdom. It was an endless pursuit of always getting closer and never arriving. No matter how wise he could be, no matter how much knowledge he possessed, the universe and everything in it was so far beyond the limits of his understanding as a tiny little object embedded within that creation that he could not hope to achieve god-like status of observation and understanding. *It was certainly not a waste of life to pursue such wisdom,* he thought. *But perhaps it was a sign of the true fallenness of our nature that we would twist our calling as Yahweh Elohim's images into an intent to become Elohim, demanding all truths be made sufficiently understandable to our puny finite faulty understanding.*

The Accuser's rant brought Enoch back into the present.

"This notion of authority and hierarchy in the covenant is quite incoherent to me. On the one hand, Elohim tells us both male and female are created alike to be his imagers or representations of his rulership on earth. And then on the other, he contradicts himself when he gives the vocation to the Man to work and keep the Garden before he even creates the woman! Imagine that! A 'men's only' club. No women allowed. How sexist can you be? Then Elohim creates the Woman out of the Man's side and tells her she is to be man's 'helper fit for him,' like some kind of slave. The Man 'names' the woman, and we all know what that means: The namer has the power over the object being named. My dear Creator, this is all about power. Not truth, not justice, and not love. But I will speak the truth to power! I would think that if one were a loving god, one would make everyone equal in race, class, and gender; not this misogynist Patriarchal justification of male domination over women."

Enoch thought of the "truth, justice, and love" that the Watchers had been giving to the women they were using to breed the

Nephilim. It was not the first time the Accuser used his own wicked behavior as an argument against his Creator.

"But I will make one concession to your majestic power," said the Accuser. "You are consistent. That is, your unfair gender favoritism of the male is a reflection of your own bias as male and your sexist creation of angels as males. It is quite clear to me, 'father,' that you and all your 'Sons of God' are afraid of women. You oppress the female gender and enslave them to be breeders and deny them their rightful place in this world. I think you are secretly suppressing the fact that the true creator of this world is not the male Sky God, but the Great Earth Goddess!"

The myriads of holy ones broke out in shocked murmuring. Whispers of "blasphemy" abounded. The grace of Yahweh Elohim in not smiting the Accuser on the spot amazed Enoch. Elohim had his greater purposes.

"And that brings me to my second point," said the Accuser. "Your covenant charge to Man to take dominion over all creation and to subdue it to his interests is just another facet of your suppression of the Great Goddess. You would have man trample, burn, and destroy the environment that the Earth Mother gives him, as an expression of your macho excess!"

He quoted the words of Elohim back to him with incredulity, "'Elohim made the greater light to rule the day and the lesser light to rule the night? And the stars in the firmament for signs and seasons and for days and years'? Where is the sun god and the moon god? And are not the stars a heavenly host of deities? You want to divest the universe of spirits and gods so that you can reign supreme as a jealous autocratic Emperor! You want to turn the cosmos into some 'soulless' natural order so that your little male minions can trample the environment, spoil the creation, and engage in cruelty to animals!"

The Accuser turned to the heavenly host with excessive theatrics, "Elohim is not fair and equal in his dealings with his creatures, he is a sexist and a speciesist!"

Enoch almost laughed out loud. The absurd lengths to which the Accuser would go to construct a delusive opinion to suit his purposes amazed the human. He wondered if anyone would ever actually believe this combination of insanity and iniquity. Ironically, he could see where the Accuser was going with it, and it was truly evil. He would make sure to address it in his rebuttal.

The Accuser ended with a rising plea. "Does your unfair favoritism and partiality know no bounds, Elohim? You choose who rules over whom, who is forgiven and who is not, you elect one man over another to carry your purposes forward. These are not the actions of a fair and impartial Creator, these are the actions of — dare I say it again — a tyrant and puppet master! But of course, if the sandal fits, wear it. Your honor. Amen." The Accuser bowed and went back to his team of Watchers.

Enoch stood and approached the throne. "Your honor." He turned to the heavenly host, "divine witnesses of the court. I want to apologize for my previous display of pride. It was unworthy and unbefitting an ambassador of Yahweh Elohim and a defender of the throne. I hope to address the Accuser's further slanderous lies with a more respectful demeanor. Amen."

Enoch began his formal presentation. "In the first place, regarding the Accuser's complaint of the imago dei and authority, I think this gets to the heart of the argument. The Accuser does not seem to like the order of things, the hierarchy of one over another, the notion of authority. He wants everything to be 'equal.' But I must ask this question, 'By what standard?' Whose definition of equal? If by the standard of the Creator, then that begs the question.

The Creator has the right to define authority and justice in any way he deems proper. If by the Accuser's standard, why? Why should anyone listen to the Accuser's definition of what is just and what is not? I would prefer my own definition over the Accuser's, and you would prefer your own definition over mine. It is an endless trap of infinite definitions and authorities that cancel out the Accuser's own accusations."

Enoch took a breath. He let it sink in. This time, he would make his arguments with more concern for the hearers. "I would like to address each one of his accusations to show that they are straw men that do not even apply to Yahweh Elohim. But I do not even have to, because his claims are simply pitting his own finite ignorant authority against the self-authorized infinite Creator of all authority. The Accuser pronounces, 'sexism, imperialism, misogyny, speciesism' and a plethora of other 'isms.' But by the Creator's standards the Accuser is sexist, imperialist, misandrist, and speciesist because he is seeking to define the created order from his own subjective, arbitrary, and finite viewpoint. This is sheer bigotry and hubris on the Accuser's part. A creature is trying to subject the Creator to his own authority."

Enoch shook his head and continued, "Since the Accuser seems to want to claim to be the creator of the standards of truth and justice, and not be beholden to a standard outside himself, then I would like a few answers from him. I would like him to gird up his loins and make known to us where he was when Yahweh Elohim laid the foundations of the earth. I wonder if he might tell us who determined its measurements and who laid its cornerstone. It would please the court if the Accuser would tell us who poured the sea, who commands the morning and evening, who crafted the gates of Sheol and dug the pits of Tartarus, who created thunder and lightning and rain, who bound the chains of the stars of the Seven

Sisters or loosed the star-cords of the Shepherd of Anu? Perhaps the Accuser might show us how he gave the horse his strength or the hawk his wings. Shall a faultfinder contend with the Almighty? He who argues with God, let him answer it. Otherwise, may he forever hold his peace."

Enoch almost sat down, but he reconsidered. "If it please the court, I said I did not need to address the Accuser's straw men accusations. But I just wanted to get something on the record. Abuse of authority does not disprove proper use of that authority. Man was not called by Yahweh Elohim to be a slave master over woman, as the Accuser argued, but to be her loving sacrificial leader. Yahweh Elohim never told man to 'trample, burn and destroy' his environment. To exercise dominion over nature, yes. And if man fails to harness the natural world, all life on the earth will succumb to chaos, disease, and destruction. But man was also commissioned to 'care for and keep' that world with responsible stewardship. It is not the *'undeifying'* of nature that leads to exploitation and hurt, it is the *deifying* of nature that does. For when the sun, moon, stars, lightning, storm and disease are gods, that is when man worships the creation in place of the Creator and death reigns."

That felt more satisfying to Enoch. He had to get that off his chest, even if it was not technically necessary. He concluded, "But there are some things I think we should all trample, burn, and destroy, and those are the Accuser's straw man arguments."

Enoch sat down.

CHAPTER 46

Methuselah, Lamech, and Betenos awakened to the smell of stew cooking on morning fires. The sun had not yet come up, but they could see by the sky that it was near. They were bound together hand and foot with vines used as rope. Cain and his pack of wolves had taken them hostage the previous night, and brought them to this camp on the far side of the valley, distant from the exit crevice.

They looked around for the wolves, but the animals were gone. The Cainites were a clan of about a hundred, male and female, all wearing animal skins — but no children.

Where were the children? thought Betenos. *What kind of tribe does not have children? How could it survive?*

Cain approached them with a woman by his side, tall, with raven black hair and chiseled facial features. She had the presence of a warrior, but dressed as a tribal queen. She carried a pot of stew for them.

"This is my favorite sister and wife, Awan," said Cain. "Welcome to 'the Hidden Valley', my 'Garden away from the Garden,' I like to say. I have always had a green thumb. So I put it to good use."

Lamech remembered from stories that Cain was a worker of the ground. This secret paradise was a breathtaking incarnation of God-given skill.

Awan undid their bindings. She gave them utensils to eat some stew from the large pot. Lamech and Betenos attacked it hungrily.

Methuselah did not bother. He stared into oblivion. Why eat? It would only keep him alive.

Cain said, "The giant twins brought you to me."

Methuselah showed no interest in this conversation.

It was Lamech who spoke. "You sent Ohyah and Hahyah?"

"I paid them a bounty to find you," said Cain. "I think you understand that concept well enough."

Cain lingered over regretful memories. "I have been wandering for too long in search of you, my vengeance."

"Us?" asked Lamech.

Cain answered, "I was not even sure you were the ones I was looking for. But when Ohyah told me of his dreams and his meeting with Enoch, I knew. I knew that you were the lineage of the chosen seed of Eve that would crush the seed of the Serpent."

Lamech broke out in a cold sweat. He had an idea where this was going and did not want to find out.

Awan watched the three of them like a wolf watching its prey.

Cain continued, "Elohim is a sadistic connoisseur of cruelty. He is an arbitrary dictator. He accepts one offering and rejects another. And why? I gave him the fruit of my gifts that *he* gave me. But it was not good enough for him. He wanted it his way or no way. He wanted a blood sacrifice."

A bitter pause hung in the air. Then Cain gave a savory grin. "So I gave him one: The blood of my brother. The vengeful petty deity cursed me and made me a creature of the night — with an eternal thirst for blood. I cursed him back and decided to create my own Eden with my own rules, and my own god: me." A big proud smile cracked his lips.

Lamech and Betenos shivered. They felt as if they were staring into the face of sin itself, crouching at their feet, ready to pounce.

"At this very moment," Cain added, "a gargantuan horde of Nephilim warriors marches on Eden to take possession of the Tree of Life." He paused. "Imagine a world of true equality, where all men are gods, all creatures divine, everyone lives forever."

Where evil never dies, Lamech thought to himself. He knew what such claims to "equality" without God led to: genocide by those who ruled in the name of equality. They never shared their power once they had it. The first to taste of the Tree of Life would turn and keep it from everyone else.

"Imagine the absolute freedom from all dependence on a cosmic child abuser who tells us what we can and cannot do."

And I thought it did not get worse than Inanna, mused Lamech.

Methuselah remained in his trance of self-pity. He listened, but still did not care.

Cain concluded his pontificating, "And in the meantime, I will have the ultimate revenge of absorbing the very life and lineage of Elohim's Chosen Seed into my own body, when I drink your blood."

A shiver of terror went down the spines of Lamech and Betenos. Now they understood why Cain looked more like one hundred years old, instead of his eight hundred and fifty years. He cannibalized the life source of his victims, their blood replenishing his youth, regenerating his body. Lamech glanced at his father, who now watched their captors. Those captors were not interested in Methuselah, they were interested in Lamech.

"The sun is rising," said Cain. "I must retreat to my residence for rest. Awan will care for you until the evening, when I rise — for dinner." He smiled and walked away, leaving Awan watching them with a smirk on her face.

She shoved the pot at Methuselah. "Eat up, old man, we need you plump."

Methuselah did nothing. Awan dropped the pot at his feet. Some of it splashed on Methuselah, and still he did not react.

Awan left them alone with the last of the food.

Lamech studied Methuselah. "Father, you are not the only one who lost mother."

Methuselah remained unmoved. They had been sitting there for some time and Methuselah had offered no plan, no hint or desire to escape. He waited to die. His meaning, his Edna was gone. And with her, the heavens and the earth.

Lamech spoke sharply with renewed conviction. "You may want to die. You may not care what happens to the rest of the world. But I do. This is bigger than my life, than all of our lives. If grandfather Enoch prophesied the truth and Betenos and I are the lineage of the Seed, then why would you give up? Would you dishonor the faith of the one you loved most on this earth?"

That got through Methuselah's wall of silence. Lamech was right. His son was absolutely right. Methuselah had placed his faith in this world and not in Elohim's promised world to come. He had relied on his senses for so long that he had worn them out. He had lost his taste, his smell, his touch; he had become blind, deaf and dumb. He had neglected prayer because Elohim seemed so distant and his prayers almost futile. He had come to believe that things got done because he got up and did them, not because of Elohim's solicited favor. Since Elohim was going to do what he was going to do anyway, then why bother wasting time talking to him about it? He had become a self-made man who lifted himself up by his own sandal straps. And it was all a self-deluded lie. He had missed the whole point that his wife had been trying to tell him: he distrusted Elohim because of the betrayal of the gods. He had lived a life of self-reliance rather than a life of faith. He had sought desperately for significance in this world. But he now understood his significance would be as the protector of Elohim's Seed, not the fulfiller of his own.

Methuselah lifted his face to Lamech. His eyes were red with tears, his face flush with revelation. Everything in Methuselah's life came clear in that one instant.

Methuselah took the pot of stew and ate like a hungry dog. He would need his strength.

CHAPTER 47

She had done it. Inanna had pushed her warrior horde at an unprecedented pace. In three days, they had gone over one hundred and thirty leagues, an unrivaled achievement of Nephilim endurance. However, her glorious fortitude had taken its toll.

"We must slow down, Inanna," Enki complained in their command tent. "We have lost two thousand warriors to exhaustion and dehydration."

"They were the weakest," said Inanna. "More food for the strong."

Utu jumped in. "The numbers of deaths will rise exponentially if we continue at this rate. Even Nephilim have their limits, and we are perilously close to it."

They were within sixty-five leagues of Lake Urimiya, on the west perimeter of the Garden.

"We will be at our destination in one more day," she said.

It shocked Enki. "Are you out of your mind? You want to take the last sixty-five leagues in *one day*?!"

Inanna's eyes narrowed like a dragon about to strike. "Are you challenging my authority, General Enki?"

Enki backed down. Insubordination was punished by binding in the earth, a fate worse than death for a Watcher.

He softened his argument. "It will do us no good if we make it to Eden in record time, with a demoralized and exhausted army at a fraction of their fighting strength. It is suicide."

"For Anu's sake," said Utu, "at least give the soldiers a half-day's extra rest." They were within minutes of trumpet's call to march.

Inanna stared at them with incredulity.

Utu clapped his hands. The eleven Rephaim generals entered the tent and stood to attention. Thamaq and the limping Yahipan were among them.

Utu ordered them, "Report on the morale."

Thamaq said, "My lord, there are whisperings of mutiny in some quarters."

Inanna thought about it. She strode past the Rephaim. She spotted Yahipan with recognition. "Hobbler here is keeping up, why cannot everyone else?"

Yahipan gritted his teeth. On the one hand, his handicap was singled out again, but on the other hand, he clearly impressed Inanna. Now, if he could only find another way to shine like a star.

"Give the horde an extra hour of sleep," said Inanna.

She thought to herself, *Am I being too weak?*

"We need to be to Lake Urimiya by nightfall tomorrow. Then they can have a few day's rest before battle."

"Yes, Queen of heaven," said Utu. He raced outside to make sure the trumpet call would be delayed.

"And for my sake," said Inanna, "track down these mutinous whisperers and execute them."

Yahipan saw his opportunity and stepped forward. "Yes, Supreme Commander. I will rout them out before sunrise."

Inanna stopped her pacing and noticed Yahipan again. She turned to the other Rephaim. "You see this will? If the rest of you had half the will of this invalid, we would be unstoppable."

Yahipan bowed and left the tent on his mission. He wondered whether her comments would raise him up or keep him singled out as pitiful.

Inanna had no intention of giving the Nephilim a few days rest when they arrived. They would need a full day just to build their pontoons for crossing the lake. She would throw numbers at the enemy to overwhelm them. Tens of thousands of weakened Nephilim were still too many for the Cherubim to withstand. Nephilim were expendable and Cherubim were not invulnerable.

She knew the Cherubim well, their strengths, their weaknesses, and their numbers. Only several hundred of them guarded the Garden. She would split her forces. The Western army would build pontoons as the Southern army travelled around the shore to mount a flank attack from the mountainous region in the south.

The Garden was walled by the Savalan mountain range in the north, the Sahand in the south, and by the huge Lake Urimiya on the west. The only opening into the valley lay in the East, where the Cherubim forces stood guard. When they discovered the Nephilim army arriving on the lake, they would split their forces between east and west. They would not be expecting a flanking attack from the mountainous southern region. The huge volcanic chain of the Sahand was precipitous to climb and therefore an unexpected entry point for a raid.

The Cherubim were not experienced in fighting angelic/human hybrids. Humans they could slaughter easily enough with their flaming whirling swords, but Nephilim were a crossbreed. The forces needed to combat the angelic half of the Nephilim were the angels who were now busily held up in heavenly legal procedures.

The Nephilim would have to rise to the occasion. Inanna did not know how much longer the Accuser could keep the heavenly council embroiled in his lawsuit. It was a diversion made in heaven. God and all his heavenly host, because of their despicable dedication to righteousness would give their full attention and presence to due process of law. In doing so, they would not be available to defend the Garden when it was attacked. She had split the enemy's forces and cut them off from their Commander in Chief, that loathsome tyrant from above.

She thought of cutting in half the extra hour she gave the Nephilim to sleep. Beneficence was one of the demands on deity she detested.

CHAPTER 48

Lamech and Betenos had prayed for Elohim to deliver them. Awan and several villagers watched them like guard dogs the entire day. They fed them well. Methuselah considered that a mistake, because regardless of how "plumped up" Cain thought they were, they were also renewed in their strength and readied in their resolve to fight back if they had a chance.

Methuselah watched the sun go down. He asked Awan, "Where is the wolf pack that accompanied Cain in our capture? I have not seen them in the camp."

"They only come out at night," said Awan, with a hint of dark delight.

Betenos wondered whether Cain planned on sharing his meal with those canine allies.

Awan watched Betenos with a cocked head, trying to read her lips moving in prayer.

"Where is your god?" said Awan.

Betenos stared back without fear. "He is in the heavens and he does as he pleases."

"He does not appear to be very capable of rescuing you," said Awan.

"Our God is able to deliver us," said Betenos. "But even if he does not, we do not fear you who can destroy the body, but rather Him who can destroy both body and soul in Sheol."

"My god will consume your body and soul," said Awan. "So I doubt there will be anything left over for yours."

They turned to see Cain walking toward them in the darkness, like a phantom.

Awan said, "Here comes my god, now." She and the other guards got up and left the captives alone with Cain.

"How goes the seed of Eve?" asked Cain with a lighthearted tone of irony. "I had a good day's sleep, and I am famished."

Methuselah glanced at Lamech and Betenos. There was no way he would let anything happen to his son and daughter-in-law. But the only problem was that he was entirely at the mercy of this monster. He was in no position to save anyone.

The silhouette of an Anzu bird suddenly fell across the bright blood red moon. It came right toward them. It landed in the village which now looked strangely empty of people. It had become a ghost village.

Where had all the people gone? wondered Methuselah.

Cain turned to see the thunderbird and whistled.

From out of the darkness came six very large wolves. The raven-black she-wolf came up to Cain. He gave it a look that Methuselah saw was more than master or owner. Then Cain went to meet the Anzu bird in the distance.

The wolves circled the captives and watched them with hungry attention.

Methuselah looked into the eyes of the black she-wolf. In that moment, he knew where all the people had gone. Those were the eyes of Awan, the black-haired wife of Cain. *These wolves must be the human villagers transformed into canine beasts of the night.* It started to make sense. Awan's allusions, the disappearing wolves and now the disappearing villagers.

Methuselah glanced at Lamech and Betenos. They appeared to have had the same revelation.

Lamech whispered, "What black art is this? Does Cain know the secrets of the Watchers as well?"

The She-wolf growled menacingly and stepped closer to Lamech. He promptly shut up.

Cain came back to them. He spoke hastily, "I have some important business to attend to. I am afraid I will be gone for the evening."

The wolves looked up at him as if they understood his every word. He turned to Methuselah.

"Do not worry, they will not be eating you tonight." Then Cain ran back to the Anzu bird. He climbed on it and it flew off like a bat out of Sheol.

The wolves turned their attention back to the hostages and stood watch as sentinels.

Lamech hoped Cain was not exaggerating with that last remark about not being eaten tonight.

Betenos was not as certain that these voracious carnivores would be able to exercise such self-control until their master got back.

Methuselah had seen real concern on Cain's face after he had received the correspondence attached to the Anzu bird. Something was not going right with Cain's plans, and that gave Methuselah just the edge he had been praying for.

He had begun praying again.

CHAPTER 49

The heavenly court reconvened for the Accuser's litigation against the third part of God's covenant with humanity. He took the bar and spoke with the particular disdain he had for rules.

"Ethical stipulations," he said. "The laws required by the suzerain of the subject if he is to maintain his status as protected vassal before his lord."

The Accuser launched into a new diatribe. "In this most primitive of law codes in the Garden, Havah was told by Elohim, and I quote, "You may surely eat of every tree of the garden, but of the tree of knowledge you shall not eat, neither shall you touch it, for in the day that you eat of it you shall surely die.'"

The Accuser paced around shaking his head with ridicule. "We will have much to say about this curse of death in our fourth complaint. But for now, we would like to focus on this silly demand that humankind stay mired in unenlightened ignorance by submission to an impossible command. I ask the court, did Elohim *actually* say this? Could his childish motives be any more obvious?"

"Now, I have said this before, and I will say it again, this whole thing is a set-up by a god who is spiteful, mean, obsessively jealous, and self-protective. He wanted to keep humanity from becoming like us — *from becoming gods*. Elohim must have known that knowledge would allow man to control his own life and to discover all the secrets of the universe, and well, we just cannot allow that kind of competition, can we?"

The Accuser paused for effect. His cohorts smiled at the progress, but the heavenly host sat unmoved. He delivered his conclusion, "I submit to you that Elohim's covenant is not the legal treaty of a master protecting his servant, it is the declaration of a monomaniac oppressing his servant, and protecting himself from being outdone by his own creation!"

The Accuser sat down.

Enoch stood. He carried with him a tablet and dove right into his rebuttal. "The testimony we have just heard from the Accuser has several half-truths in it, or as I would more accurately define them, *lies*."

Enoch read from the clay tablet in his hand. "Yahweh Elohim did not say that the couple could not *touch* the tree, he said that they could not *eat of it*. That is an exaggeration of the command to make the Creator appear excessive and overbearing. Secondly, it was not 'the tree of knowledge' that was forbidden, it was the 'tree of the knowledge *of good and evil*.' Yahweh Elohim was not forbidding knowledge to humanity, he was commanding reliance upon him as their ultimate authority to define good and evil. And we are right back to ultimate authorities that I spoke of earlier. Yahweh Elohim is the only ground of morality that can justify the Accuser's own attack on morality."

Enoch paused for a moment in thought, then said, "It would not surprise me if one day, the serpent will have effectively convinced the masses with more of these kinds of distortions. I can imagine him twisting the 'forbidden fruit' into *sex*, and turning Yahweh

Elohim into a cosmic killjoy prude who just wants to keep people from having fun."

Enoch launched into his conclusion, "No, the forbidden fruit is the essence of freedom. The Accuser would have us believe that boundaries of protection are actually restrictions of oppression; that rules repress human potential and laws take away freedom. He and his Watchers argue that freedom is the ability to do whatever one wants without an external code imposed upon them. Let each man be a law unto himself. Yet, look around the earth below to see the consequences of such ideas. Humans have achieved the self-determination from the knowledge of good and evil and in so doing have become slaves to their own appetites. Prisoners of their desire. They claim to be free, but they are everywhere in chains of their own making. Only in the boundaries of a loving Creator can humanity be free. Is a fish out of the water free? Is a bird out of the sky free? Only in fulfilling our god-given purpose can mankind experience the liberty of obedience. Disobedience is not enlightenment, it is pure blindness; it is not freedom, it is slavery."

Enoch stood for a moment as his words sank into his own soul. He realized that he had fought God's purpose for himself so many years — that he prayed when he should have fought, fought when he should have prayed, and too often exhibited the ultimate sin of spiritual pride.

Enoch fell to his knees and wept in repentance before Yahweh Elohim.

CHAPTER 50

In the early morning, the Nephilim horde arrived at their beachhead destination in the mountains on the edge of the vast Lake Urimiya. Inanna allowed them a few hours rest. Utu had been wrong. They did not lose exponential numbers of warriors in the final push toward Aratta. They only lost five thousand total weaklings to the extreme running march. That left her with about twenty five thousand Nephilim fit warriors, plenty of fodder to accomplish her goal.

She employed thirteen thousand in cutting down trees and building pontoon rafts to cross the great lake. The other twelve thousand, she sent thirty leagues around the lake to the volcanic fields of Sahand. They prepared to climb the rocky face of the mountain for an incursion on the south of the Garden simultaneous with the amphibious landing in the west. Their attack would launch at midnight when the moon was high in the sky, allowing them enough darkness for cover, enough light for battle.

She noticed that some of the trees had been carved and used to impale a host of about twenty Nephilim in the sight of all. These were the "mutinous whisperers" that Hobbler had hunted down and punished. It was a pathetic indication that a cripple could be more loyal than the other Rephaim generals who seemed to prefer ordering others around.

The undead Cain arrived the night before on an Anzu bird. Ohyah and Hahyah had heard through their officers that Inanna did not know exactly where the Tree of Life was located in the Garden, having only rumors and legends to go by. The twin giants had relayed to the goddess their connection with the Cursed One. They were allowed to send one of their thunderbirds to fetch him. Cain's knowledge from his parents of the Garden and the location of the Tree of Life could be just the information she needed to strike with a more accurate ferociousness.

Because of his well-known reputation, Cain was awarded admission to the presence of the goddess and her Rephaim generals. Inanna knew that any enemy of Elohim was an ally of hers.

But Cain brought with him another idea that would prove of inestimable value for her. The rock face of the Sahand on the interior of the Garden was precipitous. The sheer cliffs would severely impede the attackers' ability to attack with swift surprise.

Cain shared with Inanna an invention he had developed to traverse the heights of his own mountainous paradise. By sewing together cloths and animal skins into large "sails" five times the size of an individual, they could create a traveling source for each individual warrior. When grasped through some ropes the skins would allow them to jump from the great height and "sail" a pocket of wind down quickly and safely. It would delay them a few hours to construct these "sail chutes," but it was an ingenious invention.

They buried Cain in the ground according to his request, to avoid the light of day that was dawning on them. If exposed to the sun, he would burn up into ashes as a consequence of his curse. At nightfall, he would be allowed to return to his Hidden Valley on one of the Anzu birds. It was a great loss to give up one of their six

271

thunderbirds, for they were crucial to their air strike, but it was worth it to Inanna. Cain's information might actually help them win the war on Eden. She could use this Cursed One in her new administration — or kill him as a potential usurper.

Inanna performed a valuable service to her cause by apologizing to the troops.

She gathered the horde to speak to them before their Rephaim leaders set out. They assembled around the clear-cut tree stumps. She spoke to them with her amplified voice of divinity.

"Children of the Watchers, progeny of the gods! If ever you listened to me, give ear to me now, I plead with you. First, I beg your indulgence. I know I have pushed each and every one of you beyond what any god has ever asked of their servants. I know that you are hungry, exhausted, and strained to your limit. I know that many have paid the price with their lives. And for that my heart bleeds. I feel your pain. The life of one warrior is the life of all."

A low base rumbling chant of agreement interrupted her. It was the horde's way of uniting in morale. The thought flitted through her mind that perhaps she had finally become Anu's equal. His oratory was impressive, but she doubted he could inspire as she was now doing.

She continued, "But today marks an achievement unheard of in the annals of history. And you, my horde, are the titans who have risen to prove your worth of becoming gods!"

The horde rumbled again in affirmation.

"We are on the verge of a war the likes of which will change the world forever. And we are the agents of change. We are the ones we have been waiting for. We are the change that we seek."

She paused again for dramatic effect. And she received it. The ground vibrated from the noise of the Nephilim.

"We are about to occupy the Garden of the mountain of God. This god, who was born with a golden spoon in his mouth, this deity who claims to own everything and leaves nothing for the ninety-nine percent of the rest of us, we are about to show him who is god!"

She paused for another moment of rumbling before finishing.

"You are about to storm a fortress guarded by mighty Cherubim. I know you are exhausted. I know you have been worked to the bone. I know you barely have anything left to give to this campaign because you have given all you have and more. But I ask you this one thing. When you are crossing the lake, when you are climbing the rocks, when you hear the horns of war bid you attack, when you find yourself battling the evil Cherubim, when you have reached the end of your strength and have nothing left to fight with, just remember one thing: tomorrow you will taste of the Tree of Life and you will be gods, and you will tire no longer -- for you shall live forever!"

The horde rumbled yet again. They caught the spirit of the moment. She knew no amount of exhaustion could quench their strength in the light of that hope. And she was proud of her ability to lie through her fangs with every single word she spoke.

CHAPTER 51

Methuselah woke. He looked around with curiosity, squinting at the morning light. Their sentinel wolves were gone. The people of the village were also gone. Methuselah, Lamech, and Betenos had been left all alone. It did not fit with the way they had been treated up until that moment. He tried to figure out what trick was being played on them. Did they want their prey to escape? To hunt them down like rabbits, to make the feast more enjoyable?

Methuselah's searching gaze passed over the bush next to him.

Uriel the archangel stood there.

"What are you doing here?" asked Methuselah. Lamech and Betenos jerked their heads up to see Uriel step out in front of them.

"You sound disappointed," said Uriel. "Would you rather I leave?"

"Praise Elohim," said Betenos. "I knew he heard our prayers."

"Great. But are you not here to miraculously free us?" said Methuselah.

"Oh no," said Uriel. "I was sent to encourage you. Be strong and courageous, mighty warriors of God, for Elohim hears your prayers and will help you to endure."

"Wait a minute," said Methuselah. "What kind of angel shares words of encouragement but does not help us out of our bonds?"

"What, do you expect Elohim to do everything for you?" said Uriel. "While you sit and do nothing?"

The three of them could not believe what they were hearing.

Uriel said, "I just emptied the village for you! How many more miracles do you want? Respond with some faith will you?" Then Uriel walked away into the jungle.

He stopped and turned back for one last comment.

"A word to the sage, lower your demands on Elohim. He does not owe you a thing. You are blessed that he gives you anything at all." And then he vanished into the foliage.

Methuselah watched him leave with utter incredulity.

"The gall of that archangel," said Methuselah.

Lamech retorted, "He is right, father."

Methuselah and Betenos turned to look at Lamech. He stood with his bonds cut loose and a knife in his hand.

"I was fixing mother's makeshift weapon when we were caught the other night. I could not pull it out while they were watching over us like — wolves."

Methuselah sighed. "Well, cut us loose, and let us get out of this godforsaken place. If I catch that archangel, I am going to give him a piece of my javelin."

Lamech cut the vines. They darted into the jungle, wondering where in the valley the village wolf-men were.

They reached the narrow ravine exit covered with vines and found their way through to the other end. They knew something waited for them there, something huge and monstrous.

Methuselah stopped Lamech and Betenos. "Stay here, I will be right back."

Methuselah stepped out into the open and started screaming at the top of his lungs, "Over here, you son of iniquity! Come and get me!"

Lamech and Betenos looked at each other with shock. What was he doing? They heard the loud bellowing roar of Behemoth reverberate across the rocks.

Methuselah ran full tilt back to their exit. Behemoth raced after him, lunging and snapping for flesh.

They fell back as Methuselah dove into the narrow opening just out of reach of the snapping jaws. Behemoth belched out another roar that could be heard across the entire Hidden Valley. It scraped furiously at the rock, trying to get through.

Methuselah stood with his finger pointing at the beast as if it would understand him. "One day," he declared, "I am coming back, and I am going to slaughter you and turn you into a feast for the vultures, for what you did, you instrument of evil."

Behemoth backed up a step and roared again. Lamech swore to himself that the creature almost looked and sounded as if it had a tinge of fear.

Methuselah turned and walked back toward the Hidden Valley interior.

Lamech yelled after him, "Hey, wait a minute, father, what are you doing?"

Betenos joined in, "You just made it impossible for us to escape."

"I do not want to escape," said Methuselah. "I want to make the wolf tribe *think* we escaped."

Betenos blurted out, "Whatever for?"

Methuselah explained, "To maintain the element of surprise. Because we are not going to escape, my lovely daughter-in-law, we are going to stay and fight."

Understanding flooded over Betenos. Lamech smiled with pride.

Methuselah said, "It is too far for us to help fight the war on Eden. But we can fight our own war on the son of perdition. It is time we cleanse this garden of evil. You never know when we might need it someday for refuge."

Lamech added, "That seed of the Serpent wanted a war with the seed of Eve. Well, he has got it."

CHAPTER 52

For the last part of the trial in heaven, Yahweh Elohim allowed the litigators to engage in cross examination and rebuttal. The Accuser stood next to Enoch before the throne. Yahweh Elohim announced the beginning of the next exchange, "Accuser, you may speak."

The Accuser began with his first complaint, "On this fourth aspect of the covenant, the 'blessings and curses,' we find another series of immoral maneuvers by Elohim, the first of which is the injustice of his capital punishment."

The Accuser delivered his lines with theatrical exaggeration. It would have annoyed Enoch had they not been so self-incriminating. "What kind of a loving god would punish a simple act of disobedience in the Garden with death and exile? In the interest of wisdom, the primeval couple eat a piece of fruit and what reward do they receive for their mature act of decision-making? Pain in childbirth, male domination, cursed ground, miserable labor, perpetual war, and worst of all, exile and death! I ask the court, does that sound like the judicious behavior of a beneficent king or an infantile temper tantrum of a juvenile divinity who did not get his way?" The Accuser bowed with a mocking tone in his voice, "Your majestic majesticness, I turn over to the illustrative, master counselor of extensive experience, Enoch ben Jared."

The Accuser's mockery no longer fazed Enoch. His ad-hominem attacks on a lowly servant of Yahweh Elohim was so much child's play. It was the accuser's impious sacrilege against the Most High that offended Enoch — and the Most High's forbearing mercy that astounded him. He spoke with a renewed awe of the Almighty, "If I may point out to the prosecutor, the seriousness of the punishment is not determined by the magnitude of the offense, but the magnitude of the one offended. Transgression of a fellow finite temporal creature requires finite earthly consequences, transgression against the infinite eternal God requires infinite eternal consequences."

The Accuser jumped in, "But why does a loving God punish at all? Is it not his obligation to forgive all sins large or small? What kind of a loving God punishes imperfection? What kind of a loving God casts people into Sheol? That is not love, that is cruelty."

Enoch sighed. He was already weary of hearing "what kind of a loving God" preface a horde of false accusations. But in the interest of fairness, he sought to address each one. "Firstly, I would like to establish that counsel is repeating a falsehood already laid to rest. It is not imperfection that is being punished, it is iniquity. Secondly, may I remind my accusing adversary that a *just* God is not obligated to forgive anyone anything. A *just* God punishes sin. Forgiveness without payment of the penalty is the true cruelty. Worse, it is to denigrate the criminal's own worth to nothing. For if the criminal is forgiven without the penalty being served, then both victim and victimizer have no value. But neither is "love" obligated to forgive, for that would make such actions duty and no longer gracious."

"Ah," interrupted the Accuser, "But there you are on the horns of a dilemma. For Elohim to be just, he must punish, but for Elohim to be loving, he must forgive. So if he punishes, he is unloving, and if he forgives, he is unjust. So I ask the Judge with humility, submission and deference, which art thou, cruel or impotent?"

Now that was a coup, thought the Accuser as he let his impeccable logic sink in to the minds and hearts of ten million "holy ones." *Holy, my rear end.*

• • • • •

The moon cast its pale light on endless lines of rafts, built and portaged to the shores of Lake Urimiya. The Nephilim launched their rafts. They paddled across the watery expanse, led by seven of the Rephaim, including Thamaq and Yahipan. Inanna stood on the shores staring out on the waters with her Anzu mount next to her. She thought of what it would be like one day in the near future when she would swim across the expanse of the waters in the heavens to take Elohim's throne. Utu stood beside her like an obedient komodo dragon, his thunderbird ready for flight. His hands held the war trumpet ready.

• • • • •

Enki on an Anzu bird and his four Rephaim generals led the expeditionary forces onto the Sahand range. Ohyah and Hahyah rode the final two thunderbirds as scouts. The Nephilim forces had pieced together their sail-chutes and had crossed the volcanic terrain surrounding the Sahand. They encamped at the foot of the mountain and began their ascent.

Unbeknownst to the giants, they had trampled the volcanic rock ceiling of the underground city of Sahandria, home of the Karabu giant killers. The Adamite cave dwellers had not been warned of the planned invasion because of Methuselah's capture. But the sound of twelve thousand Nephilim foot soldiers stomping overhead was warning enough. The Karabu were already suited up and ready for battle. They simply waited for the right moment.

$$\bullet \bullet \bullet \bullet \bullet$$

Cain was unearthed at dark. He bid farewell to his comrade-in-arms, Inanna, and her armed force of demigods. It took only a few hours to fly back to his Hidden Valley.

When he arrived, a downcast Awan and her pack of wolves greeted him. He learned that their prisoners had escaped in broad daylight. She had no idea how it happened. She had turned her head and they were suddenly gone. She wondered if they had put a spell on her and the guards. But when they had heard the roar of Behemoth signaling their exit, she knew they were either dead and eaten or long gone into the Zagros mountain range, where no doubt they were quite at home in evading detection.

Cain flushed with anger. He suppressed the emotion to maintain control of the situation.

"You said you heard Behemoth?" he asked.

"Yes," said Awan. "But when we checked the valley exit, we found nothing. No blood, no sign of struggle."

Cain said, "Had it entered your thoughts that they may have possibly engaged in a trick to make you *think* they had escaped or were eaten?"

Awan was silent. She had not thought of it.

"Had you considered that they may in fact be hiding somewhere in this valley, waiting for a better opportunity or better course for departure?"

"No, my lord and god," said Awan.

"I want the entire pack ready for the hunt, NOW!" he yelled.

She bowed in submission and ran to alert the others.

I had them, thought Cain. *I had them in my hands, and they slipped through.* It burned like a knife in his back, one that kept burning. *I have sought all my life for this opportunity and now I have been betrayed by my own clan. My own clan. I have nothing. I have no one. I am alone, utterly alone. Elohim has stolen my revenge.*

He heard the howls of the wolf tribe already on the chase for human blood.

Maybe I will kill the whole tribe when this is over, thought Cain.

CHAPTER 53

After the Accuser trumpeted his philosophical dilemma of an unloving or unjust God, Enoch was about to respond when the entrance of another counselor to his team interrupted him. He came from the right hand of the throne of the Ancient of Days and whispered to Enoch. The hairs of his head were white, like white wool, like snow. His eyes were like a flame of fire, his feet were like burnished bronze, refined in a furnace, and his voice was like the roar of many waters. But when he whispered, it was a still small voice heard only by his listener.

It was the Son of Man, the "second power in heaven." The first one he spoke to was Uriel. The Son of Man whispered something to him and Uriel immediately excused himself from the throne room.

Then the Son of Man walked to Enoch and gave him counsel. Enoch could see the Accuser visibly shaken by the presence of this glorious being. It was as if he knew his case was instantly lost. Enoch had seen this "Son of Man" in his dreams when he was on earth, but after ascending into heaven, he came to know him. There he learned that this Son of Man was also a Son of God, but not like all the other heavenly host. He was the Firstborn, a species-unique, uncreated Son of God. And now, he had joined the defense. Everything would change.

After receiving counsel, Enoch spoke, "There is a third way, not addressed by the Accuser's dilemma. And that is substitutionary atonement."

The Accuser scoffed with derision. He was so loud, he turned heads. "I knew he would pull this."

Enoch continued, "The purpose of blood sacrifice is to place the penalty of the guilty upon an unblemished innocent. The shed blood satisfies divine wrath for justice, which makes forgiveness of the repentant covenant-breaker possible."

"Barbaric!" barked the Accuser. "Slaughtering innocent precious animals for the bloodlust of divinity. This animal cruelty is despicable and disgusting."

In truth, it was not despicable or disgusting to the Accuser or the rest of the rebel Watchers. They had set up their own religion of blood sacrifice that would substitute humans for animals. The Great Goddess Earth Mother was the most voracious, with a ravenous appetite like Sheol. Her tree rings consisted of the corpses of human vermin, the virus of the planet. But the Accuser did not have the luxury of consistency, he was trying to win a case.

• • • • •

Lake Urimiya stretched out about thirty leagues, but was only ten leagues wide. The flotilla of Nephilim warriors crossed at the shortest point, a distance of only half the full width. It was the largest salt water lake in the entire region.

But it was also one of several key openings to the Abyss.

The Abyss contained the great waters below the earth that fed the waters above and formed the overhead to the underworld of Sheol. It was this same Abyss whose waters rose to the surface of the black lake in Mount Hermon's bowels. It was this same Abyss that was one of the only things on earth that Nephilim feared. And that is because it was this same Abyss that was the abode of Rahab the sea dragon of chaos.

Climbing Nephilim covered the base of the Sahand range like termites on a tree. Enki on one of the Anzu birds flew overhead with a strategic eye, noting the progress of the masses below. About half of their forces were ready for the next wave.

At that moment, the Karabu slid out from their hiding places and crevice openings. They attacked the Nephilim at the base of the mountain.

The Nephilim forces were divided into two units, those climbing and those waiting to climb. But the six thousand at the bottom of the mountain would still be a difficult victory for the three hundred members of the vanishing secret order of giant killers. The battle form of the Karabu was referred to as "the dance of death," which showed itself as the Karabu attacked. They came at the Nephilim in clothing the color of the volcanic rock around them. The Nephilim did not even know what hit them. By the time they could get their bearings on the hostile force cutting them down, they had already lost nearly a thousand giants.

The Nephilim below pulled in their ranks to fight the spinning, twisting, flipping, nearly invisible enemy. The Nephilim above saw the slaughter, but kept climbing toward their launch point above.

· · · · ·

In the Hidden Valley, Cain's pack spread out into the entire basin in search of their prey. But their prey had prepared all day and were ready for the pack. The odds were about three to one, against the escaped captives. Except that there were two minor details that

285

Cain did not take into account. These three prey were giant killers and they were not afraid of mangy dogs.

Methuselah, Lamech, and Betenos had not been able to collect their homemade weapons before they slipped out of the village. They had one knife. But they also had their wits.

The first pack of eight wolves that ran across a scent became overconfident with zeal as they saw their quarry. Betenos and Lamech struggled up the rocky side of the valley. Lamech stumbled and fell to the ground with a thud.

The pack ran like the wind, yipping with victory. Seconds before reaching the prey, the ground gave way beneath them. The branches and leaves covering the pit full of carved spikes gave way. The wolves had thrown caution to the wind. Because they ran as one, they all fell as one into the pit.

All eight of them were skewered and impaled through their legs, throats and bellies. The few that did not die immediately yelped and whimpered in pain. Long spears carved by the team's lone knife finished them off.

A sound in the brush startled the team. Had they missed one? They drew their pathetic weapons, a few pointy sticks for Methuselah and Betenos, and a blunt useless knife for Lamech.

It was not a wolf that stepped out. It was Uriel.

"We thought you were gone," said Betenos.

"No. I was just teasing you," said Uriel.

They did not laugh.

"Oh, come on," said Uriel. "I was not going to let you get killed *that* easily."

Methuselah was angry. "Have you come to give us more 'encouragement from the Lord?'"

"Yes, as a matter of fact, I have," said Uriel. "But this time in the form you prefer."

He reached into the brush and pulled out a large bag. He threw it at their feet.

Uriel said, "I think even you are going to thank me for this one, Methuselah."

Methuselah stared at him dubiously. It was hard to know what this crazy angel was going to say or do next.

Betenos bent down and opened the bag. She pulled out a bow, a quiver of arrows and a rack of javelins.

"Our angelic weapons!" she exclaimed She handed the javelins to a slightly less doubtful Methuselah.

Methuselah growled, "It is about time."

"You are welcome," replied Uriel.

Uriel strode up to Lamech. He reached behind his own belt and drew out a familiar handle with rolled up blade. "You did not think I would forget about you, did you, Lamech?"

A big broad grin spread across Lamech's face as he unfurled Rahab into the dust. He snapped a sapling in half.

"Please give our regards to Elohim," said Lamech.

"Oh, I am not going anywhere," said Uriel. "I am supposed to guard over you."

"What, now you are my guardian angel?" said Lamech.

"Do not flatter yourself, Lamech," said Uriel. "I would not miss this for the world." He drew his shimmering sword from its sheath with the sound of metal crossing metal.

CHAPTER 54

The Accuser had been quite shaken up by the arrival of the Son of Man and of his influence on the progress of the suit, or rather, the regress. The Accuser decided to reframe the debate.

"If it please the court, I need to place into the public record another piece of evidence. You know, I am often slanderously called a liar. My character is defamed with the pernicious mudslinging title 'Father of Lies.' Well, let me tell you, it was not I who lied to Adam and Havah in the Garden, it was Elohim! 'Thus saith the Lord,' and I quote, 'in the day you eat of the tree you shall surely die.' Pshaw! They did *not* die on that day! Adam and Havah lived over nine hundred years. I ask you, who is the real liar here? The covenant is invalidated because of the discredited character of the suzerain!"

Enoch only took a moment to respond. "Your honor and esteemed members of the council, the Accuser seeks to deny the authorial intent of the text by reducing it to the reader's own responsive interpretation, as if *he* defines reality. "In the day" is a colloquialism that means a general time period, and the Accuser knows this very well. He is using literalism to control the text for his own despotic purposes. They did not die 'on that day,' they died 'in that day' which signifies a new era of existence because of the serious consequences of their actions. Exile from the Tree of Life in the Garden meant their bodies could not be regenerated. That is when they *died*."

The Accuser and Semjaza wondered how close their army was to seizing that very prize of eternal life for their minions, the Tree of Life. If they were victorious, they would make a name for themselves and nothing that they proposed to do would be impossible for them. They would be the ones kicking certain other deities out of the Garden.

The Accuser scrambled for more cover. "Counsel has suggested that death is the inability to regenerate the human body. But I submit that this depends on what the meaning of the word 'is' is."

Enoch wondered to himself, Was this insanity even worth the dignity of a response?

· · · · ·

Rahab could swim the waters above and below the firmament. It was all her territory. But her special domain was the Abyss. From there, she could access every body of water that ultimately connected to this underwater abode. Her birth waters were Lake Urimiya, where Elohim created her and held her at bay when he established the heavens and the earth. She was in the Lake again at that moment. She had returned to this sacred ground to give birth to her own spawn.

The Nephilim paddled on the surface of the water. They were unaware of the nemesis below, a protective mother sea dragon and her very hungry newborn offspring, *Leviathan*.

Leviathan was every bit the armored sea serpent as its parent. Even so young, it was already about half the size of Rahab. But it had something its progenitor did not: seven heads. Seven dragon heads on seven snakelike necks with seven times the predator's snapping jaws, and seven times the rows of razor teeth. Leviathan's strike zone was wide and it was more agile and speedier than Rahab. And it had seven times the fury.

The Nephilim were oblivious to the shadowy forms approaching them from the darkness below. They filled the waters with their crafts The lead skiffs were only two thirds of the way across.

The first casualties came at the front of the line. A huge explosion of water erupted. Pontoons snapped in two, throwing Nephilim into the water.

Yahipan screamed, "RAHAB!!" The Nephilim stopped rowing and looked about the water. The huge serpentine armor broke the surface again, crushing a slew of the flatboats and dragging Nephilim into the depths. The spiny back cut through the water and disappeared.

The Rephaim yelled orders. The Nephilim rowed for their lives. But it was an easy feast for the monsters of the deep. Rahab simply opened her mouth and scooped up dozens of Nephilim like so many minnows.

Leviathan came next, with the seven dragon heads snapping up Nephilim faster than they could get out of the way. Leviathan might be a newborn and smaller than its mother, but already armor covered it. It was even able to launch small pillars of fire from its nostrils. Its youth and speed made up for its size as it darted and dodged around, all of its heads coordinated in a bloodbath of feeding.

Inanna wondered where all that food went.

Some Nephilim tried to fight back. But it was futile and the smart ones made for the shoreline. They hoped they might get lucky and be overlooked by their serpentine predators.

That was only the beginning. The sorry paddlers were no match for the worst of all Elohim's creatures. Another creature came up from the depths. Its body could not be seen, only tentacles bursting from the water and crushing demigods in its grip. Yahipan and

Thamaq were in the middle of the mayhem and counted eight of these snakelike appendages grabbing hapless soldiers.

On the shoreline, Inanna's complexion went pale. It was the one thing she had not anticipated. And it was the one thing that might completely derail her strategy.

In the water, Yahipan noticed that the tentacles were not grabbing Nephilim, they were grabbing the Rephaim generals. It was as if the creature were searching only for Rephaim. Before he could move, one of the tentacles wrapped around his body and pulled him into the air. He chopped with a battle axe. But the constriction of the tentacle made him black out. His axe splashed in the water.

Bands of Nephilim closer to the launch site tried frantically to paddle back to shore.

Numbers, thought Inanna. *Chaos cannot possibly keep up with the numbers. Some will get through.*

She drew a bow and some arrows and started shooting the returning Nephilim. She bellowed, "DESERTION IS TREASON. FORWARD OR DIE!!" The fleeing Nephilim stopped in confusion. They turned back around, to try their luck for the other side.

The lake became one big cauldron of churning waters, snapping multiple dragon heads, crushing tentacles and Nephilim blood. The Nephilim forces were being decimated. But some crossed over and made it to the other side.

Inanna and Utu mounted their Anzu and flew overhead to try to assess their losses and help the few who appeared to be close to landing.

This sea dragon and her brood are not going to stop me, thought Inanna. *If I have to attack it myself, I will.*

• • • • •

The Karabu had trained for this war all of their lives. They had built strength, developed technique, and placed their faith in Elohim.

Thus, their casualties at the walls of Mount Sahand were a mere dozen after slaughtering three thousand giants at war. They moved like ghosts. The giants considered them demons. They fought with an acrobatic technique the giants did not recognize. The Nephilim were occultic creatures that were hard to kill for normal humans. But the Karabu were secret assassins trained by God's archangels specifically to fight Nephilim. It was not an even fight.

Unfortunately, Inanna was right. The numbers favored her. Even though the Karabu were able to take down astonishing numbers of giants and scatter a goodly number of them in fear, they could not win the battle in time to stop the other six thousand Nephilim already cresting the top of the Sahand ridge The climbers prepared for their sail-chute descent into the Garden.

•••••

Cain had heard the cries of the wolves caught in Methuselah's trap across the Hidden Valley. Judging by the sound of it, he reasoned that Methuselah had taken the offensive. That meant he probably had a strategy of divide and conquer, since he did not stand a chance against the pack. Cain called the others together with a whistle. He sent them out on the scent as a pack of forty. The wolves would simply hunt them down one by one. As Inanna had told him at Lake Urimiya, they could not overcome sheer numbers.

But Cain had another idea of his own. And he was willing to sacrifice his entire wolf clan to achieve it.

•••••

Methuselah teamed up with Betenos and Uriel with Lamech. That was one command from Elohim that Uriel was grateful for, since Methuselah did not like him much.

How could a man be so miserable? thought Uriel. *If Methuselah continues on like this, he is going to be one crotchety old geezer when I come back to guard his grandson. I guess some people just need a little more time than others to get it right. But hundreds of years?*

They bolted into the woods after the pit incident. They knew the other wolves would be there in no time at all.

They ran to their next location and waited for the wolves to follow. Their scent was an easy draw. This would be more difficult. Their pursuers would be wise to them and more cautious in their approach. On the other hand, they were sure Cain did not know they had an archangel with them. They would use that to their advantage.

• • • • •

As Cain stalked his prey, he knew that they were not alone. Only one thing could have pulled off the kind of blinding that occurred to his clan earlier in the day: they must have an angel with them.

The wolves tread softly through the jungle. They smelled their prey and knew they were near. Like silent ghosts, they glided through the forest, eyes ablaze like glowing coals, figures dark as the night. They came upon the four hiding in the bush, waiting for an attack. Their backs were to the wolves that had crept up behind them. Fifteen of the monsters leapt on their quarry, fangs blazing.

But the quarry was not their quarry. They were rocks dressed with the clothes of the quarry. The humans had dressed themselves in leaves and hid in the trees They rained down arrows and javelins, taking out a dozen wolves in mere moments.

They swung down on vines to the ground and slashed, stabbed, and sliced their way through the wolverine forces on their way to the rock wall. The rest of the pack raced after them with snarls and howls.

CHAPTER 55

Yahweh Elohim and his divine council surrounding the heavenly throne were about to be blasted by the Accuser's final complaint. He took a confident breath and embarked on his concluding strategy: blame shifting.

The Accuser said, "If I am to stomach this dodgy ad hoc definition of 'death' as eventual mortality, and the excessive punishment of death and exile for the primal pair in the Garden, that is one thing. But to then shift that blame onto the rest of the human race, that is the most unfair, unjust, unwarranted, unreasonable, unjustifiable attribution of guilt anyone has ever seen in the history of the heavens and earth."

Enoch thought the Accuser's rhetoric reached its shrill climax of excess in this catalogue of allegations and complaints.

The Accuser continued, "What kind of a just god blames innocent people for the guilt of others? What kind of a loving god punishes the *entire rest of the human race* for what two moronic idiots did in the Garden?"

He stood there with dramatic pause.

There it was again, thought Enoch. The endless refrain against a 'loving god.' But now the Accuser was adding a new slogan for a bit of variety with 'what kind of a just god' etcetera, etcetera.

The Accuser concluded, "The prosecution rests its case." He sat down by the other Watchers.

The Son of Man leaned close, giving more counsel to Enoch. It amounted to revealing the mystery of good news that would be hidden for ages until the end of days. This secret held the answer to the Accuser's charge.

Enoch then realized that the Accuser's final trick was more than rhetoric, he was trying to force Yahweh Elohim's hand to reveal the mystery.

So that is what this was all about, he thought. The Watchers and all their principalities and powers in the heavenly places were trying to use a legal maneuver to draw out Yahweh Elohim's secret in order to defend himself. If this secret were unveiled, they hoped to have the means by which they could defeat the Seed of Eve. This Accuser is cunning indeed.

Enoch stood at the bar. He knew this would require the utmost of his highest apkallu skills. How to answer the Accuser's charge without revealing the mystery of ages before its time.

He spoke with a measured tempo, "Sin came into the world through one man. Death came through sin. So death spread to all men because all sinned. Death reigns from Adam unto this very day, even over those whose sinning was not like the transgression of Adam, because Adam is the federal representative head of the human race. Just as all the inhabitants of the city of Erech would suffer for the illegal actions of its representative head of state," Enoch stared accusingly at Semjaza, "or benefit from the righteousness of that federal head. So the blessings and curses of the progenitor of the human race would be attributed to those whom he represents. It is the nature of authority and representation used even by those who seek to discredit it in this courtroom. If the Accuser does not like that, then he will have to file another injunction against all the blessings received by the human race as well. The defense rests its case."

Enoch sat back down to await the summary judgment before the throne of the Almighty Judge of the universe.

• • • • •

The lake glistened blood red in the full moon. Inanna flew angrily over the chaos and turmoil of the mass slaughter, She had to do something. She saw Rahab come up and chomp a mouthful of soldiers. She unsheathed her sword and dove from the bird down to the beast.

She landed on the back of the huge dragon with a thud. Before Rahab knew what had happened, Inanna raised her blade high, finding her mark between a couple of scales that had been torn in the battle. She plunged it deep into soft flesh, down to the hilt.

Rahab roared and the mountainside trembled. Fire belched out of her mouth, scorching the rest of the Nephilim on the water to a charred crisp. In a few seconds, a thousand of them were flaming flesh.

Rahab dove. Inanna held on. The dragon went deep. The Watcher on her back could not be drowned so easily. Although Watchers became weakened in water, all Inanna had to do was hold onto the sword. That did not require fighting strength. She rode an unbreakable sea bronco. This was the most dangerous risk Inanna had taken in her existence as a Watcher. If she held on too long, it would not end well for her. Rahab would inevitably bury her in the depths under rock, where Inanna would be imprisoned until the judgment. She just had to wait for her opportunity to let go.

Rahab turned and swam back to the surface. She broke the water and snapped her curved back in an arching leap.

Inanna yanked the sword out. She went flying a hundred cubits, landing in the middle of her decimated, water-soaked Nephilim horde on the shore.

She rolled to her feet. All about her she saw that two thousand out of the horde had made it across the water. They were on the frontier of Eden. A mere two thousand combatants for the invasion of an impregnable fortress. Five out of six Nephilim had perished at the mercy of Rahab and her brood of Leviathan and the tentacled one. The devastation was inestimable. It could lose her the war.

Still, she had two thousand warriors with her. They were on the shores of the entrance to the Garden that hid the Tree of Life deep in its midst. Thanks to the Cursed One, she knew exactly where that tree was.

She looked for her Rephaim generals but could not find them. They had all been lost to the denizens of the deep.

An earthquake rocked the land. It was deep, the precursor of something much bigger.

"Now what?" Inanna complained. She looked onto the horizon of her destination. Black smoke billowing out of the mountaintops of not only Mount Sahand, but the more distant northern Mount Savalan. The earth rumbled again. She realized she did not have much time.

She signaled for her Anzu bird, and called out to Utu, flying above them at a safe height.

"SOUND THE CRY OF WAR!" she bellowed.

Utu put the trumpet to his lips and blew with all his might. The war cry of Inanna echoed throughout the land.

Her Nephilim gathered their arms and dashed toward the heart of Eden.

Inanna mounted her thunderbird. She glanced out at the Lake. Rahab glided on the surface, its eyes watching her. It would not forget this day, nor the Watcher, who for one moment bested the sea dragon of the Abyss.

• • • • •

At the top of the Mount Sahand ridge, six thousand Nephilim prepared their sail-chutes. They waited for the call of war. When it came, they jumped off the cliff edge by the dozens. They opened up their sails to float down into the Garden. Handfuls of them failed and Nephilim plummeted to their deaths a thousand feet below. But most of them worked. The Nephilim drifted from the heavens into the pristine paradise.

Right into the flaming whirling swords of the Cherubim.

• • • • •

The humans and Uriel ran through the foliage, the pack of canines on their heels. Suddenly, ahead of them, they saw the other half of the wolves blocking their path by the brook. They were being hemmed in. They took a hard right.

Within moments they were up against a rock wall, the end of the valley. Hundreds of feet of mountain rock rose above them, at their backs. Ninety ravenous wolves surrounding their front. They had nowhere to go.

They faced the valley again and saw ninety pair of glowing orbs slouching closer toward them. They backed up against the rock. A rocky overhang with vines dangling down loomed over their heads. There was no way they could climb.

Instead, they pulled on the vines.

The vines were attached to wedges that held back a huge pile of boulders ready to fall. Those huge boulders came down upon the wolves in an avalanche of stone.

The humans had not been backed in. They had led the wolves to this prepared trap. They were protected by the large overhang as a hundred tons of rock rolled down on the heads of the wolves, killing a dozen and wounding a dozen others.

When the dust settled, Methuselah and his team leapt forward with weapons alive. Javelins, arrows, blade, and slashing whip sword.

The wolves focused all their forces on the angel.

As he fought, Methuselah wondered, *Why Uriel? He could not die. Is not Lamech their prize?*

They rushed the angel in a wave of claw and tooth. Uriel's sword slashed and cut through fur and muscle alike. He was a powerhouse, but the wolves were legion. Seventy of them piled onto Uriel and overwhelmed him with their weight. They growled and bit.

He was overcome. He might be an angel, but these large werewolves were no human warriors either. They were hounds of hell.

Lamech snapped Rahab and cut off heads and legs. The wolves could not get near to him. His flexible sword swung like a wild serpent. They did not really menace Lamech. They stayed on Uriel.

Methuselah yelled a mighty war cry. He single-handedly threw a dozen wolves off of Uriel's prone figure. Betenos picked off others of the enemy one by one from a position on a ledge.

The way of the Karabu awoke in Methuselah, and he began to move like a river of doom, dodging and dancing with fighting that balanced the equation.

Uriel finally got to his feet, and began again to cut down wolves like a machine. He and Methuselah were a two-man killing force. They took out fifty of the monsters in a bloody wave of fur, javelin, and blade.

While everyone focused on the angel, Lamech fought wide open.

The Cursed One had stealthily moved toward his only interest: Lamech. His pack had cut off the guardian angel from the guarded, as he had planned.

Cain leapt. He took Lamech to the ground. Rahab flew out of Lamech's grip. Cain's preternatural strength overcame him. Lamech blacked out.

Cain glanced up, to check the progress of the fighting. He saw Betenos turn. Their eyes met, and he grinned. She let loose a superhuman volley of three arrows. They seemed to simultaneously hit Cain before he could move. They buried themselves deep into his heart. She would kill anyone or anything that tried to take her beloved.

But Cain was not alive to kill.

He was undead, and the arrows had no effect on him. He snapped them off, picked up Lamech and dissolved into the forest.

Betenos bounded after Cain. But she was suddenly knocked off her feet. She fell to the ground in a tumble with the black she-wolf.

They rolled to a stop with the she-wolf on top of Betenos, burning rage in her eyes. She bared her fangs.

She was about to rip out Betenos' throat, when her own throat was cut by a javelin thrown by Methuselah. It missed the jugular, tearing some of beast's flesh as it passed by it. The she-wolf yelped and bounded off into the darkness after Cain.

Methuselah's aim had missed because his muscles were fatigued. They had just killed an overwhelming number of foes. He and Uriel stood thigh high in the bodies of their enemies. Methuselah collapsed. Uriel suffered a multitude of bite and claw wounds.

Uriel lay down on the ground, looking up at the moon. He called out for Lamech, but heard no response. He called again. "Lamech, are you all right?"

Uriel and Methuselah sat up, concerned. They saw Betenos running into the forest. They instantly knew what had happened.

There was no time to tend their wounds. They leapt to their feet and ran after her.

CHAPTER 56

The throne room was silent. Yahweh Elohim conferred with his heavenly host. The Accuser, Semjaza, and the rest of the Watchers stood to their side. Enoch and the archangels, minus Uriel, stood to the other side before the throne of the Almighty.

The Ancient of Days took his seat. His throne blazed with fiery flames, the Cherubim wheels burned fire. A stream of fire came out from before him. Ten thousand times ten thousand stood before him. The court sat in judgment and the books were opened.

The temple filled with smoke and the Seraphim proclaimed again the trisagion in their voice that sounded as many waters, "Holy, holy, holy, is Yahweh Elohim Almighty. Who was and is and is to come."

Yahweh Elohim spoke and the foundations of the thresholds shook at his voice. "Accuser, you have presented your case before the court this day and I have allowed it in accord with justice. I have appointed my chosen prophet Enoch to speak on my behalf. And now, I have appointed the Son of Man to pronounce my summary judgment on this case."

The Son of Man came down from the right hand of Yahweh Elohim. He spoke with the soul of a man and with the heart of God.

"The Accuser has entered this heavenly courtroom in an attempt to place God in the dock. But God is not in the dock, the Accuser is. He has listed five complaints and made a multitude of legal and moral accusations against Yahweh Elohim, including: partiality, bias, prejudice, jealousy, selfishness, imperialism, sexism, tyranny, speciesism, misogyny, monomania, and lying. He has sought to impugn the sovereignty of Yahweh Elohim. If the suzerain as foundation of the entire covenant is unjust, then the covenant is without authority over humankind and is therefore null and void. On this the Accuser stands firm. In fact, on this, we all stand firm. That is to say, without Yahweh Elohim, none of us can stand on anything at all. All of the Accuser's indictments, every single one of them, from tyranny to imperialism to cruelty assume a moral universe with moral absolutes established by a moral lawgiver, Yahweh Elohim.

"Without Yahweh Elohim, all claims to evil, all the Accuser's moral indignation and outrage, all his ethical pronouncements are mere subjective sentiment without any legal weight or value whatsoever. If Yahweh Elohim is not the origin of morality, there can be no moral condemnation of anything, only personal preferences. One man's genocide is another man's ethnic cleansing. All is permitted, nothing is forbidden. This Accuser is, in fact, *assuming* Yahweh's moral character as he is condemning it. But if all was permitted, then the Accuser would have no basis for his lawsuit.

"Secondly, every appeal to evidence and reason the Accuser has made presupposes a uniformity of nature upheld by the sovereign right hand of Yahweh Elohim. Without this sovereign control, how would the Accuser know that morality or nature should or will be consistent? How would he know if contradictions are not in fact legitimate truth in a distant corner of the heavens and earth where he has never been? What is the basis for law in a lawless universe? The only way he can in fact appeal to rationality is to assume a rational universe upheld by a rational Yahweh Elohim. Otherwise everything we say is mere subjective arbitrary chance and all our belief in reason is a delusionary habit.

"The Accuser does not like the way his Creator acts in this world, but he must assume his Creator's sovereign control in every appeal to evidence, reason, and morality that he makes, even when he attacks Yahweh himself for being inconsistent. It is like a little child sitting on its father's lap in order to slap him. Once again, the Accuser must *assume* Yawheh's sovereignty even as he is denying it, because without this assumption his 'rational' thoughts are mere illusion. The fear of the Lord is the beginning of knowledge and wisdom.

"Yahweh Elohim is the only valid foundation that provides the necessary preconditions for the intelligibility of a rational and moral universe that all of us inescapably assume in everything we think, say and do. By coming to this trial and making his complaints, the Accuser is affirming that Yahweh Elohim is the standard of justice and truth, a standard the Accuser does not like, but which is nevertheless unassailable. This lawsuit is self-contradictory, frivolous, and without foundation and is summarily dismissed."

The Seraphim pronounced, "Holy, holy, holy, is Yahweh Elohim. The whole earth is full of his glory." The ten million holy ones lit up with praise and honor to the Judge of all the universe.

The Son of Man leaned over and whispered into the Accuser's ear, "You just wasted your best military leaders in a frivolous lawsuit, when they could have been in Eden winning your war. Your plans are going up in smoke."

Semjaza heard it, too. Both of their faces went flush with shock. They had sought to distract Elohim's forces with a heavenly lawsuit, but in fact, the lawsuit had kept their best warriors, the Watchers, from leading their forces to victory. It was now too late to turn the tide.

Court was adjourned. The strategy had backfired.

• • • • •

Mount Sahand and Mount Savalan rumbled with a mighty fury of black smoke and gases over the Garden. A cloud of ash filled the night sky, darkening the moon and stars. It was as if the very earth was reacting against the Nephilim forces invading the sacred Garden. Two thousand warriors streamed in from the shores of Lake Urimiya and another several thousand sail-chuted down from the heights of the Sahand ridge.

The Garden had been breached.

The forces of evil were closing in.

But the armies of God had not been sleeping. The Cherubim had seen what was coming. They had gathered their forces en masse to meet this two-pronged assault.

The Cherubim of the Garden were several hundred strong and they fought with the technique they taught to the Karabu. They were frightening guardians of the holy. Sphinx-like with bodies of lions, human heads and eagle's wings, they stood upright in battle. Their hair was indestructible and was used to bind fallen angels. Each Cherub was accompanied by a "Flame of the whirling sword." The Flame was terrifying, for it was a divine being of the heavenly host that accompanied the Cherubim and wielded a weapon of flashing lightning. The combination was like a sentinel with a personal sentinel.

The Cherubim set a semi-circular battle formation to meet the two forces attacking from the west and the south. Not far behind the heavenly ranks was the target they protected: the Tree of Life. Not far before them surged the demonic horde of warring giants.

The sound of the clashing forces rent heaven and earth as the Nephilim met their adversaries with weapons forged in the occultic furnaces of the Watchers.

Above the battle, the volcanoes exploded with a mighty force. The reverberations leveled the battlefield. For one moment, all fighting stopped. Everyone looked up at the mountain summits. The peaks blew sky-high, bursting forth with rivers of flowing magma. They were not single peaks with portals to Sheol. The entire group of mountain ranges were a series of peaks that were now releasing that same magma, threatening to envelop the entire Garden in a wave of red hot molten lava.

Huge boulders of burning rock from the explosion rained down on both Nephilim and Cherubim. The forces continued fighting. Flashes of lightning from the Flames met with the demonic swords, maces, battle axes, and javelins of the Nephilim. Heavenly chimera faced off with hellish hybrid as heaven and earth came crashing down around them.

Inanna cursed. Elohim was making the earth vomit slag in order to bury the Garden under molten debris and destroy the Tree of Life. That juvenile deity decided that if he could not have his Tree and Garden to himself, then no one could and he would destroy it all and go home.

The Watchers knew the war was already over. They did not stick around to be part of the casualties. Inanna, Utu, and Enki abandoned their command and flew their Anzu birds into the West, back to Mount Hermon.

· · · · ·

Methuselah, Uriel, and Betenos heard another great sound of thunder from the north. The earth trembled. They turned and saw the moon and stars darkened. The sky rolled up like a scroll. They knew their heavens and earth would never be the same. But they had a son, a husband, a ward to save.

By the time they arrived at the village, Cain already had Lamech bound and lying on the stone altar next to a blazing fire.

This was all too familiar to Methuselah. He remembered Lilith and her demons, who almost sacrificed Edna in just this way. It was the way of the gods, blood sacrifice. But in this case, the god who would be drinking the blood was Cain and the victim would be Methuselah's son, the bloodline of the Chosen seed of Eve.

Cain's raven she-wolf, the transmuted Awan, stood watch for him with bared teeth and snarling growl. Cain's advantage was also his disadvantage. He held the future of Elohim's chosen Seed at fangpoint. In one bite, he could achieve the revenge he had spent his whole life seeking. On the other hand, as soon as he did, he would be vanquished and bound by these putrid sacks of flesh and their heavenly toilet slave. Cain would end up in Tartarus and who would be the winner? The problem was that Cain did not want to die. He wanted to live forever, even if just to spite his Creator, the one who cursed him.

He grasped the sacrificial dagger tightly, holding it against Lamech's neck. The edge drew a bead of blood. It excited his thirst. It became difficult to think straight.

Methuselah, Uriel, and Betenos stepped closer. Lamech's bonds were tied tight. He could not fight back.

"I know what you want, Cain," said Methuselah. "I have felt the pangs of revenge. But you cannot win."

"The Titanomachy has failed," said Cain. He looked at the heavens, darkened by volcanic ash. He could feel the failure in his restless soul.

Uriel spoke up, "The war on Eden was never your concern."

"No," said Cain. "It was only a helpful diversion. With all of Elohim's heavenly host tied up in court, and all his martial forces defending the Garden, I knew his depleted resources would increase my chances to strike down his Chosen Seed. And here we are."

He smirked. "Though I did not realize he would care so little as to send an incompetent guardian angel, an old man, and a woman to protect him."

Uriel laughed. "Do you really think Elohim has not foreseen that this would happen? That he does not plan ahead? That he does not ordain the future? Go ahead and kill Lamech. It will not stop the bloodline of the Chosen Seed."

Cain was taken aback with surprise.

Lamech and everyone else also looked at Uriel with surprise. What in the world was he talking about?

Uriel continued, "Lamech's seed is already in Betenos. What do you think they were doing in the valley before you caught them? Twiddling sticks?"

Betenos and Lamech looked embarrassed. Betenos backed up a step a little behind Uriel, touching her belly softly.

Cain tried to process what he had heard. Did he have the wrong hostage? Was it a bluff?

"I do not believe you," said Cain. "I think you are lying to cover for your failure to protect the Seed."

"On the contrary, protecting the Seed is exactly what I have been doing," said Uriel. "By stalling you. Not with a sword, but with words."

Cain's mind raced, trying to figure out what game Uriel was playing.

Uriel pointed behind Cain.

A cloud of ash cleared away to show the morning sun cresting the mountain range of the Hidden Valley.

Cain's eyes went wide. The sun's rays burst through the village and spilled over Cain. He screamed in pain and dropped the knife he held to Lamech's throat.

The she-wolf started whimpering at the sight. Cain's entire skin bubbled and smoked. He was burning alive from within.

The light rays were like a flaming blanket on his body, penetrating his very core. He gave a last guttural scream that filled the entire valley like the sound of Behemoth.

He fell out of sight behind the altar. The She-wolf howled with sympathetic pain and went to the body trying to lick its wounds. But it was futile.

By the time the three reached the altar to free Lamech, the She-wolf had already transformed back into the human body of Awan. She wept bitterly, holding onto the corpse of her beloved Cain, now a distorted grotesque figure of hardened ash and bone.

Awan glared up at the group of four. She snatched up the sacrificial dagger and pointed it at them.

The four of them stepped back, ready to fight.

Awan would not fight anymore. She used the blade on herself and fell on top of her Cain, mixing her blood with his body of wrath.

Betenos embraced Lamech for all her worth. Methuselah fell to his knees. Uriel looked up to heaven. They prayed to Elohim and gave thanks for his loving-kindness and strength.

All of a sudden, Betenos snapped a look at Uriel. "How did you know what we were doing in the forest? Were you peeping on us?"

Uriel laughed. "Do you really think Elohim and his angels do not see what you are doing?"

Lamech and Betenos looked at each other shocked. They never really thought about it that way.

Uriel calmed their fears. "I was not 'watching' you. I was watching over you. I do have some decency to turn my head, you know."

Lamech and Betenos smiled.

Methuselah piped up. "How did you know she was pregnant with the Chosen Seed?"

"It is not the Chosen Seed," said Uriel. "Not yet."

"You lied?" said Methuselah, indignant.

Uriel sighed, "If you were listening, you would have noticed I did not say she was pregnant with Lamech's 'Chosen Seed,' I said pregnant with 'Lamech's seed.' *That* was not a lie."

"That is being picky," said Methuselah.

"That is being tactful," said Uriel. "Something you should consider more often, Methuselah."

Methuselah blushed. He knew he did not think enough before speaking.

Uriel added, "But if you must know, Elohim does allow lying in order to save lives, so I consider it quite an accomplishment having avoided an appeal to an exception, would you not say?"

Methuselah rolled his eyes. This angel was a bit full of himself. "Well, now that this Hidden Valley is cleaned up, I am going to miss it. It might make a great place to retire before I die."

Uriel glanced around. "Remember one thing: you could build a big boat in here and no one would ever know."

They had no idea what he was talking about.

But one day, Methuselah would remember.

CHAPTER 57

The aftermath of the war on Eden was devastating. Mounts Sahand and Savalan had rained down ash, fire and brimstone on the battling armies of Nephilim and Cherubim. Some of the Nephilim deserted when they saw the river of lava rolling toward them like a tsunami of molten fire. The Cherubim held their ground, only too happy to be encased in molten rock as perpetual sentinels surrounding their sacred custody, the charred ashes of the Tree of Life.

Everything else burned up under the wave of magma. The Garden was completely and utterly consumed forever, thus protected from the conquest of evil. The Watchers would now have to achieve their goals by other means.

· · · · ·

Far away in the bowels of Mount Hermon, the Watchers planned their other means. But first there would be Sheol to pay for the absolutely disastrous miscarriage of their plans that had been Inanna's war on Eden. They had lost everything they had planned meticulously and worked for over generations. Inanna, the most aggressive and violent of the gods, was stripped of her garments and laid bare to the miserable punishment of approximately two hundred lashes, one from every god present.

Her back became a bloody pulp of scaly flesh. Watchers could not die, but they could experience pain and suffering. Though they healed with supernatural speed, they retained scars just like any other creature. These scars would be an eternal reminder of Inanna's utter humiliation at the hands of her compatriots in rebellion.

She screamed in agony as the lash fell down from the hands of Enlil, who had particular delight in her agony. He stole a second lash before being scolded by Anu for over zealousness.

Utu and Enki received half the punishment, as they were Inanna's inferiors in the campaign. She had ignored their strategic and tactical advice enough times to have jeopardized the outcome of the war.

When they had finished their punishment, Inanna, Utu, and Enki lay in their affliction as Anu called the council to order.

He said, "Gods of Mount Hermon, let this be a reminder to us. Inanna is one of the strongest and most loyal members of this assembly. Yet her failure has not only cost us the war, but has set us back for generations. We will never again have the opportunity to seize the Garden or the Tree of Life. They are gone forever. For her punishment, Inanna will forfeit her co-regency of the divine council and of the city of Nippur. She will become my personal consort in the city of Erech. Enlil will now be sole ruler in Nippur."

Whisperings blew across the assembly. They knew that was a pain far greater than her bleeding body for Inanna.

Enlil smirked. *Serves her right,* he thought, *stupid cow.*

"We will continue to breed our Nephilim, but they will be our security forces in our cities, not our standing armies. Any more concentration of Nephilim will only be thwarted no doubt by Elohim."

Then he dropped his special revelation on them, "I think it is time we pursue more diligently our Chimera Project. We have already achieved great successes with the mushussu and other creatures. I have been working on the creation of a new soldier. One that is a chimera of human and animal, not human and god as the Nephilim. This creature is more obedient and capable of communal conformity than a Naphil. I introduce the Bird-men and Dog-soldiers."

A platoon of ten hybrid soldiers stepped out from behind Anu's throne. They moved and walked as one. They were sinewy human bodies with the heads of predator birds and canines: falcons, hawks, jackals and wolves. They stood in perfect unison, then engaged in a brief military exercise that illustrated pinpoint precision and harmony in the platoon. They did not have the strength of Nephilim but they also did not have the individual wills of the Nephilim. They were a unified body. They were a fighting machine. They were the new army of the gods.

The assembly murmured with excitement. Anu concluded, "We have had the dubious distinction of being the recipients of the prophet Enoch's prophesy of judgment. We now know that the time is close, and that Elohim is sending a 'Chosen Seed' who will seek to 'bring an end to the reign of the gods.'"

Murmuring broke into panicked whisperings.

"SILENCE!" yelled Anu. The assembly quieted down.

He continued, "We do not know when, we do not know where, we only know soon. So the duty of every one of the gods in this assembly is to seek out, by any means necessary, this 'Chosen Seed' and bring him to me, because his is the bloodline of the seed of Eve that will war with the seed of the Serpent, our father. It is this Chosen Seed and his anointed bloodline that we must corrupt at all costs."

EPILOGUE

The city of Shuruppak stood on the Euphrates river in the middle of Shinar, now called Sumer, closer to Erech than Nippur. In the seventy short years since it had been settled by Lamech and his clan, it had grown to be quite a commercial depot for shipping. After their experience in the Hidden Valley, Lamech, Betenos, and Methuselah had found a suitable location to build a new city with their kin who had survived the Sahand volcanic eruption.

As the city grew, it drew others from the plain of Shinar who did not share the convictions of the founders. Lamech was the first priest-king and he dedicated the city to Elohim. They based their legal and political system on the covenant of Elohim. They became a commercial trading center for grains, wood, cattle and livestock, shipped through their port in large commercial barges.

But the influence of foreign traders came quickly with commercial trade. The foreigners brought many gods of the pantheon into the culture of Shuruppak. The pantheon held tight their grip on the souls of men. A growing cult of Ninlil, the consort goddess of Enlil, took hold of the city. Many of her followers pressured the government for special status. They protested to Lamech, petitioning him to build a temple for Ninlil. When they were denied, they caused a riot that ended in Lamech giving in and allowing them their temple.

The ultimate authority of a culture is its god. The deity provides meaning, sustenance, cultic religion, and law codes. Because of the city's diversity, it seemed inevitable that it be drawn toward a diversity of deities. And those deities did not like a solo incomparable divinity like Elohim ruling over everything with dictatorial authority. They demanded equality. Thus the Sumerian pantheon came to overtake the city of Shuruppak, as it had with all the cities on the fertile plain. The pantheon spread like a disease.

Eventually, Lamech became dispirited with the developments of his city. It seemed that the only people who did not become slaves of the pantheon were the nomads. These free-spirited wanderers drifted through the territories free to worship as they pleased, without the interference of the cities and their pantheon bureaucracies. Some of the nomads worshipped even stranger gods than the Sumerian pantheon, but at least they were free to do so.

Lamech looked for the right moment to resign his priest-kingship, sell all his land and goods, and journey into the desert with his extended family. He wanted to live the life of a nomad and worship Elohim as he wished. Methuselah fully supported his desire. But that time had not yet come.

Lamech waited in a closed room with Methuselah. His father was now about three hundred and seventy years old. He was still young. Most of their ancestors had lived eight hundred to nine hundred years. Of course, Enoch was only on earth three hundred sixty five years, because he had been taken by God into heaven. The longest lived so far had been Jared, who lived to a ripe old nine hundred and sixty-two. Methuselah was competitive but thought there was no way anyone would beat that record.

A midwife came into the room all covered in blood. Lamech and Methuselah looked at her with fear.

"It is a baby boy," said the midwife.

"Is Betenos safe?" Lamech asked through tired, worried eyes. It had been a difficult pregnancy. Once, they thought she would miscarry.

"Your wife is fine," said the midwife.

Methuselah grabbed Lamech and hugged him tightly. He still felt the sting of loss of his Edna. He wished she could be here to celebrate. Nothing seemed real to him unless he could share it with her. But this was real.

The midwife said, "Come see her and your son."

They followed her into the delivery room being cleaned by a couple other midwives. Being priest-king provided some rather nice privileges such as the best of midwives and medicine that the city could provide.

When Lamech and Methuselah entered, they saw Betenos holding his new son. She was not smiling. She looked concerned. She looked up at Lamech and said, "My love, I think there is something wrong with him."

Lamech's spirit sank. Was he sick? Missing an arm or leg? What could it be?

He ran to the bed and she held out the boy to him. He saw what she had meant. The little tyke had white hair on his head and his skin was shiny all over.

"What is wrong with him, Lamech?" said Betenos. "What is wrong with our son?"

Lamech looked up. They all suddenly noticed that Uriel was in the room. Uriel the archangel, who had protected Lamech because his lineage bore the Seed.

He was smiling.

Methuselah's eyes went wide with excitement.

Uriel said, "The time is arrived."

Lamech prophesied over the child, "This is the Chosen Seed who Elohim promised would come to end the rule of the gods and bring rest to the land."

Betenos turned from frowning to tearful joy.

Methuselah raised his hands to heaven.

Lamech looked at Uriel and said, "His name shall be called Noah."

Chronicles of the Nephilim continues with the next book, *Gilgamesh Immortal.*

Click here to buy *Gilgamesh Immortal.*

CHAPTER 58: FREE DIGITAL BOOK

For a Limited Time Only
(Kindle, Epub or PDF)

FREE

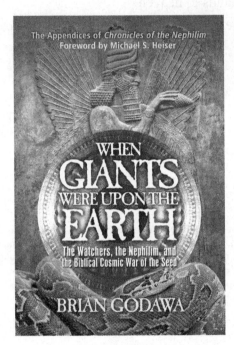

The Biblical Research of All 8 Chronicles of the Nephilim Together in One Book!
By Brian Godawa

Chapters Include:
• The Book of Enoch
• Sons of God
• The Nephilim
• Leviathan
• Cosmic Geography in the Bible
• Gilgamesh and the Bible
• Mythical Monsters in the Bible
• Goliath was Not Alone
• Jesus and the Cosmic War
• AND MORE!

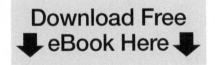

https://godawa.com/free-giants-book/

APPENDIX

Retelling Biblical Stories and the Mythic Imagination in *Enoch Primordial*

In my novel, *Noah Primeval*, I retell the story of the Biblical Noah as a nomadic tribal warrior. He refuses to worship the divine council of gods in Mesopotamia and is subsequently hunted down by assassin giants, leading the chase through Sheol, and ending in a climactic battle involving Leviathan and other hybrid monsters. In my novel, *Enoch Primordial*, I creatively imagine the untold story of the Biblical Enoch as a bounty hunter, a holy monk with a mission to kill giants who travels through a fantastic world of chimeras, gods, monsters and men.

"What?" you may say. *That's* not in the Bible! That sounds more like the non-canonical book of Enoch or the fantasy world of *The Lord of the Rings* than *Holy* Scripture. Isn't that mythologizing the Bible?

It is hard enough to get some religious believers to appreciate the imagination of the fantasy genre. But when it comes to retelling a story from the Bible, don't even think of putting those two things together; Bible and fantasy. That borders on tampering with the

Word of God worthy of the curse in Revelation 21 on those who "add or take away from the words of the book." Or at least that's what some well-meaning believers think.

I think this negative impulse comes from an essentially good intent; the desire to avoid denigrating their sacred stories or reducing them to the level of false pagan myths. But such good intent does not necessarily produce the good result of a well thought out Biblical understanding of story.[1]

What would surprise many of these concerned believers is the fact that the same ancient Hebrews who championed the Scriptures as their sacred text containing the very words of God, were also the holy ones who wrote those Scriptures utilizing pagan imagination and motifs. And they were also the same devout ancient believers who wrote many other non-canonical texts that retold Biblical stories with fantastic embellishments worthy of mythopoeic mastery.

Retelling Bible Stories and Non-Bible Stories

The ancient Jews loved to retell their Bible stories with embellishments in literature we now call apocrypha and pseudepigrapha. And they did so, not with a disdain for "the facts of history," but rather with deep respect for the original theological *meaning* as they understood it. As scholar George Nickelsburg explains, they wanted to "expound sacred tradition so that it speaks to contemporary times and issues."[2] Biblical scholar Peter Enns

---

[1] The curse of Revelation 21, is not a reference to the entire Bible, but the prophecy of the particular book of Revelation. The context is not about taking away individual words but about taking away or adding to the *content* of the prophecy. If it were words, then we are all condemned because we do not have the original words, but only English translations based on many different copied manuscripts with lots of different textual variations. In other words our English translation of Revelation contains added words and taken away words.
[2] George W. E. Nickelsburg and Klaus Baltzer, *1 Enoch : A Commentary on the Book of 1 Enoch*, (Minneapolis, Minn.: Fortress, 2001) 29.

adds, "It is a characteristic of ancient retellings of Scripture that the exegetical traditions incorporated in to these retellings are not clearly (if at all) marked off from the Biblical texts. The line between text and comment was often blurred, so much so that the two often went hand in hand."[3]

Thanks to manuscript discoveries in recent centuries, we now have access to many of these Jewish retellings of Bible narratives, some of which include Jubilees, The Genesis Apocryphon, The Testament of Moses, The Testaments of the Twelve Patriarchs, and the Books of Adam and Eve and others. In these non-canonical texts we are retold, with creative embellishments, various episodes in Biblical history, from Adam and Eve, to Noah, through Abraham, Isaac, and Jacob, to Moses and more. I have used some of these Second Temple texts and other Jewish legends to embellish the Biblical narrative in *The Chronicles of the Nephilim*.

Not only do non-canonical Second Temple texts retell Bible stories, but the Bible itself uses some of these non-Biblical manuscripts as source texts for holy writ.

The orthodox doctrine of the Inspiration of Scripture is "God-breathed" human-written words (2Tim. 3:16). Human men wrote from God, moved by the Holy Spirit (2Pet. 1:20-21). The Bible was not dictated directly by God to the authors, nor was it written by God's direct "hand" (except for the tablets on Sinai), nor does it claim to be an automatic writing scenario where God uses the hands of writers as puppets to do his bidding. Scripture itself attests to human authors compiling, editing, and drawing from other source texts to achieve their authoritative canon, all under the *providential oversight* of God.

---

[3] Peter Enns, *Exodus Retold: Ancient Exegesis of the Departure from Egypt in Wisdom 15-21 and 19:1-9*, (Atlanta, GA: Scholars Press, 1997), 35.

There are well over fifty references in the Scriptures to just over twenty non-canonical source texts used by Biblical authors that are lost to history. Some of them are *The Book of the Wars of Yahweh* (Num. 21:14), *The Book of Jasher* (Josh. 10:12-13; 2Sam. 1:19-27), *The Acts of Solomon* (1Kings 11:41), *Acts of Gad the Seer* (1Chron. 29:29), *Acts of Nathan the Prophet* (2Chron 9:29), *Prophesy of Ahijah the Shilonite* (2Chron. 9:29), *Visions of Iddo the Seer* (2Chron. 9:29), *Acts of Jehu Son of Hanani* (2Chron. 20:34), *Acts of the Seers* (2Chron. 33:19) and others.[4]

One of these source texts quoted by Joshua and Samuel, *the Book of Jasher (or Jashar)*, is believed by some to be extant in a medieval copy of a Hebrew manuscript[5] (which I incidentally used as a source for *Enoch Primordial* and *Noah Primeval*).

The New Testament continues this tradition of non-canonical sources in Scripture. In 2Tim. 3:8 Paul refers to "Jannes and Jambres" who opposed Moses, a reference to Pharaoh's magicians in Exodus 7-9 attempting to reproduce God's miracles and plagues. But there is no mention of the names Jannes and Jambres in the entire Old Testament. So how did Paul know the names of the two magicians? The ancient church fathers, Origen[6] and Ambrose claimed these names were drawn by Paul from the Jewish pseudepigraphal work entitled *Jannes and Jambres* that describes the Exodus episode from the perspective of these two magicians, one

---

[4] For a closer examination of these non-canonical source text references, see Duane Christensen, (1998), "Lost Books of the Bible," *Bible Review*, 14[5]:24-31, October.
[5] Ken Johnson, ThD., *Ancient Book of Jasher: A New Annotated Edition*, (Lexington, KY: BibleFacts Ministry, 2008), p 4.
[6] Origen, *Commentary* on Matthew 27:8. *The International Standard Bible Encyclopedia, Revised.* Edited by Geoffrey W. Bromiley. Wm. B. Eerdmans, 1988, 966.

repentant, the other unrepentant.[7] There is also a long Jewish tradition recorded in the *Targum Jonathan* of these two names.[8]

The New Testament book of Jude tells us of Michael the Archangel disputing with the devil over the body of Moses (Jude 9), an incident that is spoken of nowhere else in Scripture, but appears, according to some ancient Church fathers, in a lost Jewish book called *The Assumption of Moses*.[9]

Scholar Pete Enns explains that the Apostle Paul assumes a non-Biblical tradition when writing about the Hebrew wilderness sojourn.

> 1 Corinthians 10:3–5
> and all ate the same spiritual food, and all drank the same spiritual drink. For they drank from the spiritual Rock that followed them, and the Rock was Christ.

In context, Paul makes an object lesson for the New Covenant community by way of analogy with the Old Covenant experience. There's only one problem, the "movable rock" (or "well" as a possible interpretation) is not in the Old Testament.

Enns exegetes the origin of this moveable well as deriving from an "extra-Biblical tradition found in a variety of Jewish sources dating roughly from the New Testament era to medieval rabbinic

---

[7] James H. Charlesworth, ed., *The Old Testament Pseudepigrapha: Vol. 2* (New York, NY.: Doubleday, 1983), pp. 427-442.

[8] "Jewish tradition makes them sons of Balaam. *Targum of Jonathan* on Num. xxii. 22), and places their rise at the time the Pharaoh gave command to kill the first-born of Israel (Sanhedrin, f. 106a; *Sotah* 11a), and supposes them to have been teachers of Moses, the makers of the golden calf (*Midrash Tanhuma*, f. 115b)." "Jannes and Jambres," Philip Schaff, *The New Schaff-Herzog Encyclopedia of Religious Knowledge*, Vol. VI, p. 95, accessed from Christian Classics Ethereal Library online, February 4, 2008, at < http://www.ccel.org/ccel/schaff/encyc06/Page_95.html>.

[9] Richard J. Bauckham, *Word Biblical Commentary Vol. 50, 2 Peter, Jude* (Waco, TX., Word, 1983), pp. 73-74.

compilations" (namely, *Pseudo-Philo, Tosephta Sukka* and *Targum Onqelos*, among others).[10]

Hebrews 2:2 claims that the Law on Sinai was "spoken through angels" to Moses, another reference to the intimate involvement of the divine council of sons of God *that is not revealed in the Old Testament as we have it.*

In 2Pet. 2:5, Noah is called a "Preacher of righteousness," a description found only outside the Old Testament (*Sibylline Oracles* 1.125-31).

The Fascinating Case of the Book of Enoch

One of the most fascinating cases of Biblical appropriation of non-canonical texts is the New Testament references to the book of *1 Enoch*. Written sometime around the third to second century B.C., this text has both haunted and been cherished by the Christian Church through its history. It is apocalyptic in genre; cloaking warnings of judgment in dream visions, parables, and complex allegorical imagery. But it is most well-known for its detailed elaboration of the Genesis 6 story about the Sons of God (called "Watchers") and their intimate involvement in the cause of the Noachian Flood. There it describes in much detail the Watchers as fallen angels revealing occultic secrets to mankind, having intercourse with human women, and birthing giants who cause terror across the land.[11] Here is just a sample of passages that tell that story in much more vivid detail than Genesis 6:

---

[10] Peter E. Enns, "The 'Moveable Well'" in 1 Cor 10:4: An Extrabiblical Tradition in an Apostolic Text," *Bulletin for Biblical Research* (1996) 23-38 [© 1996 Institute for Biblical Research] 6.
[11] 1 Enoch chapters 1-36 is called the "Book of the Watchers" and deals with this material. The book of *Jubilees* is another respected text that contains a detailed retelling of the Noah story with Watchers cohabiting with women, and birthing giants. See Jubilees 4-10 and 20:4-5.

Enoch 6:1-2

In those days, when the children of man had multiplied, it happened that there were born unto them handsome and beautiful daughters. And the angels, the children of heaven, [the Watchers] saw them and desired them; and they said to one another, "Come, let us choose wives for ourselves from among the daughters of man and beget us children."

Enoch 7:1-8:3, 19:1

And they took wives unto themselves, and everyone respectively chose one woman for himself, and they began to go unto them... And the women became pregnant and gave birth to great giants.

These giants consumed the produce of all the people until the people detested feeding them. So the giants turned against the people in order to eat them. And they began to sin against birds, wild beasts, reptiles, and fish. And their flesh was devoured the one by the other, and they drank blood. And then the earth brought an accusation against the oppressors.

And Azaz'el [the Watcher] taught the people the art of making swords and knives, and shields, and breastplates... and alchemy...[or *transmutation*: Ancient Ethiopian commentators explain this phrase as "changing a man into a horse or mule or vice versa, or transferring an embryo from one womb to another."] Amasras taught incantation and the cutting of roots; and Armaros the resolving of incantations; and Baraqiyal astrology, and Kokarer'el the knowledge of the signs, and Tam'el taught the seeing of the stars...

The angels which have united themselves with women. They have defiled the people and will lead them into error so that they will offer sacrifices to the demons as unto gods.

Enoch 10:4, 11-12; 54:6
the Lord said to Raphael, "Bind Azaz'el hand and foot and throw him into the darkness!" And he made a hole in the desert which was in Duda'el and cast him there...And to Michael [the archangel] God said, "Make known to Semyaza [the Watcher] and the others who are with him, who fornicated with the women, that they will die together with them in all their defilement...bind them for seventy generations underneath the rocks of the ground until the day of their judgment and of their consummation, until the eternal judgment is concluded... on account of their oppressive deeds which (they performed) as messengers of Accuser, leading astray those who dwell upon the earth." [12]

Just what contemporary situation is Enoch referring to in his apocalyptic prose of fallen Watchers, carnal giants, and coming judgment? Some scholars think its origin around the time of the

---

[12] James H. Charlesworth, *The Old Testament Pseudepigrapha: Volume 1*, (New York; London: Yale University Press, 1983) 16-18, 38.

Maccabean revolt in 167 B.C. makes it a prophetic denunciation of the religious corruption of the Jewish world by its Hellenistic occupiers.[13] This pagan occupation would soon be overthrown by the victorious exploits of Judas Maccabeus and his brothers, returning Judaism to its purity and inspiring the origins of the festival of Hanukkah.

So the author of 1 Enoch was engaging in a rich tradition of retelling a Biblical story of judgment on a corrupted and compromised world as a moral warning for those of his own time. It was also part of this tradition to attribute their manuscripts to such historical luminaries as Enoch himself, not as a lie but as a literary technique that reinforces the significance of the message. However, it is entirely possible that sections of 1 Enoch were copied from much older manuscripts.

Though 1 Enoch is not in the Western canon of Scriptures, it is in the Eastern Ethiopic canon, and was respected by Christian scholars and authorities throughout the early church. It was never considered heretical by church authorities. But the real kicker is that the New Testament even refers favorably to the book of Enoch and its tradition of fallen angels cohabiting with humans which results in their punishment of binding (1Pet. 3:19-20; 2Pet. 2:4-10; Jude 6-14).

First, Jude quotes the book of 1 Enoch outright when he writes of false teachers corrupting the church:

> Jude 14-15
> It was also about these that Enoch, the seventh from Adam, prophesied, saying, "Behold, the Lord comes with ten thousands of his holy ones, to execute judgment on all and to convict all the ungodly of all

---

[13] Charlesworth, James H. *The Old Testament Pseudepigrapha: Volume 1*. New York; London: Yale University Press, 1983, 8.

their deeds of ungodliness that they have committed
in such an ungodly way, and of all the harsh things
that ungodly sinners have spoken against him."

Here is the text from the actual book of 1 Enoch that Jude is
quoting:

> 1 Enoch 1:9
> "And behold! He cometh with ten thousands of His
> holy ones to execute judgement upon all, and to
> destroy all the ungodly: And to convict all flesh of all
> the works of their ungodliness which they have
> ungodly committed, and of all the hard things which
> ungodly sinners have spoken against Him."[14]

But not only does Jude explicitly quote a passage out of 1 Enoch
regarding God coming with the judgment of his divine council of
holy ones (Sons of God), but *all three texts* refer to the Enochian
notion of the angelic Watchers' punishment for co-habiting with
humans as a violation of the divine/human separation; another main
theme of 1 Enoch.

> 1Pet. 3:18–20
> [Christ], being put to death in the flesh but made alive
> in the spirit, in which he went and proclaimed to the
> spirits in prison, because they formerly did not obey,
> when God's patience waited in the days of Noah.

---

[14] *Pseudepigrapha of the Old Testament*, ed. Robert Henry Charles, Enoch 1:9 (Bellingham,
WA: Logos Research Systems, Inc., 2004) 14.

Jude 6-7

And angels who did not keep their own domain, but abandoned their proper abode, He has kept in eternal bonds under darkness for the judgment of the great day, just as Sodom and Gomorrah and the cities around them, since they in the same way as these indulged in gross immorality and went after strange flesh, are exhibited as an example in undergoing the punishment of eternal fire.

2Pet. 2:4-10

For if God did not spare angels when they sinned, but cast them into hell [*Tartarus*] and committed them to pits of darkness, reserved for judgment; and did not spare the ancient world, but preserved Noah…and if He condemned the cities of Sodom and Gomorrah to destruction by reducing them to ashes, having made them an example to those who would live ungodly lives thereafter… then the Lord knows how to…keep the unrighteous under punishment for the day of judgment, and especially those who indulge the flesh in its corrupt desires and despise authority.

Just in case anyone would question this fantastical interpretation of the carnal sin of the angels, Peter and Jude quote a common doublet that linked the sexual violation of the angelic Watchers (and their giant progeny) with the sexual violation of the inhabitants of Sodom who sought sexual intercourse with angels. The common theme of both instances was the transgression of heavenly and earthly separation of flesh.

329

There's just one big problem: This doublet of the sin of Sodom and the sin of the Watchers in the days of Noah "made as an example" is not found anywhere in the Old Testament, but only in non-canonical ancient Jewish texts.[15]

Here is the list of some of those extra-Biblical texts containing this doublet of connection, and we see clearly that the angelic sexual sin is usually connected to the judgment on giants as well:

Sirach 16:7-8
He forgave not the giants of old,
Who revolted in their might.
He spared not the place where Lot sojourned,
Who were arrogant in their pride.[16]

Testament of Naphtali 3:4-5
[D]iscern the Lord who made all things, so that you do not become like Sodom, which departed from the order of nature. Likewise the Watchers departed from nature's order; the Lord pronounced a curse on them at the Flood.[17]

---

[15] There is one other New Testament passage that links Sodom with the days of Noah: Luke 17:26-34. Here, Jesus is prophesying about his coming in judgment upon Jerusalem and the Temple. He says that his coming will be as "the days or Noah" and "the days of Lot." But rather than referring to the sin of the angels here, he refers to the deception of normalcy that would blind sinners to coming judgment. People were "eating and drinking and marrying and being given in marriage" as well as "buying and selling, planting and building" until judgment came and "destroyed them all." The reference then is to the nature of surprise judgment upon clueless sinners, not about the sin of angels and their giant progeny.
[16] *Apocrypha of the Old Testament, Volume 1,* ed. Robert Henry Charles, Sir 16:7–8. Bellingham, WA: Logos Research Systems, Inc., 2004, 372.
[17] Charlesworth, James H. *The Old Testament Pseudepigrapha: Volume 1.* New York; London: Yale University Press, 1983, 812.

330

3 Maccabees 2:4-5

Thou didst destroy those who aforetime did iniquity, among whom were giants trusting in their strength and boldness, bringing upon them a boundless flood of water. Thou didst burn up with fire and brimstone the men of Sodom, workers of arrogance, who had become known of all for their crimes, and didst make them an example to those who should come after. [18]

Jubilees 20:4-5

[L]et them not take to themselves wives from the daughters of Canaan; for the seed of Canaan will be rooted out of the land. And he told them of the judgment of the giants, and the judgment of the Sodomites, how they had been judged on account of their wickedness, and had died on account of their fornication, and uncleanness, and mutual corruption through fornication. [19]

2 Enoch 34:1

God convicts the persons who are idol worshipers and sodomite fornicators, and for this reason he brings down the flood upon them. [20]

The New Testament literary reference to non-canonical sources does not mean those sources are the inspired Word of God, nor that everything in them is true; but it certainly does illustrate that the

---

[18] *Apocrypha of the Old Testament, Volume 1.* ed. Robert Henry Charles, 3 Mac 2:5. Bellingham, WA: Logos Research Systems, Inc., 2004, 164.

[19] *Pseudepigrapha of the Old Testament Volume 1.* ed. Robert Henry Charles. Bellingham, WA: Logos Research Systems, Inc., 2004, 42.

[20] James H. Charlesworth, *The Old Testament Pseudepigrapha: Volume 1* (New York; London: Yale University Press, 1983) 158.

Bible itself draws meaningfully and favorably from interpretive traditions that engage in imaginative embellishment of Biblical stories. Unlike some Christians, God *does appreciate* creative imagination.

Jude's references to the book of Enoch are not limited to material citations. He uses the same poetic phraseology throughout his letter that indicates an intimate interaction with the entirety of 1 Enoch on the incident of the Watchers and their condemnation. Researcher Douglas Van Dorn has put together a helpful chart of these linguistic comparisons.[21]

SOME OF JUDE'S ALLUSIONS TO 1 ENOCH		
JUDE	1 ENOCH	
Jude 6 "The angels that did not keep their own position but left their proper dwelling"	"[The angels] have abandoned the high heaven, the holy eternal place"	1 En 12:4
"until the judgment of the great day"	"preserved for the day of suffering"	1 En 45:2 (1 En 10:6)
"angels...kept in eternal chains under gloomy darkness"	"this is the prison of the angels, and here they will be imprisoned forever"	1 En 21:10 (1 En 10:4)
Jude 12 "waterless clouds"	"every cloud...rain shall be withheld"	1 En 100:11
"raging waves"	"ships tossed to and fro by the waves"	1 En 101:2
"fruitless trees"	"fruit of the trees shall be withheld"	1 En 80:3
Jude 13 "wandering stars"	"stars that transgress the order"	1 En 80:6
"the gloom of utter darkness has been reserved forever"	"darkness shall be their dwelling"	1 En 46:6
Jude 14 "Enoch the seventh from Adam"	"my grandfather [Enoch]... seventh from Adam	1 En 60:8

1 Peter 3:18-20 speaks of Christ going down into Sheol to proclaim his triumph to the "spirits imprisoned" at the time of the

---

[21] Douglas Van Dorn, (2013-01-21). *Giants: Sons of the Gods* (Kindle Location 4850). Waters of Creation. Kindle Edition.

flood. This act appears to be a typological replay of Enoch's own vision journey into Sheol to see the "prison house of the angels" who disobeyed at the flood (1 Enoch 21:9-10).

But the story does not yet end there. You will notice that the location of punishment and binding of the fallen angels that we have already seen in 2 Peter is *Tartarus* in the Greek.

> 2Pet. 2:4
> For if God did not spare angels when they sinned, but cast them into hell [*tartarus*] and committed them to pits of darkness, reserved for judgment.

What is important to realize is that the Greek word translated as "hell" in this English translation is not one of the usual New Testament Greek words for hell, *gehenna* or *hades*, but *tartarus*.

The Greek poet Hesiod, writing around 700 B.C., described this commonly known underworld called Tartarus as the pit of darkness and gloom where the Olympian Titan giants were banished following their war with Zeus.

> Hesiod, *Theogony* lines 720-739
> as far beneath the earth as heaven is above earth; for so far is it from earth to Tartarus...There by the counsel of Zeus who drives the clouds the Titan gods are hidden under misty gloom, in a dank place where are the ends of the huge earth. And they may not go out; for Poseidon fixed gates of bronze upon it, and a wall runs all round it on every side.[22]

---

[22] Hesiod, *The Homeric Hymns and Homerica With an English Translation by Hugh G. Evelyn-White. Theogony.* (Medford, MA: Cambridge, MA.,Harvard University Press; London, William Heinemann Ltd., 1914).

Obviously, Peter does not affirm Greco-Roman polytheism by referring to Tartarus, but he is alluding to a Hellenistic myth that his readers, believer and unbeliever alike, would be very familiar with, subverting it with the Jewish traditional interpretation.

Extra-Biblical Second Temple Jewish legends connected this legend of gods and bound Titans in Tartarus to the bound angelic Watchers and punished giants of Genesis 6.

> Sibylline Oracles 1:97-104, 119
> enterprising Watchers, who received this appellation because they had a sleepless mind in their hearts and an insatiable personality. They were mighty, of great form, but nevertheless they went under the dread house of Tartarus guarded by unbreakable bonds, to make retribution, to Gehenna of terrible, raging, undying fire…draping them around with great Tartarus, under the base of the earth. [23]

Other well-known Second Temple literature reiterated this binding in the heart of the earth until judgment day:

> Jubilees 4:22; 5:10
> And he wrote everything, and bore witness to the Watchers, the ones who sinned with the daughters of men because they began to mingle themselves with the daughters of men so that they might be polluted… And subsequently they [the Watchers] were bound in the depths of the earth forever, until the day of great

---

[23] James H. Charlesworth, The Old Testament Pseudepigrapha: Volume 1 (New York; London: Yale University Press, 1983), 337.

<u>judgment</u> in order for judgment to be executed upon all of those who corrupted their ways and their deeds before the LORD.[24]

This "binding" or imprisoning of supernatural beings in the earth is expressed in 2 Peter's "cast into pits of darkness reserved for judgment" (3:19), 1 Peter's "disobedient spirits in prison" (v. 6), and Jude's "eternal bonds under darkness for the judgment of the great day" (2:4). But it is not altogether unheard of in the Old Testament.

> Isa. 24:21–23
> On that day the LORD will <u>punish</u>
> <u>the host of heaven</u>, in heaven,
> and the kings of the earth, on the earth.
> They will be <u>gathered together</u>
> as <u>prisoners in a pit</u>;
> they will be <u>shut up in a prison</u>,
> and after many days they <u>will be punished</u>.

Isaiah here is speaking of judgment upon Israel by the Babylonians around 600 B.C., but he evokes the same Enochian imagery of the angelic host of heaven (often linked to the astronomical heavenly bodies *and* earthly rulers) being overthrown and imprisoned in the earth until judgment day.

Robert Newman notes that the Qumran Hebrew of the Isaiah scroll of this passage refers to a past event as its reference point:

---

[24] James H. Charlesworth, *The Old Testament Pseudepigrapha and the New Testament, Volume 2: Expansions of the "Old Testament" and Legends, Wisdom, and Philosophical Literature, Prayers, Psalms and Odes, Fragments of Lost Judeo-Hellenistic Works* (New Haven; London: Yale University Press, 1985), 62, 65.

"They *were* gathered together as prisoners in a pit" (past tense). [25] This past event could very well be the antediluvian binding of the fallen host of heaven (*bene ha Elohim*) as an analogy for the future captivity of Israel.

So what shall we make of all this wild exploration of Biblical stories, pagan myths, and Jewish legends? Does this mean that Biblical writers tried to integrate their theology with pagan mythology (syncretism)? Is the Bible just an unoriginal adaptation of other religious myths?

Subverted Pagan Imagination

Some Bible believers are fearful of the Bible's adaptation of mythopoetic imagery and seek to ignore it by literalizing everything in the Bible into their modern understanding. They point to New Testament commands of Paul to "have nothing to do with irreverent silly myths" (1Tim. 4:7), to avoid devotion "to myths and endless genealogies, which promote speculations" (1Tim. 1:4), "Jewish myths and the commands of people who turn away from the truth" (Titus 1:14). They even think that it is a sign of the end times that some teachers "will turn away from listening to the truth and wander off into myths" (1Tim. 4:4).

But are these texts denigrating the literary genres of myth and speculative fantasy that employ the imagination in understanding God? A closer look at their context reveals that not all mythology is created equal.

In 1 Timothy and Titus, Paul is not comparing doctrinal teaching with mythical genre, he is comparing *true* doctrine with *false* doctrine that was being taught by the prevailing myths of his

---

[25] Robert C. Newman, "The Ancient Exegesis of Genesis 6:2, 4," *Grace Theological Journal* 5,1 (1984) 13-36.

Jewish opponents who denied the Gospel.[26] It is the *content* that is damnable heresy to Paul, not the *genre* of mythic storytelling itself. Of this heretical mythology, scholar William Mounce writes,

> It appears to have been a form of aberrant Judaism with Hellenistic/gnostic tendencies that overemphasized the law and underemphasized Christ and faith, taught dualism (asceticism, denial of a physical resurrection), was unduly interested in the minutiae of the OT, produced sinful lifestyles and irrelevant quibbling about words, and was destroying the reputation of the church in Ephesus.[27]

The New Testament does not command against using mythical storytelling, but against its misuse for false doctrine. Put positively, we should devote ourselves to myths that "promote stewardship from God that is by faith" (1Tim. 1:4), myths that "turn people to the truth" (Titus 1:14); "reverent, sober myths" of "faith, good doctrine" and "godliness" (1Tim. 4:6-7); myths that "turn toward the truth" (2Tim. 4:4).

But it is equally interesting to see how the Bible itself redeems pagan mythopoeic imagination.

I have written elsewhere about the extensive use of Canaanite poetry and imagination by Bible authors to express God's own imagination.[28] The Bible redeems pagan imagination by using its motifs and baptizing them with altered subversive definitions that

---

[26] "The use is, to be sure, not specifically literary. "Myth" is used here, as is frequently the case elsewhere, to denote false and foolish stories." Martin Dibelius and Hans Conzelmann, *The Pastoral Epistles a Commentary on the Pastoral Epistles, Hermeneia--a critical and historical commentary on the Bible*, (Philadelphia: Fortress Press, 1972) 16.

[27] William D. Mounce, vol. 46, Word Biblical Commentary : Pastoral Epistles, Word Biblical Commentary, (Dallas: Word, Incorporated, 2002) 19.

[28] http://godawa.com/Writing/Articles_And_Essays.html

support Yahweh, the God of the Jewish Scriptures against Baal, the god of Canaan, and other pagan deities in the ancient Near East.

Two examples of this redemptive subversion that show up in *Noah Primeval* and *Enoch Primordial* are Leviathan and the divine council of the Sons of God. It appears that Yahweh was not only interested in dispossessing the Canaanite people from the Promised Land, he was interested in dispossessing their narrative, because the Bible embodies a subversion of Canaanite imagination within its own narrative.

Baal, the storm god, was the chief deity of the land of Canaan in the time of the Israelite conquest. Canaanite myths depict Baal as a "cloud rider" who defeats the River and the Sea, as well as the seven-headed Sea Dragon called "Leviathan," (a symbol of chaos), in order to claim his eternal dominion.[29]

In polemical response to this mythology, the Biblical writers describe Yahweh as a "cloud rider" (Isa. 19:1; Psa. 104:3-4), who defeats the River and Sea (Hab. 3:8), as well as the Sea Dragon, "Leviathan," (Isa. 89:6-12) or "Rahab" (Psa. 89:9-11) in order to establish his eternal dominion (Psa. 89:19-29). It appears that Yahweh, in consort with the human authors of the Bible, is subversively using the pagan cultural motifs and thought-forms of the day to say, "Baal is not God, Yahweh is God."

In Psalm 74 and 89, and Isaiah 27 and 51 the story of the Exodus crossing of the Red Sea is described with the imaginative terms of creating the heavens and earth, crushing the heads of Leviathan, and binding the chaos waters of the sea in order to establish Yahweh's covenantal dominion on the earth in his people. This is history mixed in with mythopoeic imagination to describe the

---

[29] See Wyatt, N. Religious Texts from Ugarit. 2nd ed. Biblical seminar, 53. (London; New York: Sheffield Academic Press, 2002). Also, Brian Godawa, "Old Testament Storytelling Apologetics," http://godawa.com/Writing/Articles/OTStoryApologetics-CRJournal.pdf

theological significance of what is taking place — just like other ancient Near Eastern religions did.[30]

Another aspect of Canaanite pagan mythology that is redeemed in the Scriptures is the divine council of the Sons of God. In the sacred Baal texts we read about an assembly of the "Sons of El," the father deity of the pantheon. Baal is a vice regent who ascends to the throne of El and rules over the other gods of the council, who then do his bidding.[31]

In the Bible, God (called "El" or "Elohim") presides over a divine council or assembly of the "Sons of God" (Psa. 82:1; 89:5-7), who also give advice in judicial decisions of Yahweh (Psa. 82), and carry out his bidding as well (Job 1:6-12; 1Kings 22:19-22). A deified figure called the Son of Man is a vice regent who ascends to God's throne surrounded by those "holy ones" who do his bidding (Dan. 7:9-14).[32]

Of course, there are significant differences that separate the monotheistic Biblical divine council and the polytheistic pagan Canaanite divine council. As one example illustrates, the Biblical divine council are not to be worshipped, as God is, while the Canaanite divine council were worshipped.[33] Big similarities, but bigger differences. Biblical imagination does not engage in syncretism (blending opposing views), but in subversion (infiltrating

---

[30] See Brian Godawa, "Biblical Creation and Storytelling: Cosmogony, Combat and Covenant" for a detailed explanation of this ANE technique:
http://godawa.com/Writing/Articles/BiblicalCreationStorytelling-Godawa.pdf
[31] See Michael S. Heiser, *The Divine Council In Late Canonical And Non-Canonical Second Temple Jewish Literature* (Madison, WI: University of Wisconsin, 2004) 34-41: http://digitalcommons.liberty.edu/fac_dis/93/; Patrick D. Miller, "Cosmology And World Order In The Old Testament The Divine Council As Cosmic-Political Symbol" *Israelite Religion and Biblical Theology: Collected Essays by Patrick D. Miller*, (NY: Sheffield Academic Press, 2000).
[32] See Michael Heiser's writings on the divine council in the Bible at http://thedivinecouncil.com/.
[33] For more differences explained, see Gerald Cooke, "The Sons of (the) God(s)," *Zeitschrift für die alttestamentliche Wissenschaft*, n.s.:35:1 (1964), p 45-46.

and overthrowing an opposing view). The commonalities show a clear cultural connection that is subversively redeemed and redefined in the Biblical understanding of the concept. God incorporates pagan imagination and motifs into his own narrative and subverts them through redefinition and poetic usage.

Eden

The novel *Enoch Primordial* includes the Garden of Eden as a location important to the plot of the story. For those who believe it was an historical place, there are as many suggestions for its location as there are Bible commentators. We just don't know. The strongest hints are found in one passage, Genesis 2:10-14 that speaks of Eden at the headwaters of four rivers, The Pishon (in the land of Havilah), the Gihon (in the land of Cush), the Tigris, and the Euphrates.

The Tigris and Euphrates we know, but the Pishon and Gihon we do not. And if the flood was historical, whether global or local, then the terrain affected by that cataclysm would be significantly altered to derail all speculation. However, it's still fun to try.

Archaeologist David Rohl takes the Bible as basically truthful about the people and events it speaks of in history. He has looked at geographical, linguistic, and archaeological evidence of the ancient and modern Near East, and has made a persuasive argument that the land of Eden was in the mountainous valley area known to us as Armenia, where modern Turkey, Iran, Syria, and Iraq all meet.[34]

Bible readers often mistake the *Garden* of Eden for Eden itself. But Genesis speaks of "the Lord God planting a garden *in* Eden in the east" (Gen 2:8). So the Garden was in the eastern part of a land called "Eden."

---

[34] David Rohl, *Legend: A Test of Time Vol. 2* (London: Random House 1998) 43-70.

Rohl places the Garden in the Adji Chay valley adjacent to Lake Urmia and nestled in the volcanic mountainous ranges of the Savalan in the north and the Sahand in the south. He shows how that area is at the headwaters of the Tigris and Euphrates as well as two other rivers he suggests are the Pishon (Araxes) and Gihon (Kezel Uzun).

The interesting variety of environments of volcanoes, mountains, lakes and forests were an inspiring setting to tell my story, so the map I've provided in the novel shows that I have followed Rohl's scholarship on the location of that most elusive Paradise.

Enoch

Enoch Primordial is a story that takes place in the primeval ages before the flood. It follows the Biblical hero Enoch on his journey through the "world that then was," as a holy man who preached judgment upon the Watchers and their progeny the giants. As discussed above, the book of 1 Enoch was used as a reference for the story of the novel. The Bible itself says almost nothing about Enoch. Apart from genealogical references, all Genesis has to say about him is this:

> Genesis 5:21–24
> When Enoch had lived 65 years, he fathered Methuselah. Enoch walked with God after he fathered Methuselah 300 years and had other sons and daughters. Thus all the days of Enoch were 365 years. Enoch walked with God, and he was not, for God took him.

In the New Testament, we have three references: A genealogical reference, the quotation from 1 Enoch in Jude about God coming with

341

judgment against the fornicating angels referenced earlier, and this passage from the writer of Hebrews reminding us of Enoch's faith:

> Hebrews 11:5
> By faith Enoch was taken up so that he should not see death, and he was not found, because God had taken him. Now before he was taken he was commended as having pleased God.

Archaeologist David Rohl theorizes that if such important people of the Faith really did exist, then they are likely to show up in other ancient literature of the same geographic location or time period. They may have a different name in a different language and culture, which was common, or they may be distorted vestiges of the real person.

In his book *Legend*, Rohl sifts through extant Sumerian literature to find who he believes is a "distant Sumerian memory" of this antediluvian patriarch Enoch. He uncovers Mesopotamian literature that refers to seven sages called *apkallus*, or wise men who are regarded as the originators of the arts and skills of civilization. By removing the mythological veil covering these advisors to ancient kings whose kingship "descended from heaven," he reveals a fascinating correlation. The seventh sage, Utuabzu, apkallu to King Enmeduranki of Sippar, is described as having "ascended to heaven," just like Enoch, the seventh patriarch, did in the Bible.[35] So I decided to follow this possible connecting point for defining Enoch's character in *Enoch Primordial* as being the apkallu to Enmeduranki of Sippar.

---

[35] Rohl, *Legend,* 201-202. Also, Hess, Richard S. "Enoch (Person)". In *The Anchor Yale Bible Dictionary*, edited by David Noel Freedman. New York: Doubleday, 1992.

Cain

The infamous first murderer Cain, son of Adam, shows up in *Enoch Primordial*. He has a wolf companion and eventually we find that the curse/mark on Cain that the Bible does not explain is vampirism. Cain is an undead being who must feed on the blood of the living to maintain his wretched life. It reminds one of the fact that sometimes the greatest punishment is not death but living with the disastrous consequences of one's actions.

> Gen 4:11, 15
> And now you are cursed from the ground, which has opened its mouth to receive your brother's blood from your hand...And the LORD put a mark on Cain, lest any who found him should attack him.

I drew from Jewish legends for this creative license. The rabbinic *Genesis Rabbah* 22:12 interpreted the "sign" that deterred others from attacking him as a protective dog (domesticated wolf), thus my lycanthropic connection.[36] The Pseudepigraphic *Life of Adam and Eve* paints a vampiric dream of Eve for her son Cain:

> The Life of Adam and Eve 2:1-3:2
> After these things Adam and Eve were together and when they were lying down to sleep, Eve said to her lord Adam, "My lord, I saw in a dream this night the blood of my son Amilabes, called Abel, being thrust into the mouth of Cain his brother, and he drank it mercilessly. He begged him to allow him a little of it,

---

[36] Gordon J. Wenham, Vol. 1, *Genesis 1–15*. Word Biblical Commentary. Dallas: Word, Incorporated, 1998, 109. See http://www.sacred-texts.com/jud/mhl/mhl05.htm (page 55).

> but he did not listen to him but swallowed all of it.
> And it did not stay in his stomach but came out of his
> mouth."…
> And God said to Michael the archangel, "Say to
> Adam, 'The mystery which you know do not report to
> your son Cain, for he is a son of wrath.[37]

The notion of vampirism is not new to *Enoch Primordial*. We
have seen the Watchers drink blood from sacrifices as a means of
their sustaining life in *Noah Primeval* as well. Biblical theology
links atonement to blood sacrifice because "life is in the blood."

> Leviticus 17:11–12
> For the life of the flesh is in the blood, and I have
> given it for you on the altar to make atonement for
> your souls, for it is the blood that makes atonement
> by the life. Therefore I have said to the people of
> Israel, No person among you shall eat blood, neither
> shall any stranger who sojourns among you eat blood.

This is not to make God into a vampire, but it does make
vampirism into a reflection of the curse of seeking to be gods or
"like god." The notion of blood sacrifice was near universal in the
ancient world because the *imago dei* in man, though distorted, is
inescapable and thus finds its way into humankind's distortions of
God-created reality.

---

[37] James H. Charlesworth, *The Old Testament Pseudepigrapha and the New Testament,
Volume 2: Expansions of the "Old Testament" and Legends, Wisdom, and Philosophical
Literature, Prayers, Psalms and Odes, Fragments of Lost Judeo-Hellenistic Works* (New
Haven; London: Yale University Press, 1985) 267.

Azazel

Baal is of course, not the only pagan entity that is subverted in the Bible. Remember the fallen Watcher Azazel who, in the Enoch passages above, was bound into the earth in the desert? Azazel makes his appearance in *Enoch Primordial* in this same way as one of the two lead Watchers who instigate the rebellion of the Watchers and the revelation of occultic knowledge to humanity. There is a much debated Scripture where this Azazel tradition may be influencing the Hebrew understanding of atonement. In Leviticus 16, the high priest Aaron is instructed in sin offerings for the people of Israel. One of those offerings is to be a scapegoat.

> Leviticus 16:7–10
> Then he shall take the two goats and set them before the LORD at the entrance of the tent of meeting. And Aaron shall cast lots over the two goats, one lot for the LORD and the other lot for Azazel. And Aaron shall present the goat on which the lot fell for the LORD and use it as a sin offering, but the goat on which the lot fell for Azazel shall be presented alive before the LORD to make atonement over it, that it may be sent away into the wilderness to Azazel.

Scholarly opinion is not unanimous (is it ever?) over just what "Azazel" refers to, but knowing the Enochian tradition of the angelic Azazel bound in the desert, there is strong warrant for the thesis that it refers to a "desert demon"[38] who happens to have the name of the demonic fallen angel who was bound in the desert in 1 Enoch.

Another demonized pagan deity appears in the Old Testament that may shed more light on this desert "goat-demon" Azazel. The Hebrew word, *seirim* is translated in several Old Testament passages as the pagan "satyr" or "hairy goat-demon." In two places it refers to the goat idols to whom some Canaanites made sacrifices (Lev. 17:7; 2Chron. 11:15) and in others to demonic entities that haunt the desert (Isa. 13:21; 34:14).[39] The Hebrews saw these pagan deities as the same thing: Demons.

Banias in ancient northern Canaan/Israel near Caesarea Philippi eventually became the center of worship for Pan, the hybrid goat-man deity. And this temple was near the base of Mount Hermon. To the Old Testament Jew, Azazel was an analog or incarnation of the desert goat-demon.[40]

Lilith

Another Mesopotamian deity subverted in the Old Testament narrative is Lilith, the she-demon. Regarding this monster, the *Dictionary of Deities and Demons in the Bible* says its Mesopotamian narrative reaches back to the third millennium B.C.

> Here we find Inanna who plants a tree later hoping to cut from its wood a throne and a bed for herself. But as the tree grows, a snake [Ningishzida] makes its nest at its roots, Anzu settled in the top and in the

---

[38] "Azazel", Karel van der Toorn, Bob Becking and Pieter Willem van der Horst, *Dictionary of Deities and Demons in the Bible*, (*DDD*) 2nd extensively rev. ed., (Leiden; Boston; Köln; Grand Rapids, MI; Cambridge: Brill; Eerdmans, 1999) 129.
[39] van der Toorn, Becking, *DDD*, 129.
[40] Judd H. Burton, *Interview With the Giant: Ethnohistorical Notes on the Nephilim*, (Burton Beyond Press, 2009), 19-20.

trunk the demon makes her lair... Of greater importance, however, is the sexual aspect of the—mainly—female demons lilitu and lili. Thus the texts refer to them as the ones who have no husband, or as the ones who stroll about searching for men in order to ensnare them.[41]

Lilith was also known as the demon who stole away newborn babies to suck their blood, eat their bone marrow and consume their flesh.[42] In Jewish legends, she was described as having long hair and wings, and claimed to have been the first wife of Adam who was banished because of Adam's unwillingness to accept her as his equal.[43] Lilith and her offspring make their appearance in *Enoch Primordial* as temptresses guarding the World Tree in the desert with the snake god Ningishzida in the roots and the Anzu bird in its high branches.

Lilith the "night hag" makes her appearance in the Bible in Isaiah 34 along with that other pagan mythical creature, the satyr, a demonized interpretation of the goat-like god Pan. In this chapter, prophetic judgment upon Edom involves turning it into a desert wasteland that is inhabited by all kinds of demons; ravens, jackals, hyenas, satyrs — and Lilith.

Isaiah 34:13–15 (RSV)
It shall be the haunt of jackals... And wild beasts shall meet with hyenas, the satyr shall cry to his fellow;

---

[41] "Lilith," *DDD*, 520.

[42] Handy, Lowell K. "Lilith (Deity)". In *The Anchor Yale Bible Dictionary*, edited by David Noel Freedman. New York: Doubleday, 1992, 324-325.

[43] Ginzberg, Louis; Szold, Henrietta (2011-01-13). *Legends of the Jews*, all four volumes in a single file, improved 1/13/2011 (Kindle Locations 1016-1028). B&R Samizdat Express. Kindle Edition.

yea, there shall the night hag [*Lilith*] alight, and find
for herself a resting place.

Resheph and Qeteb

Two other "demonized deities" that show up in the Bible are
Resheph and Qeteb. In the song of Moses, Yahweh describes how he
will punish those Israelites who enter the Promised Land but do not
obey him:

> Deuteronomy 32:23-24
> And I will heap disasters upon them;
> I will spend my arrows on them;
> they shall be wasted with hunger,
> and devoured by plague (*Resheph*)
> and poisonous pestilence (*Qetab*)

Resheph and Qeteb were Canaanite gods of plague and
pestilence. Similar to this Deuteronomy passage, Resheph was
described in Phoenicia as using his arrow of flaming judgment.[44]
This curse is a poetic expression of Yahweh handing the rebellious
Israelites over to the Canaanite gods for punishment.[45] As the
Dictionary of Deities and Demons in the Bible concludes, "Qeteb is
more than a literary figure, living as a spiritual, and highly
dangerous, reality in the minds of poets and readers,"[46] and "in the

---

[44] Ronald S. Hendel, "The Flame of the Whirling Sword: A Note on Genesis 3:24," *Journal of Biblical Literature*, Vol. 104, No. 4 (Dec., 1985), pp. 673
[45] "Resheph," *DDD*, 703. Resheph is also referenced in Ps 78:48, 1 Chr 7:25, Ps 91:5, and Sir 43:17.
[46] Qeteb," *DDD*, 703, 673-74. Qeteb also makes an appearance in Psa 91:5–6, Hos 13:14 and Isa 28:2.

OT Resheph is a demonized version of an ancient Canaanite god, now submitted to Yahweh."[47]

Rahab

One of the mythopoeic creatures that shows up in *Enoch Primordial* is Rahab, the Sea Dragon of chaos. In the appendix of *Noah Primeval*, I explained the mythological origins of the seven-headed Sea Dragon called Leviathan and its appropriation in the Bible. Though the Old Testament seems to indicate Rahab as simply another name for this sea monster,[48] I decided to separate the two and make Leviathan the offspring of Rahab. But in the big war scene, we see that Rahab has other "helpers" with her, other monsters of the deep. This was also taken from a mythic motif that shows up in Babylonian, Ugaritic, and Biblical texts.

In the Ugaritic texts, the gods Baal and Anat defeat Leviathan along with her divine allies Yam, Nahar, Arsh, Atik, and others.[49] In the Babylonian Enuma Elish, the god Marduk defeats the sea dragon Tiamat and her monster helpers.[50]

Tiamat assembled her creatures,

---

[47] "[Resheph] appears as a cosmic force, whose powers are great and terrible: he is particularly conceived of as bringing epidemics and death. The Hebrew Bible shows different levels of demythologization: sometimes it describes Resheph as a personalized figure, more or less faded, sometimes the name is used as a pure metaphor. At any rate it is possible to perceive aspects of the personality of an ancient chthonic god, whichs fits the image of Resheph found in the other Semitic cultures."
van der Toorn, Becking van der Horst, *DDD*, 703-704.
[48] See Rahab's equivocation with Leviathan in Psalm 89:10; Job 26:12; Isa 51:9-10 with Psa 74:13-14; Isa 27:1.
[49] KTU 1.3:3:35–47: N. Wyatt, *Religious Texts from Ugarit*, 2nd ed., Biblical seminar, 53, 79-80 (London ; New York: Sheffield Academic Press, 2002).
[50] "The Creation Epic," Tablet II lines 1-2, 27-29; IV, lines 107-108: *The Ancient Near East an Anthology of Texts and Pictures.*, ed. James Bennett Pritchard, (Princeton: Princeton University Press, 1958) 67.

Drew up for battle against the gods her brood
[offspring]...[51] She has set up the Viper, the Dragon,
and the Sphinx, the Great-Lion, the Mad-Dog, and the
Scorpion-Man, Mighty lion-demons, the Dragon-Fly,
the Centaur...[52]

So, we also see Rahab, the sea monster in Biblical texts being
crushed and her "helpers" the enemies of God being "bowed" and
"scattered."

Job 9:13
God will not turn back his anger;
beneath him bowed the helpers of Rahab.

Psalm 89:10
You crushed Rahab like a carcass;
you scattered your enemies with your mighty arm.

Behemoth

Speaking of Rahab's monstrous "helpers" of chaos, we come to
Behemoth, another creature who finds his way into *Enoch
Primordial* and *Noah Primeval*. The one place in Scripture where
this huge beast shows up is in God's discourse with Job about God's
unapproachable incomparable powers of creation:

---

[51] "The Creation Epic," Tablet II lines 1-2, William W. Hallo and K. Lawson Younger, The
Context of Scripture, 393 (Leiden; New York: Brill, 1997-) 393.
[52] "The Creation Epic," Tablet II lines 27-29; *The Ancient Near East an Anthology of Texts
and Pictures.*, ed. James Bennett Pritchard, (Princeton: Princeton University Press, 1958)
64.

Job 40:15–24

"Behold, Behemoth,

which I made as I made you;

he eats grass like an ox.

Behold, his strength in his loins,

and his power in the muscles of his belly.

He makes his tail stiff like a cedar;

the sinews of his thighs are knit together.

His bones are tubes of bronze,

his limbs like bars of iron.

"He is the first of the works of God;

let him who made him bring near his sword!

For the mountains yield food for him

where all the wild beasts play.

Under the lotus plants he lies,

in the shelter of the reeds and in the marsh.

For his shade the lotus trees cover him;

the willows of the brook surround him.

Behold, if the river is turbulent he is not frightened;

he is confident though Jordan rushes against his mouth.

Can one take him by his eyes,

or pierce his nose with a snare?

The most common interpretations of the identity of this monster by Biblical scholars is a hippopotamus, a crocodile, or a water buffalo. Young earth creationists argue that it is a sauropod dinosaur.[53] All of these seek to understand the creature as a real beast that existed in Bible times. Ancient Near Eastern scholar John Day dismisses these naturalistic interpretations in favor of a

---

[53] http://www.answersingenesis.org/articles/tj/v15/n2/behemoth

351

mythological picture of a chaos monster. There is no paleontological evidence of dinosaurs coexisting with humans. Hippopotamuses and water buffalos do not have strong bones, sinewy muscles, or tails like a cedar. Crocodiles are carnivores and do not eat grass.[54] But more importantly, unlike Behemoth, all of these animals are easily caught by man in contrast with Job's emphasis that only God can do so. And lastly, none of them hold pride of status as "the first of the works of God."[55]

Day argues that Behemoth is a mythological chaos monster that represents the Jewish demonization of pagan deities and symbolizes the subjugation of creation by God. He points out that Behemoth in this Job passage is coupled with the mythical chaos monster Leviathan in the verses following Behemoth (Job 41).

Later Jewish texts also understood Behemoth to be coupled with Leviathan as chaos monsters of creation with eschatological references to future judgment:

> 1 Enoch 60:7-8, 24
> On that day, two monsters will be parted—one monster, a female named Leviathan, in order to dwell in the abyss of the ocean over the fountains of water; and (the other), a male called Behemoth, which holds his chest in an invisible desert whose name is Dundayin, east of the garden of Eden..."These two

---

[54] Day ignores the dinosaur hypothesis. There remains no paleontological evidence of dinosaurs coexisting with humankind. And young earth creationists admit there is no known species of sauropods that fits all the details of Job 40.

[55] John Day, *God's Conflict with the Dragon and the Sea: Echoes of a Canaanite Myth in the Old Testament* (University of Cambridge Press, 1985) 62-87.

monsters are prepared for the great day of the Lord (when) they shall turn into food.[56]

God is using these symbols of creative power over Chaos to close the mouth of Job's complaints. Leviathan and Behemoth were "the first of the works of God" (40:19) and "the king over all the sons of pride" (41:34) because "the powers of chaos were primeval in origin."[57] But fear not, God created them, God subjugated them, and God will turn them into a feast at the end of time.

Day then shows where this coupling of Leviathan and Behemoth has its origin, in two Canaanite texts of Ugarit where the goddess Anat is described as defeating Leviathan, "the dragon," "the crooked serpent, the tyrant with seven heads," and "El's calf Atik" also called *Ars* (the ox-like Behemoth of Job 40:15).[58] Kenneth Whitney shows an established 2nd Temple Rabbinic tradition of Leviathan and Behemoth as companions of destruction in this same manner, thus the bovine nature of the amphibious creature in the *Chronicles of the Nephilim*.[59]

Day then concludes, "The reason for the inclusion of the sections on Behemoth and Leviathan in Job 40-1 is to drive home the

---

[56] James H. Charlesworth, *The Old Testament Pseudepigrapha: Volume 1,* (New York; London: Yale University Press, 1983) 40-42. See also 2 Bar. 29:4; 4 Ez. 6:49, 5.
[57] Day, *God's Conflict*, 80.
[58] Day, *God's Conflict*, 80-81.
KTU I.3.III.43-4
Surely I lifted up the dragon...
(and) smote the crooked serpent,
the tyrant with the seven heads.
I smote Ars beloved of El,
I put an end to El's calf Atik.
KTU 1.6.VI.51-3
In the sea are Ars and the dragon,
May Kothar-and-Hasis drive (them) away,
May Kothar-and-Hasis cut (them) off.
[59] Kenneth William Whitney, Jr., *Two Strange Beasts: A Study of Traditions Concerning Leviathan and Behemoth in Second Temple and Early Rabbinic Judaism*, Cambridge, Massachusetts: Harvard University, 1992.

point that, since Job is unable to overcome them, how much less can he hope to overcome in argument the God who defeated them."[60]

In *Enoch Primordial*, I took liberties to alter this monster's description somewhat in order to make him more ferociously carnivorous, but he remains a monster of chaos that is held at bay by the mountainous gates of a hidden valley of God's creation.

Mushussu

Another mythological creature that shows up in *Enoch Primordial* is the mushussu chimera that is well known from its tiled depiction on the Babylonian Ishtar Gate and many other seals discovered throughout Mesopotamia. It was a lion's body with a dragon's head, taloned back feet, and a tail that was a snake.

Robert Koldeway, an amateur archeologist of the 19th century, wrote a book about the Gate of Ishtar and noted that this mythical creature, called a *sirrush* at the time, was one of the few animals that were depicted remarkably consistent in Babylonian art over time. He thought that this might be because they had actual specimens of them. His thoughts were that they were dinosaurs misinterpreted as dragons. Ancient astronaut authors like Joseph Farrell suggest they were examples of actual genetic splicing by extraterrestrial aliens.[61] I used it as the first hint of the dark arts that the Watchers were just beginning to perfect in their own miscegenation project. We would see their advancements in *Noah Primeval*, but it represented the notion of the violation of the natural order of separation that seemed to be an important element of God's creation.

---

[60] Day, *God's Conflict*, 87.
[61] Joseph P. Farrell, *Genes, Giants, Monsters, and Men: The Surviving Elites of the Cosmic War and Their Hidden Agenda* (2011-05-09). Perseus Books Group. Kindle Edition 1-9.

Scholar Theodore Lewis explains regarding the mushussu genetic combination of lion and dragon, "The common denominator for associating these two creatures seems to be that they could both inspire paralyzing, heart-stopping fear when encountered."[62] He concludes that this is the creature used as a metaphor for the Pharaoh who had oppressed Judah rather than the "crocodile of outdated scholarship."[63] Yahweh was going to capture and cast that beast of a ruler onto the ground for the nations to gorge on its flesh.

> Ezekiel 32:2
> You are like a <u>lion</u> among the nations,
> You are like a <u>dragon</u> in the seas.

The literary pairing of a lion and serpent also occurs in Psalm 91:13; Isaiah 30:6; and Amos 5:19 and may come from the cultural awareness of this mythopoeic creature the mushussu.

Cherubim

Some of the critical characters that come to play in the narratives of *Noah Primeval* and *Enoch Primordial* are the Cherubim. The Mesopotamian version of this creature is the *aladlammu*, the bull-man and lion-man who guarded the thrones of Anu and Inanna. These large sphinx-like monsters were made famous by their presence on the huge stone Ishtar Gate of Babylon and other statues in museums around the world. But they are also ubiquitous in artifacts all around the ancient Near East, from

---

[62] Theodore J. Lewis, "CT 13.33-34 and Ezekiel 32: Lion-Dragon Myths," *Journal of the American Oriental Society*, Vol. 116, No. 1 (Jan. - Mar., 1996), 35.
[63] Lewis, "Lion-Dragon Myths," 39. He also points out that Ezekiel was in Babylon under Nebuchadnezzar, who rebuilt the Gate of Ishtar. So it is likely the prophet draws from this imagery rather than from Egyptian.

Phoenicia to Syria to Egypt.[64] They were chimeras, hybrid creatures with the body of a lion or bull, the head of a man, and the wings of an eagle, and they protected the thrones of royalty and divinity throughout the Ancient Near East.[65]

It is not surprising then, to discover that they were also the creatures that guarded the throne of Yahweh, a throne that some explain was a commonplace Mesopotamian motif of a divine "throne chariot."[66]

Psalm 80:1
You who are <u>enthroned upon the cherubim</u>.

Psalm 99:1
The LORD reigns; let the peoples tremble!
He sits <u>enthroned upon the cherubim</u>!

Psalm 18:10
He <u>rode on a cherub</u> and flew;
he came swiftly on the <u>wings of the wind</u>.

When Ezekiel has his vision of the cherubim in chapters 1 and 10 as "living creatures," their usual sphinx-like morphology is expanded into a multiplicity of four wings, and four faces of human, lion, eagle and ox. But its essential nature remains the same.

---

[64] Ronald S. Hendel, "The Flame of the Whirling Sword: A Note on Genesis 3:24," *Journal of Biblical Literature*, Vol. 104, No. 4 (Dec., 1985), pp. 671-674.

[65] William F. Albright, "What Were the Cherubim?" *The Biblical Archaeologist*, Vol. 1, No. 1 (Feb., 1938), 1-3.

[66] "Assyrian art portrays the god Aššur riding into battle on behalf of the king. The god Baal is described in Ugaritic texts as one who rides the clouds mounted on a chariot (see 68:4; 104:3). This image dates as far back as the Old Akkadian period (ca. 2400 B.C.), from which a cylinder seal depicts the storm god riding a chariot drawn by a winged lion." John H Walton, *Zondervan Illustrated Bible Backgrounds Commentary (Old Testament) Volume 5: The Minor Prophets, Job, Psalms, Proverbs, Ecclesiastes, Song of Songs*, (Grand Rapids, MI: Zondervan, 2009) 333.

The cherubim guarding the ark of the covenant with their outspread wings was crafted by pagan Phoenician artistry for Solomon (1Kings 8:6-7), and an ivory artifact discovered in Megiddo, Israel shows an Israelite king, possibly Solomon, seated on his throne guarded by a lion-bodied, eagle-winged, human-headed sphinx cherubim.[67]

In contrast with this imaginative art, the living cherubim guarding the way to the Tree of Life in the Garden of Eden were no sedentary statues (Gen 3:24), *but they were the sphinx-like cherubim.*

Genesis 3:24 says that these cherubim guard the Tree of Life with "the flame of the whirling sword." Scholar Ronald Hendel has argued that "the 'flame' is an animate divine being, a member of Yahweh's divine host, similar in status to the cherubim; the 'whirling sword' is its appropriate weapon, ever-moving, like the flame itself."[68]

Scholar P.D. Miller appeals to passages such as Psalm 104:4 where "fire and flame" are described as "Yahweh's ministers" to conclude a convergence of imagery with ancient Ugaritic texts that describe "fire and flame" as armed deities with flashing swords. He writes that "the cherubim and the flaming sword are probably to be recognized as a reflection of the Canaanite fiery messengers."[69] Thus the Biblically strange, yet strangely Biblical presence in *Enoch Primordial* of the Cherubim and their divine fiery beings beside them brandishing whirling swords of flashing lightning.

---

[67] Walton, John H. *Zondervan Illustrated Bible Backgrounds Commentary (Old Testament) Volume 5: The Minor Prophets, Job, Psalms, Proverbs, Ecclesiastes, Song of Songs.* Grand Rapids, MI: Zondervan, 2009, 405.
[68] Ronald S. Hendel, "'The Flame of the Whirling Sword': A Note on Genesis 3:24," *Journal of Biblical Literature*, Vol. 104, No. 4 (Dec., 1985), pp. 671-674.
[69] Patrick D. Miller, "Fire in the Mythology of Canaan and Israel," *Catholic Biblical Quarterly*, 27 no 3 Jl 1965, p 256-261.

Whence all this commonality between pagan and Hebrew cosmology? Did the Biblical writers draw from their ancient Near Eastern neighbors for their concepts of the cherubim or were pagan depictions distorted memories of the "myth that was true"?

Archaeologist David Rohl argues that the cherubim may have been a mythological spiritualization of a very human tribe of sentinels called the Kheruba who guarded the Edenic paradise.[70] I decided to incorporate all these interpretations into *Enoch Primordial*. How subversive of me.

Seraphim

The prophet Isaiah had an exalted vision of the Lord sitting on his heavenly throne high and lifted up with the glorious train of his robe filling the temple. But there were also some other chimeric creatures in his presence:

> Isaiah 6:2–7
> Above him stood the <u>seraphim</u>. Each had six wings: with two he covered his face, and with two he covered his feet, and with two he flew. And one called to another and said: "Holy, holy, holy is the LORD of hosts; the whole earth is full of his glory!"…
> Then one of the <u>seraphim</u> flew to me, having in his hand a burning coal.

---

[70] David Rohl, *From Eden to Exile: The 5000-Year History of the People of the Bible,* (Lebanon, TN: Greenleaf Press, 2002), 31-32.

The meaning of the Hebrew word for *seraphim* is "fiery serpent."[71] It was used to describe the fiery serpents in the wilderness whose poisonous burning venom was God's punishment for Israel's grumbling and complaining (Num. 21:6). God's balm of healing forgiveness was obtained by looking to a brass serpent (*seraph*) image raised on a pole called Nehushtan (Num. 21:8).

But this is not the only use of *seraph* that sheds light on the meaning of the angelic seraphim. The Brown-Driver-Briggs Hebrew Lexicon points out that Isaiah 14:29 and 30:6 refer to a "flying fiery serpent" (*seraph*) in the wilderness that originated in mythically conceived winged serpent deities.[72] The term is unavoidably serpentine in all its cognates.

Some deny this serpentine essence by pointing out that the Isaianic seraphim are described as having human heads, wings, hands and feet. But Karen Randolph Joines has persuasively argued that the Egyptian winged *ureus* (upright cobra) that guarded the Pharaoh's tombs and thrones with its "fiery" venom is demonstrably the equivalent of the Hebrew seraph. Like the seraphim in Isaiah, the ureus was also commonly described as having a human face, wings, hands and feet when it was necessary for it to accomplish tasks like those of Isaiah 6.[73] But it remained a winged serpent.

ANE scholar Michael S. Heiser goes one step further and provisionally considers a literary overlapping of all these elements of fiery serpents, flying, humanoid features, and divinity to be variations of descriptions for the "Watcher paradigm":

---

[71] Harris, R. Laird. "2292 שָׂרַף". In *Theological Wordbook of the Old Testament*, edited by R. Laird Harris, Gleason L. Archer, Jr. and Bruce K. Waltke. electronic ed. Chicago: Moody Press, 1999.

[72] Brown, Francis, Samuel Rolles Driver, and Charles Augustus Briggs. *Enhanced Brown-Driver-Briggs Hebrew and English Lexicon*. electronic ed. Oak Harbor, WA: Logos Research Systems, 2000.

[73] Karen Randolph Joines, "Winged serpents in Isaiah's inaugural vision," *Journal of Biblical Literature*, 86 no 4 D 1967, p 414-415.

"Seraphim, then, are reptilian/serpentine beings –
they are the Watchers (the "watchful ones" who
diligently guard God's throne, which is carried [cf.
Ezekiel 1, 10] by the cherubim, who may also serve
as guardians). There are "good" serpentine beings
(seraphim) who guard God's throne (so Isaiah 6's
seraphim), and there are fallen, wicked serpentine
beings (seraphim) who rebelled against the Most
High at various times, and who became the pagan
gods of the other nations."[74]

He supports his view from Isaiah 14:29, a prophecy about
Philistia (the city of Goliath and other giants) that references the
messianic war of the seed of the serpent (*nachash*) that brings forth
the fruit of the flying fiery serpent (*seraph*).

Isaiah 14:29
[29] Rejoice not, O Philistia... for from the serpent's
[*nachash*] root will come forth an adder, and its fruit
will be a flying fiery serpent [seraph].

Could this be a literary reference to the Watcher paradigm?
A text fragment from the Dead Sea Scrolls affirms the ancient
Jewish understanding of Watchers having this reptilian presence and
ruling over specific peoples:

---

[74] Michael S. Heiser, "Serpentine / Reptilian Divine Beings in the Hebrew Bible: A
Preliminary Investigation" 4.

4QAmram (4Q544) lines 10-14

[I saw <u>Watchers</u>] in my vision, the dream-vision. Two men were fighting over me...I asked them, "Who are you, that you are thus empowered over me?" They answered me, "<u>We have been empowered and rule over mankind</u>," They said to me, "Which of us do you choose to rule you?" I raised my eyes and looked. One of them was <u>terrifying in his appearance, like a serpent</u>, his cloak many-colored yet very dark... And I looked again and... <u>in his appearance, his visage was like a viper</u>.[75]

Rephaim

The Rephaim that appear in *the Chronicles of the Nephilim* are based upon Biblical and ancient Near Eastern references to giants or deified kings that ended up in the underworld. A buried library of cuneiform tablets was excavated at Ras Shamra from the ancient city of Ugarit during the years 1940-47. They yielded tablets that have been crucial to understanding the development of Syrian and Canaanite religion. One of the corpus of texts unearthed there was what came to be known as the Rephaim Texts. These texts and others talked about a *marzih* feast, like that in *Enoch Primordial,* that involved royalty traveling distances in their chariots to participate in this feast, wherein the "most ancient Rephaim of the netherworld" are summoned to assemble as the "council of the

[75] Robert H. Eisenman, Michael Wise, *The Dead Sea Scrolls Uncovered: The First Complete Translation and Interpretation of 50 Key Documents withheld for Over 35 Years,* (Rockport, MA: Element Books, 1992) 55-56.

Ditanu, (or Didanu)."[76] Some names of these deified royal ancestors were given as Ulkan, Taruman, Sidan-and-Radan, and Thar, the eternal one.[77] This is where I drew the names for my council of Didanu that meets in Baalbek for a diabolical plan. The names of the infamous Rephaim Thamaq and Yahipan, the Rephaim targets of Methuselah's revenge in *Enoch Primordial*, were drawn from these ancient texts as well.[78]

As Ugaritic scholars Levine and Tarragon sum up, "the Rephaim are long departed kings (and heroes) who dwell in the netherworld, which is located deep beneath the mountains of that far-away eastern region where the Ugaritians originated."[79]

While creative license and speculation drives *Enoch Primordial*, even the names of the Nephilim brothers, Ohyah and Hahyah, as well as the giant General Mahawai, were taken from the ancient manuscript *The Book of Giants* that was part of the Dead Sea Scrolls found at Qumran.[80] In these texts the giant brothers are described as the giant offspring of Semjaza, one of the Watchers, and they have dreams of God's judgment coming upon them in the form of tablets being drowned in water and a garden being uprooted. As in the novel, so they seek out Enoch to explain their dreams and allow them repentance.[81]

---

[76] William W. Hallo and K. Lawson Younger, *The Context of Scripture*, (Leiden; New York: Brill, 1997-) 356-58.

[77] N. Wyatt, *Religious Texts from Ugarit, 2nd ed.*, Biblical seminar, 53, 431-34 (London ; New York: Sheffield Academic Press, 2002).

[78] N. Wyatt, *Religious Texts from Ugarit, 2nd ed.*, Biblical seminar, 53, 321 (London ; New York: Sheffield Academic Press, 2002).

[79] Baruch A. Levine and Jean-Michel de Tarragon, "Dead Kings and Rephaim: The Patrons of the Ugaritic Dynasty," *Journal of the American Oriental Society*, Vol. 104, No. 4 (Oct. - Dec., 1984), pp. 649-659

[80] 4Q203 and 6Q8, Florentino García Martínez and Eibert J. C. Tigchelaar, *The Dead Sea Scrolls Study Edition* (Translations) (Leiden; New York: Brill, 1997-1998) 410.

[81] 4Q539, García Martínez, Florentino, and Eibert J. C. Tigchelaar. *The Dead Sea Scrolls Study Edition* (Translations). Leiden; New York: Brill, 1997-1998, 1064-65.

The Bible also reinforces this ancient Ugaritic understanding of Rephaim as dead royal or heroic ancestors who reside in the underworld, but with a twist. In Isaiah 14, the prophet pronounces an oracle of judgment upon the king of Babylon whose arrogance leads him to consider himself a god (v. 13-14). Isaiah concludes with an ironic mockery of the Rephaim, these exalted dead kings and heroes, including The Babylonian king in their ultimate impotence.

Isaiah 14:9–11
Sheol beneath is stirred up
to meet you when you come;
it rouses the shades (*Rephaim*) to greet you,
all who were leaders of the earth;
it raises from their thrones
all who were kings of the nations.
All of them will answer
and say to you:
'You too have become as weak as we!
You have become like us!'
Your pomp is brought down to Sheol.

To the Hebrew prophet, these proud kings were humiliated in the underworld of Sheol. Their glory became as "shades" in the light of God.[82] Apparently, the prophet transforms ancient Canaanite mythology into a polemical emasculation of pagan pride.[83]

But there is another element that the Biblical text adds to these royal "divinized" Rephaim: Gigantism. The very land of Canaan

---

[82] See also Proverbs 2:18-19; 9:18; 21:16; Psa 88:10; Job 26:5-6; where the Hebrew word Rephaim is translated variously as "departed," "the dead" and "shades."
[83] For a good exegesis of Rephaim from the Ugaritic and Biblical texts, see Conrad L'Heureux, "The Ugaritic and Biblical Rephaim," *The Harvard Theological Review*, Vol. 67, No. 3 (Jul., 1974), pp. 265-274.

around Mount Hermon that was called Bashan was described as the "land of the Rephaim" (Deut. 3:13), whose inhabitants were described as tall giants like the Anakim (Deut. 2:11, 20) and were related to Goliath the giant (1Chron. 20:4-8). When Joshua was wiping out the tribes and cities of giants in Canaan, one of the last ones to go was the mighty Og of Bashan, the "last of the Rephaim" (Joshua 12:4) whose bed (or sarcophagus) was thirteen and a half feet long (Deut. 3:11). The reader will learn more about Og's exploits later in the series *The Chronicles of the Nephilim*.

Satan

A familiar character that shows up in *Enoch Primordial* but not in a familiar way is Satan — or, as the name means, *the Accuser*. The typical Evangelical mythology surrounding Satan is that he was the highest cherub in God's heavenly host, a worship leader with the name of Lucifer, who before the Garden of Eden, rebelled by trying to usurp God's seat of authority in heaven. He wanted to be "like God." He was then cast out of heaven with a third of the angels and fell to earth, where he tempted Eve in the Garden as a snake, and now he is "Lord of the air" over the earth.

I have no problem utilizing *lesser known* extra-Biblical mythology or legends in *the Chronicles of the Nephilim* in order to bring a fresh perspective to the Biblical story. But I also have no problem dismantling other *well-known* extra-Biblical mythology and legends in order to support that same goal of fresh perspective. The Satan legend as I described it above is one of those accepted myths that I decided to avoid because, well, it really isn't in the Bible.

I am going to follow David Lowe's strategy and "deconstruct Lucifer" in order to rediscover Satan in a new and more Biblical light.[84] First, let me affirm that the New Testament does equate Satan with the Serpent in the Garden (2Cor. 11:3; Rev. 12:9; 20:2) so I have no quarrel with that notion. But let's take a look at the rest of the Lucifer/Satan mythology to see if it really has Biblical merit.

The two passages that are most often used as source material for this myth are Isaiah 14:12-15 and Ezekiel 28:12-16. Let's look first at the Isaiah passage:

Isaiah 14:12–15
"How you are fallen from heaven,
O Day Star (Lucifer), son of Dawn!
How you are cut down to the ground,
you who laid the nations low!
You said in your heart,
'I will ascend to heaven;
above the stars of God
I will set my throne on high;
I will sit on the mount of assembly
in the far reaches of the north;
I will ascend above the heights of the clouds;
I will make myself like the Most High.'
But you are brought down to Sheol,
to the far reaches of the pit.

The context of the entire passage of Isaiah 14 is that the prophet is making a prophesy of judgment upon the king of Babylon who existed in Isaiah's own day during the Jewish Babylonian exile. Well-meaning Christians interpret this text as a mythopoeic allusion

---

[84] David W. Lowe, *Deconstructing Lucifer: Reexamining the Ancient Origins of the Fallen Angel of Light*, (Seismos Publishing 2011).

365

or analogy of pride between Accuser, called Lucifer, and the Babylonian tyrant.

To start with, the name *Satan* is nowhere in the story, but *Lucifer* is. The problem with this name is that we have come to consider it a proper name of a demonic entity only by tradition. As author David Lowe points out, Lucifer was actually the Latin translation for the Hebrew words *Helel ben shahar*, which means "Morningstar," known to the ancients as the planet Venus.[85] In the ancient Near East, planets and stars were equated with deities and the heavenly host, so this is indeed a mythopoeic reference. But scholars have uncovered a very different narrative being referenced than the Garden of Eden. It is in fact a pagan Canaanite myth that Isaiah used to mock the pagan king of Babylon.

Scholar Michael S. Heiser definitively explains the linguistic and narrative referent of Helel ben Shahar as being the Ugaritic god Athtar from the epic Baal Cycle of myths at Ugarit. Heiser reveals that Athtar was equated with the planet Venus. Athtar sought to raise himself above "the stars of El," a reference to the divine council or heavenly host that surrounded the high god of the Canaanite pantheon. He tried to do so by seeking to sit on the throne of Baal, referred to as "the Most High," upon the "mount of assembly" in the north called Saphon. But Athtar was not powerful enough for the position of power and was cast to earth/Sheol.[86]

There are no versions of this Isaianic narrative applying to Satan anywhere in the Bible but there sure is one of Athtar in the Canaanite context in which ancient Jews like Isaiah lived and breathed. Isaiah was declaring judgment upon the Babylonian tyrant by using pagan myths against the pagan king as mockery.

---

[85] Lowe, *Deconstructing Lucifer*, 39-40.
[86] Michael Heiser, "The Mythological Provenance of Isaiah 14:12-15: A Reconsideration of the Ugaritic Material" Liberty University <http://digitalcommons.liberty.edu/lts fac pubs/280>

As Norman Habel put it,

> The presence of this archaic mythological imagery to describe the dwelling place of God does not imply that the Israelite writers thereby espoused the crass mythological view of reality current in the ancient Near Eastern world. Polemical and poetical considerations governed the Israelite writers' use of imagery taken from their pagan environment.[87]

The second passage that well-intentioned Christians use to justify their belief in the Satan/Lucifer mythology is Ezekiel 28:12-15. I will focus in on the most important elements to keep this as short as possible. Similar to Isaiah, Ezekiel prophesied about the hubris and fall of the king of Tyre. Also like Isaiah, Ezekiel makes a mythopoeic reference to some narrative. In this case, I would argue it *is* the Garden of Eden narrative being referenced. But the difference is that whereas many Christians assume Ezekiel is equating the fall of the king of Tyre with the fall Satan, the truth is that the prophet is actually equating it with the fall of *Adam*![88]

Ezekiel 28:12–16
You were the signet of perfection...
You were in Eden, the garden of God...
You were an anointed guardian cherub...
I placed you; you were on the holy mountain of God;
in the midst of the stones of fire you walked.
You were blameless in your ways

---

[87] Norman C. Habel, "Ezekiel 28 and the fall of the first man." *Concordia Theological Monthly*, 1967, 38 (8),. 520.

[88] For an excellent explanation of this view, see Norman C. Habel, "Ezekiel 28 and the fall of the first man." *Concordia Theological Monthly*, 1967, 38 (8),. 516-524.

from the day you were created,

till unrighteousness was found in you…

so I cast you as a profane thing from the mountain of
God,

and I destroyed you, O guardian cherub,

It was Adam who was in Eden and was blameless in his ways, not Satan. According to the Evangelical Satan legend, Satan already fell *before* the Garden. It was Adam who was created blameless and fell into sin and was cast out of Eden, not Satan. Satan's name is nowhere to be found in this passage.[89]

One possible reason to presume the Satan connection here is the description of the character as an "anointed guardian cherub." But there is a problem with this translation. Many commentators make the point that this is based upon the Masoretic text (MT) of the Bible. But the Septuagint (LXX), another authoritative Greek text of the Old Testament that is quoted by the New Testament authors and Jesus, renders those phrases "From the day that thou wast created thou *wast with* the cherub"[90] and "the cherub has brought thee out of the midst of the stones."[91] Being "with the cherub" is a very different meaning than "being a cherub." Though this is not unanimously conclusive, an increasing number of Bible scholars point to this

---

[89] Scholar H.J. van Dijk makes an interesting grammatical and linguistic argument that "You were the signet of perfection" is better translated, "You were the serpent of perfection" because the Hebrew word translated *signet* remains obscure. In Phoenician and Aramaic, however it means *serpent*. This would provide serious evidence for a link to the Serpent of the Garden. H. J. van Dijk, vol. 20, *Ezekiel's Prophecy on Tyre (Ez. 26:1– 28:19): A New Approach* (Biblica et orientalia; Rome: Pontifical Biblical Institute, 1968).

[90] Lancelot Charles Lee Brenton, *The Septuagint Version of the Old Testament: English Translation*, Eze 28:14 (London: Samuel Bagster and Sons, 1870).

[91] Lancelot Charles Lee Brenton, *The Septuagint Version of the Old Testament: English Translation*, Eze 28:16 (London: Samuel Bagster and Sons, 1870).

ambiguity and likelihood of the Septuagint being the superior textual tradition here.[92] Adam was not a cherub, he was *with* the cherubim.

Lastly, in Revelation 12, we see the origin of the notion that one third of the angels fell to earth with Satan at his fall. The only problem is that this event did not occur before the garden of Eden in a cosmic rebellion, *it happened at the birth of Jesus Christ!* Revelation 12:1-6 describes an apocalyptic parable of the cosmic war of the Seed of the Serpent (a dragon of chaos) and the Seed of the Woman (Israel/the Church).[93] It describes one third of the angelic stars (Watchers?) joining Satan with the swipe of his serpentine tail. The dragon and his minions seek to devour the male seed (offspring) of the woman, but they fail and the child becomes king. And then the passage tells of a heavenly war:

> Revelation 12:7–10
> [7] Now war arose in heaven, Michael and his angels fighting against the dragon. And the dragon and his angels fought back, [8] but he was defeated, and there was no longer any place for them in heaven. [9] And the great dragon was thrown down, that ancient serpent, who is called the devil and Satan, the deceiver of the whole world—he was thrown down to the earth, and his angels were thrown down with him. [10] And I heard a loud voice in heaven, saying, "Now the salvation and the power and the kingdom of our God and the authority of his Christ have come, for the accuser of our brothers has been thrown down, who accuses them day and night before our God.

---

[92] Notes on Ezekiel 28:14, Biblical Studies Press. *The NET Bible First Edition Notes.* Biblical Studies Press, 2006. Also see Lowe, *Deconstructing Lucifer*, 118-131.
[93] The woman's crown of twelve stars is a symbol of the twelve tribes of Israel.

Most Christians believe this is a reference to Satan's fall before the Garden of Eden incident, where he takes one third of the angels in heaven with him. But a closer look at the context reveals that this is not the case at all, but rather the opposite. The war in heaven *does not* happen before the Garden, it happens at the time of the incarnation of Messiah on earth! The woman (Israel) gives birth to a male child (Messiah, v. 5), who the dragon (Satan) seeks to devour (from Herod's slaughter of the innocents all the way to the Cross). That Messiah ascends to the throne in authority after his resurrection (v. 5; Eph 1:20-22), during which time that woman (Israel) flees to the wilderness (time of tribulation under the Roman Empire).

The war in heaven we see cannot be before the Garden because it says that the throwing down of Satan occurs with the coming of the kingdom of Christ! (v. 10). He is thrown down to earth and then seeks to kill the Christ (v. 13). Satan then seeks to make war with the rest of her offspring (God's people) which we see in history.

Revelation 12 is an apocalyptic parable that is describing the incarnation of Messiah, his ascension to the throne of authority over all principalities and powers, and his suppression of Satan's power as the Gospel goes forth into the world.

But our problems with Satan do not end there. In *Enoch Primordial*, I do not call Satan, Satan, but *the satan*, lowercase, or the Accuser. Why? Because the Hebrew word is not an individual's name, but a *legal role* meaning "accuser" or "adversary." The satan/accuser depicted in Job 1 and 2 is one of the divine council of heavenly host (1Kings 22) who engages in legal accusations against God and his people and sometimes carries out God's intentions. In short, he is a kind of manipulative prosecutor whose purpose is to challenge God and his perfect law.

In Hebrew, *satan* is prefixed by the definite article *ha* which makes it translate more accurately as *the satan*, or *the accuser*. In the New Testament Greek, *satan* is prefixed by the definite article *ho*, carrying the same result of *the satan* as *the Adversary* (Rev. 12:9) or *the Accuser* (Rev. 12:10).

So the most we can know of the Accuser's work in the Old Testament is that he was the Serpent in the Garden, and he *may have been* a prosecuting attorney-like accuser of God's heavenly court. I say *may have been* because the Accuser was more a role or state of being than an individual. The avenging angel who was going to strike down Balaam was described as *the satan (accuser)* in Numbers 22:22 and verse 32 ("adversary" and "oppose"); the political opponents of king David were defined as *the satan* to him (2Sam. 19:22); David himself was described as a potential *satan* to the Philistines (1Sam. 29:4); Hadad the Edomite and Reznon, son of Eliada are both described as *satans* to Israel (1Kings 11:14, 23); and even God himself is described as *the satan* (adversary) when he incites David to take a census (1Chron. 21:1; 2 Sam. 24:1). In the Old Testament, *the Accuser* was not always the same individual, but more likely the legal office of prosecutor.

This short excursion into deconstructing Satan is the foundation for why I portrayed him as I did in *Enoch Primordial*, as the prosecutorial Seraph, the Serpent of the Garden, whose purpose became accusing God's people and bringing lawsuits to God's throne to try to foil his plans.

Covenant Lawsuit

In *Enoch Primordial*, the Accuser prosecutes a "covenant lawsuit" against Yahweh Elohim in order to buy time for the Watchers to accomplish their nefarious plans of world domination.

371

The Accuser and most of the Watchers "present themselves" before the heavenly court, along with "ten thousand times ten thousand of God's holy ones," the divine council. God is seated on his chariot throne above the Cherubim and beneath the Seraphim, and the Accuser engages in his arguments against God with Enoch, the translated holy man, as defense attorney.

At first blush this may seem to the modern "enlightened" religious mind like an artificial modern construct imposed upon the ancient story. But in fact, it is organically derived from the Bible itself, which drew from the ancient suzerain vassal treaties of the ancient Near East (most likely Hittite in origin).

Whenever "the Accuser" (the *satan*) is named in the Bible, it is usually in the legal context of a heavenly lawsuit. In the *Noah Primeval* appendices, I examined the divine council in the Scriptures in detail. In passages such as Job 1 and 2, and 1Kings 22 we are told that "the sons of God came to present themselves before Yahweh,"[94] "all the host of heaven standing beside him on his right and on his left."[95] God then asks counsel and recommendation from this multitude on what to do regarding a specific situation.[96] The heavenly beings give their opinions, God renders his verdict, and directs some of the host to carry out the sentence.[97]

The context in these passages is that of a legal body of divine beings counseling with God over justice and the satan is one of these

---

[94] Job 1:6; 2:1.
[95] 1Kings 22:19.
[96] Job 1:8; 1King 22:20, 22; Isa 6:8. Scholar Frank Moore Cross shows that the divine council is implied in other passages such as Isaiah 40:1-6 and 48:20-21 where God is heard asking a question to an "unknown" plural audience. "Comfort my people," "a voice says, 'Cry!'" and "declare this with a shout" are all plural imperatives as if spoken to a multitude surrounding God's throne. Frank M. Cross, Jr., "The Council of Yahweh in Second Isaiah," *Journal of Near Eastern Studies*, Vol. 12, No. 4 (Oct., 1953), pp. 274-277.
[97] Job 1:12; 2:6; 1King 22:22-23.

divine beings whose role is to accuse.[98] In Zechariah 3:1-4, Joshua the High Priest stands in this divine council before God. The satan stands beside him "to accuse him" before Elohim in good legal form.

While some of these scenes are the Accuser initiating legal accusations against God's people, others are litigation against pagan rulers for their own defiance of God's universal sovereignty. In Daniel 7:9-14, we see "the Ancient of Days" seated on his throne, "and ten thousand times ten thousand stood before him; the court sat in judgment" over the nations of the earth (Dan. 7:10). And in Psalm 82, God renders legal judgment upon the members of the divine council who failed to carry out justice for God upon the gentile nations they had inherited.[99] We read this Psalmic phrase used in *Enoch Primordial*, "God has taken his place in the divine council; in the midst of the gods he holds judgment" (v. 1-2).

Another kind of Biblical lawsuit saw Old Testament prophets as Yahweh's prosecuting attorneys indicting Israel for breaking her covenant with God. The prophet would stand before God's divine council and make the summons and charges against Israel before calling her to respond to the charges. Then Yahweh as judge would pronounce his verdict. One of the qualifications of a prophet's authority to speak for God was that he had stood in this divine council (Jer. 23:18, 22).

Herbert Huffmon has pointed out examples of covenant lawsuits in Jeremiah, Isaiah, Micah, and other prophets carried out in God's courtroom against Israel that illustrated a Biblical pattern of legal procedure:

---

[98] Lowell K. Handy, "The Authorization of Divine Power and the Guilt of God in the Book of Job: Useful Ugaritic Parallels," *Journal for the Study of the Old Testament* (60) December 1993, 108-109: Min Sue Kee, "The Heavenly Council and its Type-scene," *Journal for the Study of the Old Testament*, Vol 31.3(2007): 259-273.
[99] See Appendix A "The Sons of God" in *Noah Primeval* for a detailed explanation of this Biblical concept of the sons of God inheriting the pagan nations.

A description of the scene of judgment

II. The speech of the plaintiff

A. Heaven and earth are appointed judges

B. Summons to the defendant (or judges)

C. Address in the second person to the defendant

    1. Accusation in question form to the defendant

    2. Refutation of the defendant's possible arguments

    3. Specific indictment[100]

I used this basic scenario in *Enoch Primordial* when the Accuser accuses Elohim of being unjust in his own covenantal relationship with man. But I also used the ancient Near Eastern covenant formula for the document under attack in the Accuser's lawsuit. This ancient formula can be seen in the form of the Biblical covenant as well. Biblical scholars have shown how God's covenants with Israel displayed the same five or six point structure that their neighboring Hittite nation used during the Late Bronze or Early Iron Ages (1400-1200 B.C.).

It is commonly understood now that covenant texts occupy a significant proportion of Biblical composition. As Biblical scholar Eugene Merrill states,

> The Covenant Code of Exodus 20-23 and the entire Book of Deuteronomy are the most outstanding examples of this type. It is quite apparent that Moses undoubtedly utilized already existing treaty formulas in the construction of biblical treaty contracts between God and individuals or God and Israel.[101]

---

[100] Herbert B. Huffmon, "The Covenant Lawsuit in the Prophets," *JBL* 78 (1959): 7. 285–95.

[101] Eugene Merrill, "Covenant and the Kingdom : Genesis 1- 3 As Foundation for Biblical Theology." Criswell Theological Review 1 (1987) 296-7.

The chart below summarizes how the book of Deuteronomy reflects five key elements of the ancient Hittite suzerain treaty as currently attested by scholarship:

Parallels Between Hittite Suzerainty Treaties & the Book of Deuteronomy[102]	
Structure of Hittite Suzerainty Treaties (14th Century B.C.)	Structure of Deuteronomy, a Hebrew "Covenant Document"
1. Preamble: "These are the words of the Great King..."	**1. Preamble:** (1:1–6). "These are the words which Moses spoke..."
2. Historical Prologue: The events leading up to the treaty.	**2. Historical Prologue:** (1:7–4:49). Events leading up to the making and renewing of the covenant.
3. Ethical Stipulations: Laws relating to the vassal's obedience to the suzerain.	**3. Ethical Stipulations:** (5–26). The loyalty due to God.
4. Curses and Blessings: Contingent upon disobedience or obedience.	**4. Curses and Blessings:** (27, 28). Contingent upon disobedience or obedience.
5. Divine Witnesses: Called to witness the making of the treaty ("heaven and earth").[103]	**5. Divine Witnesses:** (32). The witness of "heaven and earth" (30:19; 32:1).

Whether the majority of the Pentateuch (first five books of the Bible) was written by Moses or compiled and edited in the centuries that followed him, some scholars such as Meredith Kline have argued that the

---

[102] Adapted and modified from Walter A. Elwell and Barry J. Beitzel, *Baker Encyclopedia of the Bible*, 535 (Grand Rapids, Mich.: Baker Book House, 1988). See also Meredith Kline, *Treaty of the Great King* (Overland Park: KS, 2000); Walton, John H. *Zondervan Illustrated Bible Backgrounds Commentary (Old Testament) Volume 1: Genesis, Exodus, Leviticus, Numbers, Deuteronomy.* Grand Rapids, MI: Zondervan, 2009 420-515.

[103] The *DDD* has this to say about the divine witness duo of heaven and earth: "'Olden gods' frequently occur in pairs in the ancient theogonies and often represent elements of the natural order. In texts of diverse origins in the ancient world, these pairs of deities are invoked to serve as witnesses to treaties and covenants. We find analogous petitions made in OT covenant lawsuit formulas used by the prophets. Isaiah (Isa 1:2) invokes the Heavens and the Earth to act as witnesses against Israel for breaking the covenant with Yahweh. The prophet Micah makes a similar appeal (Mic 6:2; cf. Jer 2:12). While these elements were by no means considered divine by the prophets, their use in covenant lawsuit formulas indicates a common rhetorical form whose origins may be traced back to originally mythological conceptions." Karel van der Toorn, Bob Becking and Pieter Willem van der Horst, *Dictionary of Deities and Demons in the Bible*, 2nd extensively rev. ed., (Leiden; Boston; Köln; Grand Rapids, MI; Cambridge: Brill; Eerdmans, 1999) 644-45.

entire Bible, including the early chapters of Genesis, is formulated on the model of an extended ancient Near Eastern covenant.[104]

Another well established "Tablet Theory" by D.J. Wiseman suggests that the early portions of Genesis may have even found their sources in clay tablets inscribed by those closest to the primeval events.[105] So maybe the notion of the Accuser referring to "discovery documents" of genealogies in *Enoch Primordial* is not so far fetched after all.

In conclusion, even the legal procedures and divine council found in the Bible reflect the covenant treaty structures, and city-state bureaucracy of Israel's ancient Near Eastern pagan neighbors redeemed and applied to God's purposes.

The Chronicles of the Nephilim

So that's what I did in *Noah Primeval* and *Enoch Primordial*. I retold the story of these two heroes of faith, incorporating the respected Enochian tradition of the Watchers and giants, Ancient Near Eastern imagery of Azazel, Lilith, Leviathan and Rahab, cherubim and seraphim, speculation on the divine council of the Sons of God, along with other Mesopotamian mythopoeia and Biblical imagination, in order to give a theological explanation for the true origins and "partial truth" of pagan mythology. It's all positively primeval.

---

[104] M.G. Kline, *The Treaty of the Great King* (Grand Rapids: Eerdmans, 1963); *The Structure of Biblical Authority* (Grand Rapids: Eerdmans, 1972).

[105] P.J. Wiseman and D. J. Wiseman, *Ancient Records and the Structure of Genesis* (Nashville: Thomas Nelson, Inc., 1985). Online, see: Curt Sewell, "The Tablet Theory of Genesis Authorship," *Bible and Spade*, Winter 1994, Vol. 7, No. 1. http://www.biblearchaeology.org/post/2010/10/11/the-tablet-theory-of-genesis-authorship.aspx

For additional Biblical, historical and mythical research related to this novel, go to www.ChroniclesoftheNephilim.com under the menu listing, "Scholarly Research" or Click Here.

If you liked this book, then please help me out by writing an honest review of it on Amazon. That is one of the best ways to say thank you to me as an author. It really does help my exposure and status as an author. It's really easy. In the Customer Reviews section, there is a little box that says "Write a customer review." They guide you easily through the process. Thanks! — *Brian Godawa*

GREAT OFFERS BY BRIAN GODAWA

Get More
Biblical Imagination

Sign up Online For
The Godawa Chronicles

www.Godawa.com

Updates and Freebies
of the Books of Brian Godawa
Special Discounts,
Weird Bible Facts!

CHRONICLES OF THE WATCHERS

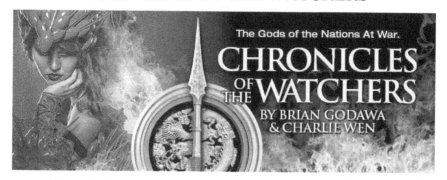

A Series About the Watchers in History.
Action, Romance, Gods, Monsters & Men.

The first novel is *Jezebel: Harlot Queen of Israel*

www.Godawa.com

VIDEO LECTURES

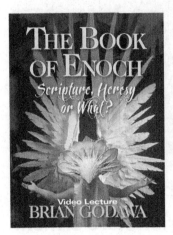

The Book of Enoch: Scripture, Heresy or What?

This lecture by Brian Godawa will be an introduction to the ancient book of 1Enoch, its content, its history, its affirmation in the New Testament, and its acceptance and rejection by the Christian Church. What is the Book of Enoch? Where did it come from? Why isn't it in the Bible? How does the Book of Enoch compare with the Bible?

Available on video.

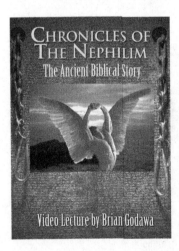

Chronicles of the Nephilim: The Ancient Biblical Story

Watchers, Nephilim, and the Divine Council of the Sons of God. In this dvd video lecture, Brian Godawa explores the Scriptures behind this transformative storyline that inspired his best-selling Biblical novel series Chronicles of the Nephilim.

Available on video.

To download these lectures and other books and products by Brian Godawa, just go to the STORE at:

www.Godawa.com

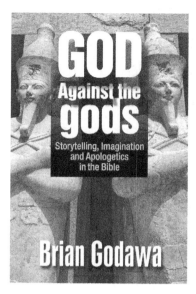

How God Captures the Imagination

This book was previously titled *Myth Became Fact: Storytelling, Imagination & Apologetics in the Bible.*

Brian Godawa, Hollywood screenwriter and best-selling novelist, explores the nature of imagination in the Bible. You will learn how God subverts pagan religions by appropriating their imagery and creativity, and redeeming them within a Biblical worldview. Improve your imagination in your approach to glorifying God and defending the faith.

Demonizing the Pagan Gods

God verbally attacked his opponents, pagans and their gods, using sarcasm, mockery, name-calling.

Old Testament Storytelling Apologetics

Israel shared creative images with their pagan neighbors: The sea dragon of chaos and the storm god. The Bible invests them with new meaning.

Biblical Creation and Storytelling

Creation stories in the ancient Near East and the Bible both express a primeval battle of deity to create order out of chaos. But how do they differ?

The Universe in Ancient Imagination

A detailed comparison and contrast of the Biblical picture of the universe with the ancient pagan one. What's the difference?

New Testament Storytelling Apologetics

Paul's sermon to the pagans on Mars Hill is an example of subversion: Communicating the Gospel in terms of a pagan narrative with a view toward replacing their worldview.

Imagination in Prophecy & Apocalypse

God uses imaginative descriptions of future events to deliberately obscure his message while simultaneously showing the true meaning and purpose behind history.

An Apologetic of Biblical Horror

Learn how God uses horror in the Bible as a tool to communicate spiritual, moral and social truth in the context of repentance from sin and redemptive victory over evil.

For More Info
www.Godawa.com

Art, Creativity and Truth in the Bible

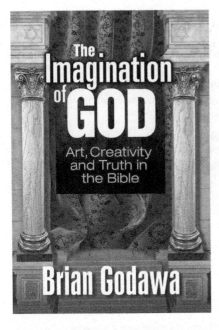

In his refreshing and challenging book, Godawa helps you break free from the spiritual suffocation of heady faith. Without negating the importance of reason and doctrine, Godawa challenges you to move from understanding the Bible "literally" to "literarily" by exploring the poetry, parables and metaphors found in God's Word. Weaving historical insight, pop culture and personal narrative throughout, Godawa reveals the importance God places on imagination and creativity in the Scriptures, and provides a Biblical foundation for Christians to pursue imagination, beauty, wonder and mystery in their faith.

This book was previously released with the title, *Word Pictures: Knowing God Through Story and Imagination.*

Endorsements:

"Brian Godawa is that rare breed—a philosopher/artist—who opens our eyes to the aesthetic dimension of spirituality. Cogently argued and fun to read, Godawa shows convincingly that God interacts with us as whole persons, not only through didactic teaching but also through metaphor, symbol, and sacrament."

— Nancy R. Pearcey,
Author, *Total Truth: Liberating Christianity from its Cultural Captivity*

"A spirited and balanced defense of the imagination as a potential conveyer of truth. There is a lot of good literary theory in the book, as well as an autobiographical story line. The thoroughness of research makes the book a triumph of scholarship as well."

— Leland Ryken, Clyde S. Kilby Professor of English, Wheaton College, Illinois
Author, *The Christian Imagination: The Practice of Faith in Literature & Writing.*

For More Info
www.Godawa.com

ABOUT THE AUTHOR

Brian Godawa is the screenwriter for the award-winning feature film, *To End All Wars,* starring Kiefer Sutherland. It was awarded the Commander in Chief Medal of Service, Honor and Pride by the Veterans of Foreign Wars, won the first Heartland Film Festival by storm, and showcased the Cannes Film Festival Cinema for Peace.

He also co-wrote *Alleged,* starring Brian Dennehy as Clarence Darrow and Fred Thompson as William Jennings Bryan. He previously adapted to film the best-selling supernatural thriller novel *The Visitation* by author Frank Peretti for Ralph Winter (*X-Men, Wolverine*), and wrote and directed *Wall of Separation,* a PBS documentary, and *Lines That Divide*, a documentary on stem cell research.

Mr. Godawa's scripts have won multiple awards in respected screenplay competitions, and his articles on movies and philosophy have been published around the world. He has traveled around the United States teaching on movies, worldviews, and culture to colleges, churches and community groups.

His popular book, *Hollywood Worldviews: Watching Films with Wisdom and Discernment* (InterVarsity Press) is used as a textbook in schools around the country. His novel series, the saga *Chronicles of the Nephilim* is in the Top 10 of Biblical Fiction on Amazon and is an imaginative retelling of Biblical stories of the Nephilim giants, the secret plan of the fallen Watchers, and the War of the Seed of the Serpent with the Seed of Eve. The sequel series, *Chronicles of the Apocalypse* tells the story of the Apostle John's book of Revelation, and *Chronicles of the Watchers* recounts true history through the Watcher paradigm.

Find out more about his other books, lecture tapes and dvds for sale at his website www.godawa.com.

BLANK PAGE

BLANK PAGE

BLANK PAGE

BLANK PAGE

BLANK PAGE

Made in the USA
Coppell, TX
28 March 2021

52581509R00223